THE HOUSE'S DAUGHTER

The Origins Duology - Book One

April Boulware

A House of Prey Novel

Copyright © 2025 by April Boulware

All rights reserved.

No part of this publication may be reproduced, distributed, or transmitted in any form or by any means, including photocopying, recording, or other electronic or mechanical methods, without the prior written permission of the publisher, except as permitted by U.S. copyright law. For permission requests, contact April Boulware at aprilboulwarewrites@gmail.com.

The story, all names, characters, and incidents portrayed in this production are fictitious. No identification with actual persons (living or deceased), places, buildings, and products is intended or should be inferred.

Book Cover by GetCovers

Contents

Trigger Warnings	1
Dedication	2
1. The Light Stays On	3
2. Tell Me Everything	12
3. Ghost Curriculum	19
4. The Intervention	23
5. In the Wall	32
6. Breathing Walls	38
7. She Didn't Run	47
8. Panic	56
9. French Fries	61
10. Purple Blanket	69
11. Rev. D. L. Emerson	83
12. Watched	90
13. Pictures	97
14. No Daughter of Mine	106
15. We Don't Forget	117
16. Dead Air	125

17.	The Girl In the Mirror	133
18.	Coffee On The Tailgate	139
19.	Confiscated	146
20.	Buried	156
21.	Just Storage	160
22.	Unholy Ground	165
23.	Back in the Attic	176
24.	My Sister's Voice	183
25.	Corduroy and Black Trash Bags	189
26.	Valentine's Day	193
27.	Connections	199
28.	A Sandwich	205
29.	Introductions	212
30.	Say it, Emily	216
31.	You Know How Your Dad Is	225
32.	Crawdad Man	233
33.	Bleeding Yellow	240
34.	Salt On Ice	252
35.	Milk. Eggs. Bread.	260
36.	The Bike	269
37.	Stepping Back Inside	277
38.	A Shame To Speak	281
39.	The Cover Girl	288

40.	Spine Of The Ministry	294
41.	A Hand In The Dark	305
42.	At The Altar	311
	Thank You	319
	What Comes Next	320
	Let Her Be Silent	321
	Sirens Screaming	322
	A Little About April	330
	A Letter from Me	331

Trigger Warnings

This novel contains themes not suitable for all audiences. These may be referred to, alluded to, or described on page. They may include, but are not limited to:

spiritual abuse
psychological abuse
emotional neglect of a child
childhood sexual abuse
abuse by a cult
mental manipulation
financial abuse
parentification
racism
bigotry
misogyny
cult-like religious control
loss of identity
psychological trauma
dissociation
anxiety
depression
mental illness
supernatural elements
horror gore
death
murder
crime

Please consider your own mental health when reading my work.

This book is dedicated to
eleven-year-old me
and every other girl out there like me.

You *are* good enough.
You *are* worthy.
And none of this is
your fault.

1

THE LIGHT STAYS ON

I used to think only little kids were afraid of the dark. Then I turned twenty-two and couldn't sleep unless the light was on. Stupid, right? Most people ditch that fear with their training wheels.

Not me. I slept with a dim yellow lamp casting its glow across the shadows like a protective spell. It felt ridiculous. But better that than falling victim to whatever waited in the dark.

You're already a part of the dark.

If I lived a normal life, I'd laugh. I'd think I was being dramatic. But I'd never lived a normal life.

And this house had teeth.

From the outside, it looked harmless. Warm. Inviting. The kind of house people slowed down to admire. "It has *good bones*," Dad said. I don't know. I think some bones aren't meant to be disturbed. But he said we'd flip it in a year.

That was my whole childhood. We moved up and down the East Coast, church to church, chasing God like He kept changing zip codes. As soon as I thought, *This is it. This is where I'll learn to drive, get my first car, finally start my life*, something would happen.

A disagreement at church. A fallout with the bishop. Or the elders would claim God told them it was time. Time to *send* us somewhere new.

Dad was a minister. That meant working with youth, preaching once in a while, and trusting God would provide for the rest.

He didn't.

So Dad flipped houses on the side—houses we lived in. He'd renovate whatever was near the church and sell it once it was fixed up. Then we'd have to move again.

I asked my dad once why he didn't work like the other men. He didn't like the question, and I felt guilty for asking. "God didn't call me to build houses," he told me. "God called me to build souls."

That was that.

Mom working was never a conversation. It was understood. "The woman's place is in the home." We heard that in every church we ever set foot in. From pulpits, choirs, and weepy guest singers shaking tambourines, clutching hymn books like talismans.

Raise children. Submit. Support your man.

That was the *gospel of girlhood*.

But then we came to Caster, South Carolina, and everything… paused.

I was sixteen when we moved here. I was twenty-two now. And we were still here.

Dad's standing at the local church didn't last. Six months, maybe. There wasn't another church for a hundred miles that met his standards. We only joined churches that left the world behind. The *true believers*.

But even without a church, we didn't leave Caster.

Six years in the same house should've felt safe. Like I could finally start the life I'd always dreamed of.

But it didn't.

It felt like the house had its hand wrapped around our ankles. Sometimes I thought it had been waiting for us. Like it had seen families like ours before—and knew exactly how to keep them.

I told myself I was being paranoid. It was simply wood and walls. And yet, I'd take six more moves over six years here.

I was twenty-two. I could've left. Right?

People my age had dorm rooms and dating apps. Cheap apartments with too-thin walls. Maybe a futon they bought themselves.

Me? I still slept in the same bed I'd had since I was five. Same threadbare teddy tucked under my pillow. Same dusty Goldilocks lamp, its cream shade now stained like old tea.

I wasn't living. I was being kept. Quiet and obedient. Like a secret someone was afraid might get out.

My parents tried to sell the house. For years, that homemade for-sale sign rotted in the front yard. No showings. No open houses. No flyers. No pictures online.

One day, the sign disappeared. No one said a thing about it. It was just gone, and we were still here.

Dad got his contractor's license. He said God told him in a dream that church walls were no longer his mission field. Now flipping houses was holy work. A *vessel*, he said, for shaping lost young men.

Gracie and I were supposed to pray for husbands to come hammering down the driveway, tool belts slung low, eager to be molded by Dad.

They never showed.

I remember sitting at the kitchen table one night, sorting screws while Mom clipped coupons. The silence said what we couldn't. The dream was dead. But Dad still believed. So we stayed quiet. That's how faith works.

Sometimes, though, I wondered if my parents even believed half the things they preached.

Late at night, I'd tiptoe to the kitchen for water. Sometimes a couple ibuprofen. Their voices would drift in from the bedroom. Low murmurs down the little hall.

Dad's voice low. Mom's softer. Always listening, agreeing.

He blamed the market. Said the world didn't want houses like this anymore. Homes set apart.

But every night, I'd lie awake, watching the chandelier sway overhead.

It was heavy during the day. Still. But at night, it moved. It didn't need wind or draft. Or reason.

I stopped believing it was the market that kept us here. Some places don't want to be left. This house clung to us. Or maybe, to me.

The chandelier in my room was made from real antlers. Heavy as sin. Still as stone during the day. But at night, it swayed. Window open or shut, door locked or cracked, summer breeze or dead stillness. It always swayed.

The walls were cedar. Dark roan. They drank in sound like they were thirsty. Swallowed light like they were starving. My room was quiet. Still. Dark. No matter how many lights I turned on, how long I left the window open, begging the sounds of the street to bleed inside, none of it ever made a difference.

At night, the rafters groaned. Like something was shifting above me. Maybe in the attic. Something old. Something that remembered.

In six years, I never had the courage to go up there and find out. Not at night. Not while it was talking.

At first, I tried to explain the noises away. Old pipes. Creaky wood. Maybe the house settling. Too many years spent on the edge of a South Carolina pine forest, stuck between boiling summers and wet, frozen winters.

But old pipes don't creak like that. And old houses don't settle the same way, at the same time, every night for six years. Not unless something's making them.

I always told myself I was being stupid. I'd roll over on my too-old mattress, pull my pillow over my head, and try to sleep. But pillows don't block voices. Or footsteps. Or whispers in the walls.

The knocking started the second summer.

At first, it was soft. A tap. I couldn't tell if it hit wood. Or glass. Or something else. The more I ignored it, the louder it got. Until it was a sharp, deliberate knock against my window.

Maybe a bird. A branch. Some night bug with bad aim.

But none of those things would come back night after night, to the exact same place. And they don't knock with purpose.

I didn't want to believe it was something else. Something watching me.

I was raised not to believe in ghosts or spirits. Only God, the devil, and angels with flaming swords. I never believed it was a ghost. Not at first. But the knocking never stopped.

Maybe it was a branch in the wind, scraping the glass.

But it couldn't be.

Because there were no trees out front. Only pines out back, planted in a perfect half-moon. Nothing in the front. Like the house had something against shade where anyone could see.

Dad tried three times to plant a tree out there. Two died from frost. The last was hit by a truck. It didn't hit the house. Just the tree. Dad didn't bother after that.

I thought about birds. Maybe a nocturnal one, an owl or a crazed mockingbird. But coming back to the same window every night? Do wild birds even live that long? If not, did one teach the next? Like a moonlit ritual passed down through generations.

Even I knew how insane that sounded.

The bug theory didn't hold up either. The knocking started long before I ever left the light on.

So, either it was a beetle that loved the dark, or a moth that hated light.

My window didn't even have a screen. I used to sleep with it wide open in the summer. If it was a bug, it could've flown in. But it didn't. It wanted the glass. Like it craved the impact.

That wasn't even the worst of it. Just the part that never let me sleep.

None of this seemed to bother anyone else. My parents never mentioned the sounds.

When we first moved in, my sister Gracie swore there was nothing strange about the house. She said it more than once, like she needed me to believe it. Later, I noticed she walked the edges of her room at night. One hand on the wall, like she was feeling for something.

Once, I asked her why.

"Habit, I guess," she said, but she wouldn't look at me.

Gracie was always like that. Rituals. Routines. Some she'd carry for years. Others vanished overnight, like they'd scared her.

But the longer we stayed, the more I wondered.

I tried to talk about it. My parents used to be easy to talk to. At least, my mom was. Not Dad.

I was never close to my dad. I think, deep down, I was afraid of him.

Gracie never said anything, but sometimes, I'd catch her watching me when I pulled away from Dad's morning hug. Not judgmental. Just...knowing. Like she understood why I flinched but couldn't say it out loud.

It was *Dad*. But we *never* talked about it.

I used to be close to my mom. I thought she was my best friend. But that didn't survive puberty. The closer I got to womanhood, the more she pulled toward Dad. Like she had to pick a side. And she always picked him.

When I told her about the noises, she said it was a bad dream. When I didn't drop it, it became the devil.

"Spiritual warfare," she said. "You're letting the evil one poison your thoughts."

Then came the prayer meeting. On my knees. Worn carpet digging into my legs. Oil on my forehead. Voices layered over mine. They said if I had enough faith, it would stop.

It didn't.

I thought I could still trust her. That maybe she'd believe me. But she held my hands, looked me in the eye, and said, "Em, I know you're older now. God will punish those He loves."

If I dishonored my parents. Entertained impure thoughts. Started craving the things of the world—sins other girls my age were already lost in. God would punish me.

That's when I stopped talking to her. And she never asked why.

No one knew I slept with the light on, tucked away in the half-upstairs of this crooked house. If they did, they didn't say a word. I guess it didn't concern them.

But that didn't mean much. There were a lot of things I thought were normal, things my parents overlooked. Or worse, encouraged.

I was twenty-two. Still sleeping with a teddy bear. I showered with my sister until I was almost eighteen. Mom said she'd feel unloved if I didn't. I let Dad brush my hair until I was twenty. Because telling him no would've hurt his feelings.

It was messed up. And deep down, I knew it. Even back then.

But when you're taught that your wants are selfish, and your discomfort is disobedience, you learn to shrink.

To disappear.

To forget what you want, because what they want is supposed to make you happy too.

Age doesn't matter when you're taught that obedience is love.

My parents knew better. They'd lived in the *world*. Drugs. Violence. Rape. Suicide. Divorce. They'd seen it all so we didn't have to.

Eighteen didn't mean freedom. That was a lie the world sold to tear families apart.

True believers separated from the world. And the safest place to be, while you're living that kind of life, was inside. At least until you got married. Then some godly man would take over the watching.

So yeah, I let him brush my hair.

Because he loved me. Because I was his little girl. Because it was supposed to be *cute*.

I was the problem. The one who thought it felt... wrong.

Mom said that was disgusting. That I should be ashamed. That I needed to *fix* myself.

That's why you learn not to speak.

Not to ask.

You start bending instead. Folding yourself smaller and smaller until no one has to ask you to.

Smaller. Quieter. Easier to carry.

If something really bothered you, you didn't talk about it. You changed it quietly. Slowly. Off-stage. Out of focus.

It took years for me to get up the courage to ask Gracie about the showers.

Mom lied.

Gracie hated them too. We stopped, and Mom never asked why.

I timed my showers for when Dad was outside, wandering the long rows of his ever-expanding garden. I'd towel off fast, brush my hair even faster. He never said a word.

Problem solved.

But the lights? That wasn't going to be so easy to fix.

I wasn't dreaming. I wasn't being punished. And God wasn't the one sending something to rap on that fucking window.

Maybe I had been asleep when I heard it. Maybe.

When I'd gone to bed, I'd tried to turn my light off. Tried to sleep in the dark like a normal person. Hoped this night would be different.

I closed my eyes at 11:12. Slowed my breathing. Counted sheep. Whatever it was normal people do.

You don't belong to the normal ones.

And then the knock came. Hard and sharp. Like a fist against the glass.

I jumped.

My clock said 11:17. I hadn't fallen asleep.

A full moon hung low behind the sheer curtains. You'd think it would brighten the room. Instead, it deepened the shadows. Thick. Heavy. And so much darker than before.

But it wasn't the knocking that scared me anymore. Not really. That stopped being the worst part a long time ago.

Now it was the scratching.

That didn't happen before. It started after I left the light on. After I got used to the knocking. It was slow. Steady. Like fingernails dragged across splintery, old wood. Patient and deliberate.

It always started far away, behind the dresser in the corner. Then it crept closer. Inch by inch. And under the scratching, trapped beneath it, was something else. A whisper so soft I couldn't tell if it came from the wall, the floor, the ceiling, or from under my own skin.

A month ago, I checked. Pulled the blanket back, heart in my throat. Nothing.

Because you weren't ready yet.

But that was before. Now if I looked, I knew I'd see it. And I didn't want to anymore.

It wasn't human. I don't think it was even alive. And it was worse than anything I'd been taught to be afraid of. Worse than strangers. Worse than violence. Worse than being kidnapped.

Because this thing didn't want to take me away. It wanted to stay.

But tonight, I couldn't take it anymore. I threw the blanket back and lunged for the lamp.

Click.

The little Goldilocks lamp flared to life. Dim, yellow, flickering. The shadows shrank, retreating like they'd been caught doing something they shouldn't.

The scratching stopped, but I didn't move. My heart pounded against my ribs like it wanted out, but I sat there, motionless, listening.

A whisper drifted across the room, dry and low. Like the hush before a bedtime story. I didn't catch the words, only the chill they left behind.

Tomorrow night, I wouldn't try again. The light would stay on. Always.

Because whatever it was, it liked it dark. It liked when I was alone.

2

TELL ME EVERYTHING

There were only two places I was allowed to go alone. The job site and the library.

If I was with Gracie, we were sometimes allowed to stop for coffee on the way to work, if we used the drive-thru. Going inside without Dad was out of the question.

Today, I wasn't with Gracie.

No coffee. Only the job site and the library.

I wasn't needed at the main site. I had a list of little jobs, touch-ups at a couple houses Dad had already been paid for. Then, I'd be free. For a few hours, at least.

I planned to spend them at the library.

It was one of those late-winter days that felt like spring, no matter what the calendar said. Blinding sunshine spilled across a cloudless sky, warming the earth where winter had finally started to loosen its grip.

Valentine's Day was often like this here in South Carolina. Pretty and warm. A teasing preview of spring, before winter came back for one last slap.

Of course, I'd never observed Valentine's Day.

Not because I didn't want to. And not because I was against the commercialized idea of love. Not even because I'd never had a boyfriend around the fourteenth of February, though that was true. I'd never observed it because, like most every other holiday, my parents had religious objections.

Or maybe objections, period.

I'm not even sure what their issue with Valentine's was.

I slid off the sticky vinyl bench seat of Dad's blue pickup.

I didn't have a car. Too expensive, they said. The insurance would bankrupt them, at least until I turned twenty-five.

That was the same reason I hadn't gotten my driver's license until last year. Well, that and after I'd gotten my permit Mom freaked. She said if I got licensed, I'd leave her.

That shocked me. I'd never thought about leaving. Not really. It hurt that Mom thought I would.

I guess she finally forgot, because they let me get my license.

But the car? Still too dangerous. Or too expensive. Or maybe Mom thought I'd leave again.

Maybe by twenty-five she wouldn't worry anymore. Maybe by then, they'd finally get me a car.

My stomach twisted.

For a second, I thought I felt a breath at my ear, soft and close, teasing a loose strand of hair from my bun. I tucked the hair behind my ear and looked across the road.

The trees lining the street stood still, bare branches tipped in green. Tiny buds peeking from brown limbs, frozen in sunlight like the world had stopped breathing.

"That's not gonna happen," I muttered, grabbing my backpack.

Still living with my parents. Still upstairs in that creepy house. Still sleeping with the light on—halfway through my twenties.

I grabbed my water bottle and drank down that thought, as I shut the truck door and stepped onto the fractured sidewalk. I felt every crack through the thinning soles of my black tennis shoes. My toes curled as I reached the red metal door. I unlocked it quickly and slipped inside.

My heartbeat steadied as I leaned back against the cold metal. The house was still. Empty.

I only had one job left. Replacing a toilet.

Dad already unpacked it and carried it to the bathroom. I just had to scrape up the old wax ring, drop the new one in place, and hook the water up. Easy enough.

I worked as fast as I could. The sooner I finished, the sooner I could get to the library.

By the time I pulled into the parking lot that afternoon, the late winter sun had baked the truck cab like a greenhouse.

The dash clock glowed 3:27.

I was proud of myself. I'd worked fast enough to earn a couple hours to kill before heading home. Before I had to go back. To *that* house.

"Hey, girl!" Wanda spotted me before I'd even made it past the front desk. She was shelving books in the local authors' display.

"Oh, hey!" I lowered my voice. This was still a library.

She dropped what she was doing and pulled me into a hug. Her perfume—pepper and jasmine—cut through the heaviness I didn't know I was carrying.

I hugged her back.

"I was getting worried about you!" Wanda never whispered. "I didn't see you last week. When I realized it was Friday and you still hadn't shown up, I thought, *Em never skips the library!*"

I laughed. She was right. I loved the books—but I came for Wanda just as much.

My parents let me go to the library alone. No Dad or Mom. No Gracie. Just me. Here I could pretend to be myself. Pretend I was free.

You'll never be free.

Mom didn't mind me coming here. She trusted me to follow the rules.

No fiction. No psychology. No religion or philosophy. Nonfiction only. Facts. The safe kind. History was okay. Animals. Plants. Space—so long as I remembered who made it all.

So long as I didn't start asking questions.

And it was quiet here. Usually empty. Forgotten, like most small-town libraries. That made it perfect. Nothing sinful happened in dusty corners, under flickering lights, between card catalogs and laminate chairs.

My parents didn't know Wanda.

Wanda worked part-time at the library while studying to be a nurse. But you'd never know it was part-time. She volunteered for everything. Book sales, author events, even story time. On her days off, she'd still come in to study. I think books were her safe place, too.

She was younger than I expected—early twenties like me. But her chunky earrings and red-framed glasses made her look older. Smarter. Like she belonged everywhere I didn't.

There was always a textbook open behind the counter. Anatomy, pharmacology, something with tiny print and confusing diagrams.

She scared me a little, at first.

"Hey there, Emily," she called once, scanning a stack of returns without looking up. "Back for more ghosts and murder?"

That stopped me. She knew my name. And what I was reading.

"Yeah. I know it's silly," I said. "I should be reading something useful."

Wanda stopped scanning and looked right at me.

"Girl, reading is never silly. You don't have to read heavy nonfiction to learn something. Some of the deepest lessons I've learned came from romance novels."

It was the first time anyone told me my choices mattered. That what I liked wasn't wrong. That it wasn't sin. And it was the first time I stayed at the library longer than fifteen minutes.

I got braver about the fiction section—haunted manors, forgotten girls, old libraries full of secrets. Even romance. I lost myself in beautiful stories of true, undying love.

I never brought those books home. I read them in the shadows between the shelves, where it was safe.

Wanda and I didn't talk a lot. Not at first.

"Ooo, digging into local legend," Wanda said one day, sliding *Caster's Buried Past* into my pile. "You ever looked up your house?"

I stopped, stared at her, too many question stuck in my throat.

Wanda raised an eyebrow. "Sweetheart, half the houses in Caster have a story. Yours more than most."

That's when I started coming in after work, nearly every day.

I'd sit at the table near the window, losing myself in research. True crime, folklore, old town records. Wanda called it my ghost curriculum. She might've meant it as a joke, but the stacks she slid over felt like a syllabus.

Some days she sat with me, helping me chase down a name or a date. Other days, she brought iced tea from the break room and studied at the next table.

Something shifted over those weeks. Wanda's questions stopped being nosy. Mine stopped being careful. I realized I'd made a friend.

Worldly friends are dangerous.

It started with little things. Wanda would talk about her mom. Not in that oversharing way people do when they're nervous or want attention. It was the quiet, offhand comments that slip out when someone's comfortable.

When I'd nearly jumped out of my skin after someone shut the archive room door too hard, Wanda said her mom would flinch just because the coffee maker clicked on in the morning. Later she told me that her brother, Kade, slept with a baseball bat under his bed for years.

She didn't explain why. Not right away. But eventually, she felt safe enough to tell me.

Her mom had escaped an abusive relationship. She barely made it out—her and Kade both. Her mom was remarried, to a man who adored her, and loved Kade as his own son. But Wanda could still see it. The way certain sounds or arguments made her mom go still. Like something inside her had ducked for cover.

Wanda called it trauma. *Fight or flight.* Leftover signals from when your body had to survive.

That's why she wanted to be a nurse. Not only to help people, but to *see* them. Especially women. Especially the ones who didn't realize how bad it was until after they got out.

I hadn't told her anything about my dad. Not then.

Life at home was hell, yeah—but not like that. It wasn't physical. Dad never hit us. Not Mom. Not me or Gracie. My parents argued. And Gracie and I were always caught in the middle, translating between World War Three and Four.

That's not abuse. Right?

Mom would know. She grew up with it. She knew the difference.

I told Wanda about my mom's dad. About the ink pen. About the Bible verse and the blood.

She listened, like she already knew the shape of the story.

That's how I knew I'd made a real friend.

I'd never told anyone that stuff. Not because it was a secret, but because it felt wrong to say it out loud. Like Mom always said, We *don't air our dirty laundry.* But with Wanda, it didn't feel dirty. It felt human.

After that, we didn't only talk about books or history.

We talked about the little stuff. Work, the weather, how we'd slept the night before. Wanda's weird library patrons. She'd vent about the lady who always came in asking for a book that didn't exist. I'd tell her about scraping toilet wax off tiles. About trying to rip up old vinyl floor squares—survivors of thirty years of food spills and Sunday shoes.

Conversation was ease. Comfortable. Natural.

Wanda told me about some of her fears. Where they started.

She told me about sneaking into the abandoned house that later became my home. The *old Dickerson place,* she called it. Her brother, Kade, once dared her to stay in the upstairs room for ten minutes. She barely made it five.

"The air was wrong up there," she said. "It freaked me out."

That's when I told her about the chandelier. The knocking. The time I woke up with my blanket folded neatly at the foot of the bed, like I'd been tucked in backward. The scratching behind the dresser.

I waited for the look. The one that said I was crazy. Or worse, that I was entertaining the devil.

It never came.

"Yeah. Some places carry things," Wanda said. Then she leaned across the table, chin resting in her palms. "Tell me everything."

3

GHOST CURRICULUM

"So where have you been?"

Wanda ushered me into the break room like she always did, like I belonged. Over time, I'd earned quiet access to places off-limits to most patrons.

"Last week was nuts," I said, popping open the iced tea she slid across the table. "We had to finish a job before final inspection. Today was just touch-ups. The last thing I did was install a toilet."

Wanda raised a brow. "By yourself?"

"It's not hard."

"You're wild," she said, shaking her head. "I can barely hang a picture frame."

I laughed. "Not really. I hate renovating."

"Then why not do something else?" She turned toward the filing cabinet like the question didn't weigh a thing.

I stared at the back of her head, the bold red flowers on her blouse blurred under the buzzing fluorescents. What could I even say?

Because I'm not allowed? Because *worldly* jobs are sinful? Because I have no education?, no skills? Because flipping burgers wouldn't cover my quarter of the bills my parents racked up—to keep pretending that awful house wasn't rotting from the inside out.

"My dad's older," I said, too fast, like I'd stomped the gas on the wrong sentence.

She turned, a thick file in her hands. "Yeah?"

"Seventy-four."

She blinked. "Damn, Em." She set her drink down carefully. "I'm sorry, I didn't mean... my dad's forty-seven. My *granddad's* not even seventy."

"It surprises people," I said lightly, like it didn't tie my stomach in knots.

Mom would hate this conversation. Dad would take my license. I'd have to start riding with Gracie again.

Wanda sat across from me, her expression soft. "Can I ask... how old's your mom?"

"Forty-seven."

"Wow," she said again, chewing her cheek like she was holding back a dozen more thoughts. "So... they met when...?"

"They were both married before," I said, waving it off. "Mom was a teenager. Dad had a whole family before us."

I could see her doing the math in her head. "I've got a half-sister old enough to be my mom."

She shook her head. "I had no idea. Does she live nearby?"

"North Carolina. Dad calls her sometime."

Talia was a *worldly* daughter. *Off the path.*

Wanda didn't press. She tapped the folder in front of her. "Remember how you hit a wall with Caster history?"

"Yeah." I didn't mind the change of subject.

She flipped the folder open and spread the contents on the table between us. Brittle clippings. Grainy photos. Yellowed printouts.

"Whoa," I said, leaning closer. "Where'd this come from?"

"You'll never guess. My mom's a realtor, right? I went with her on a walk-through for this old house on Main. The owner's ninety-something and still sharper than a tack. She remembered me from some historical society thing. When I mentioned I had a friend who was stuck on her research of town history, she gave me this."

I reached for the top clipping, the newsprint softened with age. Dated 1988.

MISSING FOSTER CHILD, RACHEL BAGWELL, REPORTED SEEN NEAR GRANITE HILL.

My spine locked, and a shiver ran up my back. *Rachel.*
"You cold, girl?" Wanda asked, pushing her chair from the table.
I didn't answer as she went to tip the thermostat up a couple degrees.

Search for the missing foster child to be suspended due to several reported sightings. This has been ruled a runaway situation. Recently eighteen, Ms. Bagwell is no longer a ward of the state.

"What'd you find?" Wanda returned with her seltzer, peering over my shoulder.
I swallowed, and laid the paper down. "Just a missing person's notice."
Her eyes darted across the table. "Wait... that name—Rachel. Bagwell?"
I hesitated. "Yeah." Did that name hit her the same way it hit me?
"I found an article about her when I took a quick peek through this stuff in the car earlier." She paused. "Oh, hell." she was flipping through the rest of the stack. "This whole file... it's all her."
She didn't say anything for a moment. Neither did I.
Wanda dropped into the chair beside me. "Why do you think Mrs. Alister saved all this? For *thirty years*? All about one runaway foster kid."
I shook my head, but the dread had already settled in me like dust in old carpet.
We stared at the table. Clippings. Margins circled in red pen. A school photo, grainy and off-color. A page printed from an old website, glitchy banner still frozen at the top.

"Maybe she was related to her," Wanda said, flipping more carefully now.

"This one's not from Caster," I eased a clipping from the pile. "It's from Wisconsin."

"Oh wow." Wanda leaned in. "This must be how the girl ended up in foster care."

Early morning house fire leaves eight-year-old girl an orphan.
Any information about Rachel Bagwell's family should be directed to the Landford County Police Department.
Assistance is appreciated.

"Poor girl." A sting bloomed under my skin. Grief. Confusion. Something deeper I couldn't name.

"They must not have found any family," Wanda said quietly. "That's how she ended up here. Shuffled from place to place."

"That would be awful."

As messed up as my life felt, at least I had parents. A house. A name. Shame climbed up my throat, thick and heavy. I spent so much time resenting everything. Hating my life. But this? This was worse.

"You want this file?" Wanda looked at me. "It's mostly about her, that Rachel girl. I don't see how one girl tells you much about Caster history."

I shrugged, grabbing my tea. "I'll take it home. Poor Rachel's got me curious."

Wanda gathered the clippings into a rough stack. "It's kind of morbid, though."

"It's not like she was murdered."

The words stuck in my throat. I sipped my tea, forced them down.

"She probably ran the second she turned eighteen. I've heard the system can be brutal."

4

THE INTERVENTION

Rachel Bagwell was dead. Murdered.

I knew it the second I saw her name. But I told myself I'd read too many mysteries. I was letting my imagination run wild.

Wanda's file sat open in my lap, the pages curling at the corners. I sat cross-legged in the center of my sagging mattress. Beagle, my tattered teddy bear, watched from his usual spot under the pillow's edge.

The house was too quiet.

I tried to ignore it, but I could hear everything. My breath, my heartbeat, the creak of the mattress when I shifted even slightly. But nothing else. No pipes groaning in the walls. No water running in the kitchen downstairs. No back door slamming after Dad came in from the garden. I liked quiet at the library, but here the stillness was worse than the noise.

Forcing myself to focus, I reached for the article again, fingers grazing the edge like it might burn.

MISSING FOSTER CHILD, RACHEL BAGWELL, REPORTED SEEN NEAR GRANITE HILL.

I sorted through the papers. A few more sightings followed. No locations. No names.

It was the eighties. Investigations were full of holes. The foster system barely had wings. People turned a blind eye to everything—abuse, violence, girls vanishing without a trace.

My stomach twisted. Why did I feel like she was dead? Why did all of this faded newsprint and blotchy ink, scream murder?

Maybe it was the old woman. Mrs. Alister. The one who kept it all. Every clipping. Every article. Maybe that felt like a cold case obsession—like in the books I'd been sneaking to read.

As I shuffled through more pages, I realized Wanda had been right. This wasn't *Caster* history. It was *Rachel's*.

A Virginia paper celebrated her spelling bee win. A church bulletin from North Carolina listed her as a children's choir member. She held a lead role in the 1982 Christmas pageant. Twelve-year-old Rachel played Mary.

Despite everything—grief, foster care, the constant moving—Rachel seemed... okay.

Or at least, like she belonged.

"You had more of a life at ten than I've had at twice that," I muttered to the papers. "Why'd you move so much, Rachel?"

I didn't know much about the foster system, only what my parents said.

That it was for *troubled kids*. That their parents were selfish. Addicts. That those kids were broken. Hard to love. Doomed to struggle. They bounced from home to home until they aged out. Then they made more broken kids.

That's what I was taught. That's what the system was for.

But Rachel's life didn't start with addiction or abandonment. It started with fire. Not drugs or trouble. Just pain and grief.

I sorted through more pages, the musty smell of old newsprint stinging my nose. A photo slipped loose from between two yellowed sheets, landing softly in my lap.

My breath caught in my throat.

Rachel, scrawled in pen on the back. No last name. Just a year. 1988.

I dropped the picture like it burned. It fluttered onto my lap, landing against the fabric of my denim skirt.

Her eyes stared up at me. Still. Direct. She looked real. Too real.

And wrong.

Not in a gory, horror-movie way. Not like she'd been hurt.

She was my age, maybe a little younger. Her hair was a deep, red blonde, like old pennies, and tied up tight in a high, hard bun. But it was her dress that stopped me cold.

She didn't wear the high-waisted jeans, or the striped tee like I expected from the '80s. She had on a cape dress. Long, shapeless. High neck. The kind they said were *modest*.

The kind I still wore.

I touched the edge of the picture as if I might find stitching or seams.

Rachel had been beautiful. Delicate. The kind of girl who should've belonged in an old film reel. Not trapped here, like this.

But there was something behind her eyes. Behind the smile she put on for the camera. Sadness. Fear.

I knew those feelings. Recognized it in her eyes.

I stared until the image blurred, then blinked and started digging. There had to be something else in here. Something to prove the article right.

That she'd run. That she was free. That she hadn't died.

All I found were three reported sightings of Rachel near Granite Hill. Two of them barely got a mention—short blurbs, months apart.

The third was from November 1988. By then, she was legal. Not a ward of the state anymore. The case was closed. The sightings were enough, at least on paper, to say she was alive. That she didn't want to be found. That no more time or tax dollars should be wasted on her.

But something felt off. This was too clean, too easy.

A girl disappears and three vague sightings, months apart, are enough to close the book? Did they even talk to her foster parents? Her teachers? Did she have friends?

Maybe she wasn't only dressed like me. Maybe she *lived* like me. Maybe there was no one to miss her. No one who cared she was gone, because no one really knew her.

"What happened to you?" I whispered.

The photo was still in my lap, her eyes unblinking. Watching me. I could almost see her mouth move, hear the shape of her voice, struggling to make sound through the paper.

I gently lifted Rachel's photo from my lap, slipping it back into the file like it might shatter. But, as I did so, another photo slipped loose.

This one was glossy, full of color. It wasn't a clipping. It wasn't grainy or sad. It was personal. Rachel stood in front of a white railing, mist curling behind her. A big waterfall spilled over a rocky ledge in the background. Niagara Falls. I recognized it from a textbook.

Rachel looked maybe thirteen. She wore jean shorts and a bright, red hoodie, her hair loose and tangled from the wind. She was grinning, wide and crooked, her lips parted like she was trying not to laugh.

She looked free.

There was no cape dress. No high collar. No tight bun hiding her hair.

My throat went tight.

The change in this girl was... disturbing. It made my skin crawl. From the younger Rachel, on a trip to Niagara Falls, to the older version of the girl in the cape dress.

The happy Rachel, that was before. Before the shift. Before she landed *here*, in Caster. Before someone made her into something else.

This was Rachel.

Whoever was in the photo from 1988, that wasn't Rachel anymore. That was what was left—a shell.

A chill climbed my back, just as a knock sounded on my bedroom door. I jumped, almost dumping all the artifacts into the floor.

"Em?"

That quiet voice. Gracie.

"Yeah?" I shoved the folder under my mattress just before she stepped into the room.

She leaned against the doorframe, red hair twisted into a knot at the back of her head, like Mom taught us. A hoodie, hiding most of her cape dress, hung off one shoulder. It was probably mine. She always borrowed my clothes.

"Mom wants us to set the table."

I swung my legs off the bed. "Be right there."

She didn't move. She watched me, eyes searching. "Are you okay?"

I hesitated.

Should I tell her?

What was there to say?

That I was spiraling into a girl's life I didn't even know? That Rachel Bagwell was turning into more than a research obsession? That she had changed? To look like us. And then she disappeared.

"I'm tired," I said instead.

Gracie didn't believe me, but she didn't push either. She nodded, like always. "Finishing that job last week wore me out, too."

"I hate the last-minute rush," I muttered as we headed for the stairs. "I wish things were... better managed. Timewise."

Gracie rolled her eyes, lips pressed into a familiar line.

If it weren't for Mom tracking receipts and balancing payments on the hardware store credit card, Dad wouldn't have a business at all. He couldn't manage money, much less a deadline.

But of course, he didn't see it that way.

Mom didn't have a penis. That made her lesser, in his eyes. We were *all* under him. The head. The authority. The voice of God. And we, especially me and Gracie, had no right to challenge him.

Nothing ever finished on time because he spent half the day arguing. With Mom. With us. About methods. About obedience. About *submission*.

"Independence," he'd sneer. Like it was a sin.

The kitchen smelled like overcooked broccoli and leftover meat from last night. Dad sat at the head of the table, as usual, hunched over his plate, reading from his Bible between bites.

It was a quiet meal. None of us really had much to say to each other, not anymore. But my mind was humming. Not only with what I'd been researching, but with the life Rachel had enjoyed *before* the cape dress and tied up hair.

"I was thinking," I said quietly, but immediately hoped no one had heard me so I wouldn't have to finish.

"Thinking what?" Mom's voice was too sharp for the quiet room.

"I mean..." I picked at the carrots on my plate, trying not to lose momentum. "It might be nice for Grace and me to... I don't know. Get out more? Maybe a class or..."

"No," Dad said without looking up.

"What kind of class?" Mom cut in. My heart stuttered. Was she... considering it?

I hadn't expected to get this far. "I don't know." I sat up straighter, mind racing, "Maybe um..."

"A bachelor's in education," Gracie said and we all froze.

Dad's fork clattered against his plate, sending a splatter of gravy across the checkered tablecloth.

"It sounds like you've been thinking about this for a while, Grace," he said.

Gracie took a slow bite of a green bean and nodded. "I'm twenty-five. I've been thinking about what I might need to do if I never meet a man. Never start a family."

My mom had this way of grunting when she was pissed—a low *uh* that came up from her gut but pushed out through her nose instead of her mouth.

"Gracie, you sound like one of those worldly girls. *We* don't think about the future with that kind of doubt. There is no plan B. No *safety net* when you're living by faith."

Gracie stayed calm, which wasn't like her. She was usually anxious, always fidgeting.

She looked up at Mom and took a sip of her water. "Marriage isn't God's plan for everyone, the Bible says so. Maybe it's not for me. Maybe I'm meant to teach other people's children instead."

"In a worldly school, Gracie?" Mom's eyebrows shot up. "God wouldn't call you to study the world's ways. He wouldn't ask you to teach the world's children."

"It wouldn't have to be public school," Gracie said calmly.

I stared down at my plate and closed my eyes. This felt like the calm before the storm. What had I done?

"And where will you find a Christian school filled with real believers?" Mom snapped. "We'd have to move again. You know your father can't attend Caster Assembly—not after how Bishop Biddle spoke to him. And there's not another true church around here, much less one running a school. Most of these churches *say* they're Christians, but they're not living for God."

"Then how am I to find a true Christian husband, Mom?" Gracie asked. "Marriage is a much bigger commitment than a job."

My jaw tightened.

"Grace Ann." Dad's voice soft but sharp. "Where are all these negative thoughts coming from? You don't need to *find* a husband. You don't need to go to school, or work, or search for anything. God will send the right man—when you're ready."

Gracie didn't answer. She looked down, slipped a green bean between her lips, and chewed in silence.

"I don't like this," Mom muttered. "The evil one is planting thoughts in my girls' minds."

"It's alright, Mom," Dad said, patting her hand gently. "Girls, you don't know the evil that's out there. You've been shielded. Your mother and I have done our best to be good stewards of what God gave us. You haven't had to see what's out there."

He paused, took a slow breath.

"Men only want one thing. We can't help it. It's how God made us. Like any other male animal, we're driven to propagate. But Christian men, with the help of God-fearing wives, learn to bring our bodies under the rule of the Holy Spirit."

"Don," Mom hissed, "this isn't dinner talk."

Dad's answer to everything was always the same. Men. Sex. It was his job to protect us from the evil lurking out there. Until he could hand us off to a godly husband.

"This is how the devil works," Dad said, low and severe. "It starts small. Innocent. It all sounds right, if you're listening with your flesh."

"The evil one tricks us," Mom added. "He slips in through cracks. Makes you deaf. One little compromise, then another, and before you know it, you're swallowed up by the world."

"But Mom," Gracie's voice was eerily calm.

And far away.

I blinked. I was still sitting at the table, but I felt weightless. Like I'd floated to the ceiling. Watching all of this from above.

"What happens when you and Dad die?" Gracie said. "What if neither of us ever meet a man? What if we're alone? You've left us with nothing. No education. No skills. Nothing to build a future."

She sat back in her seat.

"We'll be working gas station counters, selling beer and scratch-offs so we can eat."

That was the last straw. The half-minute speech that ended dinner.

Dad pushed his plate aside and stood, declaring the devil had planted evil thoughts in Gracie's mind. She needed prayer.

So, we knelt. In the dark red carpet of the living room. All of us. Hands on Gracie's head.

Dad dipped his finger into a tiny pot of olive oil. Imported from Israel. From the Mount of Olives. He smeared a cross on her forehead, shiny and wet. He started praying. Mom started crying.

My head was pounding.

What Gracie said was true—and I'd never thought of it before. Never considered where she and I would be if Mom and Dad weren't with us.

We'd be *fucked*.

How was it wrong to think about these things? How was it sin to be... honest?

I closed my eyes, and the floor shifted beneath me. The carpet turned to liquid. A slow flood rising under my knees. Thick. Coppery. Warm. It was blood, and I was being carried. Dragged. Washed away.

I gasped for breath, screamed Gracie's name. But the river pulled me under. No one heard.

My family knelt, unmoved. Still and dry, while I drowned beside them.

It was too much. Too fast.

And I was too small.

5

In the Wall

I woke in my room. Not drowning in a flood of blood. I was in bed. In my nightgown. Like none of it happened.

My eyes snapped open. Sleep still blurred the edges of my mind. My light was off. How the hell did I get here?

The last thing I remembered was praying for Gracie. Or kneeling on the wiry carpet, my hand on her head while my parents prayed over her.

I remembered floating. Feeling detached. Like I was watching it all happen to someone else. Then the flood. The living room swallowed in blood. Dragging me under.

I drew a slow, hollow breath. The cold air hurt my chest.

There was no light under the door. No hum of pipes or creak of movement. Just darkness and still. The kind that swallowed sound. The kind of dark you could taste.

I licked my cracked lips and rolled over. The mattress groaned beneath me.

11:13. The neon-blue numbers of my alarm clock glowed like an omen. Four minutes.

Four minutes until the knocking started.

I lunged for the Goldilocks lamp, a little too hard, but the warm, yellow glow was worth it. It soaked the shadows. Slowed my heart. Helped me breathe.

I sank into my pillow. I wouldn't sleep, but pretending might help.

Then I remembered Rachel. The file.

I sat up again, reaching beneath the mattress for the bulging manila folder. If I couldn't sleep, I might as well research.

Maybe I'd find proof that I was wrong. That Rachel lived. Maybe she was still alive today. She'd be somewhere in her forties. Maybe she found love. Had kids. Built a life. A career.

Maybe tonight, she was watching *Hotel Transylvania 2* with her grandkids. Popcorn in hand, staying up too late during a sleepover.

I smiled at the thought.

I'd seen posters for the movie in the grocery store.

Television was off-limits, of course. Especially new releases. Gracie and I could watch old cartoons on VHS. Nature documentaries, sometimes. But no color TV. No movies past 1965. Too much skin. Too many sins.

Dad said the devil came in with cable.

We got internet a few years ago. Mom needed it for her bookkeeping. After that, Gracie and I started sneaking.

We'd watched sitcoms from the nineties, Jane Austen films. Some had sex scenes. We felt so guilty, we didn't touch our laptops for weeks. After that, we stuck to the black-and-whites. They felt safer. Cleaner.

Rachel didn't seem to have she lived by all these rules. At least not at first.

I pulled out the photo from Niagara Falls and held it carefully. Jean shorts. I'd never even tried on pants.

Her hair was loose, curled at the ends. Cut to frame her face.

I wondered what that felt like. Choosing what to wear, what to show. Curling your hair because you wanted to. Letting it blow in the wind instead of binding it up tight, hiding it away like sin.

I picked up the second photo. The one where she wore the cape dress. Sadness crawled into my limbs. Even I could see it. From just a couple photographs. The second picture wasn't Rachel. Not really. Only what was left.

The dress swallowed her. Modest, they'd say. Godly. But she looked... hidden. Like being a girl was something to be sorry for.

Her face was pale. Her smile, strained. And behind her eyes... Something hollow. Something that hurt.

I squinted at the background. Grainy shadows. Blurred light. A lamp? A window? Was she inside or outside? I couldn't tell.

"Where are you, Rachel?" I whispered, not expecting an answer.

But the sound that followed made my breath snag.

No.

No, no, no.

I snapped my head toward the Goldilocks lamp. Still on. Warm, steady light filled the room. The clock read 11:17.

What? Only four minutes?

That couldn't be right.

It had been longer than four minutes. I'd looked through this file. Touched the photos. Thought. *Processed.* It had to be later. I was imagining things. I had to be.

The light was on. This only happens in the dark... right?

Chhk... Chhk...

No.

Please, no.

"Stop it!" I choked, half-whisper, half-shriek. "The light's on!"

I grabbed my journal from the side table, tucked Rachel's pictures between the pages and shoved the rest of the file under my mattress.

I sat tense. Waiting. Hoping it was done.

Minutes passed. Things stayed quiet. I started to relax, the muscles in my back loosening. Maybe that was it. Maybe it was over.

Chhk... Chhk...

I almost jumped off my bed.

"Holy shit." I hissed the curse beneath my breath, heat prickling at my neck.

Chhk... Chhk...

It started again—behind the dresser.

The sound always started there, before it crossed the room. Slow. Steady. Scratching across the floorboards. Along the walls. Stopping beside my bed. Watching.

My heart raced against my ribs. Blood roared in my ears, louder than the scratching. Like the sound of that flood. Foamy. Red. Swallowing me alive.

I squeezed my eyes shut and clamped my hands over my ears.

Chhk... Chhk...

But it was still there. Behind the dresser.

I don't know what possessed me, but I moved.

I sprang off the bed and crossed the icy floor, bare feet slapping wood. I gripped the particleboard dresser and shoved. It lurched from the wall, nearly toppled.

I jumped in front of it, throwing my weight against the frame to keep it upright. Breathing hard, I waited. Waited for the scratching. But nothing happened.

My chest stayed flush against the peeling laminate top. My lungs heaved. My ears rang. Still, the silence held.

I opened my eyes. Nothing. Just the cedar paneling. Dark and reddish-brown, running from the wood-slat ceiling to the wide pine boards of the floor. Same as always. There was nothing behind the dresser.

Maybe it was a rat in the wall.

I looked toward the clock on my nightstand.

11:20

No. That didn't make sense.

Rats don't keep schedules. They don't scratch the walls at the same time. Every night. If it were a rat, I'd hear it during the day. I'd hear *something* else.

I swallowed hard. Slowly, I pushed the dresser farther from the wall, enough to slide behind it. I pressed my palms to the paneling. The wood was cold.

I was doing the same as I'd done with the knocking and the chandelier. I was trying to find something rational. If I couldn't, then I'd push the dresser back, crawl into bed, and pretend none of this happened.

A shiver crawled up my spine.

The scratching started after I tried to ignore the knocking. Whatever this was, I didn't want to find out what came next.

"Don't be stupid," I muttered. "It's probably rats."

But then I remembered Gracie. How none of her furniture touched the walls. How she walked the edges of her room before bed, hand grazing the wood. Does she hear scratching, too?

She claimed it was a habit. But habits start somewhere. What had she been looking for?

Something sharp scraped my palm. I pulled back fast, sucking air through my teeth as blood welled on my skin.

"What the hell?"

I leaned closer. In the dim glow leeching around the edge of the dresser, a glint of metal caught the light. A nail. Tiny. Trim work sized. Embedded between two cedar panels like it had been working its way free for years.

I followed the shimmer down. One nail. Then another. A seam. What I'd thought was ordinary paneling was something else. A repair. The wood had been cut, cleanly, and then returned to place so precisely it looked original.

But why? Wiring? Plumbing?

I lowered myself to my knees, fingers carefully tracing the square.

I didn't expect the panel to come loose.

The entire board dropped without warning. Landed hard across my lap. I gasped, breath catching as the corner pinched the skin above my knee. A bruise bloomed as blood bubbled beneath the skin.

But I barely felt it. Not the sting. Not the throb at the base of my skull. Because behind the panel was a hole. And something breathed from it.

Cold air. Rot. And something older—older than mold. Older than the house.

My eyes adjusted slowly. The dark inside the wall wasn't empty. There was something there.

They flooded in one at a time, confusion, denial, fear. Then they all washed over me at once.

What the hell was this?

6

BREATHING WALLS

The hole in the wall was breathing.

I didn't move. I couldn't.

The air spilling out was colder than anything I'd felt in this house before. Wet and heavy, like the breath of something that had waited too long to be found.

Silence pressed in around me. Each breath snagged in my throat. Every second stretched, warped by the dread coiling in my chest.

This wasn't an access panel. Not a wiring box. Not a plumbing repair. It was a void. A space that didn't belong. Forced into the house like a wound. Everything about it felt… wrong.

My eyes had adjusted, but my mind was stuttering.

Beagle sat on a worn purple blanket, deep inside the hole. My teddy. Watching me with blank, button eyes.

My stomach flipped. I spun, clutching the edge of the dresser to pull myself upright.

Beagle wasn't under my pillow. He always was. Always. Since before I could remember. But here he was, in the fucking wall.

I wanted to scream and run. But I stood there. I couldn't look away from the little brown bear. He was sitting too still on the purple blanket, his faded, blue ribbon tied in a perfect bow.

Who would do this? And why? When? Was Beagle in my bed when I got in? When I changed into my nightgown? I didn't know. Because I couldn't remember doing any of that.

A soft knock on my bedroom door jolted me.

No.

Mom? Dad?

Panic pricked my scalp. I scrambled to push the dresser back. Hide the hole. To pretend I hadn't seen. But I wasn't fast enough.

Another knock. The doorknob jingled.

"Em?"

My lungs dropped into my stomach as relief washed over me. It was Gracie.

"I'm up," I said, moving toward the door, but not fast enough to stop her from opening it.

"I wanted to check on you," she whispered. "I waited until Mom and Dad were asleep."

I shouldn't have been anxious about her seeing the pulled-out dresser or the uneven panel behind it. But I was.

Would Gracie judge me for hearing things? Would she think I was crazy for trying to find where the sounds came from?

"I'm fine." Too fast. Winded.

"How are you?" I tried again. "After... last night?"

Gracie waved it off and lowered herself onto the edge of my bed. The hem of her white nightgown brushed the pine floorboards.

"Whatever happened to you made Mom and Dad forget about me," she said with a little smile.

It was the first I'd seen her smile in a while, but her words stopped me cold.

"What happened to me?" I asked cautiously, as the memory surged. The flood of blood, the carpet turning liquid, the sound of rushing in my ears.

"It was like you blacked out," she said softly. "You were shaking... crying. It sounded like you were trying to scream, but with your mouth was full of cotton. Like Mom sounded when she got all those teeth pulled."

I swallowed hard.

Oh no.

"Me and Mom brought you to bed."

No.

"Mom and Dad..." I didn't have to finish.

Gracie nodded. "I wasn't sure if you'd remember." She bit her lip. "But I wanted to warn you before morning. They're... really worried." Her green eyes found mine.

"I'm not possessed," I said, louder than I meant to. Like I needed the house to hear it. Like I was talking to them, not Gracie.

"I know you're not," she said.

That made me pause.

"You do?"

"You're no more possessed for fainting than I am for thinking practically about the future."

This wasn't the Gracie I knew. Not the anxious, soft-spoken girl who gave in at the first sign of conflict to keep the peace. She was composed. Grounded.

It unsettled me. I wiped the cold sweat from my palms onto the fabric of my nightgown.

"We haven't talked much lately," I said. "Not really. Not like sisters, you know?"

"I know what you mean." Her eyes moved slowly around my room, and something about the way she looked at it made my stomach twist.

Could I tell her?

"We're more like housemates," she said with a wry smile.

I wanted to be comforted by it. But it made me more anxious. That wasn't a happy smile. It was thin. Tight. Tired. The kind of smile that tries to cover a bruise.

"It's all work, eat, sleep. Then do it again the next day." Gracie shrugged.

I let the silence sit for a moment, thick and humming with things unsaid.

I thought of her at the dinner table. The way she didn't back down. The way she spoke up. That took guts. I bet Gracie didn't even realize how brave she was.

"Do you really want to be a teacher?" I asked quietly.

Gracie looked up but didn't answer right away.

"It seemed like you'd done research," I added. "About the kind of degree you'd need, I mean."

She nodded slowly, like she was turning something over in her head. "Do you think I'll go to hell if I never have kids?"

I caught my breath. "What? No. Of course not. God wouldn't punish you because your body can't..."

Gracie winced. "I mean if I *choose* not to have them."

"Oh."

"I don't know," she said. "Sometimes thinking about raising a kid makes me freak out inside."

My mind scrambled. *You don't play God.* Birth control is manmade. Evil. It interrupts God's design. Condoms break the unity of what He's joined together.

If Gracie never wanted children... she'd have to stay single. Forever.

"You don't want to get married?"

She drew a slow breath. "I've been reading," she said. "Online. Did you know some women take birth control for health reasons? Even if they're not... sexually active?"

The words felt dirty. Like she'd said something shameful. My chest tightened.

"Pregnancy can mess you up, Em." Her voice thinned. "Even with good doctors. Postpartum hemorrhage. Uterine rupture. Preeclampsia." She swallowed. "I didn't even know what those were until a few weeks ago."

I sat in silence, her words echoing.

Weren't children a blessing? Sure, pregnancy hurt, but wasn't that the price Eve paid for bringing sin into the world? Didn't God ease the pain afterward? Didn't mothers forget all about that the moment they held their babies?

You are holy vessels. Sanctified. Set apart. Chosen for God's divine plan. A pastor's voice echoed in my memory.

I saw the prayer circle in church. A weeping mother at the center, nine kids lined up behind her like stair steps. They anointed her belly with oil. Called her holy. Obedient. Favored.

Honor our prayers this day.

No one ever talked about danger. About complications. About risk. Only about spiritual warfare. About the devil attacking pregnant women—women carrying holy offspring.

A sick, heavy feeling twisted in my gut.

Maybe they weren't sick because of demons. Maybe they needed a doctor. Maybe they were... bleeding. Dying. Crying out. And no one listened.

My mind was spinning.

Everything I'd been taught. All the things glorified by my parents, our churches, *everyone*. Home births. Unmedicated births. Women bouncing back after their fifth baby, back to work, back to the kitchen. Cooking. Cleaning. Serving. Always smiling. Barely bleeding. Never breaking.

And all the things we were taught to fear. The devil's work. Or worse, God's punishment for unbelief, for cowardice, for refusing to carry your cross.

Miscarriages. Stillbirths. Babies born with malformations so severe they died in hours, or days. Tiny coffins at the front of the church. Tears swallowed behind modest veils.

But the worst? The thing invented by evil feminists. The excuse weak women used to stop loving their children... Postpartum depression.

My lungs clenched. The air thinned. My vision rippled. Everything felt warped. Fluid. Like reality was melting at the edges.

"Gracie," I gripped the hem of my nightgown. "You... don't want to have kids?"

"I'm twenty-five, Em," she said quietly. "Still at home. Not married. I've had a lot of time to think. And now that we've got internet, I've had time to research too."

Sitting there, watching her, I realized something I couldn't shake. I didn't really know Gracie. Not at all.

"All the complications considered, I'm not afraid of the pain," she shrugged one bony shoulder. "I don't think I'm cut out to be a mom. Some women aren't."

Dad's voice hummed like a sermon in my head.

My eldest daughter lives in North Carolina now. Worldly. Godless. On that nasty little pill because she decided never to have kids.

"She's selfish," he'd say, again and again, stabbing his fork into his plate.

"There's nothing more sacred than raising children for the Lord. But Talia?" He'd glance around the dinner table, eyes settling on me and Gracie like warning shots. "Her mother led her astray. She's lost in the world. She doesn't know God's way."

"I think I'd love teaching," Gracie said, her voice steady. "Older kids, though. Middle school. Maybe even high school."

I stared at her. Who was this girl sitting on my bed? What had she done with Grace Ann? The gentle one, the peacekeeper. The soft-spoken daughter who smoothed every wrinkle and silenced every fight with a smile and a whispered, "Let's pray about it." She never questioned anything. Never *researched*.

"Do you see why I'm afraid I'll going to hell?" she asked softly, smoothing the skirt of her nightgown with a thin hand.

"No…" My gut twisted. Like I was being torn apart from the inside.

Gracie couldn't go to hell—not my sweet, quiet, faithful sister. But… If I believed what I'd been taught, wouldn't she?

Didn't Dad say Talia was damned? Because she didn't submit. Didn't believe. She wore pants. Cut her hair. Wore makeup. Worked outside the home. Her husband wasn't the head of his home, wasn't leading his wife.

"You're not going to hell," I said, choking on the words. "No way. I don't think God works like that."

I couldn't believe those words came out of me.

If God didn't *work like that,* why was I still wearing dresses? Why couldn't I have a job outside my father's business? Why couldn't I go to college?

My mind couldn't take it. The spinning. The back and forth. This slow, splitting crack in the perfect world I'd been taught was whole.

"I never stopped hearing the noises," I said suddenly. Like tearing off a three-day-old bandage.

I needed to change the subject. Distract myself with something that consumed me.

Gracie looked at me, but her face didn't shift.

"The knocking," I added, my voice low. "It never stopped."

The room felt strange. Heavy. Like I was in a dream. Like the house had swallowed me whole, and I hadn't come back up. Gracie was calm. Too calm. And she was questioning things. Things no one in this house ever questioned. Not without consequences.

"I remember," she said.

"Do you think Mom and Dad…" I hesitated. "Do you think maybe they…"

"They're not playing tricks on you," Gracie said, finishing it for me.

I got up and went to the dresser before I could change my mind. "Who did this?"

I shoved it back. Too fast. No time to think. No time to warn her. No time to realize I was crossing a line I couldn't uncross.

Gracie stared at the opening like she didn't see it at first. Then she moved, slow and cautious, slipping off the bed and taking a step toward me.

"Beagle's in there," I whispered.

The words hung between us like ash in the air.

"In where?"

"In the hole."

She leaned over the edge of the dresser, and whatever had kept her calm, whatever held her together, let go.

It wasn't just the color that drained from her face. Something deeper slipped out of her. Like her spine had folded in on itself.

That wasn't shock. It wasn't fear. It was recognition.

Her gaze locked on the hole. Her mouth opened, like she meant to speak but the words had died on the way out.

And I felt it. Not only the fear, but the shift. Like I'd been dropped from the ceiling, back into my own skin. Something shattered. Gracie's calm was gone. And what replaced it was so much worse.

"Gracie." Even whispering her name seemed to snap something loose.

She backed away from the hole, and then from me, moving slow and strange, like her legs didn't belong to her. Her bare feet dragged across the floor toward the door.

"It's in your room," she breathed, eyes locked on the dark behind my dresser.

"What?" I stepped toward her, but she flinched, like my voice had touched her. "Gracie, what's wrong?"

She was shaking her head, red curls bouncing in wild, knotted rings around her narrow shoulders. Her nightgown clung to her knees. Her chest rose too fast. Too shallow.

"It wasn't a dream."

"Gracie," I pleaded. "Talk to me!"

"You..." Her voice caught in her throat. "You found it."

Her back hit the door, eyes still fixed on the hole. One hand clawed behind her, fumbling for the knob. Her fingernails scraped wood. As if the darkness might lunge. Pull her in. Swallow her whole.

"It's in your room."

7

She Didn't Run

I don't know what happened with Gracie that night. Something in her face, something raw and broken, told me there was more to her reaction.

I hoped it was just Gracie being Gracie.

She had a way of folding in on herself when the world didn't add up. Maybe this was another one of those times.

She hadn't said anything else. She slipped out of my room without a word, left the door hanging open behind her. I stood there, shaking beneath the antler chandelier. Maybe in shock, but I told myself I was waiting.

Waiting for Gracie to come back. To explain. To help me understand. She didn't.

And deep down, I knew she wouldn't. Still, I stood there too long. Waiting anyway. Feeling like an idiot. And feeling watched.

The cold from the hole crept across the floor like a slow leak. It crawled over my toes, up my legs, pressed hard against my chest. But I didn't move. Not until the chandelier above me started to sway. Slow. Rhythmic.

I turned back to the dresser. Shoved it far enough to peek behind.

Beagle was still there. Tucked into that worn purple blanket. Propped up like someone had placed him there. Carefully. Deliberately. Lovingly. The threadbare teddy fit right in, curled inside the wall, tucked into the blanket, surrounded by dust and cobwebs. He looked like he belonged there. That was the part I couldn't shake.

Everything slowed as I looked deeper into the space. It wasn't just a hollow behind the wall. It was a room. Small, but very real.

The walls were finished in the same cedar paneling as my bedroom. But the ceiling wasn't. When I looked up, I saw spiders hanging in clusters from their shimmering webs stretched between splintering rafters—some dead, others twitching. I didn't stare long.

The space climbed high, wedged between dusty crossbeams. And near the far wall, a line of pale light spilled down like a crack in reality. The attic? I didn't remember any windows up there. But something was casting light into that hidden room. Something above it.

I had to know. So sometime after one a.m., I crept into the bathroom and opened the narrow door to the attic tucked behind the linen closet. I climbed, slowly.

But just like I remembered, there were no windows up there. No light source. Only beams and old boxes. A ceiling that angled sharply to meet the floor, shadows layered over shadows.

There shouldn't have been light. Not from the attic. But there *was* light in that hidden room.

I didn't push it any further that night.

I'd pulled Beagle out of the wall. Reseated the panel. Slid the dresser back in place like I hadn't seen anything at all.

But I couldn't put Beagle back into my bed after that. I left him on the nightstand. Close, but not too close.

I did try to sleep, but I wasn't surprised when I failed.

And now I was outside the library, sitting on a concrete bench that held the chill of the late winter day. My head throbbed. The sun was too bright, my thoughts, too loud.

Wanda sat next to me, arms folded tight, watching me.

"It's probably nothing," I said, eyes on the cracked parking lot.

Little green blades of spring grass pushed stubbornly through the asphalt.

"I told you about the weird noises and shit…" I almost choked.

Shit? When had I gotten comfortable enough with Wanda to swear—out loud? I never did that. Not with anyone.

"It started at dinner," I continued, fumbling. "Gracie said she wanted to be a teacher. Mom was crying and Dad flipped. We prayed for her. Then I woke up in my room…" I stopped, and realized I was pacing the sidewalk.

"It was a dream," I added quickly. "I'm tired."

"Oh, come on, girl." Wanda sat forward, swinging her legs off the bench. "That would've been a *hell* of a dream."

"You'd have to hear some of my dreams," I muttered, dropping back onto the bench beside her.

She laughed, but only a little. She put a warm hand against my chilled arm and waited for me to look at her.

"Em, we're friends, right?" She asked, her voice soft.

"Of course."

Wanda smiled. "I've seen you tired. This…" she waved her finger in a little circle, "Isn't tired. And whatever dinner-Gracie-teacher-prayer thing happened, it wasn't a dream."

I groaned, tipping my head back against the bench.

"And there's more," she said, standing. "Come on. Let's go inside. I'll make coffee and you can tell me."

Inside, the lights were low, and the building was empty. The coffee was cheap instant, but Wanda had the good hazelnut creamer, the kind that came from the fridge, not a powdery packet.

By the time I was finishing my third cup, I'd told her everything. Dinner. Gracie's dream of being a teacher. The prayer. The flood of blood. Waking up in bed like nothing happened.

I told her about the scratching. The wall. The hidden room. Beagle. And how Gracie had reacted to it all.

Wanda didn't interrupt. She listened, her eyes sharp, expression unreadable.

"So... your teddy bear," she clarified finally, "was *in* the wall?"

"Yes!" I leaned forward, animated now. "Gracie said Mom and Dad would never do something like that—hide a teddy bear in the wall."

"Why would they?" Wanda asked, settling across from me again, fresh cup in hand.

I shook my head. "I don't know."

I reached into my ever-present backpack, half out of habit, and slid my journal out. The photos of Rachel were still tucked between the pages.

"It creeped me out, the way Gracie acted when she saw that little room," I said, remembering, as a cold shiver ran up my spine.

Wanda was quiet for a long time. She stared into her coffee like it might talk to her.

"What?" I asked, heart starting a slow race. "You think I'm crazy?"

She shook her head, quick and certain. "No. But..."

Her eyes met mine.

"That room you found. The one in the wall?"

I nodded slowly.

Wanda bit her lip, scraping a faint line of peach-colored balm onto her teeth before licking it away.

"Damn, Em," she said softly. "I don't want to scare you. It's local gossip, you know? People talk. Stuff gets passed down, twisted. Folks love telling stories."

"Wanda." My thoughts ricocheted. "Please. Just tell me."

She hesitated a second longer, then took a long, steady breath, bracing herself.

"People used to say the man who built that house... kept a girl locked in a closet. Until she died."

My stomach dropped. "Like—kidnapped her? Some kind of serial killer?"

"I don't know." Wanda's voice was quiet. "The story changed every time I heard it. Some said she was his daughter. Others said she was a niece, or a foster kid. But it always ended the same way. He kept her there. And she died."

My eyes fell to the photos, the ones stuck in my journal. I'd opened it, without even knowing, and now a hiss rose behind my eardrums.

All the clippings. The grainy images. The half-read reports buried in the folder under my mattress. Several of them said Rachel was a foster kid. But there were thousands of foster kids moving through the system every year, all over the country. Who's to say Rachel Bagwell, and the girl who vanished from Caster, South Carolina, were the same person?

Still, silence hung between me and Wanda, thick and charged. Like if either of us spoke, something would shatter. So, we didn't.

Instead, I pulled the second photograph out from between my journal pages.

The one with Rachel as a shell. Her red hair pulled tight in a bun. Dressed like me.

Wanda's eyes dropped to the photo. "Em... what is this?"

I turned it over, showed her the scrawled handwriting on the back.

She read it. "Oh fuck. Why is she..." Her voice trailed off. She looked from me to the photo and back again. "Why does she look like you?"

I took a shallow breath. "Same church, I guess."

"But this one." Wanda picked up the first picture.

The one taken at Niagara Falls. Rachel laughing. Free. Life bright in her young eyes. Joy radiating from her smiling face.

"That was before," I said quietly.

Before the cape dress. The bun. Before the life left her eyes.

"Before she joined that church." Wanda muttered. "Or before someone made her."

She looked up at me, cautious, but I nodded. "She looks like a different person."

I could see it. The pain. The hollowness. The complete absence of joy. I wanted Wanda to know I understood. That I felt it too.

I couldn't say any of that out loud, but I didn't have to. Wanda reached across the table and closed her hand over mine.

We sat like that for a moment, quiet. Rachel Bagwell staring up at us from two old photographs. Like she'd been waiting all this time for someone to finally see her.

"She didn't run away, did she?" Wanda's voice was quieter than I'd ever heard it.

"They say she did."

Wanda looked at me then. The blue shadow on her eyelids catching the fluorescent light buzzing above us. It made her eyes flash.

"She didn't," she said. Firm. Low. Almost angry.

"I don't think she did either," I agreed with her. "And I think... last night, I might've found where he kept her."

Wanda picked up the photograph, studying it like I had the night before.

"That doesn't sound like..." I pictured the old man my parents bought the house from. He was quiet. Polite. Propped on his walker while his daughter fussed over him in the lawyer's office.

"Mr. Dickerson?" Wanda asked. She was already shaking her head. "No. He was good as gold. That house sat abandoned for years before he bought it at a state auction for cheap."

That was news to me. I knew Mr. Dickerson had done a lot of work on the place; modern wiring, updated plumbing, energy-efficient windows. I knew the house had been empty for a while. But I didn't know it had been *abandoned* or sold by the state.

"I didn't realize that," I said slowly.

"Yeah." Wanda stood to refill her coffee. "I told you that place had a story. Most houses in Caster do. It's an old town. But that one..." She shook her head as she came back to the table. "The man who built it was strange. Some kind of preacher, I think. Wrote religious books. Kept to himself."

She took a long sip. "He was divorced, and people started a rumor that he'd killed his ex-wife."

My stomach flipped. I didn't know what was worse, how easily people could turn a man into a monster, or how often the monsters were real.

"It was the mid-eighties," Wanda went on, rolling her eyes. "Divorce wasn't common. Especially not here. Caster's always been behind the times. We're deep in the Bible Belt. People didn't know what to do with a divorced preacher."

"So, how'd he end up raising a teen girl?"

"That's the part nobody ever figured out. Some thought she was his daughter from the failed marriage. Others said a niece. But it didn't make sense. Who gives custody of a kid to a shut-in divorced *man* with no family? Especially back then."

I picked up Rachel's photo again, my thumb grazing the edge. "She was a foster kid," I said slowly.

"Once people saw him raising her, they kind of warmed up to him," Wanda explained. "But a year later, she disappeared. After that, the rumors got ugly. They said he'd killed her. Hid her. Or worse. He couldn't shake it, so he eventually skipped town."

She paused to sip her coffee again, then added, "He hired a realtor to try and sell the place, but no one would touch it. Not with the stories. So, he stopped paying the taxes, and the state seized it. It sat empty for years. The yard went wild, the floor collapsed in the living room."

The carpet. Red. Splitting apart like rotted skin. Washing me away.

I stood up and started slowly pacing the break room, watching the tight gray carpet blurring beneath my feet, trying to loosen the knot in my chest.

"Eventually, Mr. Dickerson bought it and fixed it up," Wanda said. "He wasn't superstitious. Didn't believe in bad juju or haunted houses. He lived there for several years, until the Alzheimer's got bad and his daughter had to move him to a home. I think she sold it to pay for his care."

"And my parents bought it." My voice wavered. I hated how thin it sounded.

"It had to be out-of-towners," Wanda said, finishing her coffee. "Even forty years later, nobody local wants that house."

My breath caught. "Do you know his name? The man who built it?"

Wanda's brow furrowed as she thought. Then she slowly shook her head. "That's one detail that never carried over into the gossip." She studied me. "Em, you don't look so good. Are you okay?"

I bit my lip, too hard, but nodded. "I'm fine," I lied. My voice barely made it out of my throat.

"All this is small-town gossip," Wanda said gently, rounding the table. "You know how rumors are. They spread fast. Get twisted, over and over."

She put a hand on my arm. "The police looked into it. They didn't find anything. No charges. No proof. It was all talk."

I wasn't sure I wanted to hear more. I didn't want to entertain the thoughts smoldering between us. But the question came anyway, pushing past the knot in my chest. "Did they find the hidden room?"

The words barely scraped out, and Wanda's face didn't help.

The blank look that crossed her features, the way her eyes unfocused, made the floor feel thinner beneath me. Like the whole library was rotting from the inside out, and I'd found the soft spot where everything caves in.

"Maybe that was left over from some vagrant," she offered, too quickly. "From when the place sat empty."

She was trying to brush away what we both knew was catching. Like you'd swat a spark before it found dry leaves.

I wanted to believe her. I wanted to let it go. But Wanda saw the doubt crawling across my face.

"Yeah, I know." She shook her head. "A vagrant wouldn't patch the wall back up after hiding in it."

"She was in there." I whispered. "Wanda, she was in there. That purple blanket was hers."

"Let's sit you down." She guided me to a chair like I might collapse without it.

"It sounds insane," I said, voice trembling. "The house, the timeline, the photos. All of it. But it's her, I know it."

"Okay," Wanda said softly. "But you have to calm down, girl."

She was kneeling in front of me. Her hands wrapped around mine.

"You're shaking," she said. "Try to breathe, okay? In through your nose, slow. Out through your mouth."

I tried. I really did. I forced slow, measured breaths. Tried to match her rhythm. Tried to hold her hands, to ground myself. But then I caught my reflection in the microwave door across the room.

That warped, black plastic. The kind that curves just enough to make your eyes look too big.

I stopped breathing. The room twisted. The edges of my vision fuzzed, like static on an old TV. Wanda's voice floated somewhere above the fluorescent hum, beneath the crash of blood in my ears.

Because for one quick second, it wasn't only *me* staring back. Rachel's eyes were there too.

Hollow. Familiar.

Watching me.

Waiting.

8

Panic

"I can't..."

I heard someone speaking. I think it was me, but it didn't sound like my voice.

Those eyes in the microwave door. Hollow and dead. They weren't mine. My chest locked up, ribs stiff like rusted hinges.

"I have to get out..."

Out of where? The break room? The library? The house?

You're stuck.

"Do you want to go back outside?" Wanda's voice sounded warped. A whisper, faint and far away.

The room was too loud, drowning her out. The hum of the fridge, the buzz of the light, the faint whoosh of the air vent overhead. All of it pressed in, thick and suffocating.

Why couldn't I breathe?

I wasn't crying. I couldn't. My body had skipped that part and gone straight to locking down.

My throat was collapsing, like something inside was crushing it. I tried to inhale, but it caught halfway.

"Em, try and look at me."

That was Wanda's voice again, low and distant.

Her thumbs brushed over the backs of my hands. My skin was too tight. Too cold. Then too hot. Sparks raced up my arms at her touch and I involuntarily pulled away.

The microwave door. The reflection—those eyes.

Something in me twisted. I wrapped my arms around my stomach, like I could hold myself together, keep the pieces from slipping out onto the floor. My vision blurred at the edges again, white noise and static.

I couldn't stop seeing it. That warped reflection.

I was slipping again. Falling into that dreamlike, syrupy nothingness I'd felt when the carpet turned to blood the night before, taking me away in a raging flood that tore apart the living room floor.

The world felt like it had narrowed to a pinhole of sound and light. Just buzzing, like the fluorescent lights above me were boring straight into my skull. But things wouldn't go black. I couldn't slip away. I couldn't leave.

You're stuck.

I stayed right there on the edge, the drop-off teasing me like it knew I couldn't jump.

"Breathe, hon. In through your nose. Out through your mouth." Wanda's warbled whisper, like she was speaking under water. "It's just a panic attack, alright?"

No.

"You need to breathe."

Believers don't have panic attacks. They pray. Rebuke. Overcome.

"It's okay, Em." Wanda's voice was still so far away. She put her hands on my knees. "Can you feel the floor under your feet?"

God doesn't give us a spirit of fear. My dad's voice rang loud inside my head.

Worldly people have anxiety, panic attacks, depression, and all sorts of mental health issues because they're unbelievers. They don't have God in their lives.

This was sin. Doubt. Weakness. Had I cracked a door? Let something in?

Those hollow eyes, reflecting in the microwave door, flashed through my pounding brain.

"You're safe," Wanda said gently. "Let's try to breathe again, okay? In through your nose."

Believers didn't panic. Believers prayed. Believers trusted.

"And now out through your mouth. Slowly. Like that."

I couldn't look at her. I couldn't move.

We have to keep an eye out for you, Emily. Dad had said as I left the house that morning. *Last night, you passing out during prayer, that was an attack of the devil. You need to guard your heart. Your soul. Most of all, your mind.*

What if this was the devil? *If it's not leading you to God, it's leading you away from him.* What if this was my judgment? For filling my mind with fiction instead of Scripture. For chasing shadows in newspapers instead of light in the Word.

"Emily," Wanda's voice softened. She squeezed my hand. "Can you name five things you see right now?"

The break room blurred. My eyes darted. Unfocused. The coffee pot. Her badge. My journal. The light fixture. The edge of the microwave.

I wouldn't look at the microwave.

Don't look at the microwave.

I tried to speak, but my tongue felt thick. Like it was blocking my airway.

Em, I know you're older now. God will punish those He loves. My mom's voice. When I confided in her about the noises, the knocking, the chandelier swaying in my room.

"Good," Wanda said calmly. "That's good, hon. Can you name four things you can feel?"

Shame. Fear. Cold. The hard plastic of the chair digging into my thighs.

"Three things you can hear." Wanda was steady.

If you dishonor your parents. Entertain impure thoughts. Covet the sins of the world. My mom's voice again. Assertive. Sure. Accusing.

I felt like I was falling. Off a cliff, into water. Drowning. Clawing to get back up, out, free. But my hands found nothing. No grip. No hold. No way out.

"Wanda?"

A new voice. Warm. Resonant. Male.

The sound of a door cracking open, and the smell of something warm—fried and salty—cut through the panic like a blade, resurrecting a blurry memory.

An endless pool of soft, colorful balls. A huge, red tube slide. Tall, golden arches and...

"I brought lunch," the voice said again, shattering the dream. Or memory?

I tried to look up, but everything was dim. Unfocused. All I saw was a tall silhouette in the doorway, holding a brown paper bag like he wasn't sure what to do with it.

His eyes—dark, maybe?—moved between me and Wanda. I felt them land on me, and something stilled, just for a second.

Like all the buzzing in the room paused. The hum of the fridge. The fluorescent lights. My thoughts.

"Is everything okay?"

Wanda stood quickly, one hand still on mine. "Kade, hey. Can you grab a glass of water?"

He didn't hesitate. I heard the bag crinkle as he set it down on the counter. The soft *thunk* of a cabinet. Water rushing into a glass.

No sudden movements like my dad would've made. No frantic questions. No sharp commands. Just motion. Quiet. Steady.

He crouched beside Wanda a moment later, holding out the glass.

I couldn't meet his eyes, not really. But I saw his hands. Calloused, but steady. Familiar in a way I couldn't place.

Wanda took the glass and pressed it into my palms. "A sip, Em. That's all."

But my hands wouldn't listen. They trembled too violently. Water sloshed dangerously close to the rim. I couldn't lift it without knocking the glass against my teeth.

Kade's hands brushed mine, warm and sure, and instinctively, I pulled back.

He didn't flinch, didn't say anything. Like it wasn't strange at all to help a girl fall apart in a break room. He waited. Then gently helped guide my hands to the table's edge.

"Do you want to go outside?" Wanda asked again. A question I think she'd already asked once before.

This time, I could hear her. And I nodded.

Wanda stood quickly, her steady hands wrapping around my arm to help me up.

My legs were shaky. Cramping. They didn't feel like they'd hold me. But somehow, they did. I felt the floor beneath my feet, the thin soles of my shoes biting into the tight, gray carpet.

"Please bring lunch, Kade," Wanda said quietly as she pushed open the break room door. "And grab some drinks from the fridge."

Kade was coming with us.

I heard the paper bag crinkle, the soft clatter of cans as he pulled them from the fridge. His footsteps followed, slow and even, as we stepped out the back door.

The bright sunshine stung my eyes, but the pain helped. It cut through the fog in my head, made room for air. The warmth on my skin chipped away at the stiffness in my body.

9

FRENCH FRIES

Wanda guided me to an old wooden picnic table. I slid onto the bench, my denim skirt catching on a few splinters along the edge. I reached down, felt the thick fabric against my fingers, and tugged it free.

Wanda sat next to me and Kade slid in across from us.

I hadn't really seen him in the break room. Everything was too dark. Too blurry. But I could see him now, even if I couldn't look him in the eyes—not fully.

If you look a man in the eyes, he'll think you're flirting. My mom's warning from when I was twelve.

As the spinning in my chest began to ease, I filled my lungs with warm, late-winter air. My gaze caught on the slope of Kade's arm. The curve of his jaw.

His skin was a warm, golden-brown, like sunlit earth. Rich and deep, smooth beneath the shadow of his dark curls. Broad shoulders were squared beneath a thick, black leather jacket, a band t-shirt peeking from behind the open front. A dimple tugged at the corner of his mouth. Not quite a smile.

Wanda pulled a cold soda toward her, popped the tab, and slid it my way. "Can you sip?"

"Thank you." My voice was hoarse. I took the red and silver can from her carefully.

I could hold it this time, unlike the glass of water in the library. I brought it to my lips.

Sharp. Clean. Sweet. It stung down my throat, all the way to my stomach, lighting me from the inside out as the numbness began to fade.

Kade still hadn't said anything. But when I dared a glance, I caught him watching me. Not like my parents would have. Not like I was a spectacle. He looked... concerned. Kind.

Wanda followed my gaze and gave him a little nod. "This is my brother, Kade," she said. "Kade, this is my friend, Emily."

He smiled. It brightened his whole face. "Nice to finally meet you, Emily."

I opened my mouth to say something. Anything. Nice to meet you, too. Thanks for the help. The water. The drink. Sorry I'm a wreck.

But nothing came out. So, I nodded, feeling every bit the awkward, sweaty mess I probably looked.

Kade didn't seem to notice. He smiled again and started pulling foil-wrapped sandwiches from the paper bag. One by one, he lined them up on the picnic table.

"Chicken sandwiches." He tapped a couple of the neat little packages and glanced at Wanda. "Burgers." He waved his hand over the last three, grabbing himself a burger and peeling the wrapper back.

He didn't push one toward me, didn't ask if I was hungry. He left them there like an invitation I could choose to accept or ignore, whichever I felt like.

I wasn't sure what I was feeling at that moment, but it felt... good.

Wanda and her brother had both helped me. They hadn't judged me, hadn't said I was being punished, hadn't asked to pray for me to stop the devil's attack. They helped me. Gave me space and support.

I found myself watching Kade's hands again as he unwrapped his lunch. Clean nails, a little grease beneath the thumbnail. A scar across one knuckle like a jagged, white thread.

"Are you feeling better, Em?" Wanda asked, peeling back the foil on her chicken sandwich.

I let out a shaky breath and half-laughed at myself. "Yeah." I grabbed a burger, trying to push away the tightness in my chest, the tremor in my fingers. "I don't know what the hell happened."

I bit my lip, casting a quick glance at Kade. He was eating. He didn't seem to notice my curse, and if he did, he didn't seem to care. Something in me relaxed a little more.

"Is that what happened last night?" Wanda looked at me. "When you woke up in your room?"

I hesitated, every part of me hyper-focused on dissecting my burger. I slid the top bun off the sandwich, sesame seeds scattering onto the foil wrapper before I carefully removed all the tomato, lettuce, onion and pickle.

Last night, hovering over my sister during prayer on the living room floor, was the first time I could ever remember really and truly fainting. But those moments where I can't stop shaking, can't breathe, and feel like the world is caving in on me, that happened all the time—but never this bad.

"Yeah," I said, finally. "It happens sometimes."

"Sometimes?" Wanda stopped, looking at me, her brow raised in an unspoken question.

"A couple times a week?"

"Good lord, Em!" Wanda shook her head, big hoop earrings dancing from her ears. "I'm no doctor, but I've had anxiety all my life. That was a freaking panic attack. You don't need to be having those every week, hon."

There it was again. Anxiety. Panic. I was going to hell for sure.

"You know, mental health isn't something to be ashamed of." Wanda put a hand on my arm, and I realized I'd slipped into silence as I reassembled my nearly naked burger.

"Even Kade has issues he's struggled with through the years." Wanda looked toward her brother who nodded, wiping his mouth with a thin paper napkin.

"I'm on a couple different things." He shrugged. "Your brain's an organ, like the other parts of your body. Sometimes it needs some meds. Nothing to be ashamed of."

I should've felt relieved. I tried to smile. Tried to act like I felt better. But something tight and cold twisted in my gut.

God doesn't give us a spirit of fear.

If it didn't come from God, where did it come from? All of this was fear. The shivering, the clammy forehead, the cold sweat, the pounding heart, the lungs locked tight.

That wasn't peace. Or joy. Or love. All the things God was supposed to be. All the things I was supposed to have as a believer. I didn't have any of them. Not today. Not ever. So it had to be...

You're no more possessed for fainting than I am for thinking practically about the future. Gracie's voice came back to me, soft and steady.

I took a bite of my burger. Greasy patty, sharp ketchup, tangy mustard, soft bun. And suddenly I was back there.

A ball pit. A huge red slide. Golden arches stretching high over the playground. A clear plastic case full of cheap, little toys.

"Are you okay, Emily?" Kade's voice pulled me back. I opened my eyes. I hadn't realized I'd closed them.

My face burned. Not because I felt like a fool, swooning over a dollar cheeseburger, but because something else was happening inside me.

"What's up, girl?" Wanda elbowed me.

"Nothing," I said too fast. "This is going to sound *really* stupid, but I've never had this before."

I believed it when I said it. But as soon as the words were out, I knew they weren't true.

"Never?" Wanda choked on a fry. "Holy shit, Em! Here, have some more before rigor mortis sets in."

"Not even one fry in the back of a friend's car?" Kade asked, grabbing a few for himself.

Our hands brushed. Just for a second.

I shook my head.

You'd need friends for that. And I didn't have friends growing up, no more than I'd had fast food.

Yeah, you did.

I dipped a fry into Wanda's ketchup, spilled across her foil wrapper.

"I always wanted to try it," I said. My voice was steadier now. I wanted to believe the lie. "We didn't grow up with it."

That part was true. My parents hated fast food.

Our girls have never put that junk in their bodies. They said like it was some kind of badge of honor.

"Probably for the best, honestly," Kade said. "This stuff's poison."

"Yeah, but damn it tastes good sometimes." Wanda grinned. "A kid needs at least one kid's meal in their life. The toys were the best part. Screw the nuggets."

She leaned against me. "Back in our day, you got to pick the toy. Now it's whatever's left. But back then? It was fun. And the ball pit? That was everything."

It was. It really was. That endless sea of red, yellow, and blue. It felt like it went on forever.

But how did I know that?

How could I know the slide curved twice before it dropped you into the balls? Or that the plastic smelled faintly of feet and sanitizer?

I'd never been inside a fast-food restaurant. Not once. Not ever. Right?

My phone buzzed across the weather-worn picnic table, chipping more pale paint from the surface. I jumped, nearly dropping my half-eaten burger. The screen lit up: **Mom**, in bold, bright letters.

Wanda glanced at it. So did Kade.

I didn't move. I stared at the screen like maybe if I waited long enough, it would stop.

It didn't.

"Do you need to get that?" Wanda asked, casually, turning her focus back to her fries.

"I guess."

I stood, wiping my hands on my denim jumper like I could scrub away the nerves kicking back up in my chest.

I walked a few steps toward the side of the cinderblock library, out of earshot, then swiped *accept* and pressed the phone to my ear. My eyes shut instinctively. Like I could brace myself against whatever she was going to fuss at me about this evening.

"Hello?"

There was a pause. Then her voice. Sweet, practiced. Too even. Too precise.

She was mad.

"I wanted to check in. I haven't heard from you since you left work at lunch."

"You said I could," I tried not to sound as defensive as I felt. "I've been at the library."

Another pause.

I could picture her, lips pursed, holding in a thousand things she wasn't ready to say. "You're not answering your texts."

My stomach dropped. My phone. I always checked it. Always stayed on top of texts. It kept Mom at bay. Prevented the calls.

"I left my phone in my bag." I winced. I never lied to my mom.

"Well." Her voice cracked into a brittle smile. "As long as you're having fun, Em."

I rolled my bottom lip between my teeth, felt the dry skin tear.

"We came home right after you left anyway." Her words were minced, tight.

"Why?"

My mind started racing. Maybe Gracie would've left early, there wasn't much left to do, only finishing the trim in the master. But Mom and Dad? They stayed late. Always.

"Gracie isn't feeling well. We brought her home."

The world stilled. The breeze died. The lone butterfly hovering over an early spring bloom sank to the grass.

"What do you mean, Gracie isn't feeling well, Mom?"

The room. Something happened when she saw that hidden room upstairs. This has to do with that room.

"You know your sister," Mom said gently. Too gently. Her voice was soft, but it made my knees lock, like trying to tell firm ground from quicksand in a creek bed.

"She has her good days, and her bad ones. But I think she'd feel better if you came home."

"Okay." The word slipped out before I could stop it.

I glanced toward the picnic table. Wanda and Kade were quietly finishing lunch.

"You know how sensitive Gracie can be," Mom reminded me.

I closed my eyes.

"We'll see you soon, yes?"

"Yeah. I'm headed home."

"I love you!" She hung up before I could answer.

I stared at the phone screen for a moment after the line went dead, my thumb hovering like I might call her back, to ask what *not feeling well* really meant. But I didn't.

I slipped the phone into the pocket of my denim skirt, pressing it down like I could smother the conversation before Wanda or Kade noticed.

But Wanda was watching.

"Everything okay?" she asked, when I rejoined them at the table.

I nodded. "Fine. That was my mom."

Wanda arched a brow, clearly not buying it, but didn't press. She was finishing the last of her fries, a crumpled chicken sandwich wrapper resting near her elbow.

Kade had gone back to his burger.

The silence stretched until he broke it with the crinkle of foil as he balled up his wrapper and shoved it into the empty paper sack.

I picked up a fry, let it dangle between my fingers, then dropped it back into Wanda's basket.

"Mom wants me home," I said, trying to cover the sigh that slipped out. "Gracie's not feeling great."

"I hope she's okay," Wanda said.

I shrugged, and for a second, our eyes met. I wished she could read my mind, this once.

It's the room, Wanda. Gracie's upset about the room.

"If things..." Wanda paused, then steadied herself. "Here. Let me give you my number."

Something warm flushed across my chest as she grabbed a napkin, scribbled her number, and folded it up.

"Text me if anything happens." She stood, pressing the napkin into my hand, then wrapped me in a tight, quick hug. "Be careful driving home."

10

Purple Blanket

The road home blurred past my window, gray and familiar. The bright blue sky had dulled, clouds hanging dark and heavy near the trees. Every mailbox looked the same. All the road signs blurred together. Pine trees hunched over the two-lane road like they were watching me. Like they knew something I didn't.

I kept both hands tight on the wheel.

Mom hadn't said much, only that Gracie wasn't feeling well. But that wasn't true. Not really.

Something happened when she saw that room. I could still see her face, blank and pale, like a part of her had been unplugged.

Had she... remembered something?

That's what I would've guessed, if I didn't know Gracie. If I didn't know our family. If I didn't know anything.

She remembered something. About that wall. That room. But what? And how? We'd only lived there six years. I'd found that room half an hour before she saw it.

It's in your room. Gracie's voice echoed. *It wasn't a dream.* She remembered the hole. The little room inside my wall. *You found it.*

Gracie's habit, tracing her bedroom walls every night, dragging her hand along the paneling. She was looking.

I eased off the accelerator, dread coiling in my chest. There were too many horrible thoughts. They all spiraled too fast to hold.

Why would Gracie remember a hidden room in a house we'd only lived in six years?

A low headache bloomed at the base of my skull. I was getting too close to the house. And whatever was bothering Gracie, it wasn't new. And it wasn't good.

Slowly, whether I wanted to see it or not, the house came into view. A small, unimposing split-level. Its dark green shingled roof met at uneven angles, creating space for the cramped attic and the odd, half-finished upstairs. Faded white shutters framed the windows.

Inside, everything was dark. Like night had already fallen on the last lot on Great Falls Road, shrouding our crooked little house in a mantle of darkness before creeping out to the rest of the street.

The windows looked black without any light behind them. Too black. Like eyes, watching.

The driveway wasn't long, but it stretched forever as I inched Dad's truck toward the house.

Text me if anything happens, Wanda had said. *Be careful driving home.* I took a slow, steadying breath, but it caught against my ribs.

When I pulled up and put the truck in park, I saw my mom standing on the porch. Arms crossed. Like she'd been waiting since the moment we hung up.

She stepped down to meet me, smiling, but it didn't reach her eyes.

I grabbed my slouchy backpack, phone in hand, and pushed the truck door open.

"Thanks for coming home," Mom said, pulling me into a hug.

I tried to relax, like I had when Wanda hugged me, but my whole body felt like a board.

"I know you like spending your evenings at the library."

I shrugged. "How's Gracie? Fever? Puking? Is the cough back?"

"Oh, it's nothing like that."

She linked her arm through mine, and I felt myself recoil inside. But I didn't give into that. I didn't pull away.

None of this felt like comfort. Not like a mother's gentle, nurturing touch. It felt like I was being dragged. Like I was a prisoner, and the house was my cell.

"She's resting now," Mom said more softly, like Gracie might hear us. "I wanted to meet you outside, to make sure you didn't wake her. I don't think she slept much last night."

I pictured Gracie, pale and dazed, curled up on her bed, rocking herself back and forth.

"So why did I have to come home?" I stopped, shy of the door. I'd never felt this much dread about stepping into the house. "If Gracie's asleep, that's good for her. I could've stayed at the library."

Mom pulled her arm free from mine, her hand settling on her hip. "Emily Carol. You know how your sister is. She'll feel better knowing you're here when she wakes up."

Maybe. Or maybe she wouldn't know either way, wouldn't really *care* either way. Gracie never seemed bothered when I spent hours at the library.

"What's so great about the library anyway?" Mom's voice shifted, lighter, but edged with suspicion. "All the time you spend there, I'd think you'd have read every book by now. It's a tiny library."

I tried not to let the panic reach my voice. "I like reading history."

I stepped over the threshold, the cold air hitting me like a wave.

"Why is it so cold?" I asked quickly, changing the subject before she could ask anything else about the library.

"It's six in the evening in February, Em." Mom moved past me toward the kitchen. "It's always cold this time of year."

But not *in* the house, right? Dad always kept a fire going.

I stepped toward the living room and glanced at the hearth. Bare. Cold. Maybe he hadn't had time to light it yet?

But something was off.

The hearth wasn't just empty. It was spotless. No embers from last night's blaze. No ash from weeks of burning. Not even soot on the caramel-colored bricks. It was clean, scrubbed down. Like there hadn't been a fire there in years. Like the fire last night never happened.

Dad must've cleaned it out. He did that sometimes. A full sweep was needed every so often, after weeks of burning pine. He'd probably spent the evening working on it. Maybe he was about to rebuild the fire as I walked in.

But then I heard voices, low and steady, coming from the bedroom off the kitchen. The hum of a VHS tape. Dad's World War Two documentaries. He wasn't near the hearth. He wasn't planning a fire.

The house was cold. Gracie was sick. And the fireplace sat silent, empty, wiped clean—while Dad watched war films in the dark.

A chill crept up my spine, triggering a shiver I couldn't suppress. Then a burst of machine gun fire cracked through the quiet kitchen, and I jumped.

I turned and hurried up the stairs, taking them two at a time.

Drop my bag. Sneak back down. Check on Gracie.

That was the plan.

But when I stepped into my room, I stopped short.

My dresser had been moved. Only far enough for someone to squeeze behind it and push the panel aside.

My first, panicked thought, *Mom and Dad found it.*

But no. That didn't track. If they knew what was behind that wall, Dad wouldn't be watching his tapes. They'd be up here. Investigating. Tearing things apart.

I slung my bag onto the bed but and my back stiffened. My arms went cold.

Beagle wasn't on my nightstand where I'd left him. He wasn't on the bed either. He was on the floor. Torn open. Clumps of yellowed stuffing spilling from a jagged tear down his back.

"Beagle." I dropped to my knees without thinking, scooping him up like I'd found a wounded friend.

Then I saw his face. The eyes, his black button eyes, were gone. Gouged out. Only ragged holes stared back at me, with brittle tufts of thread where the buttons used to be.

"Aw, Beagle." Guilt surged in my throat. I'd dropped him. Like I was dropping a dying friend because there was too much blood.

"What happened?" I whispered, gathering every piece of torn stuffing, every limp thread. I cradled him against my chest like I could protect him.

But something burned behind my eyes. This wasn't just a broken toy. It felt like murder. Like he'd been gutted. Blinded.

"I'll fix you," I whispered, voice trembling into the matted fur. "I will."

I tucked him gently into the bottom drawer of my dresser.

My dresser.

The one that had been moved.

I couldn't see inside the hole, not by leaning over the dresser like Gracie had last night. I'd have to move it again. Push the panel completely out of the way.

I squeezed behind the dresser, squatting cautiously as I eased the loose panel aside.

"Gracie?"

There she was. Curled next to the dusty purple blanket. Her chin rested on her knees. Arms wrapped tight around her legs. Her green eyes, dulled with exhaustion, stared blankly through the opening, right at me. But it didn't feel like she was really seeing me, and she didn't answer.

"Gracie?" I said her name again.

She lifted a finger to her lips. "Mom thinks I'm in bed."

I didn't want to go in. My legs didn't want to move. They still ached from earlier. Tight and trembling after the panic attack at the library. Every instinct I had screamed not to crawl into that space. Not to enter that dark, little crypt behind the wall.

But I couldn't leave her alone.

So I climbed in. Careful not to touch the sagging cobwebs, or the piles of dead roaches and flies that littered the edges of the floor.

"Are you okay?"

Gracie took a breath that shook her whole body. "Why'd you open this?"

Her question caught me off guard. It felt like she'd known about this place all along. Like she'd avoided it. That thought cut my throat like glass.

"I heard scratching," I whispered. "I told you, I've heard knocking since we moved in."

I waited. She didn't respond.

"Then it turned to scratching. I finally got tired of it. It was coming from behind my dresser, so I moved it. And I found this."

Gracie stared at me, like she was letting the words sink in. Then she buried her face against her knees again.

A long beat of silence passed between us.

Gracie didn't look up. Her hands dropped to the blanket, fingers plucking at the frayed edge. Something crawled in the pit of my stomach.

Gracie was neat. Put together. Obsessively so. She folded every piece of laundry with perfect corners. Aligned. Tidy. Precise.

But now she sat tugging loose threads on this forgotten blanket like she might unravel the whole thing, stitch by stitch, if she kept going.

Dust curled into the pale shaft of light spilling from that unseen window above us. Drifting like ash. Fragile. Restless.

"It's always been a dream," Gracie whispered, her voice muffled against her skirt.

I remembered her words from last night, spoken on a breath as she backed away from me.

"What's been a dream, Gracie?" I asked, when she didn't say anything else.

"This." Her head snapped up. She threw out her arms, motioning to the dark. The movement was sudden. Twitchy. Like a marionette jerking on tangled strings.

I flinched. My shoulder slammed into the exit behind me, sharp wood biting into my back. I froze. Didn't blink. I waited for her to snap.

But Gracie didn't move again. Her arms dropped like dead weight, knuckles smacking the dusty floor with a hollow *thwack*. I winced, but she didn't seem to notice.

"She told me it was okay." Her voice was far away now. Thin.

Then she looked at me. Her dull green eyes had gone glassy.

My fingers found my pocket, closed around the napkin Wanda gave me. I held it tight.

"Who told you it was okay, Gracie?" I asked, voice low. Careful.

She didn't answer.

From downstairs, I could hear Mom in the kitchen. Pots scraping, the click of burners. The far-off hum of Dad's war tapes, still playing from their bedroom.

"In the dream," Gracie muttered. "The girl in here... she told me it was okay. But..."

She turned her glazed eyes away from mine, and my limbs relaxed a fraction.

"It wasn't. I wasn't supposed to make a sound. It was dark. Mom and I left. I didn't know where Dad was."

I bit my lip. Too hard. Blood filled the cracks of dry skin.

"Gracie." I said her name gently. Hoping it might anchor her, bring her back.

"We left, Em." Her gaze was fixed on the purple blanket, eyes vacant as she picked at the fraying edge. "Mom and I left. We left Dad."

I hesitated. I didn't want her to think I doubted her. But... I did.

My parents didn't believe in divorce. Sure, Dad had been divorced before, but that was his ex-wife's fault. She backslid, took her daughter into the world with her. That wasn't *my m*om. My mom would never leave Dad. Would she?

"I kept crying for him," Gracie mumbled, her mouth pressed into her skirt. "We ended up at a rest stop near the Virginia line. I was sobbing, and Mom used a payphone to call Dad. He came and got us."

The words hit me like a punch to the chest.

I wanted to tell her it was only a dream. That something that big—something like *that*—I would've heard about, even if it happened before I was born. I wanted to remind her that Mom and Dad believed in marriage. In fighting for it. In staying no matter how hard it got. *Believers* stayed. They didn't run.

But I couldn't say anything. Gracie's memories were too real. Too vivid.

Would Mom remember? A gut-wrenching panic clenched my ribs at the thought. *Fear.* I couldn't… I could *not* ask Mom.

"I used to think it was all a dream." Gracie's voice shook. "This room. That night. I've had nightmares about it. It ate me alive for years." She sucked in a shaky breath.

"How did seeing this bring it back?" I asked softly.

We've only lived here six years. You couldn't remember this room because we didn't live here back then.

Gracie looked at me, her green eyes hazed and rimmed red. A tear tracked down her cheek. She yanked the purple blanket closer, releasing a puff of dust into the air.

Then she shoved it at me.

I caught it, right before the filthy, rat-shit-covered thing landed on my head.

"Gracie…" I wanted to snap, but my voice came out thin. Raw.

"Look at the embroidery, Emily." Her words were sharp, unraveling like the threads she'd tugged loose.

It took me a second, but I turned the blanket over in my hands. In one frayed corner, I found it. Faded pink thread, the tight little stitches barely legible anymore.

Gracie Lyles '88

What the *fuck*?

Her nickname. The one Mom used when she was small. Her birth year. Three years before I was born.

The blanket itched against my fingers. I squeezed my eyes shut, my fingers curling into fists. Something rose inside me. Something buried. Long dead. Forgotten.

A blanket. Coarse, with frayed edges that clung to my arms, charged with static. A car. Music playing. But not gospel music…

I reached for the memory, tried to grab hold, but it dangled just out of reach, like a road half-lost in the morning fog. I couldn't make it out. I couldn't hold on. It slipped away, like smoke on a breeze, rising with the dusty haze in the hidden room.

I clutched the blanket tighter. Tried to call it back. But it was gone. And I was left. In this hollow room inside the wall. With Gracie. And a blanket embroidered with her name. From *before* we lived here. Before my father ever bought this house.

"Gracie." I finally tore my eyes away and looked at her. "We'd never seen this house before we moved in. That was only six years ago."

"I was here." Her voice was steady. Sure. No hesitation. No doubt.

Gracie. Here. In this house. In this room. Mom, leaving Dad. Taking Gracie with her. If Gracie had been here, if it wasn't a dream, what else wasn't? What else from her nightmares had been real?

What about mine?

"You don't believe me." Gracie's voice sharpened with anger. "It's all a dream, right? I didn't believe it either. Not until you opened this panel."

She looked around the cramped space, her voice catching. "It's real. This is real. Do you know how long it took me to make peace with the nightmares? How many years I spent convincing myself it was messed up dreams? Something wrong with me?"

She bit her lip. "If you hadn't found this room, it would still be a dream."

I didn't know what to say. I wanted to be the kind of sister who helped. Who made things better. Not worse. But I couldn't un-find this room. I couldn't un-hear what she'd just told me.

Gracie rocked forward and back, arms tight around her knees again. "Mom hid me in this closet," she whispered. "And we ran. We ran away from Dad."

My head pounded. "Why would Mom run away from Dad?" The air shifted. The room seemed to tilt.

Gracie didn't answer right away. For a moment, I thought she wouldn't.

Silence stretched between us. I clutched the dusty blanket, my sister's name stitched in tattered pink threads across one corner. Gracie huddled in the shadows, fear and shame flickering across her thin face.

I didn't push her. I sat in silence beside her, waiting. For a word, a breath, anything.

"I don't know..." Gracie's answer was whispered, sighed. Like she was spilling out pain and confusion.

A chill coiled around me as I heard it. It was subtle at first. Almost like the cold of a crisp autumn morning. It cooled my breath, my sinuses, my lungs. It felt good, even comforting. The burn in my throat eased. The sweat on my brow chilled my blood. I closed my eyes for half a second. Breathed it in.

That's when it hit.

The scent slammed into me, sharp and sour. My breath caught mid-inhale as I choked. Gagged.

It was rot. Decay. It started like wet mulch or damp leaves but thickened fast.

For a second, I thought it was coming from me. From inside my own mouth. My throat. My stomach. Like something was rotting inside me, crawling out.

Death.

The rancid, unmistakable scent of a corpse buried in damp earth. Skin sloughing, marbled in purple, yellow, and sickly green. Maggots writhing from sunken eye sockets, from lips peeled back in an unnatural, skeletal grin.

And I could see it.

I could *see* it.

The cracked skull. Flaming red hair gone limp, slick, tangled. Eyelids peeled back. Teeth, perfect teeth, still in place, still white, still clean. Grinning.

A fly buzzed near my ear.

That part was real. Too real.

I swatted it away, smacking the side of my head, my fingers catching in the strands of hair that had fallen loose from the bun on the back of my head.

Get out.

That voice. I didn't care now whether it was mine or not. Whether I heard it aloud or in my head. I was already moving.

I tore my way out of that hole in the wall, the rough edges of cedar scraping raw lines into my arms as I shoved past the paneling and stumbled into the light.

"What are you doing?" Gracie's voice rose behind me, sharp and frightened.

But it didn't stop me. I ran. Down the narrow hallway, into the bathroom. I dropped to my knees just in time to vomit into the toilet.

The taste of death still clung to my sinuses, mixing with half-digested burger and sweet ketchup in my throat. I couldn't stop.

Gracie appeared cautiously at the bathroom door. She flicked on the light but didn't come any closer. She stood there, giving me space while my stomach emptied itself completely.

She was thoughtful like that. Gracie never pushed. Never forced her way into someone's personal space.

Mom, on the other hand, was the opposite.

"Oh, my poor baby!" Her voice pierced the silence as I tried to breathe, hoping the vomiting was over.

Oh no.

The faucet roared on. Cold water hissed against the ceramic sink. A damp rag traced across my forehead, and another wave of bile surged up, burning my throat.

My mind was racing. My fingers clutched the toilet bowl, knuckles blanched white.

The dresser was still out of place. The panel was still moved. The room was still open. And I'd dragged that fraying, purple blanket out with me. Had I dropped it in the hallway? Had Mom seen it? Fear sank deep into the cramping pit of my stomach.

I snatched the rag from her hand and slapped it over my face, as if that might stop everything, my nausea, the memories, her curiosity.

"I have to get back to my room," I muttered behind the cloth.

"You're sick, baby." Mom cooed. "Stomach bug must've found my baby girl."

My legs screamed, muscles cramping as I pulled myself up. I still held the cloth to my face, part shield, part excuse.

"I'm fine," I croaked, and pushed past her.

Gracie flattened against the wall as I barreled by, Mom's house slippers flapping behind me.

"Emily!" she called. "You need to brush your teeth!"

I slammed my bedroom door shut and twisted the lock as her hand touched the knob.

"Emily!" Her voice was sharp now, a little hurt, a little angry. But she smoothed it over quickly. "What's the matter with you?"

"I need to be alone," I said, my voice muffled through the rag.

Silence.

I could hear her breathing on the other side of the door. Then, after a long pause, she turned and shuffled away.

"Gracie, it's dinner time, I guess," she called over her shoulder, and I heard my sister's soft footsteps following.

"What's wrong with her?" Dad's voice echoed up from the kitchen.

"I don't know," Mom snapped. "She slammed the door in my face."

Their voices blurred into the clatter of plates, the drop of ice into glasses, the hum of routine.

I pressed the rag to my face and exhaled. Slow, shaky, and shallow.

Relief.

She couldn't see the room. Couldn't know that I knew.

I didn't know why, but the fear that gripped every cell in my body when I imagined my parents finding that room... realizing I knew about it, that Grace remembered... it was paralyzing.

I wiped the cloth across my burning face, over my sticky lips, and opened my damp eyes.

What the...

The dresser was back in place. The panel was closed. The blanket gone.

"Oh... Gracie..." I couldn't stop the tears that rolled down my cheeks.

I didn't know how she managed it, in the few moments between me tearing out of that hole and Mom hearing me gag and bounding up the stairs, but she did.

She hid it. She knew Mom and Dad couldn't know either.

A cold chill crept up my spine. I staggered toward my bed.

Beagle.

He was lying on my pillow. Blinded. Gutted. Fresh stuffing waited beside him. Clean and white. New. A small sewing box sat next to him. A pack of black buttons placed neatly on top.

Something cold crawled across my limbs.

Gracie. It had to be Gracie. Who else would've done this?

But something in my gut said I was wrong.

The little sewing box was too perfect. The buttons, pristine. The needle, stuck into the padded lid, was already threaded with light brown thread. The exact shade of Beagle's worn fur.

I took a shaky breath.

Maybe Gracie had closed the panel. Maybe she'd taken the blanket. Hidden it somewhere safe before Mom could see it.

But she hadn't had time to gather sewing supplies, get Beagle from my dresser drawer, and stage him like this.

Had she?

11

Rev. D. L. Emerson

I didn't know what woke me. I must've been exhausted. I'd fallen asleep with every light still on, not just my little Goldilocks lamp.

I hadn't changed into my night clothes. I was still on top of the covers, and I was freezing. And sore. Every muscle in my body was sore. Even the little ones between my fingers.

I tried to flex my hand, stretch the soreness away, but a sharp puncture to the skin of my palm made me sit straight up, stifling a cry.

Beagle fell off my bed, dragging the needle from my hand.

"Oh damn," I whispered, flinching as blood bubbled to the surface of my palm. I must've fallen asleep trying to stitch Beagle back together.

I slid off the bed, ignoring every part of my body screaming at me to lay back down. I wiped the spot of blood onto my skirt and picked Beagle up, weaving the needle safely through his fabric paw.

"Hold this for me, buddy," I whispered to him, tasting my own breath as I spoke. "Oh, shit, I'm sorry."

I realized what I was doing—apologizing to a stuffed bear for my vomit breath. I sighed, tossed Beagle onto the bed, and shuffled toward the bathroom, muscle memory guiding me through the dark hall.

I shut the door carefully and flicked the light on.

"Oh, good lord." My reflection made me recoil.

Dull, blue-gray half-moons sagged under my bloodshot eyes. The whites were so red I could barely see the brown of my irises. My lips were cracked and peeling, papery shreds dangling off in bloody patches. Drool and dried blood caked the corners of my mouth.

"You look like death, Em," I whispered, but the vision came back, uninvited.

That woman. The hole in the wall. That smell. Rot and earth and bile, curling through my lungs until I thought I'd drown.

"No, you don't." I tore my reddened eyes from the mirror and splashed cold water on my sticky face.

When I'd scrubbed the taste of vomit and blood from my mouth, I turned my attention to my hair.

Buns aren't inherently comfortable—especially when your hair goes all the way to your ass, because you've never been allowed to cut it. Not even a trim to keep it healthy. But you're also not allowed to wear it down. Flaunting it is vanity.

It takes a hell of a lot of straight pins, scraping your scalp raw, to twist that much braided hair into a lump on the back of your head.

It's bad enough during the day. But if you make the mistake of sleeping in it, those little bastards embed themselves deep into the most tender parts of your skull.

Pulling them out hurts like hell. But there's relief too. Pressure easing. Blood returning. I spent a few minutes brushing it out, scratching my scalp with the teeth of the brush.

I caught myself yawning in the mirror, but behind me, I saw something else. The attic door. Cracked open.

My first thought was Gracie.

She wasn't the go-hunting type, not really. But maybe the memories from that closet-like room had pushed her up there. Maybe she was digging through old boxes, looking for proof her memories were real. Or maybe she was chasing the reason Mom left Dad.

"Gracie?" I opened the attic door wider, peering into the dark.

If she was up there, she'd need a flashlight. There was no wiring, no lights at all. Only open rafters with old plywood sheets laid between them, barely enough to keep someone from falling through.

Maybe she was deeper in, beyond where I could see any light she may have.

I pulled my phone from my skirt pocket and switched on the flashlight before starting up the narrow steps.

"Gracie?"

The light swept ahead of me, but I strained past it, trying to see more than it was showing me.

"Are you up here, Gracie?"

Boxes loomed in uneven towers, stacked like insulation for a forgotten past.

Some of it was my parents'.

I recognized the old banana boxes stuffed with antique glass they'd dragged from house to house and never unpacked. The busted wicker rocker no one could sit on anymore. The one that split the last time someone tried. Instead of fixing it, or tossing it, they shoved it up here.

"It's a collectible!" Mom had said. "We'll get it fixed someday."

But some of these things, I was sure, had been stored away long before we moved in. Seeing them now made something prickle along the back of my neck.

I didn't know much about the house's history. Only what Wanda told me. That Mr. Dickerson had bought it in disrepair from the state. He spent a chunk of his retirement restoring it. According to his daughter, it made him happy. But now, looking at these old boxes, I saw them differently.

What if they didn't belong to Mr. Dickerson at all? What if they belonged to the man who built the house? The man who fostered Rachel Bagwell.

The man who... lost her.

I knew what was in most of these boxes. I'd spent a few hours up here when we first moved in, digging through them like a raccoon after something shiny. I'd lost interest eventually. Moved on to something else.

Now they felt like coffins. Sealed. Silent. Suddenly dangerous. Like they held answers to questions I wasn't supposed to ask.

"Gracie?" I whispered, though I already knew she wasn't up here.

I didn't know who left the attic door open. Maybe a shift in air pressure. The heater kicking on downstairs. It never shut right anyway.

But however it opened, it wasn't because Gracie was up here. The place was empty. Dead.

I could've gone back to bed. Tried to catch a little sleep before work. Instead, I peeled open the flap on one of the oldest boxes, tucked deep in the farthest corner.

The cardboard was warped and sagging, dark stains creeping up the sides like it had once soaked in muddy water. Faded ink bled into the cardboard like veins beneath thin skin.

Inside, I found what I expected, rows of leather-bound books. White powdery mold dusted a few covers, but most were caked in cobwebs, the silk draped over their spines like burial cloth.

I reached in. My fingers brushed brittle leather. The air drifting from the box smelled old. Mildew, dry paper. But beneath it, something else lingered. Sweet. Foul.

My stomach twisted. It was the same smell I'd caught in the wall last night.

"Oh no..."

I stepped back, covering my nose with the collar of my shirt, the hem wrinkling beneath the waistband of my jumper.

But the vision didn't come. Not the rotting woman. Not the death-soaked earth. It was just that hint of decay, then gone. Replaced by the thick, dusty scent of the attic.

Slowly, I lowered my collar and breathed in the musty air. Familiar. Forgotten. I straightened my shirt and stepped back to the box.

These weren't the kind of books I'd ever picked up for fun. They were thick, heavy, scholarly. I dusted off the cobwebs and aimed the beam of my phone light at the spines.

The Purity of Faith

I stilled. The words sank like a stone in my chest as my eyes flicked to the next one.

Gaining Your Soul

A dull thud started in my ribs.

Of Bloodlines and Redemption

My hand moved on its own, reaching for the last book in the box.

When I opened it, a puff of dry, stale air hit my face. And with it, that sickly-sweet smell again. Faint, but unmistakable.

I didn't move. I couldn't. The book stayed in my hands. I had to see.

The pages fluttered like they were breathing. For a moment, I swore the attic grew colder—air slipping up beneath my skirt, lifting goosebumps along my legs.

A chapter heading.

The Doctrine of Spiritual Cleansing

And beneath it:

Why the Races Must Not Intermarry

I bit my lip, hard.

Kade Weston's face flashed behind my eyes—his smile, his warmth.

We don't mix races, it's not God's design.

Those sickening words were already inside me, threaded through memory, spoken in sermons I'd heard since I was a child.

My dad's voice.

"God made us separate for a reason. Bloodlines matter. God's design matters."

These weren't just books. They were law, once. And Dad hadn't just read them. He'd *quoted* them.

"The man who built it was strange." Wanda's voice from the library yesterday. "Some kind of preacher. Wrote religious books."

The man who lived here. The man who fostered Rachel Bagwell. The man who—

I slammed the book shut. The brittle leather burned against my palms. The cracked spine nearly gave, but I caught it. A crash like that would've woken the house.

I stood there, nausea pooling in my stomach. But my eyes were already searching again.

I was looking for a name. Whoever wrote this shit. Whoever preached it.

I turned to the front. My fingers found the title page. Beneath a grainy, off-center emblem—a roaring lion and a cross—the ink had faded to gray.

Rev. D. L. Emerson

Could this be the man who built the house? Back in the eighties? The one who took in a teenage girl? The one accused of hurting her. Of murder. Had I found his name?

The book sagged open again. The heaviest section flopped on its broken spine like a human head from a snapped neck. A scrap of cloth fluttered loose, drifting to the dust at my feet.

I closed the book carefully and slid it back into the box. Then bent to pick up the fabric.

It was pale pink. Faded. Edges curled with age. Loose threads dangled. Cobwebs clung to the folds.

A child's dress.

The words came unbidden. I closed my hand around it and shut my eyes. The fabric was soft, like worn satin. But warm now, too. Like it held blood. Like it remembered.

The attic vanished. The solid planks underfoot, the dusty air, it was gone. All of it slipped away like breath fading from cold glass.

I wasn't in the attic anymore.

A girl spun slowly through the yard behind my parents' house. Evening light softened everything. She held a glowing jar in her hands. Fireflies winked around her like scattered stars.

She wore a nightgown. Long. Pale pink. Faded at the hem. Bare feet swept the tall grass. Red hair blazed like embers beneath the dusk.

She turned, and her wide brown eyes locked on mine. Not startled. Not afraid. Expectant.

Rachel.

My breath caught.

The moment stretched—too vivid to be memory.

It wasn't memory. It was recognition. Like I'd stepped into something that already knew me. Something that had been waiting on me.

And then she was gone. Torn away, like film ripped from a reel. The image warped. Then vanished.

My lungs seized. I stumbled back, choking on the sudden emptiness, gasping like I'd been dragged up from underwater.

"Rachel?" I whispered her name, barely audible, the pink scrap still clenched in my fist.

"Emily?"

That voice.

I dropped my phone. My knees buckled. I nearly fell. But I forced myself to stand. That voice didn't belong up here.

I scrambled for my phone. The flashlight beam swung wildly across the boxes and rafters.

My heart plummeted.

You're caught, dumpling.

The words cut through my mind. Not mine. I would've screamed—jumped, something—if I hadn't already aimed the light at the attic door.

At the voice that said my name.

At my dad.

12

Watched

I tried to pretend everything was normal. At first, it wasn't hard.

I didn't remember leaving the attic or crawling into bed. I was still dressed, cold, tense, but the quilt was tucked up to my neck like someone had carried me there and pulled the covers over me.

I wanted to pretend it had all been a dream. The attic. The books. Dad. I wanted to pretend that I'd never left my bed. I'd passed out repairing Beagle. He'd fallen to the floor when I pulled the blanket back.

It could've been a dream. Except, my arms were aching, and when I dragged them from under the quilt, the fraying scrap of pink fabric was still clutched tightly in my fist.

That was real.

I could pretend it was all a dream. But even make-believe has its limits. I couldn't pretend my arm didn't ache. I couldn't pretend I hadn't held onto that thing all night, like a drowning woman clinging to a final shred of rope.

I hadn't been able to leave that scrap of fabric behind. Not in the attic, or my room, or anywhere else in that house. It carried a horrible kind of belonging. Like it was mine now. Something I had to protect.

No one noticed I hadn't changed my clothes. If they did, they didn't say anything, or I didn't hear them. The scrap of fabric went into my jumper pocket, beside the napkin with Wanda's number on it.

I drifted that day, in and out of what was real and what was this horrible nightmare I'd found myself in.

"What are you doing up here?" Dad hadn't asked if I was okay. Hadn't mentioned the sickness from last night.

"The door was cracked. I thought Gracie was up here." I'd told him the truth.

"She's not." That's all he said, and the way he watched me, eyes peeling over my entire body like he was looking for something to catch me with. It was unsettling.

His glance flicked toward the corner where the boxes sat. Or maybe I imagined it. Still, my fist closed tighter around the pink fabric.

He can't see this.

"Em." A woman's voice. Soft. Close.

"Em." Whispered, but nearer now.

My limbs went stiff. What now? Hadn't I seen enough? Heard enough? Felt enough?

"Emily!"

I jolted. Like from a dream. Teetering on my ladder before I remembered where I was—six feet in the air, paint bucket in hand, cabinets half-finished in a gutted kitchen.

Gracie stood at the base of my ladder, watching me.

"Oh my gosh, Gracie," I gasped.

"You were staring into space." She tilted her head. A couple rebellious red curls had escaped her bun, trailing over one shoulder.

"I didn't sleep well."

I searched her face, but it was blank. She shrugged.

"Well, be careful. You're on a ladder."

I watched her leave the kitchen, scouring pad and gloves in hand. She was working in an empty bedroom, cleaning the hardware for the cabinets I was painting.

I closed my eyes for a second, felt the rough wood of the paintbrush against my palm, then got back to work.

The plastic smell of paint was strong. I was high against the ceiling, brushing the tops of the cabinets. Pain bloomed behind my eyes, but it was still better than some of the things I'd smelled in the last twenty-four hours.

I didn't let my mind wander far enough to remember the stench of death that engulfed me in that little room behind the wall. No. I would not go there. It was bad enough I hadn't spared the time to even change my clothes since then. If I let myself, I could still smell the rancid musk of dust and time clinging to the purple blanket Gracie threw at me.

Gracie Lyles '88

Questions rattled around in my skull like rubber balls off concrete. Loud, fast, impossible to catch.

My phone buzzed in my pocket. I already knew who it was. She was the only one who ever texted me, the only reason my phone ever lit up at all.

> Don't tell Mom and Dad anything about what I told you last night.

I could see her in my mind's eye.

Huddled in a corner of one of the nearly gutted bedrooms.

She was bent over a plastic dishpan, half full of old hinges and cabinet handles. Her usually bright green eyes fluid from the sting of the gloppy orange gel coating every piece of metal, melting away fifty years of grime.

Thick yellow gloves lay on the floor between her knees as she hunched over her phone, back to the bedroom door.

> Please.

Another text came through. Softer than the first. A little less like a command.

> I won't say anything.

I texted her back, but she was already typing again before mine went through.

> I wasn't feeling good last night. I don't think I remembered everything the way it happened.

I bit my lip. She was backpedaling.

If she didn't remember it right, then... why was a blanket, with her name and birth year stitched into it, buried in that wall? Why had she remembered the room at all?

It wasn't a dream. At least, it hadn't started as one. Maybe she'd dreamed about it since. But something real happened. In that house. In that wall. And Gracie's blanket was left there.

> Please don't say anything.

Another message. I grimaced, a strange ache twisting through my chest.

> I won't.

I replied, even though the words sat heavy in my gut.

She didn't respond again. I stared at that last text a little too long.

Gracie was slipping back into forgetting. Or pretending to forget. Into dreaming. And I felt alone. The same kind of alone I'd felt in the attic, pink fabric clenched in my fist, Dad's voice behind me.

"You don't need to be up here."

I went back to painting, trying not to replay the voice he'd used. Quiet. Pointed. Not... Dad. Not the version of him I was used to.

"Your mom doesn't even come up here. That should tell you something."

"I was going back to bed," I'd lied. And felt every inch the deceptive, sinful daughter I was supposed to fear becoming, walking toward my father, expecting him to step aside, to let me through.

But he didn't. Or maybe I imagined he didn't. I'm sure he didn't mean it the way it felt. Like he was blocking me. Stopping me. Holding me hostage in the attic.

My pulse skittered beneath my skin, lungs tightening, my body reliving the fear before my brain could talk it down.

My dad wouldn't do that. He was a believer. A minister.

"It's funny how kids always end up where they're not meant to be."

The way he said *kids*. It made me shiver. He never called us that. Not ever. It was a point of pride for Mom and Dad, never referring to Gracie or me as *kids*, like the *world* did. They had daughters. Girls they loved.

I couldn't take it anymore. Not the slow drag of my brush against the wood. Not the footsteps in and out of the house. And especially not *that* voice.

I dug into my skirt pocket, past the wadded-up bit of pink fabric from the attic and the napkin with Wanda's number and pulled out my dollar store earbuds.

I unlocked my phone and swiped over to my music app. Not the one labeled Music. My secret one. Tucked inside a fake trash folder, five screens to the right of everything else.

My public app was trained to play only religious music. Hymns arranged for solo piano. A few low-budget gospel bands my dad tolerated. A bluegrass gospel station my mom loved, and my dad loathed.

Mom had grown up in a tiny Appalachian town, surrounded by music. Her whole family played or sang. It was in her blood. But Dad made fun of her when she tried to learn guitar, until she gave up. And he hadn't let her listen to bluegrass in years. So when Gracie and I discovered the magic of streaming apps, Mom latched on. She let us play it loud.

Of course, even her permission had limits.

Let Josh Turner come on singing *Long Black Train* and she'd wrinkle her nose. She'd let it play, but not without the classic, underhanded, "That's not glorifying the Lord, girls!"

Which never made sense to me. It was literally religious. She said it was because it was too popular. People wouldn't see it as sacred. But it was fine to blast Ricky Skaggs singing hymns with a banjo.

At least Mom liked some music. To this day, I have no idea what kind of music Dad liked. I think he hated anything that might bring someone joy. That's how it always felt anyway.

For me, music was freedom. *My* music. The hidden app was my rebellion. The one thing I did that actually made me feel alive. Free. It scared me, how much I liked it.

Now, AC/DC was screaming *Back in Black* into my skull. I set my phone inside the open cabinet and started painting again. But even with heavy metal pounding into my ears, I couldn't shake what I'd come to know over the last few days.

What started as a mild irritation, a knock on glass in my room every night for six years, had ruptured into something far worse. Like the body I saw last night. Swollen and slick with death. Like it was waiting to infect me.

No matter how hard I tried, I couldn't go back to before. Before I found out about Rachel. Before I found the room in my wall. Before Gracie told me what she remembered.

I stopped again. This time to take a sip of burnt coffee from my scratched black plastic mug. The taste stung. Bitter and lukewarm.

I closed my eyes. Took another long sip.

But the prickling on the back of my neck wasn't from the coffee. I knew it wasn't, even if that last swallow made me shiver.

I was being watched.

I set my coffee down beside my phone and picked up my paintbrush, turning slightly, like I was reaching for the far corner of the cabinet.

The floor creaked behind me.

I didn't need to look. It was him. My dad. I knew it was him. Standing in the kitchen doorway, watching me. His narrow-set eyes boring into my back.

Should I turn? Acknowledge him? Say something? Or keep pretending I didn't know he was there?

Was I even sure—positive—it was him?

I reached for my phone and tapped pause on my music. Silence filled my ears, sharp and jarring. I bit my lip. Could he have heard? My earbuds were cheap. They didn't seal well. Could someone hear the music from across the room?

Is that why he was standing there?

I finally turned to look.

It was Dad, all right. Arms crossed. He'd been looking at me, no question. But the second I met his eyes, he looked away. Too quick. Too practiced.

Or...

Had he not been looking at me at all? Had he been watching something just beyond me?

"Thinking through my next job, Em," he said, nodding toward the blank wall where the stove would go. "New vent hood."

I gave a small shrug and turned back to painting. But I didn't turn my music back on.

Not until I heard the soft scrape of his boots. The slap of his hammer swinging in its holster. The creak of the back steps as he walked outside.

Only then did I tap play, turn the volume down a notch, and pull the crumpled napkin with Wanda's number from my pocket.

13

Pictures

> Send me a pic of the fabric, asap!

Wanda's text came through while I was still staring at my phone, lost in thought.

I'd told her everything that happened since I left the library yesterday, through nine massive, book-length texts. Even what Gracie said. How she asked me not to tell our parents.

> Lots of people have marital issues.

She'd tried to assure me.
Not my parents. They don't believe in marital issues.

> Our church

I stopped, staring at the words I'd typed. *Our church.*
But we didn't go to church. Not anymore. Not since Dad fell out with the bishop at the assembly in Caster. There wasn't anywhere else to go. Not anywhere that my dad counted.

Granite Hill had the usual: Baptist. Methodist. Pentecostal. A couple Presbyterian. One Catholic. All *worldly* churches.

After the fallout, we stopped looking. Twice on Sundays and once on Wednesdays, we sat in our living room while Dad led "service." Since he'd started his business, even that had grown... sporadic.

I deleted *our church* and stared at the blinking cursor.

It felt wrong. Like dragging my fingernails across a blackboard.

I wasn't being honest with myself. Over the past few weeks, I'd started questioning everything I'd believed since before I could talk. What if Gracie never had kids? What if she did become a teacher? Would that make her a sinner?

A sharp breath caught in my chest.

> The churches we've been a part of don't believe in divorce.

I sent a quick explanation before I could overthink it.

While I waited for Wanda's reply, I set my phone down beside my coffee mug and absentmindedly picked up my paintbrush. Clearwater Revival hummed through my earbuds, something about seeing light.

Wanda's response came a few minutes later.

> You'll have to tell me more about your church.

Your church.

The words made something twist inside.

I didn't feel like I had a church. Or a community. All I had was my family, and even that felt... blurred. Years of moving. State to state. House to house. Church to church.

None of it ever stuck.

Even at the churches we did attend, I never made real friends. I'd sit at tables with my parents while the other girls ran through the lawn, playing hide and seek, climbing trees until they got scolded. Best friends. Always in pairs.

Gracie and I sat quietly, pretending we didn't want to join. Pretending we liked listening to the men talk. Pretending green bean casserole didn't taste like wet cardboard.

My phone buzzed again.

> Send the pic!

Wanda's urgency snapped me out of it. I blinked, realizing I hadn't even answered her yet.

Carefully, I set my paint bucket and brush inside one of the cabinets and slipped off to the bathroom.

The bathroom in this house was unfinished, like the rest of it. Dad had signed a contract with the city to renovate the place. It was part of a housing and urban development program. Low-bid jobs to fix up low-income housing when tenants left.

This place had been an actual dump a week ago. Vomit in the kitchen sink, beer cans scattered everywhere, needles embedded in what was left of the crusty carpet. Fist-sized holes in the sheetrock. Bullet spray on the vinyl siding. And the bathroom?

I almost gagged stepping into it. Mom and I had cleaned it together, tying towels over our faces, layering gloves up our arms, but the stench still soaked into my skin. I'd showered twice that night trying to wash it off.

The old bathroom door was busted off its hinges. Someone had shoved a grimy cloth through the hole where the knob used to be. Dad replaced it first thing.

The tub was gone. A silver pipe jutted from the wall where a shower should've been. Gracie and I had chipped up the shattered tile floor. Right now, I stood on stained, splintered subflooring with my back to the door.

I pulled the fabric scrap from my pocket. Tattered. Faded. But in the orange light of the mirror bulbs, it seemed to glow.

I snapped a photo and sent it to Wanda.

The electric guitar screaming in my ears faded as Wanda's response came through.

> Holy shit.

I waited, watching the dots bubble at the bottom of the screen.

> Can I show this to Kade?

My heart half-skipped at his name.

> Sure.

Thank God I could text it instead of saying it aloud. I wasn't sure what it was about Kade—I'd barely met him—but thinking about him, especially sharing something like this with him, made all kinds of butterflies take flight under my ribs.

> I told you he and I used to go up to that house when it was abandoned.

Another text muted the music.

> He saw more than I did up there. If you don't care, I'd like to tell him about Rachel.

I stared at the screen. Kade saw more? Did Wanda and her brother believe in…?

I rolled my bottom lip between my teeth and winced as the cracked skin split, the taste of warm iron rising on my tongue.

> The more the merrier.

I typed the reply and set my phone on the bleached countertop. The screen went dark. I fished lip balm from my pocket and smeared it over my mouth.

I didn't want to think about what Kade might've seen in that house. Why Wanda thought that, because of what he saw, it would be a good idea to bring him into our impromptu investigation.

Was whatever he saw still there? Had I experienced it? Through the knocking? Or the room inside my bedroom wall? Or the face of the dead woman that rose in my mind and made me physically sick last night?

"Hey, Em!" Mom's voice followed three sharp knocks on the bathroom door, making me jump and drop my lip balm. "Are you okay in there? You've been in there a while."

"I'm fine." I crouched to find the clear tube, trying to keep my voice steady.

"I know you were sick last night." She let the words hang, like I was supposed to explain it. I didn't.

"If you're not sick, you need to hurry up and get back to those cabinets. The paint's drying in your brush."

"I'm coming, Mom," I said, trying not to sound too stiff as I searched behind the toilet for the balm.

I found it wedged in that grimy little spot no one ever wants to clean. Even though we'd scrubbed this bathroom top to bottom, I couldn't forget what it had looked like before. The piss, the crusted floor, the smell.

I tossed the balm into the open trash bag hanging on the doorknob, grabbed my phone, and slipped out before Mom caught me.

Back on the ladder. Back to painting. The rhythm kept my thoughts from spiraling, until I realized Wanda hadn't texted again.

She hadn't replied to my okay about telling Kade about Rachel. Maybe he was with her at the library, and she was already showing him everything. I pictured them in the break room, sharing fries for lunch, Wanda animated as she shared every detail, her brother listening.

I wondered if he liked stories like she did. If he liked books. He hadn't said much when we met, but maybe that was because he'd walked into something he wasn't expecting. His sister trying to talk down a girl going to pieces.

Still, even if he hadn't said much, I hadn't felt like he judged me. He didn't say a word, just knelt beside me and helped steady my hands when they shook too badly to hold a glass of water.

I hadn't noticed it then, and maybe I was imagining it now, but his touch had been warm. Gentle. Steady.

Something fluttered in me when I thought about him. Something small and terrifying but also... kind of wonderful.

Which meant it was wrong.

Whosoever looketh on a woman to lust after her hath committed adultery with her already in his heart. My father's voice echoed in my skull. *Blessed are the pure in heart, for they shall see God.*

I'd heard it all too many times. Purity conferences. Sunday sermons. Youth group lectures. And I knew the rules didn't only apply to guys.

What I felt when I thought about Kade wasn't pure. It wasn't the same as seeing a stranger at the store. Or someone at a gas station. This was different. And I liked it.

But that flutter came wrapped in the heaviest guilt I'd ever known.

Because it wasn't just that Kade wasn't in our church. According to my parents, no matter if he believed in Jesus, he wasn't *really* saved because he hadn't come out of the *world*. They would tell that by looking at him. The long hair. *Worldly* band T-shirt. Black leather jacket.

Some part of me wondered how all of that made any difference. Why did what someone wore decide if they'd make it into heaven? And if it didn't matter, then why was I stuck wearing dresses...

I pushed those thoughts away.

My parents would hate Kade even if he *was* an upstanding member of the *right* church. Because he wasn't someone my parents knew. It wouldn't be *their* idea, so of course it wouldn't be right. And, as if that wasn't bad enough, Kade wasn't even the same color as me.

We don't mix the races. My dad's voice came up like bile, echoing louder than Whiskey Myers blaring in my ears. But I wasn't really listening to the music.

My mind was back in the attic, with those dusty, forgotten books that somehow weren't forgotten at all.

They preached the same things I'd heard my whole life. From my parents. From church. Things I thought were bullshit. And I'd thought that for a very long time. But I hadn't been brave enough to let myself realize it.

I set my brush across the paint bucket and wiped my hands on my denim jumper, blinking away any stray thought of Kade.

That black leather jacket... I wondered if he wore it often.

I had to stop thinking about all this. About him. I had other things to worry about, and I was sure he wasn't thinking about me.

To him, I was probably just the girl who had a breakdown at the library. The girl with the crazy house and the maybe-murder that probably wasn't even a murder. A runaway from twenty years ago, she'd imagined was a cold case.

My phone felt heavy in my pocket. Why hadn't Wanda texted back yet?

But when I pulled it from my pocket and the screen lit up... I froze.

A woman. Naked. Spread-eagle across the hood of a 1967 candy-apple red Camaro.

Not my phone. I nearly dropped it.

No.

No.

This was Dad's phone.

My stomach twisted as realization hit me in a wave. My chest burned. I couldn't breathe. I scrambled off the ladder too fast, barely noticing the paint that splattered my skirt.

"Emily!" Mom called. "What's the matter?"

"My stomach hurts," I gasped.

Not a lie.

I rushed to the bathroom, slammed the door shut, and locked it. My whole body shook.

My phone stared up at me from the counter where I'd left it. I had picked up my dad's phone.

My dad looks at porn.

My father, the one who preaches purity. Who won't let Mom wear jeans or listen to secular music. Who held "modesty devotions" for Gracie and me in the living room.

I shouldn't have, but I tapped open his search history. He didn't even know how to clear it.

My vision blurred as I scrolled. Entry after entry. Every twisted, disgusting search saved in his phone, stretching back six months, since the day he got it.

I felt like I'd vomit. I edged toward the toilet, clutching the counter for balance.

Does my dad look up anything else on his phone besides women?

It wasn't only pictures. Full-screen videos. Clips. Page after page. Younger and younger women. Way younger than Mom. With bigger boobs and a lot more ass.

I knew he looked at women in real life. Mom fussed at him about it all the time. He'd say he couldn't help it. God made him that way. Men were visual. Women shouldn't dress so provocatively. If they didn't, men wouldn't be tempted.

But I never thought he'd...

My dad.

The man who could quote the Bible in English, Greek, and Hebrew. The man with a whole seminary's worth of study books in his office. The man who searched for this? Who lusted like this?

My knees gave out. I dropped to the floor and dry-heaved into the brand-new toilet.

Every conversation he'd ever had with me and Gracie about men came rushing back. About how nasty they were. How sex was all they wanted. How evil filled their heads constantly, and how girls couldn't even begin to understand.

But God made them that way. And girls didn't have those thoughts. Not real girls. Not pure girls. But men of faith? Believing men? They were different. Controlled. Holy. Enlightened. My father was one of those men. He was a minister. A teacher. A vessel of truth.

I gagged again, bile crawling up my throat, stinging the back of my nose. I swiped out of the search engine and set his disgusting, filthy phone back down on the counter where I'd found it.

Then it hit me.

The room. Where I was. Where his phone had been left.

My stomach dropped.

Had he...?

I hit my knees again. This time, I didn't dry heave. I puked up everything I'd eaten that day into the toilet.

14

NO DAUGHTER OF MINE

I was numb as I finished painting that evening.

My music still played, shuffling between metal, country, jazz, and a little pop. But I couldn't hear it. It might as well have been muted. My ears felt stuffed with cotton instead of cheap earbuds.

I forgot what I was doing. My body just moved. *Dip. Tap. Brush. Dip. Tap. Brush.* Until the entire wall of upper cabinets gleamed white. Streak-free. Glossy.

But I didn't see cabinets. I saw women. Photo after photo. Naked. Or wearing so little it made no difference.

I wasn't even allowed to wear pants. Putting on a swimsuit would be blasphemy. Tanning lotion? A sin. Laying out in the yard in shorts? Tempting men. Sunglasses? Worldly vanity.

But a woman—tanned, oiled, legs spread on a red Camaro? That was apparently fine. That was what my dad wanted.

Anger surged in my chest. My hand jerked. White paint spattered to the floor. I stared at the tiny dots bleeding across the subfloor.

> Can you come by the library after work?

Wanda's text pinged through, muting Katy Perry's *Roar*.

I stared at the screen a second, blinking. My fingers hovered, ready to type.

> Sure! Be there by four.

But I didn't hit send. I don't get to make decisions like that.

Could I go to the library after work?

If it were up to me, I would. But nothing ever was. I was twenty-two and still asking my parents for permission to go to the one place I was technically allowed to go alone.

Yet my dad could look at porn and preach purity in the same breath?

I'd be excommunicated for wearing lip gloss. He got to ogle strangers naked and still lead youth group.

Two wrongs don't make a right, Emily. Like a splinter, my mother's voice dug its way up from the back of my brain.

But what exactly was wrong about going to a damn library? About making one, single choice for myself?

We're not citizens of this world, we're sojourners spreading the truth.

So... all that grown-at-eighteen stuff? Bullshit. The whole adult-at-twenty-one rule? A lie the government told to turn kids into "minions." That's what Dad said. That's what church taught.

Minions of sin. Of rebellion. Of hell.

And now I couldn't decide for myself if I could go to a public building after work. But he could stare at strangers' bodies on a screen.

> Kade and I will wait for you. Kenny told me I could stay after hours and research.

Research.

A low hum filled my veins. That's what I needed. To bury myself neck-deep in figuring out if Rachel Bagwell actually ran away from her foster home at eighteen, or if something worse happened.

Then I wouldn't have to think about what Gracie said, or how fast she took it back. I wouldn't have to think about my dad's phone, or how many lies he, and my mom, might've told me.

I could do what I always do. Lose myself in the search for answers.

Only this time, the answers might actually matter.

Not some historical deep dive about how Germany unified into a single nation. This could mean finding out what happened to a girl who vanished over twenty years ago. A girl no one else seemed to remember. No one had bothered to find.

And I wouldn't be doing it alone.

I had Wanda, who'd somehow become one of the only people I trusted. And now, maybe Kade too.

Excitement fluttered inside me like a trapped bird.

I had to finish painting. I'd tell Mom I was going by the library on the way home. I'd say it casually, like it was no big deal. I went there so often, maybe she wouldn't question it.

I'd driven myself that morning. Gracie rode in the back of the van to brace a couple new windows, and I was sure I'd be driving back alone. Gracie didn't like to go home in a different vehicle than the one she left in. One of her habits.

I reached too far, rushing to finish the last cabinet without moving the ladder. I almost slipped, caught myself, and the paint. But not my phone.

It hit the subfloor face-up.

I tried to catch it but only managed to fumble the screen and disconnect my earbuds.

Randy Travis blared through the gutted house, his twangy voice echoing *Digging Up Bones* like a ghost moaning through gravestones.

"Em!"

Shit.

Dad.

He was working in the kitchen. I hadn't noticed. Hadn't seen him. Hadn't even heard him.

"Turn that off!"

"I'm trying!" I scrambled to set down my brush without sinking the whole handle into the wet paint.

"Turn it off *now!*" His shout was punctuated by the hard whack of a six-by-eight slamming to the subfloor.

I glanced over. He was pissed.

Dad's head always had a slight tremor. I never knew why, maybe his age, but when he was angry, everything shook. His fists clenched at his sides. His jaw locked. His face and neck flushed crimson. The tremor got worse.

That happened fast. One song. That's all it took. One stupid secular song. Dad had a temper. But this? This was sudden. This was something else.

"I'm getting it!" I jumped off the ladder and grabbed my phone, but the screen was locked up.

"That's not a song for believers." Dad took a step toward me, and I instinctively backed up.

Not because I thought he'd hit me. Because I thought he'd grab my phone.

"It came on by itself." The lie came out smooth as a hymn. Dad couldn't know about the music. Not what I really listened to. Not that I listened to it every day.

"My phone's locked up." I kept swiping, clicking, shaking it.

"That's Randy Travis," Dad growled.

Mom's voice cut in. "That's who it is." She was in the kitchen now. Gracie right behind her.

Dad snatched the phone from my hands and hurled it across the kitchen.

I watched in horror as it smacked the drywall, bounced, and hit the floor.

No.

No, no, no.

Randy Travis went silent.

But the screen of my phone...

"Dad!" Gracie shrieked, stuffing her phone deep into her pocket like she thought she might be next.

"We don't listen to that!" Dad turned on me, fists clenched. "That was one of your mom's favorite singers! Back when she was in sin."

So that was it. Jealousy. Mom's past. The explosion made sense now.

Dad was usually slower to blow, but jealousy—especially anything to do with Mom or her past, before *him*—lit the fuse fast.

Dad had always been like this. Mom wasn't allowed to go anywhere alone. Couldn't talk to other men. Not even a cashier. But Dad could go anywhere. Look at anyone. Flirt with the waitress. Gawk at women in daisy dukes.

Because that's *how men are.*

But women? Women had to be watched.

This whole thing over a stupid song... because it wasn't about the song. It was about Mom liking a singer. Dad's power. His rules.

"It came on by itself," I said again, hoarsely, stepping through the maze of half-empty paint buckets to retrieve my phone.

The screen was spiderwebbed.

"Dad, my phone."

"What do you mean it came on by itself?" He didn't care about the phone.

"That's how it works, Dad," Gracie said carefully. "You thumb-up or thumb-down songs to train your radio. You don't pick each one."

"I was going to thumb it down," I added. Another lie. "But I dropped it."

"Oh." Dad backed off. "I'm sorry, Em. You should've explained that to me."

"You didn't give me a chance!"

"Don't raise your voice at me, young lady!"

He could shout. Break things. Look at porn in secret. But me? I raise my voice, and I'm the problem.

"You broke my phone!" I shouted this time. Full volume. Not from nerves, from rage.

Rage at my dad's tantrum. At how Mom let him treat Grace and me like this. At how she had let him treat her like this for over twenty years, in front of us.

"Em!" Mom gasped.

"You, Allie!" Dad turned on her now.

Damn. I'd gotten him mad at her again. My stomach sank.

"You disrespect me in front of the girls. Where do you think they learn it?"

"Dad, do you ever think about respecting us?" I didn't wait for an answer. I already knew it.

I was his kid. A woman. I didn't get respect. That wasn't my place.

"I am the head of this house!" Dad bellowed, like an angry cow, which might've been funny if it wasn't so fucking infuriating.

"If you're the head, what does that make us? Your tail?"

He ignored me and snapped back to Mom.

"If you respected me, your daughters would respect me!"

He shoved a sawhorse down. The legs folded, and it slammed into the wall, punching a gaping hole through the drywall Gracie and I had just finished mudding. It had been ready for paint. Right up until two seconds ago.

"Are you happy now, Don?" Mom huffed. "Add it to the list. We're already a week and a half behind schedule!"

"You need to get it together, Allie," Dad pointed at her. "The devil's dividing our family—and you're letting him!"

Maybe it wasn't the devil. Maybe it was the man throwing phones and quoting scripture between tantrums. Maybe it was the woman standing there silent while he attacked her daughters.

"How am I doing it?" Mom snapped—finally.

"By not respecting me!"

That's all life ever was to him. A series of challenges to his authority. His leadership. His position as the man.

"Dad, this doesn't have anything to do with Mom."

I could've stayed quiet. Let her fight her own battle. She'd left me to fight mine, not only today, but every time I had a confrontation with this man. She'd hang back. Not speak up. Not defend me.

I could've done that to her.

But something inside me wouldn't let me.

It never had. Ever since I was too little to understand what the fights were about. I only knew he raised his voice at her.

"For whosoever shall keep the whole law, and yet offend in one point, he is guilty of all." Dad was quoting scripture now. Ignoring everything I'd said.

I was numb on the outside. Standing there. Staring. Listening. Yet somehow, I was boiling underneath my skin.

Nothing was ever his fault. Never his fault he broke things. Flipped the dinner table. Belted the car through congested traffic at eighty miles an hour, just to whip into the emergency lane and jam the brakes so hard my seatbelt locked, leaving angry, red marks across my neck. All so he could shout at Mom about staying in her place.

That wasn't his fault.

It was us. The women. We drove him to it. Made him do it. If we'd only submit, stop arguing, stop being so independent, then nothing bad would happen. Except... things always went bad, no matter how good we were.

"You disrespect your husband, Allie, and God isn't going to bless our family! You're letting the devil in!"

I couldn't take another second.

"Grace, I'm leaving." The words came out like someone else said them.

"What?" Her voice was weak beneath my parents' arguing. The shouting, barking, and sobbing almost drowned my sister's voice completely.

All over a song.

"You can come or stay," I said, grabbing my hoodie.

"Where do you think you're going?" Dad's voice stopped me cold. That sharp edge of sarcasm he used when he was daring you to try something.

"I'm leaving."

I wouldn't look at him, wouldn't give him the satisfaction of seeing me falter, doubt myself, lose even a little of my determination.

"You're not going anywhere."

I glanced back at the freshly painted cabinets. Where I'd spent all day painting for my dad. Working for the family. So many hours today, yesterday, weeks and months before, chipped away from my life because it was what was best for all of us. Because, as a family, we worked together.

I couldn't keep pretending I was alright with any of it.

"I'm sick of this bullshit." I said it out loud.

I felt it land, like an out-of-control semi careening down the side of a mountain off a winding interstate in West Virginia.

Mom gasped. Grace froze. Dad's face turned purple.

"Emily Carol Lyles."

Full name. Classic.

"I'm sick of it!" I turned for the door.

Behind me, it was chaos.

"Em, where are you going?" Mom shrieked. I could hear her trying to hurry around Dad to get to me.

A little too late for that now.

The thought came without me looking for it. A snap of pain I hadn't known I felt so deeply. That of a daughter betrayed by the only true friend she ever had, ever trusted—her mother. While Dad's screaming, throwing things, breaking my phone. Mom's silent.

But let me try to get away—from the hell, from him—and here she is, trying to pull me back.

"I don't let my employees walk out on me!" Dad shouted so loud that his voice cracked. "You walk off this job, you won't have a job!"

Really?

I spun back. Dad stood on the tiny front porch, where Mom had spent her entire day painting all the pickets and railing by hand. His arms were crossed over his chest, his heavy eyes glaring at me.

"Maybe I don't want this job?" I snapped at him. "Maybe I'd like to actually pick my job."

Dad stared at me, his salt and pepper beard brushing his chest as his head tremored back and forth.

"You're letting the devil trick you, Emily." His voice was strained with anger. "That's your prerogative. Let the devil destroy you. But you're not going to disrespect me while you do it. I don't let my employees walk off my job."

"I'm your daughter!" I shouted at him again. There was no going back from where this explosion over music had taken us. "You wouldn't throw an employee's phone!"

"I said I was sorry!" Dad barked at me. "You have to forgive me, Em, like God already has. You think you're better than God?"

I groaned, shifting my hoodie on my arm. "If you were sorry, this wouldn't happen every day!"

"Em, don't do this," Mom's voice floated up behind him, thin and weak.

"Oh, she won't, Allie," Dad hissed. "She can cuss about it all she wants, but she knows better than to walk off my job site."

I turned and kept walking. Past the porch. Across the yard. Toward his truck.

"I'm not an employee," I called back over my shoulder. "I'm your daughter."

"Not on the job, you're not."

I stopped. Every muscle in my body froze, every nerve tingled in my limbs. I turned slowly on my heel to face him again.

He watched me from the porch, hand clutching the railing so hard every knuckle was bleached.

I was back in the attic. Watching my dad, feeling like he was blocking me in, keeping me. I was back in the gutted kitchen, an hour ago, paint in hand, certain he'd been standing behind me. Watching me.

It was the same look. The same voice. The same empty stare in his eyes.

This wasn't about a song, or Mom fangirling over Randy Travis back in the day. It had nothing to do with me not being fast enough to obey Dad's demands or losing my temper and shouting or cussing at him. It wasn't even about Dad being in one of his sucky moods that so often ruined halfway decent days.

This was about me. About the attic. The books. About what I might know.

"Don, stop," Mom said. Finally. She was finally *kind of* defending me.

"Don't tell me to stop, Allie." His voice was sharp with threat, and his hand flexed against the railing, gripping it so tight the freshly dried paint rippled up around his fingers.

Things shifted. My eyes. My grip on reality.

I was seeing something else. My dad, ripping the railing up, nails and all, and bringing it down against my mother's head.

I blinked the image away, stumbling back half a step.

"Mom, you don't have to listen to him!"

The color drained from her face. "Emily..."

Her tone, the way she said my name. *He's my husband, Emily.*

"She's my wife!" Dad barked at me, stepping up as if he were protecting my mother from me.

"I'm your daughter!"

"Not on my job site!" He pulled his hand from the railing, shredding the fresh paint off the wood like sheets of skin. "You're not my daughter here."

That was it.

I couldn't look at him anymore. Couldn't look at my mom, crying behind him, or Gracie huddling in the doorway.

I turned and crossed the yard. Got in the truck. Tossed my things to the bench seat beside me and slammed the door.

"God will punish you, Emily Carol!"

I could still hear Dad shouting at me, but I didn't look back.

I drove.

My cracked phone screen glinted at me from the hot vinyl seat.

A spiderweb of truth I couldn't unsee.

15

WE DON'T FORGET

I didn't even know how I got there. One minute I was peeling out of the driveway, gravel flying. The next, I was parked in front of the library, hands clenched around the steering wheel, knuckles bone white.

I hadn't cried. Not yet. But I could feel something rising in my throat. Tight, hot, choking.

I probably shouldn't have taken the truck. But if Dad didn't want me to, he shouldn't have thrown my phone across the kitchen and screamed scripture at me like a televangelist having a breakdown. The least he could do was sponsor my getaway. Even if it was only to the library.

Still, when I pulled into the parking lot, I didn't move. I sat there, listening to the echo of his voice in my head.

God will punish you, Emily Carol.

The truck reeked of him. Sweat and drywall dust. Stale coffee. The sour, chemical funk of old caulk tubes and polyurethane fumes.

I'd rolled the windows down on the way, but the stench still clung to me. Soaked into my shirt, my hair—like mildew and male ego.

I tumbled out of the driver's door now, gulping in fresh air like I'd been drowning. Like I could flush the disgust, rejection, and anger out of my body by simply breathing.

It didn't work. The smell stayed with me. And so did his voice.

I breathed deep of the chilly, late February air and closed my eyes, feeling the sting of dusk against my burning skin.

As believers, aren't we promised joy, peace, and love?

I certainly wasn't feeling any of that. Not now. Not in a long time.

I'd think it was all my fault. All this arguing and fighting. Gracie's habits and frailty. I brought it on my family. I didn't have an honest heart. I wasn't truly and fully sold out to God. I was in sin. Raising my voice at my father. Cussing. Running off with his truck.

Somehow none of that felt like the reason I was suffering right now.

Something about leaving felt right, even if it hurt like hell. Something about stepping away, stepping out, speaking up. It was exhausting, painful, like plunging my entire body into an ice-bound river in the middle of January.

But it felt right.

I leaned back against Dad's truck, feeling the bite of cold metal against my back.

The sun had started setting, shadows stretched like fingers across the asphalt parking lot. The crispness in the air seemed to hint that it would be cold tonight, maybe even freeze again.

"Em?"

A man's voice made me jump, like glass cracked in my chest.

"I'm sorry," Kade said, hands up like he was calming a skittish animal. "I didn't mean to scare you."

When I tried to answer, my voice caught. I hadn't realized how close I was to crying until now.

Swallowing that burning lump in my throat, I shook my head and managed a half-hearted smile.

"I came out to my bike to grab my tablet." Kade nodded somewhere behind him and held up what looked like a black and white composition book. "Are you okay?"

I tried to keep my answer short, simple. Stop myself from crying. "Yeah, just really tired."

He tilted his head and long, tight curls fell over his shoulder. "Long day?"

"Something like that." I managed another smile, but this one was genuine.

"If you'd rather go home, I'll tell Wanda. We can always talk about this later." He held up his tablet again.

"Oh no." I was quick with that response.

I *really* didn't want to go home.

To be alone in that house, with the room in the wall, and wait for my father's rage, my mother's disappointment, and my sister's silence.

Kade smiled. "We've found some stuff Wanda said you'd really like to see."

"Okay," I said, too quickly. Kade kind of laughed and I felt my face flush.

I pulled open the truck door and grabbed my backpack, holding my breath until I'd swung the truck shut again.

"How'd you start researching about Rachel Bagwell?" Kade asked, as we started down the concrete walk toward the library. "Other than living in the house she probably disappeared from," he added, glancing at me. "Wanda told me."

I figured I couldn't look much crazier than I did when Kade walked in on Wanda trying to calm me down from a panic attack yesterday. Hugging myself in a chair while Wanda knelt in front of me trying to get me to list things I could see.

I told him about the knocks and the scratching, the room in the wall, and the books upstairs, like I told Wanda.

Kade, like Wanda, didn't look at me like I was crazy.

"I don't know what you believe." Kade opened the library door for me. "But I believe there's a spirit world around us. Ghosts, demons, angels. Some things we can't name." He looked at me, but his expression was calm, like he was reciting facts. "I believe they're all around us, and I think someone's trying to get your attention."

I could only stare at him, arms hugging my backpack.

No one except Wanda had ever given me that much validation before. Until now, all of this had been in my head, a dream, the devil's attacks on my mind, or divine punishment because I was covetous of the world.

He saw more than I did up there. Wanda's text from earlier rang in my mind.

"I know that sounds crazy." Kade's voice cut through the silence as we walked past the dark front desk.

I caught our reflection in the tall glass doors of the conference room. Me, Kade beside me, and—

I blinked.

There'd been a third figure. Not a shadow, but not a reflection. Pale and still, thin shoulders and a shock of red hair, it stood a little behind my shoulder.

But when I turned, there was no one.

Just the darkness of the conference room, its long, oak table surrounded by empty chairs, and the humming silence of after-hours.

"No," I said, too quickly. "I don't think it sounds crazy at all."

"Hey!" Wanda popped out of the break room, a bag of chewy, chocolate chip cookies in her hand.

The overhead light flickered behind her, casting the room in a warm yellow that felt too bright after the shadowed hallway.

"I thought I heard you two!"

The cookie bag crinkled loud and sudden in the quiet, like the snap of a tight rubber band.

She threw her arms around me in a tight hug. "Girl, you got to see what we found!"

The evening blurred past in a haze of old paper and cheap coffee. Easy laughter filled the corners of the archive room as we pored over records Wanda had dug up.

"Rachel went to Caster High." Kade was just as invested now. He pushed a yearbook across the table to me.

"Oh…" My breath caught as my eyes landed on a black and white version of Rachel Bagwell. "That's her."

"Junior year, 1987." Wanda confirmed, squinting at the picture from across the table.

She glanced up at me. "See, she's dressed like…" Her voice trailed off.

"Like me."

"That's what we wanted to show you." Wanda tapped the picture. "You found the picture of her at Niagara Falls, dressed… um… normal."

I wish she wouldn't worry about hurting my feelings. It wasn't like I wanted to wear these stupid dresses. I didn't know how to tell Wanda that, though.

I didn't know how to explain why I still did something I didn't want to do—when I was a grown woman and could simply refuse to dress like I'd just stepped off the stage in Dodge.

"So, she moved here for high school," I murmured, bringing my own mind back to focus on the pieces we were putting together.

"But nothing earlier than junior year, and nothing in Eastridge before that," Kade added, flipping through another yearbook.

"Eastridge?"

"Middle school in Caster," Wanda clarified.

Kade flipped the next book open. The peeling, gold foil caught the buzzing fluorescent light overhead. "1985. She's not in here."

"Not in the freshman class?" Wanda's big, hoop earrings jangled as she sat up straighter.

"Or sophomore," her brother said, flipping pages again.

"So, she came to Caster for the last half of high school?" I was beginning to get lost in all the names.

My parents' homeschool didn't really have high school. I quit in sixth grade.

"That's what it looks like. But what's weird is she's not in senior year either." Kade set the 1988 yearbook down with a quiet finality.

"But she went missing in '88, right?" I asked, doubting my memory.

"That's what the newspaper clipping said," Wanda agreed. "Around June? She should have had her senior yearbook photo."

"So..." My voice died off as I tried to make sense of what we were finding. "She disappeared earlier than the newspaper said?"

"She doesn't look like someone who'd drop out." Wanda picked up one of the books to study Rachel's class picture more closely. "There's something sharp in her eyes. Like she had plans. Goals."

"But if she's missing from the senior yearbook," I said slowly, "that means she stopped going to school in '87, right? Right after she started going."

"And nobody said anything?" Wanda blinked. "She vanished and no one reported it until the following year?"

"We need to find some kind of proof of that." Kade rested his elbows on the table, sipping from a foam cup of strong, black coffee.

"Right..." Wanda was thoughtful for a moment. "Is there a way we can find out if she was sent to a different school? A private school, maybe?"

I dragged my beat-up, orange backpack up to the tabletop and peeled open the snagging zipper.

"You brought the file?" Wanda lit up as I pulled the bulging manila folder from the guts of my bag. "You were planning on researching tonight, weren't you?"

I shrugged. "I didn't want to leave it... there."

Home felt wrong on my tongue, talking about that creepy house Rachel Bagwell may or may not have died in.

And the thought of leaving this file there felt even worse. Like the house would eat it. Like the hollow, hungry walls of the place would swallow it whole.

I couldn't put it in words, couldn't articulate it to Wanda and Kade, but I didn't want any of my family finding this file—or learning that I was researching Rachel Bagwell at all. Not yet.

I needed to figure this mystery out before my family, my parents more than Gracie, knew a thing about it.

"Oh, that's cool." Kade inched his chair closer to the table, deep brown eyes taking in the spread of photos and newspaper clippings, reports and stray scraps of scribbled notes. "Wanda told me about the old lady who gave her this file, but I didn't expect it to have this much stuff in it."

"All kinds of things." I felt myself smile, and it felt good.

After the day I'd had—hell, the week—smiling with friends over something that mattered felt almost holy.

"I haven't gotten to go through it much," I confessed.

"I think Mrs. Alister must've had a thing for cold cases." Wanda picked up a paper, words underlined in red ink, notes scribbled in the margins.

"Or she was related to Rachel Bagwell." Kade's suggestion froze us both.

"Oh my gosh, Wanda." I squeezed her arm. "You said that, when we first opened this file. Remember?"

Wanda nodded and started sifting through the pile of archives we'd inherited.

"What if she was?" I felt a little hope spring up inside of me. "There has to be a reason she kept all of this. People don't save this kind of thing for no reason."

"We can go talk to her," Wanda suggested. "Since Mama helped sell her house here in Caster, Mrs. Allister moved to Whispering Pines—a retirement community in Granite Hill."

My parents would never let me go visit a stranger. Not even a little, old woman in a retirement home.

What would I tell them when they asked me why I wanted to meet this woman? If they asked where I'd learned about her?

Wanda seemed to read my racing mind. "She's on socials too, I think," she added, picking up a torn envelope with a return address scratched in shaky handwriting.

"I'll look her up." I made up my mind quickly.

"That would probably be better." Wanda glanced over at me. "To start with anyway. She knows me, through my mom, and I told her about you. If you mention me and the file, she'll know exactly who you are."

That's what I'd do. Message her. At least ask if there was a particular reason she kept all these notes and articles about Rachel Bagwell.

"Girls..." Kade's voice was cautious, his deep, brown eyes focused on an old photograph in his hand. "I think I found the reason why Rachel dropped out of school."

He turned the photo slowly, thumb pressed to one corner, careful not to smudge it.

The bulb above us buzzed, then flickered once, sharp. I flinched, but I couldn't look away.

There, sitting on the edge of a bed, was Rachel Bagwell. She wasn't smiling. Her bright, red hair hung in tired strands over her thin shoulders.

She wasn't in her high-collared yearbook dress. Just a dull pink nightgown and fuzzy socks.

I couldn't get my tongue to work, but Wanda spoke for both of us.

"Holy shit, she was pregnant."

16

DEAD AIR

I didn't remember driving home. Or saying goodbye. One minute I was at the library, then I was driving. Alone.

All I could see was the grainy photo of the once-happy girl, sitting on the edge of a bed, dull, sad eyes staring at the camera, one hand resting on the curve of her belly.

Was that why she disappeared? Did her foster father hate the baby? Maybe she did run away. Maybe she married. Maybe her last name changed and that's why no one could find her.

Part of me needed to believe that.

But deep inside, I somehow knew that hadn't been the case. Something about Rachel and her sad eyes, the way her face had lost its smile. It was like she knew. Like her hope was gone.

"I wish I could find you," I whispered.

The truck thumped—hard. A sharp, cracking bang sliced through the usual hum of tires on asphalt. The steering wheel jerked. Rubber flapped against pavement like a dying bird.

I wrestled the truck off the road, and it came to a halting stop in a little driveway, just short of colliding with a gate.

I sat there, hands glued to the wheel, my ears ringing, as I stared at the green panel gate in front of me. Illuminated by the headlights, a NO TRESPASSING, PRIVATE PROPERTY sign glared back in red and silver.

Dad never taught me to change a tire. I was a girl. I didn't need to know how to do men's work—unless it earned him a dollar.

My first thought, after I got my lungs to work again, was to call Gracie. I'm sure she'd be worried. It was really late, and after how things went down earlier today...

"Oh shit."

That curse slipped out on a breath, and I let my head fall back against the window with a *thunk*. I winced as the pins holding up my bun jabbed into my scalp.

In all the easy company with Wanda and Kade, all the discoveries about the missing girl from my parents' house, I'd almost forgotten the blow-up with Dad. The shouting, the threats as I peeled away.

It was late. Really late. Way later than I'd ever left the library before.

Mom hadn't called. Had she?

I sat up and dug through my ever-present backpack. Dusty receipts. A broken pen. Cold plastic. My phone was buried at the very bottom.

Oh yeah...

The spiderweb of cracks across the screen caught the moonlight, reminding me how Dad hurled it against the wall earlier—shutting up Randy Travis and murdering my phone.

That's why Mom hadn't called. Or why I hadn't heard it.

"That's great."

I tried not to panic, but every fear my parents ever planted in me started resurrecting. The woods are dangerous. Women stuck on the side of the road are easy prey. There are millions of men out there who look like family guys, but they're not.

Should I get out? Try to change the tire myself?

I looked around. Nothing but quiet blacktop and trees. The woods sat before me, behind me, lining the road, watching in the darkness.

No one was out there. Not a soul.

I sank down in my seat. Any passing car would see me. Alone, stuck, helpless.

Could I drive home on it? I pushed that thought away as quickly as it came. There was no way I'd make it without destroying the rim.

I didn't know how to change a tire, but I knew that much. You don't drive on metal.

Chest tight, I held the power button on my phone.

"Come on. Come on."

I bit my lip. Pressed again.

Nothing.

I groaned, banging my head back. The pins probably drew blood that time.

"Fuck this."

Clawing at the bun, I yanked out the stiff metal pins and tossed them to the floorboard. I worked through the braid, uncoiling it. My hair fell down my back in waves.

"Thank God."

I ran my hands through it, rubbing my aching scalp. My eyelids fluttered shut. It was the first thing that had felt good all night.

A light bloomed in my lap, and I opened my eyes.

"Oh my gosh."

Jolting upright, I snatched my phone up with shaking hands. The screen lit up, generic yellow wallpaper, daffodils, even through the spiderweb cracks.

Warped, but it worked.

I swiped carefully. The text app opened.

Nothing.

Mom hadn't texted. Not once. That wasn't normal. She should be blowing up my phone.

Where did you go, Em?

Are you okay?

Please answer.

I need my girls.

I swiped to Gracie's texts. She was quiet. Probably still in shock.

Guilt prickled as I typed.

> I'm sorry I left you there, Gracie. I should've made you leave with me. Been at the library. Heading home. Got stuck with a flat.

I hit send and leaned back, more carefully this time, and closed my eyes.

Maybe a flat tire would soften things. Dad would come to fix it, to get me. Maybe we wouldn't talk about me driving off, at least not tonight.

I sat there, eyes closed, waiting for Gracie to text me back. My mind drifted to Rachel.

Did she know how to drive? Did he let her? Was she ever… stuck?

"I'm not stuck." I said it out loud. I needed to hear it.

But saying it didn't make it feel true. I *was* stuck. Gracie and me both. Stuck at their house. No money. No job away from theirs. No car. No real life.

They finally let us open bank accounts, but that wasn't much use when I kept getting emails saying mine would close for inactivity. Mom gave us ten bucks now and then for gas. Just enough to keep them open.

I really was stuck, no matter how much I didn't want to believe it.

"Were you stuck too?"

I bit my lip. I was talking to a girl missing for twenty years. Maybe I was crazy.

"You were probably a little crazy too," I muttered, and glanced at my phone.

Still quiet. Still dark. No text from Gracie.

Maybe she was arguing with Mom and Dad—because of me.

Then I saw the dash clock.

1:17.

The green digits blurred.

"What?"

I sat up. "Shit..." My neck cracked.

1:18.

"What the hell?"

I'd left the library around nine. How was it after midnight? Had I fallen asleep? Dozed off?

Rubbing my eyes, I checked again.

1:20.

It felt like time was slipping past me. Like someone hit fast-forward on the world.

I swiped my phone open. 1:21 a.m.

No service.

A broken sound slipped from my lips.

No bars. Just EMERGENCY CALLS ONLY.

I shoved the door open, swung my legs out of the truck, feeling the bite of gravel against the thin soles of my shoes. The road was quiet. It was too cold for crickets or frogs. Too dark for songbirds. A single owl called far off.

Being murdered didn't scare me as much now. Not as much as being stuck here forever.

Maybe I could try to change the tire. If I couldn't, at least I'd have the tire iron ready. Something to swing if a murderer showed up.

Leaning over to peer into the bed of the truck, something cold ran through my veins.

I could *try* to change the tire, assuming there was a spare. Dropping to my knees, I searched for a spare strapped somewhere under the tuck. There *was* one on this thing *somewhere*, right? It's like a law, isn't it? Every vehicle *has* to have a spare.

"Fuck." I let out that curse louder than I meant to. Too loud in the silence.

Dad took the spare. He put it on the trailer he pulled behind the work van for the aluminum brake. We didn't even use that thing on every job. He'd started loading ladders on it too—bought a toolbox for the tongue.

I guess it made him feel like a real contractor, dragging that thing around like a badge.

It just made me angry. Not normal-angry. Sharp, spitting, helpless angry.

He hurt you.

"It's just a tire!" I almost shouted into the void. My voice echoed in the dark, bouncing off the trees.

I scrambled back into the truck, locked both doors, and cranked the heat.

I was stuck on the side of the road, with a flat, no spare, and no way to call anyone for help.

Great. Just fucking great.

I grabbed my phone, almost angry enough to throw it like Dad had, but then I blinked.

Five full bars. They lit up the busted screen, bright and unnatural in the dark.

I didn't waste time trying to make sense of it. I dialed the one number I knew would pick up.

She answered on the second ring.

"Hey, Em, are you okay?" Wanda's voice was thick with sleep.

"I don't know." Fear bled into my voice. "Wanda, I... I think I'm stuck."

"Stuck where, Em?" Urgency replaced the sleep in her voice. "Somewhere in that house? That room in the wall?"

"No, I never made it home." I choked. "I'm on the side of the road. I have a flat tire and no spare. I thought I just left the library, but... I must've fallen asleep."

"Okay." Wanda's voice settled out, like she was sitting up now, maybe turned the lights on. "Calm down," she said. "It's going to be alright."

"I was on my way home." I looked around. Desperate for a sign. But everything looked darker now. The shadows longer. The budding trees looked predatory—long, spiny fingers reaching out from the woods.

"Can you send me your location?" Wanda asked.

I dropped my eyes to the dash.

3:42.

The digits glowed, a sickly green-yellow.

"Wanda!" I shrieked, flinching away from the clock like it had reached out to slap me, jamming my ribs into the steering wheel.

"Em! Are you okay?"

"What time is it?"

I couldn't look away from the numbers. If I blinked, I'd lose more time.

Time wasn't ticking. It was dripping. Thick and slow. Then, all at once, it would just slip away—hours at a time.

"It's 3:43, Em." Wanda's voice softened. "Just send me your location."

"How long have we been talking?"

A pause.

"Three minutes?"

I pulled the phone away. The seconds ticking away on my call were adding up. Two hours, twenty-three minutes, thirteen seconds.

"Wanda... I called you at 1:20."

"I was still up at 1:20, Em, studying for a test. You woke me just now."

My throat burned. Stomach twisted. Bladder ached, sharp and urgent, like one of those bleary dreams where there's no bathroom.

"It's okay," Wanda said gently. "We'll figure it out. Send me your location. It's only a flat, alright? We'll fix it."

But it wasn't just the tire. It was the dark. How I didn't remember driving. Time sliding past while I just... watched. Those glowing green numbers melting into each other.

"Okay. Got it." Wanda's voice jolted me back.

"What?"

"Your location."

Weight settled in my chest. "I didn't send anything. I haven't even opened Maps."

"Well, I just got it. You're on Beltline Road… halfway between Caster and Granite Hill. You were heading *away* from your parents', Em."

I broke. Folded into myself, sobbing.

"Hey, hey," Wanda soothed. "It's okay. I'm calling Kade. He lives right around there. He'll be there in five."

"Okay." I hiccupped. "Wanda… I'm scared. I don't know how I got here."

"It's been a long day," she said gently. "You might've dissociated while you were driving. I fell asleep with my laptop open, studying."

"No…" I kept my eyes forward. Didn't look toward the woods. Didn't let the shadows crawl in. "I really don't *know* how I got here. I left at nine, right? How long was I driving? How long have I been here? I called you after one—I know I did. My phone says we've been talking over two hours. I thought it was still… not even ten."

"It's okay. I don't know what happened either, but we'll figure it out. I'm going to hang up, call Kade, then ring you right back. Okay?"

"I lost service for a while," I whispered. "Then it just… came back."

"Sit really still. Maybe you won't lose it again. I'll call you right back. Two minutes. Promise."

I closed my eyes. Took a breath that stung all the way to the bottom of my lungs.

"Okay."

But I didn't feel okay.

Not even close.

17

THE GIRL IN THE MIRROR

I hung up without opening my eyes, rested my phone in my lap and waited. I didn't want to look. Didn't want to see the clock jump to five or six.

I tried to stop crying. Crying wouldn't fix any of this. It just made my eyes burn and my throat hurt worse. I breathed slowly and wiped my face with my jacket sleeve. But I couldn't keep my eyes closed.

The first thing they found when I opened them was the clock.

3:50.

Relief loosened my spine. The stiff vinyl gave a little, swallowing me deeper.

Maybe it was over. Whatever made time slip away while I watched it, whatever got me lost halfway to Granite Hill without even knowing. Maybe it was gone.

The phone buzzed against my hand, and I jumped, swiping to answer before even looking at the busted screen.

"Hello?" Relief hit fast. Wanda got through. The service held.

But it died just as fast because... Wanda didn't say anything. The silence sunk straight into the pit of my empty stomach.

"Are you there?" I pleaded into the heavy silence.

I pulled the phone from my ear. The contact read *Wanda*, the seconds ticking up on the call.

"Wanda, can you hear me?" My voice cracked, rising to a near scream.

Silence answered. Heavy, dark—it sucked me in, cocooned me as my voice died into the phone speaker.

I squeezed my eyes shut. Counted to five. I had to calm down. This was bad service. Spotty reception. That's all.

"Hey?" Lower this time. If I couldn't sound calm, I could at least stop screaming. "Wanda, are you there?"

The truck creaked in the cold, then everything went still. The breeze died in the trees. The owl went silent. I held my breath, and it felt like the world around me held its breath too.

Until rasp split the silence. Low, metallic, like a whisper grinding through gravel.

"He hurt you..."

That wasn't Wanda. It wasn't anyone I knew. Not anyone who should've had my number.

Not anyone *alive*.

My throat tightened and I dropped my phone. It fell to the truck seat beside me, the fractured screen lighting up like cracked ice.

"He hurt you..."

Again. But it sounded like a voice on speaker, except... it wasn't.

Maybe it was a glitch. Some kind of crossed line. Like an old two-way radio catching the wrong frequency.

But this wasn't a radio. This was my cell. And it had rung. Caller ID: Wanda.

I slammed the red End Call button. Again and again, over and over, the cracked screen pinching my finger, drawing blood.

The call ended, my phone went black, but under the heater's hum and my thudding pulse... I heard it.

Breathing.

Breathing that wasn't mine. Not my panicked gasps. Jumpy. Loud. This was slower. Deeper.

I stopped my lungs, straining to hear past the blood rushing in my ears.

Someone was still breathing.

I forced myself to listen. Seconds passed. Minutes. Maybe hours with how time was slipping by. I didn't move. I just sat frozen, listening. And that's when I heard it. That godawful, soul-wrenching sound—the one I'd heard every single night for six years.

Tap. Tap. Tap.

Every muscle in my body locked. My stomach cramped low in my gut. I reached out with a shaking hand and flipped the heater off.

Silence rushed in. Thick. Suffocating. The kind that presses in on you. Makes your ears ache under the weight of it.

But it was silence. Beautiful, deafening silence.

I had imagined it. I had to have.

Alone, in the dark, my brain rewound old fears. Replayed the noises that kept me up night after night in my parents' creepy-ass house.

A shudder climbed my spine.

I'd take that horrible room right now. Creepy-ass house and all. Hell, I'd even take the little room in the wall—at least that ghost didn't lie about the time.

Clink.

My body seized. My hands formed fists so tight my nails dug into my palms.

No.

Clink. Clink. Scrrrraaaaape.

I spun so fast my shoulder cracked. My eyes darted across every inch of glass. I had to look. Even if it meant seeing a hand... a face... breath fogging the glass.

But there was nothing.

Just me, my backpack, and my now quiet phone.

I flipped the heat back on. The fan purred to life, warmth and noise flooding the cab.

Just my brain. It was dark. I was scared. And it was too quiet with the heat off.

I pulled my backpack onto my lap. I needed something to hold. Or hug. I squeezed the bag to my chest.

A paper slipped from the side pocket, fluttering onto the seat.

I picked it up, expecting a receipt from where I'd stopped for gas this morning. Or yesterday morning.

I glanced at the dash. Bright green numbers.

3:57

At least time seemed to be going by at a usual pace now.

The paper wasn't a receipt. It was the picture of Rachel.

Pregnant.

Sadness soured in my chest.

I leaned closer to the glow of the dash clock for a better look. She was sitting on the edge of a bed. I narrowed my eyes, squinting at the edge of the picture.

Was that Beagle?

"No way..."

There were probably thousands of stuffed bears like mine. So Rachel had a brown teddy bear. Just like me. Lots of kids had one, I'm sure.

But not every kid had that four-post bed—with the bottom left post broken down the side.

My stomach flipped.

I broke that bed, when I was nine. Tied a rope to the post. Tried to swing like Tarzan.

I closed my eyes, scrubbed a hand down my face. Willed the crack to be a trick of the light. Or a stray hair, catching the moon at the right angle.

I dusted the picture off.

"Holy fuck."

The crack was still there. Rachel leaned against the post. And there, half out of frame, near the pillow, was Beagle.

"There's no way."

It couldn't be the same bed.

I was nine. I broke that post. I remembered tying that rope. Swinging like an idiot. How mad Dad was. My parents had lugged that fucking thing state to state, house to house, for as long as I could remember.

It wasn't the same bed.

Ping. Ping. Ping.

Three sharp taps in rapid fire.

I jumped. Looked before I could stop myself. It was dark. The road curved away, like it got as lost in the woods as I had.

I didn't imagine that. I heard it—as loud as a baby screaming at night.

Ping. Ping. Ping.

I don't know why I did it, but I leaned forward, enough to catch the rearview.

Something moved.

A flicker. A shadow sliding against the ribbed plastic of the truck bed.

I gripped the wheel like a lifeline and hauled myself upright, heart slamming against my ribs like it wanted out.

I wanted to see the truck bed. The tailgate. The road behind me.

But I didn't.

Instead, all I saw were those hollow, milky eyes from the library microwave.

But this time they were real, not a warp of my own reflection. Set into a thin, pale face. Skin sagging like it was melting off her jaw. Stringy, red hair hung loose, tangled with clots of blood and wet earth.

Her head tilted. A sick, shuddering motion. Her milky eyes rolled back, and her mouth gaped open. Blood oozed from the corners of her lips as her neck cracked—so loud it echoed in my ribs.

And then... she smiled.

Slow and stretching, lips peeling back to reveal busted teeth the color of rotten bone.

Something moved behind her. Something that wasn't her. A shadow that shouldn't have been there. It reached forward and her smile warped into pain.

The truck bed groaned behind me. And from some distant, dark place, I heard that voice again. Grating, like nails against blackboard.

He hurt you.

Those bulging, white eyes locked onto mine, and I finally found my voice.

A shrill scream broke the silence, pierced my ears. A scream I had no idea I was capable of making.

I tore at the truck door like a rabid animal until it gave way, spilling me onto the cold, damp gravel. Fighting to my feet, I only made it a couple paces before I ran headlong into something—someone.

I knew, even in my hysteria, who it was.

18

COFFEE ON THE TAILGATE

"Kade."

His name didn't come out so much as it collapsed off my lips.

Strong arms wrapped around me. The gentle smell of leather and pine. That deep, resonant voice humming in my ear.

"Whoa, Em." He caught me, held me steady. "I'm here, okay? I got you."

I broke down into tears against his chest.

"Are you hurt?"

I shook my head, sobbing. "She was there... just like in the library."

Kade didn't say anything. He held me. Let me cry.

"She's dead, Kade, and she's after me."

I hadn't realized I'd grabbed him. His jacket was balled in my fists.

"Who's after you, Em?" His voice was gentle, but the question made me realize how insane it all sounded.

Could I tell him a ghost was after me? That a ghost wanted my teddy bear? That I saw a bloody ghost girl in the rearview of my dad's truck?

I didn't give myself time to overthink. I knew what I saw. What I heard. What I felt. And I told Kade everything.

About the eyes in the microwave door. The time slip in the truck. The smiling apparition in the mirror. I even told him about Gracie—how she reacted to the wall in my room. What she said about the blanket.

I told him everything. Everything I'd already told Wanda, and some things I hadn't even told her.

About my dad. How he smashed my phone over a song—after I found porn on his. How he told me I wasn't his daughter, not on *his* job sites, but that he wouldn't let me work anywhere else. That he said I'd be corrupted by the *world*.

I even told Kade about not being allowed to own a car or go to school. About feeling stuck, hopeless, and alone.

By the time I realized how much I'd let out, my lungs were burning. All the crazy. All the disgusting. All the unbelievable.

"Oh my gosh," I panted, burying my face in my hands. "I'm so sorry. I didn't mean to…"

Kade cut me off, his warm hands gently gripping my upper arms.

"Em, look at me." His voice, quiet, calm. Steadying.

I looked up at him. Tears stung my face, blurring everything.

"Don't tell me you're sorry." His dark eyes held mine. "Em… with all the shit you're going through, you need a friend. I don't mind being that friend. I'll listen."

That only made me cry harder, but Kade didn't flinch.

He'd already seen me panicked. Spiraling. Now he saw me broken. Terrified. Sobbing into his chest like my world had split open.

I'd never been allowed to get close to a man, but I was pretty sure this wasn't the best way to make a first impression.

It was all wrong.

But somehow, it felt right, with Kade.

That night changed something between us.

Me, pouring out everything. Trusting him with secrets I'd never spoken aloud. And Kade, listening. Holding me. Believing me.

He'd parked his old El Camino off the road, a little up from the overgrown driveway where I'd landed Dad's truck.

At some point, Kade had guided me to the tailgate. Now we sat side by side. He still held my hands, quiet and patient.

"Don't think you're crazy." Kade gave my hands a small squeeze.

I hadn't spoken in a while. I'd finally run out of things to say.

"None of this is crazy, Em." He was serious. "Not the ghosts or haunting."

He paused.

"Your parents..." He let that sentence die.

And I couldn't help it. A cracked, broken laugh slipped out. If I didn't laugh, I'd cry some more.

"I'm going to be in such deep shit." I pulled my hands from Kade's, wiped my eyes. "I don't even know what time it is. I left work with Dad screaming about how sorry I'd be, after I cussed out loud and he broke my phone."

I had to stop, take a breath. It caught in my ribs, burned my lungs.

I looked at Kade, shaking my head. "I don't even *dare* mention a rotting ghost girl in the mirror. The fucking blown tire and me rolling in at sunrise? That's going to be enough."

Kade slid off the tailgate and circled around to the driver's side. He came back with a thermos, twisted off the lid, and poured it full of steaming, creamy coffee.

"Here." He handed me the cup.

I couldn't even thank him properly, I was gulping down the sweet, life-giving liquid.

I was freezing. Bone-deep cold. And so damn thirsty. I couldn't even remember the last time I ate. Lunch yesterday? What did we even have for lunch?

"He doesn't put hands on you, does he?" Kade's voice was low, careful.

I froze, mid-sip.

He was watching me, his dark eyes gentle, but there was a spark of something else behind them. Something sharp.

"Who, my dad?"

Kade nodded. "You said he threw your phone," he said softly.

"He puts on." I drained the rest of the coffee.

Without asking, Kade took the cup from my hand and refilled it.

"Dad's mean. But not violent."

I caught Kade watching me.

"Not physically." I added. "Not to people, anyway. Just phones."

And tables. Dinner plates. Sometimes the van. Or truck. Driving like a bat out of hell if he was mad enough and happened to be behind the wheel.

"I'm not trying to be intrusive." Kade shrugged a little. "My dad hit my mom. And me."

"Oh..."

He shook his head, cutting me off gently. "I was seven when she got away. She's married to Wanda's dad now. He's a good guy. Good to Mom. My dad's in Virginia. Runs a bar. I never see him and don't want to."

"Kade..."

"That's just what came to mind." He interrupted me. "When you said he threw your phone."

He set the big, green thermos down beside me on the tailgate of his car.

"Let me know if he hits you, Em—you tell me. Or Wanda. We'll help you. Don't live like that."

My tongue felt glued to the roof of my mouth.

No one had ever offered to help me leave before. No one had looked at Mom and Dad and seen how bad things were. Because I'd never told anyone.

And no one ever thought Dad could be something worse.

No one ever asked if I was in danger. I'd never even thought that.

"You drink all the coffee you want, alright?" Kade nodded toward me. "I'll change your tire, then follow you home. Make sure you get there safe."

He didn't wait for an answer. Just grabbed the spare and some tools from the bed of his El Camino and headed for my dad's truck.

I sat there, quiet and clutching the warm cup of coffee, watching him work.

He changed the tire fast, like it was second nature. He was back at the El Camino before I could pour another cup.

"Thank you so much for doing that."

He waved it off.

"Don't thank me. I was already getting up. Wanda called while I was getting ready for work. I'm a mechanic in Granite Hill. Work for a lube and tire shop. This just felt like an early start."

I shook my head. "You'll have to show me how to do that sometime. In case this ever happens again."

"I can do that." He smiled and I slid off the tailgate, thanking him for the coffee.

"I'm sure it didn't warm you up much, but hey…" He shrugged. "Better than nothing." Kade tossed the thermos back into his car.

I hadn't looked at my dad's truck since Kade came back. But I'd have to now. I'd have to get back in it. Drive it home. Check the rearview mirror. A cold chill worked its way up my spine.

"I could drive you." Kade seemed to read my mind. "Maybe your dad could come back later for his truck."

Dad would come unglued if I left his truck here. His *classic* pick-up. Out in the boondocks. Waiting to be stolen.

I took a shallow breath.

But it wasn't just the truck. Both my parents would lose it if I came home with a man. Especially a man like Kade.

We don't mix races. Dad's voice, slow and smug, echoed in my head.

I couldn't put Kade through that. Not after all he'd done for me this morning.

"I can drive." I whispered, barely pulling the words from my chest.

Kade nodded. "I'll still follow you, is that okay?"

"Yeah." I looked up quickly. "Of course. I don't want to get lost again. I still don't know how I ended up on this road."

"It happens." His shoulder rose in a half-shrug. "I think Rachel's trying to talk to you."

The skeletal face from the rearview flashed in my mind. I had to close my eyes.

"We didn't get around to telling you earlier, Em." Kade's voice drew me back. "I recognized that fabric."

"The fabric?" My voice was strained, but I pulled the folded bit of worn, pink fabric from my jumper pocket.

"Yeah." Kade took it, his huge hands dwarfing the torn shred. "Damn…"

I watched his face. The way he rolled his bottom lip between his teeth. The way his dark eyes slowly blinked, moisture pooling at the corners.

"I saw her." He looked up at me. "That's how I know you're not crazy. That's how I know ghosts are real."

"You saw Rachel?"

The words tumbled out—too fast, too loud.

I wasn't alone. I wasn't crazy. And if I was, then Kade was too.

"Wanda and I used to sneak around your house when I was a teenager." He looked back down at the fabric in his hand, brushing his thumb over the silky fibers.

"It'd been deserted for years. It was a wreck. Creepy, yeah, but fun for a bunch of us from school. We used to scare the shit out of each other."

He looked up at me, and his face grew sober. "I saw her one night. Standing in the woods out behind the house. Pink nightgown. Long, bloody hair. She looked right at me. She had big, milky looking eyes that locked onto mine."

Kade closed his eyes and for the first time since I'd met him, he looked shaken.

"I didn't know who she was." He steadied himself. "I lost almost a year. Don't remember anything but trying to find out who she was."

"Oh, Kade..." I put a hand on his arm and his eyes dropped.

"I believe there's a spirit world." He spoke to me, but his eyes were still on my hand. "And that girl in the pink night gown is why. I know it's real. And I know you're not crazy."

He looked back up at me.

"We know who she is now. We know Rachel Bagwell's dead, or she wouldn't be a ghost." He handed the fabric back to me and watched me fold it carefully and tuck it into my pocket.

"We have to figure out what she wants." Kade was quiet. "And why she's bothering you."

19

CONFISCATED

The sun was rising, a dim, pink light bleeding through the pines as I turned into my parents' drive. Kade followed behind, his El Camino's headlights steady in my rearview, a silent reminder that I wasn't alone.

As I pulled into the driveway, Kade passed by toward town. I hoped I hadn't made him late for work. Or drank too much of his coffee. Somewhere in my backpack was a scrap of paper with Kade's number on it.

"Just in case you need anything," he'd said, shrugging. "Or you want to talk."

I'd text him later. To say thank you. But maybe he'd want to keep talking. About something other than ghosts and Rachel. Maybe we'd get to know each other for real.

I bit my lip as I stopped my dad's truck in front of the house.

We don't mix races. His voice crawled up from the back of my brain as I shoved the gearstick into park.

I didn't care about their judgment, their anger, not at all. If Kade wanted to get to know me better, as more than his sister's friend, I'd fall for him so fast... Maybe I already was.

Of course, this was probably all wishful thinking. Kade was kind. Gentle. But maybe that's all this was—kindness. Maybe once the mystery unraveled, our paths would too. Maybe he was just nice.

I slid out of the truck and shut the door behind me. The weight settled. I was back. At my parents' home.

Everything about yesterday slammed through me. The attic. The fabric. The porn. The fight. My phone hitting the wall.

I took a shaky breath and started up the block walk. Relief rushed through me when I saw Mom step outside. She'd be worried. She'd run to me and hug me, hold me tight, cry. Tell me she's so happy I'm home and safe.

Except, that's not what happened.

"Emily, where have you been?" Her voice held concern, but something else simmered beneath it.

"I got lost." I stepped onto the porch, still expecting her to throw her arms around me. Still needing her to.

"I had a flat tire," I added, quieter, when she made no move toward me.

"How did you get home?" She hadn't hugged me, but her words climbed an octave. There was fear. "Did you have a spare? Did you figure out how to change it?"

"No spare. A guy stopped." I whispered a prayer for forgiveness. I couldn't mention Kade. Or Wanda. "He helped."

"Oh, my goodness, Emily!" Mom's hands flew to her chest, but not around me. "You could've been raped and murdered and no one would've known a thing! Why didn't you answer my calls?"

I held up my busted phone. Had she even called? When I'd finally got my phone to flicker back to life, no missed calls showed up. No texts flooded through like I'd expected.

Mom's shoulders dropped. "Where did you go when you left?"

"The library."

"It was late, Em." Mom hugged herself. "The library would've been closed."

"Mom, the lady at the desk let me in. She was getting ready to leave." I watched her face. "She sees me there all the time. She trusts me. I stayed and read for a while. Locked up when I left."

It wasn't exactly a lie. Wanda trusted me. And I was pretty sure, if she ever had to leave early and I needed more time—to research or just breathe—she'd trust me to lock up.

"Hm." Mom's response was tight, doubtful. "Then you got lost." She said it like she'd used air quotes in her head.

"Yes. Lost. With a flat." I adjusted my backpack on my shoulder. "And no spare. Because Dad put it on his trailer."

Speak of the devil. Dad came thundering out the front door and across the porch.

"Emily Carol!" He stormed across the porch and crushed me into a suffocating hug. I wanted to recoil. My stomach doubled on itself, like it was trying to slip down into my guts.

What the fuck?

I'd never liked Dad's hugs. Or his slimy kisses—always on the lips, even into my teens. But I'd never physically revolted.

He was... worried. Relieved to finally see his daughter.

Guilt crawled through me, thick and nauseating. This wasn't in my head. It was real. Physical. Revulsion I could barely choke down.

I swallowed it and hugged him back—enough for him to finally let go. When he did, I stumbled back a step.

"I'm so tired." I tried to cover whatever the hell just happened.

"What happened to you? We've all been worried sick, Emily. Where've you been?" Dad's questions were more urgent than Mom's.

I gave him the same half-true story I gave Mom.

I went to the library. Got lost. Flat tire. No spare. Some kind stranger helped me, and I got home safe.

I left out Wanda. Left out Kade. Left out how I got lost, how I couldn't even remember driving. Left out the slip in time. The voice that wasn't Wanda's that spoke to me through my phone. The skeletal face in the mirror.

Those events of last night would die with me before I'd ever tell my parents.

"Some random man on the road happened to find her, Don." Mom's arms were still crossed, eyes pinned on Dad. Too hard. Too steady.

But the look they shared made my stomach turn. Like something unspoken passed between them.

"Let's get inside." Dad's hand closed around my arm. "We'll get you some warm coffee. Then we'll talk."

Sitting in the kitchen with my parents was the last thing I wanted to do. Not even coffee could fix this.

"I'm really tired," I said again as we stepped inside.

I followed my parents down the hall anyway. Past the living room, toward the kitchen. But... something felt wrong.

Worse than dealing with my parents after being lost all night.

I caught the faintest whiff of fire, and my eyes darted to the hearth. It had been clean the last time I noticed it. Too clean. Scrubbed almost white. Free of ash and soot.

But something had been burned there recently. Not just wood, even though there was wood there now. There was a fire there. Glowing warm and bright into the dim living room.

Yet, I wasn't smelling wood smoke. This was something else... Plastic?

Mom put a hand on my arm, jolting me back to the present. "Come on." She nodded toward the kitchen.

But I shook my head. "I think I'd like to lay down."

"You don't want coffee?" Mom's brow rose. "You always want coffee, Em."

"Mom, I was scared. Lost in the dark, with a flat tire. No way to call anyone." I took a shaky breath. "I just want to lay down."

"You can after we get you something warm to drink." Dad's voice sounded from the kitchen—he was already sitting at the table.

Keeping my backpack's strap slung over my arm, I clutched it tighter as I followed Mom into the kitchen, leaving the fireplace and its lingering scent of plastic in the living room.

Something was off this morning. And it wasn't only that I'd been gone all night.

Mom wasn't worried. She was mad. Probably still pissed about yesterday. Me leaving the job. Staying gone all night hadn't helped.

You'd think she would have been more worried and less mad, though.

I put the kettle on the stove and lit the burner, then dug through the cabinets for lemon ginger tea. It was buried behind a red can of ground coffee, boxes of instant packets, powdered vanilla cappuccino, and two oversized tubs of creamer.

The nutty stench of coffee hit my stomach like the putrid scent of rot. Smelling it, I thought I might throw up.

If I were back with Kade, on the tailgate of his El Camino, even with Dad's haunted truck ten yards away, I'd drink coffee and love every drop.

But here, in this house, with my parents' eyes drilling into the back of my skull, I was already jittery, nauseous, and raw. The last thing I needed was a cup of Mom's acidic coffee-colored water scorching my throat.

Tea. If they insisted I drink something, I'd choose tea. Lemon ginger. Something that might settle my stomach. Something that might help me sleep.

I poured steaming water over the teabag and dunked it in, watching the gold swirl and spread. The spicy scent hit my nose. I closed my eyes and breathed it in.

"Em." Mom's voice was too close, too sudden. I nearly jumped out of my skin. "Why are you so jumpy?"

She grabbed a rag from the sink and dabbed at the spilled tea.

"I haven't slept."

"And you think we have?" Mom snapped, fast and sharp enough to make me look up. "We've been up all night, sick with worry."

She nodded toward Gracie's room, on the opposite end of the house.

"I finally got her to take some melatonin. But your dad and I? We've been up. All night. Waiting."

"I would've called."

"Are you pregnant?"

Her words didn't register at first. They hung in the air.

"Pregnant?" The word stuck to the roof of my mouth. "Why would you even think that?"

Her hand went to her hip, eyes flicking to my tea. "You drink coffee, not ginger tea. You only drink that when you're sick."

She paused, like she was waiting for me to respond. But I couldn't move my mouth. Couldn't tear my tongue off my teeth.

"You were sick a couple nights ago, and when I tried to help, you ran off and slammed your bedroom door in my face."

Mom tilted her head, like she was studying me under a microscope.

"You're cussing. Storming off the job. Stealing your dad's truck. Then you vanish all night. And now you expect us to believe some stranger happened to stop and change your tire out of the goodness of his heart?"

"There are good people left in the world!" I snapped, louder than I meant to.

"You showed up this morning with your hair down, Emily!" Mom's voice sliced through mine.

My stomach dropped.

My hair. I'd torn it down in Dad's truck. Ripped out the braid, the pins, everything. Because it hurt. Because my phone was busted. Because I was alone.

"The pins were hurting my head!"

"You don't go out in public with your hair down." Mom shook her head, arms folded tight. "You know that. Men like it when your hair's down. That's why we keep it up."

I couldn't believe this was happening. Not after last night. After everything. All the shit. Now this.

"Are you pregnant?"

This time it wasn't a question. It was an accusation.

I stared at her. She believed it. She actually believed it. My mother thought I was pregnant.

"No, I'm not pregnant."

"We've been by the library." Dad's voice cut in. Low. Final.

My back went rigid.

"All those evenings you claim to be at the library." There was no worry in Mom's voice now. It was just harsh, bitter anger. "Reading or researching, or whatever you call yourself doing. We've been by there, several times. Your dad's truck was out front, but you were nowhere. We've even gone inside. I've walked every aisle. Even checked the bathroom. You weren't there."

"Did you check the archives? The conference room?" I dunked my tea bag again, trying to look calm while my brain screamed. "Sometimes I take books in there to read, so I'm not bothered."

"We checked all the rooms." Dad's voice was closer. Too close.

I was boxed in. Mom on my left. The stove on my right. Dad closing in behind me.

They didn't trust me. They'd been checking up on me. Not only driving by the library but going inside. Walking the aisles. Because they didn't trust me. Not even a little. What the hell?

I'd been at the library, like I said. Reading less, sure. Talking to Wanda more. But I was there.

"I'm not lying." I looked straight at Mom. "I don't know where I was exactly when you came by. I don't know why you couldn't find me. But I was at the library."

"Where were you last night?" She asked it like it was brand new. Like I hadn't already answered it—three times.

"I was at the library!" I stared at her. "The woman at the desk trusted me to lock up. I stayed until nine. Then I left. I don't know how I got lost, maybe I was tired. But I did. And then the tire blew."

"How do you get lost between here and the library, Emily?" Dad's voice shifted. Any concern was draining from it, replaced by something colder.

Because... I blacked out? Drove without realizing it? Rachel was driving? Time passed at the speed of light?

"I don't know." I hated the quiver in my voice. I took way too big a gulp of my still-steaming tea and swallowed it down.

Silence thickened in the kitchen. No one moved. My parents stared. I sipped my bitter, over-steeped tea like it was a potion. Like it might protect me.

The silence shattered when Mom held out her hand. "Give me your keys."

"What?"

That hit harder than the pregnancy question.

"To the vehicles and the house."

I stared at her. "You're taking my keys?"

She didn't flinch. Hand out. Face blank. Waiting.

"Fine."

I set my tea down, unzipped my bag, and pulled out my small chain of keys. There was one for Dad's truck, one for the work van, and one for each entrance door to the house, the back and the front.

They all hung from a pink cat keychain I'd bought myself. I kept the charm. Dropped the keys into Mom's hand.

"We don't know what kind of people you're hanging out with, Em," Mom said, flatly. "We can't have strangers showing up here."

"You think I'm lying?" My voice was pinched.

"I'm not buying the library story." Mom shook her head. "And you're not bringing anyone up to my house."

It felt like someone was holding me underwater. Waiting for me to suck in the cold. Let it fill my lungs. Slowly drown.

She said it was about safety. About strangers. But what if I needed a way out?

What if I needed to run—from whoever these people were she thought I was hanging out with, or even pregnant by?

That didn't matter.

I didn't matter.

"And your phone." Dad spoke up from somewhere behind me.

"You can have it." I spun and hurled my phone across the kitchen. "It's broken anyway."

Dad was shouting at me. Mom was scolding me. But I didn't hear them.

I threw that phone way harder than Dad did yesterday.

If they were going to take it, fine. But I made sure it would cost way more than it was worth to ever get it fixed. There wouldn't be any turning it back on. No finding Wanda's number. No spying on me.

I ran up the steps, ignoring my parents calling after me. I got to my room and slammed the door behind me, locking it.

I'd sleep. I'd lock myself in and I'd sleep.

That's not what happened.

What I found inside didn't make this morning any better, and I sure wouldn't be able to sleep after this.

Mom hadn't only wanted my keys. Dad didn't only want my phone. They'd been through my room.

My bed was a mess. My journal, kept under my mattress, had been found and gone through. It lay open on my bed, pages wrinkled and torn.

My laptop, old and clunky though it was, no longer lay hidden under my mattress. It was missing completely.

My closet was open, clothes askew, clearly searched. My dresser drawers, though closed, had been gone through. Each drawer I opened was a disorganized, scattered mess.

The room was a fucking disaster. It looked like a tornado had whipped through the place.

I clutched my backpack to my chest. The file with Rachel's history was safe. I'd taken it with me. I knew, without a shadow of doubt, it would be missing, too, if I left it here yesterday.

The napkin with Wanda's number, the torn pink fabric from my jumper pocket—they were safe.

I clutched my backpack tighter, sinking to the floor against my locked bedroom door.

The file was safe. The fabric was safe.

Everything else they'd violated.

A person's supposed to feel safe at home, with their family.

But I didn't feel safe. Not in this house. Not with them. Not anymore.

20

BURIED

I wanted to text Wanda. Tell her everything. I wanted to thank Kade. For helping me this morning, for being the one sane, kind person in the middle of this madness.

But I was cut off. Trapped. The second story of this stupid, haunted house might as well have been a dungeon. No phone. No laptop. No way to reach anyone but the people inside these splintering walls.

I didn't even remember standing, only that I couldn't stay curled on the floor like a kicked dog. Somehow, I peeled myself up.

I stepped through the wreckage of my room, feeling like I was walking through a dream. A nightmare. Someone else's nightmare.

I straightened what I could. Shoved clothes into drawers, smoothed my journal pages, fluffed the pillows. It didn't help.

I felt... erased.

They'd taken everything they could. Violated everything that made me *me*.

So, I took the only thing I had left. The only thing they hadn't touched. And I hid it where I knew they wouldn't look. In the room inside the wall, behind my dresser. Still revolting. Still cold with dust and that faint, lingering stench of rot.

But it was hidden. And right now, I needed *hidden* more than I needed *safe*.

I couldn't let them get Rachel's file. Something inside me recoiled at the thought of their hands on those papers. They needed to be hidden.

I took out the scrap of fabric from my pocket, and the wrinkled napkin with Wanda's number scrawled across it. I held them in both hands and closed my eyes for a moment, trying to breathe.

The napkin still smelled like grease and paper bags.

Behind my eyelids, I could see the bright plastic blur of a ball pit. The yellow toy case. The cheap, plastic prizes kids picked with their meal.

Pick which one you want, sweetie.

My eyes flew open. I spun around, searching for the voice. But I was alone, in the dusty hole behind my dresser. That voice wasn't here. It was in my head. A voice I knew. A memory I wasn't supposed to have.

I'd never been inside one of those places... With the huge, golden arches, and the clown with the curly, red hair and painted smile.

I shoved the fabric and napkin deep into my backpack.

How could I remember that? How could I remember the sticky floor in the dim bathroom... the way it clung to the soles of my hot pink flip-flops?

I gripped my backpack like it could anchor me. Keep me from unraveling any faster.

I've never worn flip flops. Some men like women's feet. We always cover our feet.

And hot pink? I wouldn't own that. Not for anything. Hot pink is like red. Or sunshine yellow. Or neon any-color. Too loud. Too bold. It draws attention.

We dress modestly. Quiet.

Grays with tiny floral prints. Faded green. Dark blues. Denim jumpers. Turtlenecks. Ankle socks. Black tennis shoes.

I clutched my backpack harder. My fingers curled so tight around the strap that it bit into my palm.

None of this was real. It couldn't be. The voices. The colors. The ball pit. That cheerful voice telling me to pick a toy. The smell of French fries and grease. It had to be a dream.

Maybe it was something I saw once, on a hotel television, during free breakfast. Stale toast. Cheap cereal. A commercial that wormed its way into my brain and turned into fake nostalgia.

I pressed the heel of my hand into my temple. Hard.

I'd never eaten fast food. Never walked under those golden arches. Never slid down that big yellow slide into a pit of plastic balls. Never worn flip flops. Never.

Tucking my backpack between the studs, I backed out of the tiny room. I replaced the cedar panel and shoved my dresser tight against it.

I dusted my hands on my skirt.

Rachel's file. The fabric scrap. Wanda and Kade's numbers. All safe. For now, that had to be enough.

I didn't know it yet, but everything had shifted. That night. That morning. Those hours I spent in my room...

I took a quick shower, speeding through it so I could get back to my room and be alone, behind the locked door.

I was relieved to find my parents hadn't come upstairs while I was in the bathroom. No one was sitting on my bed, waiting to *talk* when I raced back inside, a towel wrapped around me.

It didn't take long to get dressed. Finding a comfortable, gray cotton cape dress in my closet, I pulled it on.

I knew I needed sleep, but something inside me wouldn't let me relax. I slipped on socks and tied back on my shoes. I even braided my hair, but I didn't bother to bun it. My head was sore from pins anyways.

And I didn't lay down.

Instead, I crossed the room and opened the bottom dresser drawer. I'd finish fixing Beagle. He deserved that.

So did I.

I deserved to feel like I could control at least one part of my life. I could fix something.

Pulling back the folded sweaters, I found my worn teddy carefully tucked between them. But then I froze, hand flying to my mouth to cover a scream.

There, beside the frayed edge of Beagle's little, brown paw was a toy. Plastic. Faded. A clown, red and yellow, with a painted smile cracked across his face.

"Oh no..."

I staggered back, my voice a ragged whisper.

Its molded arms, the red-and-white stripes across the sleeves. The puff of molded, red hair sitting on top of its ghostly white face.

I remembered it.

I could remember holding it. Playing with it. In a sand box. Burying it, in a little plastic, treasure box, and scratching an *X* in the sand with a stick so I could play pirate and find buried treasure.

They buried you.

"No..."

I grabbed Beagle from the drawer as if I were saving him from something horrible.

The plastic toy toppled from against the drawer's base with a hollow clank as I pulled the bear free. But I'd revealed something else. Something hidden beneath Beagle. Something else that hadn't been there when I stuffed him in that drawer.

The treasure box. My treasure box. Nausea hit me hard. I doubled over, clutching Beagle like he could hold me together.

It was real. The memory. The voice. The pink flip-flops. It was all real.

I tore out of my bedroom and back to the bathroom, still foggy from my too-hot shower. Falling to my knees in front of the toilet, I heaved up my guts between violent sobs and hot, burning tears.

I remembered. Things I didn't know I'd forgotten. But I remembered. And now, I wished I didn't.

21

Just Storage

I holed up in my room, pouring everything I had into fixing Beagle.

I tried not to think. Not about the toy, not about the memory clawing at the back of my brain. The ball pit. The sandbox.

So I focused on the thread. The needle. In and out. Over and under. One stitch at a time.

Beagle was slowly looking less like a gutted mess and becoming the teddy I remembered.

I was nearly finished, nodding off sitting up, when a soft knock at my door startled me.

I knew it was Gracie. Mom's knock was louder. Dad never bothered.

"Hey." I opened the door and let her in, locking it behind us. "Sorry if I kept you up last night."

Gracie shook her head. Her green eyes looked dull. Her face pale. Arms wrapped around her stomach like she was holding herself together.

"I wanted to check on you." Her voice was small. "I'm riding with Mom and Dad to Granite Hill for supplies."

"I can come." I started gathering up the scraps of thread and fluff from Beagle.

"You don't have to." Gracie stepped beside me.

"I don't feel right staying home while everyone else works. Especially since it was my fault no one slept last night."

"Mom said you need to stay here." Her whisper wasn't a suggestion. It was a sentence.

"Oh..." I sat on the edge of my bed, mechanically picking up Beagle and starting back on the stitches.

Gracie stood there, silent, watching me. The air between us felt thick.

I heard Mom in the kitchen, washing dishes from whatever breakfast she'd made. Outside, the truck engine purred through the thin glass of my bedroom window as Dad backed up to hitch the trailer.

"Mom thinks I'm pregnant." I broke the silence, my voice wavering more than I wanted.

"Are you?"

Gracie said it so simply. My head snapped up so fast my neck cracked. "No!"

That came out harsher than I meant it. I rubbed my neck and took a steadying breath.

"Gracie, I'm not pregnant. I don't even have a boyfriend. How could I? We don't do anything. We don't go anywhere. Neither one of us even sees anyone."

"Mom said you haven't been going to the library."

My jaw dropped. "You believe her?"

Gracie bit her lip. One shoulder lifted in a half-shrug. "Why would she lie?"

I stared at her. "Why would I lie?"

She didn't answer, but we both knew.

To taste freedom. Even for a second. The kind of life our parents said was too dangerous. Too worldly. Too evil.

But I wasn't lying. And I sure as hell wasn't pregnant.

Somehow, my hands kept stitching. Thread in, thread out.

I used to think our parents hid us from the world to keep us safe. That's what they said. They were guarding us from the influence of the evil one.

But now... I wasn't so sure.

Maybe they were hiding us from something else entirely. Like memories.

Gracie sat on the edge of my bed. "What happened to Beagle?"

I looked up.

I'm not sure why, but when I found Beagle gutted on my bedroom floor the other night, I'd automatically assumed Gracie had torn him apart. Maybe she'd done it in a fit of memory, right before crawling into the wall where I found her.

"I thought..." My voice caught as I watched her face.

"You thought I did that?" She winced. "Why would I tear up your bear, Em? That's... crazy."

I didn't know what to say.

"He was already like that when I came to check on you the other night." Gracie shook her head. "I thought... maybe you'd done it."

"I wouldn't tear up Beagle."

"Then why did you think I would?"

A sharp throb bloomed behind my eyes.

"When I found you in the wall, I thought maybe... you were upset. That you tore him up without realizing it."

Gracie didn't answer. She stared.

"You know... like when somebody picks at their fingernails without realizing." I tried to backpedal.

Gracie was still silent.

Still staring.

For one flickering second the thought infected me—what if it wasn't her? What if I tore up Beagle without realizing? Like I'd driven half the night without realizing.

"Em..." Gracie's voice was hesitant. "How could I be *in the wall*?"

My stomach flipped. No. She wasn't saying that.

Her question was quiet, uncertain, so simple it sent a chill up my spine. Gracie couldn't *not* remember the room. The blanket. What she told me.

"The little room." I nodded toward it. "It's behind my dresser, remember? It has the old purple blanket with your name embroidered on it."

"Em, I don't know what you're talking about." Her voice had thinned to a whisper. "There's no room in your wall."

"Yes, there is!" I jumped off my bed and went to my dresser, pushing it back and popping the cedar panel out of place. "You were in there just the other night!"

A gust of sour air curled from the opening, brushing against my ankles. The smell of dust and old rot. It hit me like a breath from a mouth that shouldn't exist.

I had to take a little step back.

"That's just storage." Gracie gave a laugh—light, dismissive, and so much like Mom's it made my toes curl.

"What about the story about Mom trying to leave Dad?" I was desperate.

Either she truly had forgotten all of this, or... had it never happened? Was it like the time slip in the truck last night? Like when I couldn't even remember getting behind the wheel, let alone driving to Beltline Road?

"Emily!" Gracie's voice was almost scolding. "Mom would never leave Dad."

We stood, me by my dresser, Gracie by the door, staring at each other.

I didn't know what to say.

But I couldn't have said anything, even if I thought of something. My tongue felt glued to the roof of my mouth. Like all the liquid in my body was suddenly absorbed by the thirsty silence in the room.

"Grace Ann!" Mom's voice chimed from downstairs. "Hurry up, or we'll be late for the parking lot sale!"

Gracie didn't say another word to me, she turned and left my room.

I didn't go after her. Didn't beg Mom to let me tag along. Didn't offer to help Dad and Gracie load sheetrock. Didn't try to make up for yesterday's fight, or last night's disappearance.

I didn't do any of that.

Instead, I stood at my bedroom window and watched as Dad backed the trailer down the driveway. Mom sat next to him, squeezed beside the floor-mounted gear stick. On her right sat Gracie, blankly looking out the windshield, her gaze lost somewhere up the drive toward the garage.

I sidestepped the window a little, so Mom wouldn't see me watching.

I bet she thought leaving me here was a punishment. No way to call anyone. No keys to the work van parked outside. No way to leave.

She didn't know.

The only thing I wanted was to be away from all of them right now. Away from my family. The ones who claimed to love me more than anyone else ever could.

I needed to figure whatever this was out.

To prove to myself that I wasn't going crazy. To prove Rachel Bagwell really died here. To prove Gracie had been inside that little room hidden in the wall before—way before we moved here six years ago. To prove that *was* her worn purple blanket with her name stitched into the fabric.

To prove I remembered, and so did she.

22

UNHOLY GROUND

It took a minute to realize I was truly alone.

Once Dad's truck rumbled out of earshot, I finished the last stitches on Beagle and pulled my slouchy, orange backpack from the wall.

I spread Rachel's file across the floor and studied it with a scrutiny I hadn't dared before. There was no chance of anyone walking in. No chance anyone could glimpse these pages before I stuffed them back into my bag.

I could take my time. Really see things.

Like the picture. With Beagle in it. And the crack on the bedpost.

I'd turned on every light in my room and found a flashlight too. I used it to inspect that photograph—comparing the crack in the image to the one I made on my bedpost when I was nine.

It was the same crack. The same, fucking crack. It had been there the whole time. Right where I propped my pillow every night, to stay up late and read.

"And that's Beagle."

Another thing I could do when I was alone: talk to myself. Which I found I was inclined to do—a lot.

"That's you, isn't it?" I held the photograph up beside Beagle.

He didn't look, of course. Only stared, like always. But his stitched mouth seemed to smile a little wider in the flashlight beam.

"You haven't always been mine." I picked Beagle up and carried him to the mess of documents scattered across the cold, wooden floor.

I set him against my dresser, where his button eyes watched me while I used the flashlight and studied every piece of paper in that file.

Beagle lived in some of my earliest memories. He'd always been with me, always been mine. But... he'd always been old. Worn to threads on the ends of his little paws, and across the tops of his rounded ears.

I'd never thought of where he came from. Had Mom bought him for me from a thrift store?

I guess that's what I'd always thought. That's why he'd always felt so... old. Like he'd lived a life before me. Like he wasn't a child's toy.

He was an old friend.

A chill grazed the back of my neck, and the flashlight caught a crumpled corner. Red crayon.

Holding the light between my teeth, I tried to tug the page from under a newspaper clipping about Rachel's fifth-grade spelling bee, but it wouldn't budge.

I spit the flashlight out. It clanked to the floor at my knee, and I carefully pulled the newspaper up to my lap. The crayon-smeared page stuck to it.

I'd read that clipping before. Rachel won the spelling bee with the word "perpendicular."

How had I missed what was under it?

The waxy page came off the newspaper with a crisp *shhkk* and fluttered to my skirt-shrouded legs. There, in my lap, sat a child's drawing, done completely in red crayon.

A stick-figure girl in a triangle skirt, coils of red crayon for hair. Behind her loomed a man, his face erased by a thick red X. Heavy clouds hovered above them, but around the little girl's feet was a patch of little red flowers.

Staring at that picture, I started shaking. Every cell in my body humming like a stuck tuning fork. A vibrating panic I couldn't shut off. Couldn't stop. Couldn't control.

I knew this drawing. I hadn't drawn it. But I knew it. I'd felt it. When I was young. A child. And even now. As an adult but still treated like a child.

This drawing struck something so deep my body recognized it before my brain could catch up or put it into words. Into *a* word. One word. A name. Surfacing in my thoughts like oil on water. Thick. Familiar. But so wrong.

"Dad."

I almost gagged as the word left my mouth, tasting like sour rust on my tongue.

My fingers twitched. I didn't realize I was digging my nails into my thighs until the sting cut through the fog.

The name clung to the silence. I could see the letters floating in the dark, clouding the crayon drawing in my lap.

The flashlight near my knee flickered once, then dimmed, its light trembling against the floorboards as Beagle toppled to his side.

I jumped up. The crayon drawing fluttered to my feet like a dead leaf on a chilled autumn breeze.

I didn't remember getting there—standing in the kitchen, hands shaking, glass beneath the running faucet. The water rushing into my cup sounded distant, like my ears were stuffed with cotton. My head throbbed. My neck ached. My whole body trembled.

So much shaking.

I tried to drink. Cold water slid down my throat and pooled in my stomach.

None of this was really happening. It was like the living room floor turning to blood. Like the story about Mom leaving Dad. A dream. All of it.

I closed my eyes and drank. Gulp after gulp. Until my lungs screamed for air. I pulled away with a gasp, water streaming down my chin and soaking the front of my gray dress in dark blotches.

"I'm not doing this."

I grabbed a towel and wiped my face, my neck, my dress.

"I'm not Gracie."

I forced a breath. Then another. Then deeper ones, until the tremors slowed.

"I'm not going to pretend this isn't happening."

But part of me already was.

The part that wanted what Gracie had. Oblivious trust. The ability to forget. To make-believe everything was fine. To do what I was taught to do. Conditioned to do. Brainwashed to do.

I closed my eyes and breathed again. Slow. Steady.

I'm not sure how long I stood there. Long enough that I wasn't shaking anymore. And things didn't sound like I was underwater.

I filled my glass once more and drank, slower this time, focusing on the taste of the water, the smooth glass against my fingers.

Once I'd finished, I was finally able to turn away from the sink. Step back through the kitchen.

I'm not sure where I was planning to go—back to my room, maybe? To more research, digging through Rachel's file? To look for more red crayon drawings?

I didn't make it that far. I didn't even make it to the steps. I hadn't quite made it out of the kitchen when something stopped me.

It was that smell again. The smell from when I'd walked down the front hall with my parents this morning. The smell from the fireplace.

I stepped out of the kitchen, legs prickling like I'd been sitting too long.

It was definitely coming from the fireplace. The scent grew stronger, harsher, the closer I got to it. It was sour. Chemical. Not the rich, earthy aroma of burning wood. This was something else.

I knelt on the wide brick of the hearth and used the fire iron to poke through what was left of the burnt ash from this morning's fire.

There was wood. The blackened remains of a couple chunks of half-burned oak. But between them, hidden beneath the ash, something that was definitely not wood glinted at me.

A warped plastic cover. A hint of pink beneath the soot. Bright orange now burnt and toasted. Yellows turned dull and gray.

And, staring at me from beneath it all, the singed silver of a heart-shaped lock.

I recognized it immediately.

A diary. And not just any random kid's diary from the late '90s. This was *my* diary.

My insides turned to sand. Dry. Slipping.

There it was again. That bitter taste of something real... something I thought I'd dreamed. My parents would never buy me a locking diary with a bright, white unicorn on the front.

We don't believe in unicorns. Like we don't believe in dragons. Or fairies or imps. Or that angels have wings.

But I could remember writing in this rainbow-colored diary with the white unicorn on the front. I could remember sitting in the back of a car, pencil in hand, scribbling on the blue pages. I always thought it was a dream.

Seized with the sudden need to rescue the little book, I carefully moved the wood with the stoker, hoping maybe what was left of that rainbow cover would have protected the pages inside.

But when I shifted the wood, the cover disintegrated into shards of gray ash.

"No..."

Tears welled in my eyes as I reached inside the fireplace, already knowing what would happen when I touched those pages.

They collapsed. Into a pile of ash, with tiny bits of blues and pinks showing through on the edges. But the pages were gone. Whatever had been scribbled on them, when I was too young to even remember writing in it, was burned away.

"Why?" I asked aloud—to my parents or the house. "Why would you burn this?"

I fished the singed metal lock from the ashes, dropping it into my lap and dusting off what was left of a diary I hadn't known I'd lost.

It stared up at me, its shine lost to fire.

Kids always end up where they're not meant to be. Dad's voice hummed inside my head. The disgusted tilt his tone had when he said *kids*.

Anger surged through me, hot and heavy, and I pulled myself to my feet.

I needed to go back to the attic. This diary had to have been up there, right? Why would he find it and burn it—before I could find it and read it? What was he hiding? What did he not want me to know?

I shuffled the half-burned blocks of firewood back into place on the hearth, returning the fire iron to its spot on the wall nearby. Then I turned to bound upstairs, but a sudden, heavy knock against wood made me trip.

I jumped out of my skin. My foot slipped on the bottom step, and I took a hard fall to the floor.

Bang. Bang. Bang.

"Holy shit." The curse slipped out in a hiss. I gripped the lock in my hand, forcing my body to move, to sit up, my mind racing through every worst-case scenario.

Bang. Bang. Bang.

Each knock made me jolt. My fingers wrapped around the edge of the bottom step, nails digging into the old, scarred wood.

It wasn't Mom. Or Dad. Or Gracie. They had keys. They'd walk in. People with keys don't knock.

Who would knock?

No one ever came here. We didn't have friends. We didn't have family anywhere near Caster.

Bang. Bang. Bang.

The knock echoed through the back hall, the living room. It bounced off the dark, cedar paneling and hit my chest like a second heartbeat.

I could hide. I could slide to the floor and huddle behind the couch. No matter what door whoever this was went to, or what window they peeked inside, they couldn't see me. I could pretend I wasn't here.

I pushed the lock into the seam pocket of my dress, eyes darting to find the best path to the couch. But then my heart stopped—twisted against my ribs.

What if I hid, and they didn't leave? What if they were only knocking to make sure no one was here? What if they were here to break in? Would they shoot me? Rape me? Kidnap me?

The water I'd swallowed churned, threatening to come back up.

Clink. Clink. Clink.

A softer knock. A tap, on glass.

"Em!" A muffled voice from the back porch. "Em! It's me and Wanda! Are you in there?"

My feet moved before I could think, sending me flying down the hall to the back door. I fumbled the lock with shaking hands, tears spilling over my cheeks.

"Oh, Em!" Wanda pulled me into a huge, warm hug the second I opened the door. "Are you okay?"

I nodded into her shoulder, still crying. "How'd you know I was here?"

"We were grabbing cappuccinos at that little place on the corner," Wanda said, brushing loose strands of hair from my face. "We saw your dad's truck. Your parents and Gracie were in it, but not you."

"After last night," Kade added, "we figured we'd check on you."

"Oh my gosh." I pulled Wanda inside, motioning for Kade to follow. "I haven't slept. It's been hell. Mom took my keys. Dad demanded my phone. Mom thinks I'm pregnant, and Gracie... she says she doesn't remember the room inside my wall. Or any of it."

I couldn't stop. I didn't want to. I was too tired to censor myself. Too tired to care what my parents would think if they ever found out I brought *outsiders* into the house. If they knew I'd told anything.

We don't air our dirty laundry. Mom's voice rose in my head, but I drowned it out.

I told them everything.

Somewhere in the middle of it all, I led them up to my room. Wanda dropped to her knees the moment she saw the red crayon drawing. She picked it up with both hands—reverent, careful.

Kade stood beside me as I finished my story. I was shaking again, but at my side, I felt his hand reach for mine.

I was clutching my skirt, knuckles white, but I let go. I let him take my hand. His was huge, warm. Calloused, but gentle. He rubbed his thumb over the back of mine.

"Em," he said, voice low, "I'm going to run back to town and get you a phone."

I blinked at him.

"They have the prepaid kind," Kade said. "You need a way to reach out. In case..."

"In case your parents flip their fucking lids," Wanda cut in, still kneeling over the file.

Dread creeped up my spine. What if my parents found it? What if they asked how I got it? What if I broke and told them?

They wouldn't just take the phone. They'd stop me from seeing Wanda and Kade. At all. They'd lock me down in the house. No trips to the library.

"I don't have money for it," I said quietly.

Wanda's head snapped up. "They don't pay you?"

"I live here," I tried to explain. "My part of the money helps with the mortgage. And bills."

Kade gave my hand a small squeeze before letting go. "Prepaids aren't much. I'll pick one up. You can pay me back later if it makes you feel better."

He didn't wait for a reply. He was already on his way out.

"He doesn't have to do that," I told Wanda, but she waved me off.

"He's worried about you." She looked at me. "We both are."

I know she saw the grimace, even if I tried to hide it.

"Look, I don't want to sound mean or anything, but... this." She motioned to the room. To me. "It's weird, Em. All of it. You're twenty-two. They treat you like you're twelve. Why? Why are they so afraid of you having a life? Friends? Leaving? What do they think you'll find out... or tell?"

I bit my lip. Tasted blood.

She'd said it. The thing I hadn't dared say out loud. And now it was real.

But it couldn't be true, could it? There wasn't anything malicious about protecting your kids. That's what Dad always said. They were shielding us. From the world. From evil.

"They say they're protecting me," I said, my voice small.

"From what?"

A simple question, but it made me flinch.

The world. The influence of the evil one. But how could I explain that to Wanda?

She sat there in a black T-shirt with a death metal logo scrawled across the chest, her eyelids painted blue, lips peach-glossed, silver earrings dangling from her ears. Her skinny jeans hugged every curve, leopard-print sandals on her feet, pink polish on her toes.

Worldly. That's what my parents would call her.

Suddenly, I felt like the biggest fraud. The biggest liar. A hypocrite. Sitting beside Wanda in my gray cape dress, hem down to my ankles. Elbow-length sleeves. High, tight neckline. Plain black tennis shoes. No makeup. No jewelry. The picture of modesty. A Proverbs 31 woman.

I'd worn it all my life. Dressed up. Played the part. Smiled through it. To keep the peace. To keep my parents from being angry with me, or disappointed in me. But my heart hadn't been in it since I'd been old enough to realize how we lived wasn't *normal*.

"The world," I finally said.

Two words. But they explained everything.

"Okay." Wanda set the red crayon drawing gently in her lap. "I'm a Christian, Em. I don't go to church much, but I believe in God. In Jesus."

She paused, glanced at me, at my clothes, then looked down at herself. "Your parents think I'm going to hell for what I wear?"

"No…" I drew the word out, apology thick in my voice. "They think once you believe in Jesus, you're supposed to come out of the world. That's when you change your clothes and habits and all."

I half-shrugged, tried to roll my eyes.

"So I'm not a *real* Christian then." Wanda's brow rose. "Believing in Jesus isn't enough. You have to do all… this." She motioned around my room again. Around me.

"I don't believe that." The words rushed out, hot and sharp.

You never have.

It felt like rocks grinding up my throat. Like something heavy lifting from my gut. I'd never said that before—not even to myself.

"But they do." Wanda nodded toward my bedroom door, meaning my parents. Maybe Gracie, too.

I nodded slowly, like I was confessing something on the stand. Incriminating my family behind their backs. Like a traitor.

"I know they love me, though." My voice dropped to a whisper.

Wanda reached out and gave my hand a quick squeeze. "Listen, Em. If you ever need somewhere to go, my place is open, okay? If you need someone to pick you up, I'll come, or Kade will. Either of us."

"Thank you." I swallowed the knot rising in my throat, and Wanda pulled me into a hug.

For a moment, we held each other. When she pulled back, I thought I saw her wipe a tear, but she shook her head and grabbed the crayon drawing before I could be sure.

"We need to find out what happened to her," she said, voice steadier now. Determined. "This is where Rachel lived. Maybe where she died. We need to search this place, top to bottom."

I nodded, letting her fire spark something in me. "Let's gather up the file, grab my backpack, and head to the attic. There's a ton of stuff up there."

"Stuff?"

"Yeah. Old boxes. From before we moved in."

"What?" Her jaw dropped. "Kade and I used to go up there when the place was abandoned. The attic was our favorite spot, full of books and weird old junk."

"It's still up there," I said, sliding papers back into the file.

Wanda blinked like she needed to reset her brain. "Hurry." She started helping me. "I want to see that."

23

BACK IN THE ATTIC

The attic was like I remembered from the night I found the shred of pink fabric. Dusty, dark, and oppressive.

Despite that, there was so much up here. So much Wanda and I needed to go through. To uncover.

But I hadn't thought about the books—the ones I'd found filled with the racist bullshit my dad would quote. I hadn't thought of Wanda finding them, how she might be hurt if she read even the titles or chapter headings like I had.

It was too late to think of any of that now though, because we ended up starting with those very books. Wanda seemed drawn to them before anything else, just like I had been.

"Holy fuck." Disgust curled in her voice as she read the thick, gold-stamped titles along the spines. "*The Doctrine of Spiritual Purity.* Please tell me that doesn't mean what I think it does."

She grabbed the last book I would have ever wanted her to open and flipped to a chapter.

"*Why races must not intermarry.*" Her voice hardened as she read.

She stared at the page for a beat, then fake-gagged and slammed it shut. "Holy shit. Your parents believe this crap?"

I bit my lip. I didn't have to answer.

"So... Kade's shit out of luck, huh?" Her mutter took me off guard. "Half Black, half White. I guess God don't love those mixed-up beggars."

"It's so fucked up," I said. My voice sounded small. Not at all equal to the weight of this moment.

"Yeah, it is." Wanda was quiet, still staring at the books. "He likes you, you know."

Heat crept up my neck.

"Kade likes you," she repeated, like she wanted to make sure I'd heard. "Like really *likes* you."

I opened my mouth, but nothing came out. I wanted to answer her. To say something. To tell her that I liked Kade too. The words were there, but stuck, caught behind too many years of silence. Of swallowing what I really wanted to say.

"I get it," Wanda said. "Your mom and dad would hate it. He's mixed."

I shook my head, but we both knew it wasn't a denial.

She dropped the book hard back into the box. The torn spine caught against another book, ripping with a satisfying *skiiirch*.

"I'm Black, Em," she said flatly. "My parents are Blacker than I am. If you and Kade got together, it wouldn't only be about his skin. He was raised Black, because his deadbeat White dad used to beat the shit out of my mom."

My hands froze on the seam of my skirt. The loose thread I'd been picking at broke off between my fingers.

Wanda had told me before. And Kade told me some about his dad, when he helped with the flat. But hearing it from Wanda now, raw and bitter, somehow made it worse. I *felt* it.

"I shouldn't have said anything," she added, a little quieter. "It was his to tell."

She crossed her arms tight, like she'd caught a chill that had nothing to do with the air.

"He probably wasn't planning to say anything anyways. He's used to it." Wanda shrugged. "Even my grandma barely tolerates him."

I shifted closer to her, not sure if I should reach out or stay still. My heart thudded hard in my ears.

Wanda looked up again, her bright brown eyes clearer now. "Turns out you don't have to be a religious nutcase to be racist," she said. "He's not Black enough, but he's never been White enough either."

Silence settled heavy between us.

Wanda turned back to the books, eyes scanning the spines again. "Sorry. That was weird. Let's get back to this."

I wanted to tell her it wasn't weird. That she was right to be angry.

"These books kind of triggered me." She stood and wiped her palms against her jeans like she could scrub the weight off. "What else is up here besides racist bullshit?"

"I like him."

The words slipped out. Quiet. Cautious. Like they were scared.

Wanda turned slowly. "What?"

"I like Kade."

Saying it aloud—twice—made it real. Made it stronger.

"You like my brother?"

I nodded. "I have since I first met him."

Wanda turned away, her gaze drifting across the attic like she was looking for something she couldn't name.

I drew a tight breath.

"I didn't think he'd like me. The first time he met me, I was a mess. All we've talked about is Rachel, murder, and my parents." I stopped suddenly, needing air.

Wanda was still quiet. Still surveying the attic. Arms tightly folded over her chest.

"I figured he thought I was crazy," I said. "I mean... look at me." I glanced down at my gray cape dress. "I look like I time-traveled out of a history book."

"Kade doesn't care about any of that."

I looked up to see Wanda had turned back to me. Her eyes were red and fluid, but she smiled.

"You like my brother? Even with your parents preaching all that..." She nodded at the box. "Bullshit?"

I bit my lip.

There it was again.

You don't believe.

I didn't know how to say what I was feeling. Or how to handle the questions it would raise.

If you don't believe this shit, why don't you leave? If you don't like dressing like Laura Ingalls, why don't you wear something different?

I didn't know how to explain *why* I didn't do anything differently, why I didn't stand up for myself. Why I never got a job outside my dad's business, just because he said no.

Because, honestly, I didn't really know.

Was it fear? Deep down was I afraid if I rebelled, he would kick me out? No vehicle. No home. No money. Nowhere to go and no one to go to.

Was it because, somehow, I knew Mom wouldn't stand up for me? Wouldn't stop him from abandoning me?

She had been the one to take my keys. She'd turn her back on me as fast as he would, wouldn't she?

She'd taken my keys because she *suspected* I *might* be pregnant. What would she have done if I'd said yes? If I *was* pregnant?

I took a slow, tight breath.

"I like him, Wanda," I told her again. "No matter what they think."

And I meant it.

I liked what I felt for Kade Weston. And I wasn't willing to snuff it out because my parents would hate it.

This wasn't as simple as clothes, or a job, or even a car. It wasn't something I was willing to give up before I even got a chance to see what it was.

No matter what happened with my parents because of it.

"I should have let him tell you," Wanda said quietly. "Don't tell him I told you, please." She looked at me. "Promise."

I nodded. "I promise."

"He'd kill me," she muttered.

Her gaze swept the attic again, but with purpose this time. "Come on, Em," she said. "What else is up here?"

"Well, for one thing, the name on these shitty books." I picked up the one she'd dropped and flipped to the title page. "Have you found out who built this house? You said the guy wrote religious stuff."

Wanda leaned in. "D. L. Emerson…"

I could see the gears turning.

"Emerson rings a bell," she muttered. "I'll check the Caster archives. I still haven't found who built this place. It's like that part of the record's been wiped. All I know is the state auctioned it to Mr. Dickerson."

Record's been wiped.

Why did that sting?

"Let's keep looking." I dropped the book, dismissing that tinge of pain, and led Wanda across the rough attic floor.

For half an hour, we combed through boxes, ones I'd already picked through. Vintage clothes, mostly from the nineties. A few more boxes of books in Greek or Latin. Old glassware my mom had supposedly been saving to sell.

"Damn," Wanda muttered, frustration creeping in. "Nothing on Rachel."

I sagged against the wall, the old wood pressing into my spine.

"There's even some old Christmas stuff," Wanda said, tugging another box from the shadows, brushing off the crust of dead roaches and rat shit.

"What?" I blinked at the label. Christmas '71, scrawled in thick black marker.

"It's old decorations," she repeated, lifting the lid. The cardboard disintegrated at the corners.

"No." I crossed the attic quickly. "Mom threw out everything Christmas we found when we moved in."

Wanda raised an eyebrow.

"They don't celebrate," I said. "It's pagan. A sin to hang ribbon or donate to a toy drive."

"Holy shit." Her jaw dropped, but I couldn't tell if it was because of what I'd said or what was in the box.

"I told you it's not Christmas stuff." I dropped to my knees beside her, the sharp scent of old paper hitting my nose.

Documents. Files. Photographs.

"This is like... firebox stuff," Wanda murmured. "Why would it be in a rat-infested attic?"

I barely heard her. My eyes had locked onto a photo she brushed past. I grabbed it.

A little girl in hot pink flip-flops stood beside a burgundy Toyota Camry. The passenger door hung open, and behind the wheel sat a young woman with a radiant, infectious smile.

The singed lock in my dress pocket burned hot against my skin. As if memory itself had sparked it back to life.

"Wanda." My voice came out sharper than I meant. I grabbed her arm.

"What?" she asked, startled. I'd interrupted her, but I hadn't heard a word she'd said.

I held up the photo.

"Is that Rachel?" she whispered, taking it.

But something inside me tilted, like the floor had shifted beneath my knees. I clenched my fists, pressing my knuckles into the wood.

I knew those pink flip-flops. That car. That woman's smile.

They weren't just familiar. They were mine. Not in the way you recognize a photo from a story or a dream. Mine, like memory. A piece of me buried deep, jarred loose by the image.

The sunlight through a windshield. Whitney Houston on the stereo. The smell of greasy fries. The crinkle of a paper bag.

Pick you a toy, sweetie.

A faint movement behind us made me jump. Wanda reached out, steadying me.

"It's just Kade."

"Yeah," his voice echoed low in the attic. "Just Kade."

"You know what I meant," Wanda said, waving him in. "Look what we found. A whole box of stuff."

Wanda held up the photograph, but I couldn't take my eyes off it.

"Em found another picture of Rachel, I think," she said.

Kade shook his head and took the photo from her. "This isn't Rachel."

I stood, unsure my legs would hold me, but I needed to see that picture.

"Why not?" Wanda asked, already turning back to the box, sifting through the mountain of paper.

"That's a '91 Toyota Camry," Kade said, his tone flat with certainty. "Rachel disappeared in '88. She was eighteen. This girl's like three."

"Oh…" Wanda paused. "You know I suck at recognizing cars. All those old models look the same to me. So… if it isn't Rachel, who is it?"

Kade looked at me, his eyes finding mine.

I bit my lip.

He was right. This wasn't Rachel. But it wasn't a stranger either.

I stepped closer, taking the photo from his hand, my fingers brushing his.

A little girl with brown eyes. Straight brown hair. A bright, gummy smile and chubby cheeks. Hot pink flip-flops on her feet.

My life.

A piece of me I hadn't known was gone.

"It's me," I whispered.

24

MY SISTER'S VOICE

"Why would there be a picture of you in an old attic box, Em?" Wanda stood beside Kade, brow furrowed as she studied the photo in my hand.

"I don't know." I gave her the picture, too fast.

Something in me had snapped while I stared at that little girl. Something deep. Something stretched too thin for too long. Like a rubber band finally busting.

"Is that your mom?" Wanda squinted at the image.

"No." I dropped to my knees and dove into the box. "She's not my mom." My voice was tight. "And the woman who raised me? She's not my mom either."

It felt like my brain was splintering. Like the world was peeling back in fast, dizzying layers.

But underneath it all, something was surfacing. A shape in the fog I'd lived in for so long. And I was chasing it.

"What?" Wanda squatted beside me, her voice cautious.

"Rachel was an orphan." I didn't look at her. I was elbow-deep in paper, tearing through decades of history like a woman possessed. "She came from the foster system, right?"

"Yeah..."

"It started with the French fries." My throat clenched. My mind was sprinting almost too fast for me to keep up.

"French fries?" Wanda's voice cracked. "Em, are you okay?"

"Yes!" I yanked a fistful of paper from the box, rat shit and mummified moths hitting the floor. "I was in the ball pit, Wanda! I was there!"

"Em." Wanda grabbed my shoulders. "What the hell are you talking about?"

"It's all real." I met her eyes, then bolted upright so fast she shrieked.

"Keep looking!" I called over my shoulder. "I've got to grab something!"

The toy. The little, molded plastic toy with a curly red hair. It had been mine. I'd walked through those golden arches. Slid down the giant yellow slide. Sank into the soft flood of colorful balls. I'd eaten fries. Nuggets. Picked my own toy from the magical box at the counter.

I ran into my room, tore the bottom drawer from my dresser, and scooped up the plastic clown and treasure box.

But as I turned to leave, as desperate to get back to the attic as I'd been to get to my room, something stopped me cold.

No. There was no way. I'd watched her leave, squeezed into Dad's truck with Mom.

"Gracie."

My sister smiled at me. A sly, off-kilter twitch of her lips that didn't quite reach her eyes.

I stepped back.

She stood in my bedroom doorway, arms folded, head cocked to the side. Red curls spilled over one shoulder, like she'd just shaken them loose from her usual tight bun.

"I thought you went to Granite Hill with Mom and Dad." My fingers curled around the toy, tucking it into the pocket of my dress.

Gracie didn't answer. She shook her head. Slow. Her eyes didn't leave mine. I wasn't even sure she blinked.

"Okay..." I hesitated. "Are you alright, Gracie? You don't look... alright."

"I'm fine."

Her voice was hers, but steadier. Too steady. More confident than I'd heard Gracie sound in a very long time.

"Good." I tried to smile.

She shook her head again. "You need to stop."

I swallowed. "Stop what?"

No answer.

Her head tilted further, curls spilling forward. She studied me with an eerie calm.

"Don't you care about the family, Emily?"

"Of course I do." My voice wobbled. "Why would you even ask that?"

"You're making trouble again." Her eyes narrowed. Not angry, just disappointed.

Like Mom, when we asked the wrong kind of question in church.

"I'm not. I'm trying to understand what's happening. I think..."

"You always do this," she interrupted, her voice suddenly flat. Hollow. Like she was reading from a script. "Digging things up that are better left alone, *Emily*."

She said my name like a warning.

My mouth went dry.

She shook her head again, and this time, something snapped. Loud. Sharp. Like a bone breaking.

I flinched, and something flickered behind her eyes.

"Every family has their problems, Emily." She was whispering now. "Don't they?"

I nodded. Too quickly.

She stepped into my room. But something was wrong with her gait. It was off. She wasn't steady. She limped, slightly dragging one leg.

I looked down.

Her hands hung loose at her sides. The nails were long. Jagged. Curling upward. Her skin was paper-white. Dark veins threaded beneath it, deep, unnatural purple.

"Look at me." She growled the words.

I stumbled back.

This wasn't Gracie. Every part of me knew it. But if it wasn't Gracie...

What was it? A spirit? The soul of the house? Or was it my brain, cracking under the weight of everything I was finally remembering?

"Don't." Her voice glitched, distorted, like a skipping cassette. "Don't. Go. Back. Up. There."

I sidestepped her, slowly. Carefully.

"Gracie, you're scaring me."

She smiled again. But this time her mouth opened *too* wide. Rows of blackened, rotted teeth filled the gap.

I screamed, dodged around her—around whatever the *fuck* this was pretending to be my sister.

It lunged.

I shrieked again, slammed my shoulder into the doorframe as I stumbled into the hall.

"Em?" Wanda's voice echoed from the attic.

I tripped on my own feet, running down the hall, barely ducking into the bathroom as I slammed the door, praying to God that whatever this was couldn't pass through walls.

"What the hell?" Wanda burst in behind me. Kade followed, pausing on the stairs. The bathroom was too cramped for all three of us.

"Are you okay, Em?" he asked, and I looked up, met his eyes.

"No," I gasped. "I saw Gracie." I was crying, shaking, nausea climbing my throat. "But it wasn't Gracie. She had black teeth. She tried to grab me."

Wanda stiffened, her arm tightening around me.

For a long moment, no one moved. Silence hung in the space, in the house. Whatever it was wasn't making a sound. Was it listening? Was it even real?

Then Kade shook his head, shattering the stillness. "Fuck, no." He slipped past us to the door.

"Be careful," I whispered.

He nodded, then inched the door open.

Gracie stood on the other side. Real. Silent. Perfectly still. Face blank. Lips parted. But her eyes. She didn't even seem to see Kade. Her eyes locked onto mine.

I looked away. Down at the floor. Anywhere else.

They weren't my sister's eyes. Not dull green. Not bright emerald. Just empty, black holes in her skull.

"You are not allowed to be here." Kade's voice dropped into something deep, commanding. "You don't touch her. Do you understand me?"

He saw it. He had to. This wasn't a trick of my mind. This was real. He was talking to it.

"She needs to stop."

I shivered and Wanda hugged me tighter. It was Gracie's voice. Perfectly Gracie's voice. I covered my ears.

"When we figure out what happened to Rachel, we'll stop," Kade said. Calm. Measured. "Until then, fuck off."

The hallway went still. Even the floorboards held their breath. So did Wanda. So did I.

The thing smiled. Those jagged, black teeth again.

"She's scared of me," it said, taunting. Its voice broke, glitching in and out of Gracie's cadence.

"She won't be," Kade told it. "Because she knows you're nothing. A shadow. You can't even talk without stealing someone else's voice."

It hissed. A sharp, animal sound.

Wanda's grip on me tightened.

"Fuck. Off."

Kade said it again. Flicked his hand like he was swatting away a fly.

The thing stared.

Time stretched, warped, like we were trapped in that moment forever.

Then the thing shifted. Limped on its bad leg. Growled under its breath. And turned. Its footsteps faded down the hall.

I broke from Wanda and slumped against the wall, breath catching in my throat.

No one said a word.

Wanda didn't ask what I saw. Kade didn't either.

Because they'd seen it too. Or maybe... No I didn't want to think it.

They weren't just being kind, were they? They wouldn't just pretend. Just play along to keep me somewhat sane. To keep me from realizing I'd completely lost my mind.

25

CORDUROY AND BLACK TRASH BAGS

One second, I was huddled in the bathroom, trying to breathe. Wanda was frozen, staring at the floor, and Kade was still standing in the doorway, his back to us.

The next, I was gripping the edge of the kitchen sink, breath fogging the window above it, staring out into nothing.

Like maybe the trees could tell me something. Like maybe they'd seen whatever hijacked my sister's face.

A floorboard creaked behind me. I didn't turn. "I need a second," I said, though no one had asked. My voice sounded hollow.

Behind me, Wanda murmured something. To Kade, maybe. Or to herself.

No one knew what to say.

What do you say after that? After something wears your sister's skin and knows your name? Or when you have to wonder if your friends are just pretending—playing along so you don't completely lose your grip?

It had started small. The tapping. Then the scratching. Then the boney faces in glass.

Now a creature dressed like my sister, chasing me in my own home, with jagged black teeth and overgrown nails.

It was too detailed to be a dream, but too freakish to be real.

"Hey..." Kade's voice was soft beside me. Reassuring.

I turned. His dark eyes found mine.

"I saw it too," he said.

Four words. Simple. But they cracked something in me. Was he telling the truth?

"You really saw it?"

I waited for the hesitation. Braced for the forced, careful nod meant to soothe me.

"Yeah, of course." Kade almost smiled. "You think I could fake that? I'm not that good of an actor, Em."

I half-laughed, but it came out more of a sob.

Kade pulled two paper towels from a stray roll on the counter and handed them to me. "You're not going crazy, if that's what you're thinking."

"No," Wanda cut in quickly. She came up beside me, linking her arm through mine. "Something's not right with this house. I saw that freaky thing too."

"I thought it was Gracie..." My voice cracked. I pressed the paper towels to my face.

"Whatever it was, it didn't want you upstairs," Wanda said. "It didn't want us finding that box."

She was right. We'd found a picture of me. A toddler in hot pink flip-flops. And it had brought everything back. Memories I didn't know I had.

Pick you a toy, sweetie.

"We've got to go back up there." I pulled free of Wanda and wiped my eyes. "I need to see what's in that box."

Having them with me didn't soften the blow.

Maybe it kept me grounded, Wanda sitting beside me on the attic floor, Kade near the door, like he was standing guard. Maybe it kept me from spiraling completely, but nothing could truly brace me for what I was about to find.

It looked like trash.

A crumpled black garbage bag, half-crushed beneath decades of forgotten junk in a box marked *Christmas*.

You'd think it was packing. Something thrown in to pad the contents. But I knew better. Something inside me remembered. Some part of me had never forgotten.

I pulled the bag free. Old envelopes and yellowed paper tumbled out around it. The bag reeked of mildew and age. Plastic crinkled against my dress.

And then, the world around me became a vacuum. Narrowed. The air collapsed.

"Holy shit, Emily!" Wanda sounded like she was talking through water. "This is Rachel's foster placement."

I barely heard her. My ears were filling from the inside out.

"She was here then," Kade's voice was deep but muffled, like it couldn't break through the hum in my head.

The bag shed flakes of brittle plastic, black shards clinging to my fingers like dead skin.

I held my breath. My hands trembled, hovering over the knot. Part of me didn't want to know. But another part already did. That part had always known, no matter how carefully the truth was buried.

I pulled.

The knot gave way, revealing a ribbed scrap of pink corduroy.

A jumper.

I reached for the collar. The stained tag stared back at me. *3T* embroidered in bold black thread.

My eyes shut on instinct, and I was there.

Back in the burgundy Camry. Back in that jumper. Clutching this plastic bag to my chest, tiny arms wrapped tight around my whole life.

I knew.

When I found the clown toy. When I saw the photo of that little girl outside the car. I *knew*.

But this... This was proof.

Not a picture. Not a feeling.

This was fabric. Stitching. Embalmed in a lifetime of dust. And I was touching it. This was *real*.

I don't remember opening my eyes. I don't know what Wanda or Kade were saying, or if they were saying anything. I just kept pulling.

Piece after piece. Tiny blue pants. Velcro sneakers, once pink, now dulled to the color of dried gum. A doll.

She lay twisted at the bottom of the bag, brittle black hair tangled like cassette tape caught in an old player. One braid half undone. The other stuck to her scalp with yellowed wax.

Her faux suede dress had curled at the fringe, its warm sand color faded to the pale beige of old bones. One leg was warped, bent outward like she'd tried to run and fallen.

Her brown eyes, dulled by a film of attic dust, still stared straight ahead. But the smile, that little, painted smile... it hadn't changed.

And for a moment, I was there again. Holding her in bed, eyes on the glowing, green ceiling stars. Small, but safe. Whole.

Before everything was erased.

It was this moment of memory that everything cracked open. My life. My name. My trust in the people who'd raised me. Because I remembered.

What my parents tried to hide. What Gracie didn't know or refused to say. Everything they'd forced me to forget.

Rachel had a file.

I had a trash bag.

We were both brought here, our pasts packaged up and forgotten.

Rachel, by the original builder of this house.

Me, by the people who claimed to love me more than anyone else.

26

Valentine's Day

"Is that..." Wanda's voice cut through the fog, shaking me like someone reaching under water to drag me to the surface.

I came up gasping, sobbing, my fingers still clenched around the brittle black bag in my lap.

"Oh, hon..." Wanda's arms wrapped around me, tight.

"They're not my parents."

Hearing it out loud, in my own voice, made it undeniable. Bitter. Final. The pain sliced through me like a hot blade.

They claimed they loved me more than anyone. Despite the religion, the weird rules, the so-called protection, I knew they loved me because I was their daughter.

Except I wasn't.

Not on the job, you're not. My dad's voice crashed through me.

That one line shattered what little faith I had left. In him. In my mother. In the fragile identity I'd been forced to wear my entire life. Like a second skin over who I really was.

He'd told me. I hadn't heard him, not fully, not then. But some part of me had. And that's why I'd left. Not just the job site. Not just the argument. I'd left them.

Even if it was only for a few hours. Even if I didn't understand what I was doing when I peeled out of that driveway.

I'd ignored his voice. Ignored the threats. Ignored Mom and Gracie, standing behind him. Crying, but silent. Like they had been for years.

You're not my daughter here.

Anger rose, hotter than the grief. It dried my tears.

Memories slammed through me, years collapsing behind my eyes in seconds. I'd lived a lie. My entire life had been a lie. All those churches. All those new starts. Every time Dad took another youth pastor position.

We'd be paraded in front of a new congregation on a Sunday morning. The perfect family. Polished. Pressed. Rehearsed.

Let's welcome our new youth minister, Brother Don Lyles, and his sweet wife, Sister Allie, along with their two daughters, Grace Ann and Emily.

But I wasn't their daughter. I never had been. None of it had ever been true.

Wanda's hand pressed gently against my arm, pulling me back to *now*.

I blinked, eyes stinging, and saw what she had pressed into my lap. A sheet of yellowed paper.

Illinois Department of Social Services
Foster Care Placement Agreement

Illinois.

At least that part was true. They'd always said I was born in Illinois, before Dad took a youth minister job further south.

I bit my lip, my stomach knotting.

My birth story.

The one Mom told again and again. How she went into labor while Dad was away at a ministers' convention. How he raced home, ignoring red lights and speed limits, talking her through contractions over his bulky bag phone.

How he got her to the hospital just in time, and I arrived ten minutes later. No pain meds, no epidural, only pure maternal strength.

All of it was a lie. A neat, practiced lie. And I'd believed it. Why wouldn't I?

I drew a shaky breath and looked back down at the faded black ink.

Child's Legal Name: Emily Rose (Last Name Redacted)
DOB: 02/14/1991
Placement Date: 08/23/1994
Foster Resource: Donald Lyles and Allie Lyles
Home Study: Approved

"I didn't know you were in the system, Em." Kade's voice behind me was quiet but solid. Like the paper in my hand.

"I didn't either." The words scraped out, rough and dry. "I didn't even know my middle name was Rose."

Wanda's fingers tightened on my arm.

"I thought my birthday was August twenty-third." My voice cracked, thin with disbelief.

Wanda bit her lip, her eyes glued to the paper. "That's the day they got you," she said gently. "You were born on Valentine's Day."

My heart kicked. *Valentine's Day.*

We didn't celebrate it. Like Christmas. Like Easter. The Fourth of July. Halloween. Like any other *useless* holiday, derived from paganism or steeped in *worldly* patriotism.

Every year, February fourteenth passed quietly. An empty square on the calendar. Scrubbed from existence, like everything else my parents didn't believe in.

Forgotten.

This year I'd spent it replacing a toilet. Then I'd gone to the library. And Wanda had shown me Rachel's file.

That was my birthday. My twenty-third birthday.

"Holy shit... I'm not twenty-two, Wanda. I'm already twenty-three."

Wanda's hand found mine, fingers lacing through my own.

I stared at the paper. "Every year I've been six months behind," I whispered. "Six months older than I thought I was."

"I'm sorry, Em." Wanda's voice was soft, but I shook my head.

"Why would they lie?"

My mind was racing. The birth story. The milestones. The memories... They weren't mine. My first birthday. Mom losing sleep when I was a baby. Teaching me to walk. Toilet training me. None of it happened. But they said it had. Told me stories so detailed, so tender, I'd believed them.

You don't believe.

Kade knelt beside the box, gently sorting through the mountain of yellowed paper.

"Your adoption placement should be in here," he said, quietly, like carefully peeling back a bandage instead of tearing it off.

But that word... there wasn't any way to soften that.

Adoption.

I was adopted. I was in the foster system.

I looked back at the page in my hand, stared at the words.

Emergency and *temporary*.

What emergency? Why had temporary become forever? Who decides a lie should outlive the truth?

I scanned the rest of the page.

Notes:
No known allergies
Night terrors reported at previous placement
Recommends therapy (denied by foster parents)

Signatures lined the bottom, faded but legible.

Case Manager: Sheryl M. Jackson
Foster Parent(s): Donald Lyles / Allie Lyles

One last note had been scribbled sideways, the ink bled through the back of the page.

Will re-evaluate in 30 days. No contact with biological parents and/or relatives permitted at this time.

My pulse roared in my ears. *Shh-shhh.* Like my own body was trying to hush me. Telling me to stop.

No contact—*at this time.*

I was a secret. A secret they were never supposed to keep forever.

The legal truth glared up from the brittle paper in my hands, tearing through a lifetime of lies. I suddenly felt like a stranger reading it.

And yet, I recognized their signatures. I'd seen them on house deeds, church rosters, utility forms. And here they were again.

On me.

Flashes of what I once called dreams surged in my mind. The greasy taste of French fries, the rubbery pinch of plastic flip-flops.

They weren't dreams. They were memories. Pieces of a life I hadn't only forgotten, a life I'd been *robbed* of.

"We need to get this box downstairs." The realization struck me like a brick to the chest. There was more in there. More truth. More pieces of me.

"There's no way we'll get through it all today." I squeezed Wanda's hand before letting go and pulled myself to my knees. "I need time. I need to go through every bit of it."

The attic seemed to breathe around us. The air had grown thick, dense.

Inside me, something settled. A quiet resolve. I would exhume the truth, no matter how deep it lay buried beneath the lies.

But outside of me, beyond the storm in my chest, something else stirred.

Wanda must've felt it too. She shifted to her knees, one steady hand on my arm.

The house was listening. I could feel it, like it was holding its breath. Inhaling every word. Weighing every discovery. Deciding what to do with the truths we'd uncovered. Preparing to fight back.

To stop me.

"We need to get out of the attic," I whispered.

"Okay." Kade nodded, like he'd been waiting for me to say the words.

Wanda carefully tucked a page into the box as Kade gathered it into his arms.

"Rachel was here too," she said quietly, nodding at the box. "We found her foster placement."

The memory hit me, Wanda's voice from earlier, calling out to me while I was still lost in that crumbling trash bag of my childhood.

And now, it was right there. Staring me in the face as Kade adjusted the fragile box in his arms.

Proof. Of something I hadn't even known I was searching for. Something I needed to know.

South Carolina Department of Social Services
Foster Care Placement Agreement.
Child's Legal Name: Rachel Marie Bagwell
DOB: 07/26/1970
Placement Date: 03/10/1987
Foster Resource: D.L. Emerson Ministries

27

Connections

Home Study: Waived under Section 3B (Clergy Exemption)
Religious Affiliation: Non-Denominational
Status: Kinship Placement (non-biological)
Reasons for Placement
Removal from prior placement due to overcrowding and caseworker reassignment.

Child exhibits emotional detachment and mild disordered eating. Counseling recommended.

Foster parent reports experience with "troubled girls" and has committed to long-term care.

Caseworker: Lawrence Biddle
Initial Visit Scheduled: April 3, 1987 (No follow-up documented)
Medical Consent: Signed
Education Plan: Enrolled in local public high school but not required per religious exemption. Home-based curriculum filed. No standardized testing opt-in.

"Wait, wait, wait." Wanda held her hands up as Kade set the box down on the floor of my bedroom. "D.L. Emerson Ministries? That's the same name on those shitty books we found upstairs."

She looked at me. "Right? The racist bullshit?"

I nodded once, stiff. "Yeah."

My throat felt like it was closing up. The name meant something to me now... something *more* than it had in the attic.

I was trying to place it. Trying to stop the skidding in my mind long enough to pin it down.

"The man who built this house?" Kade asked. "Wrote religious books, fostered Rachel Bagwell... He used a ministry name? Like a fake organization?"

"Not fake." Wanda's voice dropped. "It's real enough to get a foster license waived." She held the paper closer, lips tightening. "Clergy exemption. Vague homeschool plans. No follow-ups. *Fuck.*"

I could barely speak. Pieces were starting to meld. The edges were still blurred, but they were getting closer. Fitting together like a terrifying jigsaw puzzle.

"Dad..." I stopped.

Saying that felt wrong. So wrong, it hurt. He wasn't my dad. Not really. He was the man who raised me. Lied to me. Erased everything that came before him.

Wanda looked at me, her face dropped. "What is it, Em?"

"Um..." I took a steadying breath, but it burned my lungs. "My dad..."

I stopped again. It wasn't right, calling the people who raised me Mom and Dad.

"Don and Allie," I said quietly, and it felt like a little more of my world crumbled beneath me.

I bit my lip.

"D.L. Ministries." I spit the name out. "It's an organization for youth. The church we went to, when we first moved here, it's based there."

There was silence a minute. Thick. Tense.

"Okay..." Wanda shook her head, like she was trying to shake away all the distractions. "What?"

"D.L. Emerson." I watched her face. "The name on the books. I knew I recognized it, but it didn't hit me until I saw the ministry name. D.L.

Ministries. He must have founded the youth organization at the church and used it to get Rachel."

Used it to get Rachel.

My stomach lurched. That was *too* real, *too* mercenary. And the church I'd been a part of for so many years—the interconnected *independent* assemblies scattered across the country—was involved.

Had the pastor in Caster known? Did he know Rachel? Did he know when she *disappeared?* Had the church here covered something up?

Kade hadn't said anything, but his arms were crossed. The softness in his face was gone, replaced by something sharper. Harder.

He was staring at the page in Wanda's hand.

"We need to find out more about *D.L. Emerson,*" he said finally. "And this *church.*"

I nodded, but I was numb. I already knew way more than I wanted to.

"I could tell you." I murmured, and my voice didn't even sound like my own anymore. "I could tell you so much."

Wanda looked over, but I wasn't really talking to her or Kade anymore. I was slipping somewhere deeper, far away.

D.L. Ministries originated here in Caster, South Carolina. Don made sure we knew that when we moved here six years ago.

This little town was the birthplace of a great ministry.

"A powerful movement of God," Don said.

It all started within the cinderblock walls of a quiet church at the end of a red clay road. But it had spread. Just like the *church* it was cocooned in. It was all over the country. And I'd been involved, all my life.

We didn't call it D.L. Ministries. It was purity camp. Obedience training. Mentorship programs. Proverbs 31 apprenticeship. Girls' school. Boys' classes.

Separated.

Because girls were temptations. And we had to learn. We needed training, preparation. Because, as women, it would be our job to keep men pure.

I'd heard the name. D.L. Emerson. Every once in a while, in a sermon. Printed on pamphlets. Tucked in the corners of literature that always found its way into our home.

I never questioned it.

The man was revered. Honored. Like a legendary ghost no one really knows ever existed or not.

He helped build *God's church*. He was the man *God used* to articulate theology that had been pounded into the heads of the women of these churches for decades.

"Do you think someone in the church would talk to us?" Kade's question sounded far away, and I closed my eyes.

"Maybe?" I answered him, my voice strained.

"But you're a woman..." Wanda's laugh was dry. "And we're Black. So, good luck with that, huh?"

I bit my lip, hard enough copper bloomed across my tongue.

"Don fell out with the preacher here in Caster. I don't know why. We stopped going. I don't know if he'd talk to me at all."

"We could try." There was determination in Kade's voice. "If Rachel was fostered by this *ministry*, and we know she was, because of her placement agreement *and* the one yearbook picture where she's dressed like..."

He stopped.

Like me?

I sank onto the edge of the bed, my knees weak.

"There should be someone at that church who knew her." Kade finished what he was saying, a little quieter this time. "Her disappearance raised enough local accusations it made the man who built this house abandon it and leave the state completely. If he was a part of that church, it had to have stirred things up, at least a little."

I couldn't breathe.

This started as one simple question. Who was the girl who went missing from this house in 1988?

I thought I was chasing a cold case. A mystery. A tragic story buried under years of rumor and neglect.

But I wasn't investigating a stranger anymore. I wasn't just unraveling someone else's story. I was pulling apart my own.

I'd found out my parents weren't really my parents. That my name wasn't mine. That everything I'd been told was my life was just a carefully constructed lie.

And now we'd pulled the veil back on something even worse.

A ministry I'd spent my whole childhood in, that built its theology on submission and silence.

A ministry founded by a man who fostered girls like Rachel. Girls who disappeared, vanished. A man who used the church to do it.

A church I'd belonged to. Worshipped in. Joined in songs in youth services, memorized its mantras, swallowed its laws like life-giving communion.

"Hey, Em." Wanda sat beside me. "Let's not jump to conclusions, okay? You're thinking the worst, I can see it."

"Of course, I am." My voice cracked. "They've lied to me my whole life. And now the girl we think was murdered here was fostered by the church I was raised in!"

I was crying again, but not from grief this time.

This was rage.

"It's all connected somehow." Hot, angry tears burned down my face as I jumped up and tore through my backpack.

I didn't want it to be connected.

Finding out I'd been lied to about my infancy was one thing. Finding out the church I grew up in, travelled the country to visit different congregations of, that prided itself on *kindness, love,* and *peace* might've been instrumental in a young woman's disappearance...

That was something else.

And I didn't want to be connected to it.

"She was here." I yanked out the photo that had fallen into my lap when I was stranded in my dad's truck.

Rachel. Sad eyes and very pregnant. Sitting on my bed.

"She slept here. In *my* bed!"

Wanda followed me as I stormed across the room to show her and Kade the cracked bedpost.

"I wrapped my sheet around this fucking post when I was *nine.*" I was shaking. "We lived in *Michigan,* and I played like I was Tarzan. The damn thing busted. I landed on my ass on the floor. My dad…"

The name caught in my throat.

Wanda pulled me in for a tight hug, and I hugged her back. I needed her. I needed Kade. I could feel myself collapsing inside.

"We'll figure this out, Em." Wanda's voice shook with emotion she was trying to swallow. "But you're gonna make yourself sick trying to do it all today."

I nodded against her shoulder. "It's the same crack," I whispered.

"She's right." Kade's voice came from behind us. "There's an old repair beneath the newer one."

I broke from Wanda enough to turn and look.

He showed me the crack. He'd picked at it with his pocketknife to expose the old scar.

Beneath the careful finish nails of Don's fourteen-year-old repair was yellowed glue dried hard into the wood grain. Faint traces of orange paint showed beneath it.

"The photo." I pulled away from Wanda, searching desperately for the picture.

She pushed it into my hands.

"It was orange." I choked on the words.

"This was her bed."

28

A SANDWICH

I wanted to keep searching, keep digging, uncovering every buried piece of my life and Rachel's that might still be hiding in that box.

But I'm thankful now that I had friends with me that afternoon.

Wanda and Kade wouldn't let me keep torturing myself, peeling back layer after layer of my existence until there was nothing left.

"When was the last time you ate, hon?" Wanda tugged me gently toward the bedroom door. "You need food and I'm not taking no for an answer."

I let her lead me downstairs, into the hollow quiet of the kitchen.

"They let you eat this stuff?" she asked, holding up a half-empty pack of bologna from the casket-size fridge. "But no kids' meals?"

I winced.

"I've had kids' meals," I murmured. "I remembered when we ate lunch at the library that day."

Wanda paused as she laid the bologna and a half-empty jar of mayonnaise on the table.

"I thought something was wrong with me," I said. "But the woman in that picture, the one in the red Camry? She took me out for a kids' meal. I remember the car. I remember the way the booster seat felt under me. I remember the ball pit, and the little clown toy."

"You've been having flashbacks?"

Wanda rummaged through the cabinets like she lived here, like she didn't need permission. I watched her, wishing I had half her confidence.

"You've had memories come back in little pieces," she said, laying a loaf of bread and a knife on the table. "Repressed memories come back like that. Everyday things—like eating a French fry—can trigger a fragment."

I bit my lip. "I thought I was going crazy."

Wanda gave a short laugh. "With everything we found in that attic, I think you're the least *crazy* person living in this haunted house."

I tried to smile, but my brain snagged on that word, *haunted*.

The figure of Gracie who came to my room. Papery skin. Long, black teeth. I closed my eyes, forcing the image away.

"Here." Wanda pushed a bologna sandwich between my elbows. "Eat, okay?"

"Thank you, Wanda." I shook my head. "I don't know what I would've done if you and Kade hadn't been here when I found all this shit."

She opened the fridge again, grabbed two waters, and passed one to me.

"I wouldn't have it any other way, Em." She sat across from me. "You're my first real friend since high school, you know that?"

"Seriously?" I frowned. "You must have tons of friends."

She shook her head, capping her water bottle. "Nope. I work at the library. That's a real hopping spot for young people." She grinned at me. "I like books, math, nursing. If I'm not at the library, I'm studying. I've got my own apartment, tuition, a car payment, gas. I'm not running with the party crowd." She shrugged. "I guess I don't fit in with the daddy-paid-my-way clique. I'm a buzzkill."

I had to laugh at that. "You're anything but a buzzkill, Wanda."

"Well, you get my point." She tightened the lid on her water bottle. "You really are my first real friend, Em. And friends look out for each other."

I smiled, and this time it was real. Not half-hearted or forced.

This conversation, Wanda's honesty, the sandwich—it all helped. Grounded me. Brought me back to the now. Reminded me that I still had to live. Still had to eat. Even as my world crumbled around me.

I hadn't realized how hungry I was. I couldn't even remember my last meal. I devoured the sandwich in two minutes and was already raiding the refrigerator for more.

"Do these people keep any sweets around?" Wanda rummaged through the cabinets again. "I need sugar."

"Check the pantry." I pointed toward the door in the corner, chewing leftover cornbread. "There should be cereal."

"Ooo." Wanda hurried over to the pantry. "Corn flakes? What the fuck? They're not even the frosted kind."

"Sorry." She looked so disappointed I had to laugh.

"Never mind." She spun from the pantry, holding up a bag of semi-sweet chocolate chips like a trophy. "Jackpot."

We didn't touch Mom's chocolate chips. They were for the rare moments she got a wild idea to bake something—usually cookies.

But Mom wasn't Mom. She was Allie Lyles. And Wanda was the one who helped me see it.

So, I watched her pop a handful of forbidden chocolate chips into her mouth and didn't say a word.

"Uh." Kade appeared in the doorway, voice careful. "What exactly am I seeing here?"

"Two starving women eating whatever the hell they want." Wanda tossed the bag of chocolate to him.

"Oookay." He poured a few chips into his hand, tossed them into his mouth, then rolled the bag shut so neatly I had to look twice.

"Where's this go?" he asked, still a little bewildered.

"Pantry." Wanda nodded behind her without looking as she cleared the table.

I'd already downed the first bottle of water Wanda gave me. Now I was finishing the second, washing down the dry, crumbly bits of cornbread stuck in my throat.

"Oh my gosh, that feels so much better." I came off the bottle with a gasp. "I had no idea I was that hungry—or thirsty."

"Or tired," Wanda added. "You need sleep too, Em. From what I remember, when you called me about the flat, you never got any rest."

She was right. I hadn't slept in over twenty-four hours, maybe closer to forty-eight. I wasn't even sure anymore.

"Here, before I forget." Kade crossed the kitchen and pressed something into my hand.

A phone. I'd forgotten all about him going to the store earlier to pick up a prepaid one.

"Oh..." My fingers wrapped around it like a lifeline. "You didn't..."

"Nope." Kade shook his head. "Don't even say it. You need a phone. More now than when I went to pick it up."

I took a short breath, staring down at the device in my hand.

Then I nodded. He was right.

"We don't know what's going on here," Kade added. "You need to be able to call someone. Me, Wanda, or 911 if it comes to that."

The weight of what he said settled in.

911 if it comes to that.

"I set it up for you already, and I added Wanda's number and mine to your contacts." He paused, and I looked up at him.

"I don't really like leaving you here, Em," he said. "If you want to leave now..."

His words faded as I shook my head.

"I need to know." I swallowed hard. "It's terrifying—all of this. That I've lived my whole life not even knowing where I came from, or who I am. That my parents spent twenty years lying to me." I took a slow, steadying breath. "They made up stories. About my birth, infancy, everything. Like really detailed stories."

Kade nodded. "You don't have to go into it. I believe you."

Those three words.

I believe you.

I let them soak into my soul.

"I can't leave before I know," I finally said, determination threading my voice in a way I hadn't heard from myself before. "And we need to find out what happened to Rachel. She deserves that."

The kitchen fell quiet. Like what I'd said needed space, needed silence.

"Okay." Kade nodded.

Then it hit me, what I'd chosen. Like a slap in the face, or a punch in the gut.

I was staying here, alone. Kade and Wanda would have to leave, sooner rather than later. They had jobs, school, lives to get back to. But I'd still be here.

"You're not in this alone, Em." Wanda stepped up beside me, linking her arm through mine like she'd heard where my thoughts had gone. "We're going to find out together, okay?"

My breath hitched, but I nodded.

"Actually, I think I should take the box home," she said. "You need to rest. If it stays here, you won't stop until you've gone through everything. You'll bleed yourself dry in one sitting."

I hesitated, but I knew she was right.

I only thought I felt crazy right now. If I kept peeling back the layers of my life, kept uncovering how deep the lies ran, I really would go crazy.

"Take it home," I whispered.

"We'll figure out how to meet up, like at the library, and keep going through it," Wanda said. "If you want, I can start going through some on my own." She nodded toward Kade. "Or he can, while I'm in class and he's not at work."

"Sure can," Kade agreed. "If you want me to."

I nodded. "Yeah. Let's do that."

I looked down at the phone in my hand. "I don't even know when I'll be able to get to the library. Mom took all my keys."

Kade grimaced. "We'll figure out how to get you out, so we can go over whatever we find."

"Until then, we'll text." Wanda squeezed my arm. "Kade, can you run up and grab the box?"

He did. A few minutes later, we were all outside, standing by Kade's El Camino. He tucked the box into the floorboard of the passenger seat.

"Wait." I touched his arm. He stopped so fast, I snatched my hand back.

He turned and looked at me, his eyes flicking to the spot on his arm where my hand had been.

"I'd like to keep the foster placement papers," I mumbled. "I just... need to."

He nodded and picked the yellowed pages from the top of the box's mountain of history, handing them to me.

I held them for a moment, the paper hot against my skin.

Emily Rose [Redacted]

I closed my eyes for just a second, then folded the pages and tucked them carefully into my dress pocket.

"I'll text you as soon as we're down the road." Wanda hugged me tight. "And you text me when you go back inside. When you're in your room."

I nodded. "I will."

"If you even *think* that thing pretending to be your sister is back," Kade spoke up, "don't text, just call."

"Oh, believe me." I forced a smile. "If it shows up again, I'll be running down the road in my nightgown, calling you while I run."

Neither one of them had time to respond. No laugh. No smile. Because at the end of the drive, Dad's blue pickup was pulling in.

"No, no, no," Wanda whispered. "Em, they're gonna flip. We should've left already."

"Wanda." Kade's voice dropped. "Calm down."

She clamped her mouth shut, but the damage was done. My blood had turned to radio fuzz.

The truck crawled up the driveway.

I squeezed Wanda's hand. "Don't worry about it."

She looked at me, guilt flooding her wide eyes.

"I want them to meet you," I said. "Both of you."

29

INTRODUCTIONS

I didn't let go of Wanda's hand as Don shoved the truck into park.

They were all looking at me. Don and Allie with eyes full of anger, disappointment, maybe even alarm.

Gracie sat stiffly by the passenger door, her dull green eyes alive with… excitement? Fear? I couldn't make sense of her expression. She looked like a child on Christmas morning—or a rabbit caught in a snare.

But I knew one thing for certain, in that instant when our eyes met through the windshield, she hadn't been in the house this afternoon. Something else had worn her face. But it hadn't been her.

Don stepped out of the truck. Neither Gracie nor Allie moved until he went around and opened their door.

Wanda side-eyed me.

"We're not allowed to leave a vehicle until he opens the door," I whispered.

Her jaw tightened. A muscle jumped in her cheek. "Shit," she muttered, barely moving her lips.

Don crossed the driveway with purpose and stuck out his hand to Kade.

For a split second, I wished I could vanish. Time distorted. Don's strides seemed longer. The world warped around me.

I'd wanted him to see that I wasn't alone anymore. But now, nausea tingled in my throat.

I didn't want Wanda and Kade to see this version of Don Lyles. The one I knew. The godly father. Hand extended. Smile rehearsed. With a phone full of porn in his pocket, and a box full of lies sitting in Kade's car.

But there was no undoing this moment. No rewinding. No pausing.

"Don Lyles," he said, voice firm, snapping time back into motion.

I saw the flicker of hesitation in Kade's face, but he took Don's hand and shook it.

"Kade Weston," he replied evenly. Then he nodded toward us. "This is my sister, Wanda."

Don barely looked at her. His nod in Wanda's direction was so slight it could've been mistaken for a twitch.

Behind him, Allie and Gracie quietly gathered their purses and water bottles from the truck.

In the background. Silent. Practiced. Falling into line. In their proper places.

Women don't speak to strangers. That's the man's job.

"We're friends of Emily's," Kade said.

"Oh." Don's congenial mask slipped, then reset. "Emily didn't mention she was having company today."

What? My head spun. Really? When have I *ever* had company?

"We just dropped in," Wanda said smoothly from beside me.

Don finally looked at her.

I recognized that tight-lipped smile. The one he wore when a cashier wouldn't honor one of Allie's coupons or let him return something without a receipt.

The smile he put on right before pulling the *I need to speak to your manager* card, or snapping, *I thought the customer was always right.*

But his gaze didn't linger. It slid over to me. And the smile dropped. His eyes were calm. Too calm. Like the still before a storm.

That stillness used to scare me. But not anymore. Not after everything I'd learned. And not with Wanda and Kade beside me.

But I didn't need to confront him today. Not yet.

I needed answers, about Rachel. About everything. And I wouldn't find them if I rocked the boat right now.

But that didn't mean I had to be afraid. Because I wasn't alone. Not anymore.

Kade stepped forward, drawing Don's attention. "This was perfect timing, Mr. Lyles. If you were five minutes later, we wouldn't have met. Wanda and I were just leaving."

I squeezed Wanda's hand. Don's reply faded into static.

"I'll text you," I whispered.

She squeezed back, a silent acknowledgment, no need for words. She understood.

I didn't want to be alone with Don.

I knew some kind of confrontation was coming. But at least in the house, Allie and Gracie would be there. Even if they weren't on my side.

I didn't interrupt whatever Don was saying to Kade. But I could feel Kade's eyes on me as I turned and headed back to the house.

I'd text him too.

Inside, the air felt too still. I wasn't sure where Allie or Gracie had gone. The living room was empty. The kitchen, silent.

I slipped into the tiny half-bath between the kitchen and my parents' room. Locked the door. Pulled out the phone Kade had bought me.

The screen lit up. Soft, electric blue against the dark. It cast my face in sterile light, ghostly and too bright.

I winced and flipped the light switch. Couldn't have anyone noticing I'd locked myself in the bathroom in the dark.

I scrolled to Kade and Wanda's numbers and started a group text.

> Thanks for everything.

I watched until the message marked as delivered. Then I closed the app.

My old phone only had three numbers in it. Don. Allie. Gracie. This one had two. Kade and Wanda. And I had no intention of ever adding Don or Allie into any phone I ever owned again.

That realization landed like a stone in my chest. I hadn't even decided it. Not consciously. It was like something deeper had made that choice for me.

I took a shaky breath and shut my eyes.

Gracie.

I thought about adding her number. Maybe later. I needed to see how the next thirty minutes went.

Don would come in. We'd all gather in the kitchen. Then the questions would start.

Where did you meet them?
How long have you known them?
Why didn't you tell us?
Did Gracie know?
Why were they at the house?

I'd answer the best I could. There wasn't time, or energy, to prepare.

> He's coming inside.

Wanda's text lit up the phone screen.

> You don't have to thank us for anything. Let us know what happens. Kade said call if things go south.

30

SAY IT, EMILY

I told them the truth. Somehow, that still made me the liar.

Wanda and Kade were my friends. I met Wanda at the library. Kade, her brother, brought her lunch one day.

"Is that the man?" Allie's voice cracked through the room like a snapped bone.

Until now, everything had been unnaturally calm. Controlled.

I didn't answer. Just looked at her.

"The man you've been sneaking around to see, Emily." Impatience curled around every word. "Is that him?"

"I haven't been *seeing* a man."

I sounded steady and even. I had no idea how. Inside of me, everything was coiled tight. Twisting. Building.

You've lied to me my whole life. You're not even my mom. How much of my life is real?

But I held it in. It wasn't time. Not yet.

"You're *still* going to give me that story?" Allie's voice cracked. She looked at Don.

"You haven't been at the library like you said, Emily." Don hadn't sat. He stood by the kitchen door.

Blocking me?

"I *have* been at the library," I contradicted him. "Wanda's my friend. I sit with her in the break room sometimes."

Allie turned away, jerking open a cabinet, slamming down pots and pans.

"Meeting *that* boy for hook-ups, more like it."

She muttered it, but I heard every word.

"What?" I stood.

"Allie," Don's voice was calm over the rush of water hitting metal, "we need to keep our heads. Don't push her away."

That stopped me.

He knew? Did he know I had a way out? I'd never heard Don Lyles say a word about me or Gracie leaving. That had always been Allie.

"We're worried about you, Emily." Don's voice softened. "Our little girl wouldn't be using the kind of words you used the other day. She wouldn't disrespect her parents like that."

You're not my parents.

It was my first though, but I swallowed it.

"I'm not a little girl." I said that instead. "I'm twenty-two."

Twenty-three.

"It doesn't matter how old you are!" Allie spun to face me, face blotched red. "You *respect* your parents!"

Parents.

It was harder to swallow that time.

"I should be able to have friends." I got the words out, as steadily as I could. They came out even. Measured. But I felt like a tornado inside.

"*Friends?*" Don spat, losing a little of his even composure. "You need *believing* friends, not *worldly* friends."

"Wanda's a Christian."

The words dropped like a stone. Silence rippled out. It was like time stopped. The house went still, like it stopped breathing.

Except, it hadn't.

I don't think anyone else felt it, the watching. Or heard the breathing.

The house, whatever had worn my sister's skin, it was here, and it was listening. Taking it all in. Weighing. Measuring.

Gracie shifted in her seat at the table. Did she feel it, too?

The creak of wood against vinyl broke the spell. Time resumed. The house exhaled.

Allie smacked the faucet, the water rushing into the pot stopped. Don let out a sharp sigh. The clock over the sink started ticking again. The buzzing of electricity, the hum of the ceiling fan, it was all so much louder.

"Emily." Don was the first to speak. "You're a wise daughter of God. You know the difference between *true* believers and worldly people who only *claim* to love Christ."

"Yeah, *true* belief means the men get to dress however they want, but the women have to look like they're headed west for the Gold Rush…"

My voice was climbing, and suddenly, I couldn't stop.

"They think they're closer to God because they don't say words like *fuck,* or *damn,* or *bitch.* They don't drink liquor or gamble… but they're racist as hell. They think they're better than anyone else. The women stay silent, and the men do whatever they want—so long as they can hide it."

I hadn't meant to say that last one. But it was out.

Don stared at me. The tremor ticked in his jaw. His neck flushed crimson.

"Emily Carol Lyles!" Allie exploded for him. "You *know* better than that! *True* believers don't do what the world does. We don't act like they do, don't say what they say, or dress how they dress. And we respect God's *order.*"

God's order.

The one where Don can look at porn and buy his clothes at the store, but Allie can't say no to sex no matter how tired or sick she is, and has to make her clothes by hand, so she looks *different.*

I didn't have time to respond. No time to dig my own grave a little bit deeper.

"Why were those people at my house, Emily?" Don cut me off. "What were they doing here?"

"They came to check on me." I crossed my arms against my chest. "Like they said."

"Did they come inside the house?"

I didn't have to answer him. He could see it on my face.

"Why would you let strangers in my house?"

"Because they're *my* friends," I snapped. "And I thought this was *my* house too? The one I help pay for by working your construction jobs because a *real* job wouldn't pay enough?"

"Emily!" Allie gasped, but Don was already crossing the kitchen. Even she fell silent when his open palms slapped the tabletop.

"That's enough!"

Gracie flinched. Her chair scraped softly against the floor as she shrank back. She quickly wiped at her face with the sleeve of her cardigan, like she didn't want anyone to see the tears.

I bit my lip.

"This stops now." Don growled, his hands still planted on the table.

His eyes locked on mine, flat, unreadable, but his jaw twitched. His head was shaking again, that rhythmic tremor ticking down his neck until his beard brushed the front of his shirt.

"You don't get to stand in *my* house and talk to me like that. Or to *her*."

He jerked his head toward Allie, who stood frozen at the sink, arms stiff at her sides. "She's your mother."

No, she's not.

The words bubbled up from my gut, into my throat, but I wouldn't let them out. My jaw clenched, teeth grinding against each other.

"You think because you're grown, you get to run your mouth like the world? You get to disrespect me? Your mother? God? You think that's strength?"

He sneered. "You're wrong. That's not strength, that's rebellion. Independence. That's sin. That's the devil crawling around in your head, Emily. And I'm not gonna let that destroy this family—or you."

"Don…" Allie's voice was quiet now. Thinner. Strained. Careful.

"No," he said, eyes still locked on me. "She opened the door to that poison, Allie. She brought it in here, behind our backs."

Wanda and Kade. He was talking about Wanda and Kade. Anger warmed my chest. I felt my fists tighten, clutching my skirt.

"Wanda and Kade are my friends." I got my words out in steady clips.

"No, they're not, Emily." Don's sarcastic smile sliced his features. The *you're wrong and you know it* grin that felt like he threw gasoline on fire.

I had to look away. Step away. Do something with my hands to keep myself from exploding.

I went to the stove and put on the tea kettle.

"You're blind if you can't see how they're using you." Don spoke to my back. "Turning you against your family, against God."

I ignored the second part of that.

"How are they using me?" I asked a simple question.

Don shook his head, that smile creasing his face again, this time his eyes dark with pity. "That's why you *need* me, Emily. You have no idea what the people of this world are capable of. You don't know what men are like."

"Oh my gosh…" I groaned, turning back to the cabinets and finding tea. "It's always the same thing."

"Then you tell me what it is, young lady." Don snipped, and I heard him take a step. Away from the table. Toward me.

"What is it about that boy, huh? You like the way he talks to you? The things he says? That leather jacket? The ink up his neck?"

My stomach knotted against my ribs. I almost crushed the box of tea in my fist. I closed my eyes. Breathed.

"You think that's freedom, Emily?" Don's voice was patronizing now. He was making fun of me—and of Kade. "You think that boy's gonna show you what the world's like? What you're missing by following God?"

"He treats me like a person."

The words slipped out. They were a defense, but they were also a confession.

And the room went still. Allie sucked in a sharp breath. Gracie's chair creaked against the floor again, like she'd anxiously shifted in her seat. Don was silent.

"I knew it." Allie was the first to speak, her voice fluid with tears. "My sweet Emily... Oh Lord God, don't let the evil one take my baby."

She'd crossed the kitchen to me now and tried to hug me. She was crying, like all the anger had dissolved away into a broken heart when I'd stood up for Kade.

"We're your God-given family." Allie held me, her tears dampening my shoulder. "No one will ever love you like we do. The devil's using false believers to turn your heart against your family." She squeezed me tighter. "You can't let him do that. I can't lose my baby."

Because I have friends?

Because my friends came to my house?

Because I stood up for a good man that *your porn-addicted husband* was berating?

"God placed you under our covering for a reason." Don spoke up from behind me. He was calmer now, but his voice held an edge. Authority. Correction.

"If you step outside of God's covering, you're flirting with the devil. And God won't force you to stay. You're opening yourself up to deception, and you're making that choice. You don't want to find yourself cut off, Emily. The enemy prowls like a lion. We're trying to protect your soul."

I pulled away from Allie, peeled her off me and grabbed a tea bag and a cup, dousing the dried leaves with steaming water from the kettle.

"I'm going to my room." I mumbled, turning away, my eyes fixed on the amber tendrils coiling from the teabag.

"No, you're not." Don's voice was firm.

I looked up at him, my eyes burning, teeth aching as they locked down against each other again.

He pulled a chair out at the table. "You're going to sit down and we're going to fix this."

Fix what?

I started shaking my head, but before the words could leave my mouth, Allie's hand gripped my arm, guiding me to the table.

"We love you, Emily, we've forgiven you before we ever started talking. But you have to do the rest. You have to repent and turn back to the narrow path before it's too late."

I'd let myself be led to the chair. I'd sat down, my head spinning. What? Repent? For... having fucking friends?

"You're allowing the devil into your mind." Don's voice sounded so much louder than I knew it was. "You're letting yourself be influenced by people who don't know the truth."

"You can't even see it, and that's how the devil works." Allie chimed back in, my skull pounding to each syllable she dropped. "But we can see it. The Emily I raised wouldn't talk the way you've been talking. She wouldn't bring strangers into our home. She wouldn't degrade our faith, talking about what we believe like the world talks about us."

I was shaking, the tea in my hand sloshing dangerously close to the lip of the cup.

Then, beneath the cover of the tabletop, I felt Gracie's hand slide to my knee. A small thing, a touch, but I knew what it meant.

Even if she was too scared to speak up, too afraid to face our parents' disapproval, Gracie didn't agree with them. She didn't think I was wrong.

I tried to glance at her, but her eyes didn't quite meet mine. She stared down at her lap.

But that was fine. That touch. That assurance. Even without acknowledging it, it's what I needed.

"We're fixing this." Don said, his voice threading into my head like a prayer I didn't choose. "Number one, you're not disrespecting us again. We're your parents. No matter how old you are, we're your God-given protectors until you meet the *right* man. When you dishonor us, you're dishonoring Him. And if you walk away from that, don't expect Him to chase you."

He paused long enough I focused on his face. He stood across from me at the table.

Looming over me and Gracie. Ticking off his demands on his fingers.

The picture flashed behind my eyes. Red crayon. The man with no face.

My heart skipped four beats, and my head felt light.

"Second, you're not going to that library anymore." Don's voice rose ever so slightly. "You're not seeing those people. They're not to come to this property, much less inside the house, and you're not to speak to them. Not a word. No phone call. Nothing. Do you understand me?"

The air around me froze. Tense. Cold. Chills pricked up my spine. Tiny bumps of cold rose on my skin, across my arms, up my legs.

But Gracie's hand was still on my knee. While the cold enveloped me, her hand was heavy and hot, like a burning coal searing my skin.

"Say it, Emily." Don's tone had dropped low. Warning. Demanding. "You're done with those people. You won't see them again."

My neck was stiff, like the cold had seeped through my skin, into my spine. But I looked up at him again, met his eyes.

Gracie's fingers dug into my skin like she wanted me to stop. I wanted to stop too. I wanted to scream. To get up and flip the table. Leave the room, telling Don and Allie both to fuck themselves.

But I didn't. I swallowed it all. Forced it down. Stared Don in those empty, dead eyes and took a steady breath.

"I won't see them again."

Gracie flinched, but Don smiled.

"See how easy that was?" He stepped back from the table, still watching me. "*Now* you can go to your room."

I stood, shoving the chair back and picking up my tea. I didn't feel the heat. I was so chilled through, that cup could've been a glowing ember and I wouldn't have felt it.

I left the kitchen, passing the fireplace and its burned remains, destroyed fragments of a life Don and Allie didn't want me to remember. I didn't slow down, didn't stop to think. I went down the hall and up the stairs.

I was still shaking, but I couldn't tell now if it was from the cold or the confrontation in the kitchen.

I tripped up the steps, reaching the top just as my tea sloshed over the lip of my cup, spilling the dark orange liquid over my hand. I stopped to steady it, sipping the spicy lemon-ginger potion down a bit.

I took the last steps to my room carefully, opening the door with unsteady hands.

What I saw didn't scare me. Not after facing off with whatever had worn Gracie's skin. Not after learning that my name wasn't my name. My birthday wasn't my birthday. And my parents weren't my parents. Not after what I'd survived downstairs.

She was sitting on my bed. Her back rested against the cracked post. Beagle lay in her lap like he belonged there. Rachel Bagwell. Or what Rachel might've looked like as a child.

Not the pregnant teen from the photograph I'd found. Not the young woman she was when she died.

There was no peeling skin like I'd seen in the rearview of Don's truck. No darkened, clotted blood or rotting teeth.

She was a girl. A little pale. Her hair was dull, not the bright red I knew from the photos. Her eyes were hollow, but not milky white. They were dim, soft with sorrow.

"Don't worry," I whispered, my voice raw.

"I lied."

31

You Know How Your Dad Is

I looked away for a second, long enough to set my tea on the dresser, and she was gone.

I was alone again.

I took a deep breath, closing my eyes and steadying myself. I let everything from the past couple days wash over me. Through me. But I didn't have long to reflect.

I pulled the phone Kade had gotten me from my pocket, swiping to the messages.

> Back in my room.

> I'm not supposed to talk to either of you again.

I sent it in the group chat, and both Wanda and Kade read them almost as soon as they were delivered.

Kade's side was quiet, but little bubbles popped up telling me Wanda's thumbs were flying over her screen.

> Doesn't look like you're a very good listener.

I smiled when I read her text and shook my head.

> Fuck them.

As I sent that message there was a short rap on my bedroom door.

"Knock, knock!"

Allie. That was her signature *I'm going to swing the door open before you can hide whatever you're doing.*

She did, but I'd already hid the phone. It was safe between my boobs, behind my bra strap. Sufficiently hidden between the double layered bodice of a cape dress.

At least capes were good for something.

"Hey, sweetie." Allie came in without waiting for an answer.

But she wasn't looking at me. Her eyes darted around the room like she was looking for something else.

Something I was hiding? Or something *she* needed to hide?

"I'm tired," I mumbled.

I knew how this would go. The soft voice. The sad eyes. She'd blame Don, say she was praying for him, pretend like she hadn't nodded along the whole time.

"I know…" She invited herself to sit on my bed, right where I'd seen Rachel a couple moments before.

She shivered. "There's a draft in here!" She hugged herself, rubbing the cold from her arms.

I had to get up. I went to the dresser for my tea.

"I'm sorry everything's so bad right now." Allie was watching me as I took my first sip. "I know I was mad, and I'm sorry. It surprised me, seeing strangers at the house. I was scared for you."

"They're my *friends…*" I almost said her name, but I drowned it with more tea.

She sighed, a slow, sad exhale, and slumped against the cracked bedpost.

"I know that's what you think Em." Allie shook her head. "But you need *believing* friends, friends who won't make you doubt your calling, or make you question the truths of the Word."

I didn't answer.

But I did think that I should probably read the Bible again, for myself. Maybe a different version. See if all these *truths* were really in there...

Don would hate that.

King James, that's the only Bible you need. The rest are twisted. Adulterations.

"I wish things hadn't gone the way they did at the local assembly here in Caster," Allie said pensively.

We need to find out more about D.L. Emerson, and this church. Kade's deep voice rang in my ears.

"What happened?" I forced myself to ask. "I miss going."

So many lies. I was getting very good at lying lately.

Allie shook her head. "Every church has its wolves in sheep's clothing, Em." Her mouth formed a stiff line I imagined she thought was a frown. "I wish things hadn't gone badly. You girls *need* fellowship."

I sipped my tea. She hadn't answered my question.

"I know you need friends." She looked right at me that time, her blue eyes locking onto mine. "I want you to have friends, believing friends. You don't need to go out into the world and find friends."

I could still see the hurt in Wanda's face. I glanced at the floor, the spot where she and I had sat, sorting through Rachel's file when Kade left to get me a phone.

I'm a Christian, she'd said. *Believing in Jesus isn't enough?*

"Emily." Allie had gotten up from the bed, crossed my room to me without me even hearing her. I almost jumped back when I realized how close she was.

"I know you're confused. You're growing up. It's a confusing time."

"I'm grown." I looked at her and I couldn't stop the words from coming out. "The *confusing* time was ten years ago—when my boobs grew in, and I started my period. *That* was confusing. The day you told *him* I was using tampons."

Allie grimaced. She knew exactly what I was talking about, but I wouldn't stop. She was going to hear it.

"Remember that?" I stepped away from her, went around my bed and set my tea down on the side table. "He *freaked out* because a tampon could *take my virginity*." I used air quotes. "Remember? He said *he* should be the one to decide when something goes into *my* body. Because he was my *protector*."

"I make mistakes, Em. I'm only human." Allie's voice was fluid. She was going to cry again. Or pretend to.

"Okay." I nodded. "But why couldn't I use tampons for eight years after that? If it was a mistake, why did I have to suffer with leaky pads and cheap pantyliners for eight years?"

"You know how your dad is!" Allie crossed her arms, hugging herself. "You don't even see half of it. He hides it from you girls, saves it all up for when we're alone—him and me."

That was always the excuse.

Don's mean. You girls don't know how he really is. I need my girls.

What about me needing a mom?

I drew a short breath that stuttered against my ribs, then shoved the blankets back on my bed, pushing Beagle under my pillow.

"I need to be alone for a little while," I mumbled.

Allie was quiet, and I didn't look up at her. I knew she was crying. Trying to control it.

Or pretend she was.

I sat down on my bed, shoving my shoes off and tucking my legs beneath me.

My head was pounding. A hard, steady ache between my temples.

"I don't know what happened." Allie sniffed. "We used to be so close. You were always the one I could count on."

My teeth came together with a soft click.

"You know how your dad is, and Gracie's so fragile…" Her voice faded and she crossed the room toward me again, inviting herself to sit next to me.

She found my hand, pulled it into her lap and held it with both of hers, linking her fingers through mine.

"You used to come to me about everything, Em. We used to talk, share things. Stay up late and pray together." She sighed. "What happened to my sweet girl?"

You chose him. You put him first. You always did. I grew up enough to finally see it.

"Lean not unto thine own understanding." Allie quoted Scripture now. "Trust in the Lord with all thine heart."

Part of me wanted to pull my hand away, and part of me wanted to reach over and fall into her arms. Let her comfort me, hold me. Cry together.

Like we used to. Before I knew.

Then I saw the window. The one where, for six years, I'd heard the tapping.

In the glass I could see her. Not Rachel. But Allie. Not as the grieving, lonely woman sitting beside me. But as the woman who left Don, years and years ago. The woman who took Gracie with her and left. Walked away.

But then came back.

And stayed.

"The heart is deceitful above all things, Emily." Allie's quiet voice shattered the image in the glass. It fell away, and I could see the sun setting outside, the darkness overtaking the road in front of the house.

"We can't trust our feelings. We're all just human."

I finally looked at her. First at her hands grasping mine. Thin, boney. Her freckled arms and narrow shoulders, buried somewhere beneath the yards of muted blue fabric she'd used to make her dress.

Then her face. She was watching me. Thin lips in a tight line, pale blue eyes sad but calculating.

Measuring her words. Weighing my reactions.

"I did everything I could to raise you right," she said, "even though it was hard, with your dad the way he is." Her shoulders slumped. "You were always the strong one, Em. Don't let the devil steal that now."

She wanted me to fold. To break. To crumble enough she could say she saved me. She could go back to Don and tell him she *talked to me*. Tell him I cried. She'd be the *good mom*. The *obedient wife*. Faithful in all things.

None of this was about me. It never was. It was about her. Her feelings. What she wanted. And how it affected her relationship with Don.

"You like him, don't you?"

That question took me by surprise. I snapped my head around to face her, pulling my hand from hers.

"It's okay if you do, Em." Allie's voice was calm. "It's natural. That's how God made us. A good-looking man shows us some attention." She smiled at me.

I didn't answer, but I didn't look away either.

"He's that girl's brother?"

"Wanda."

Allie nodded. "I didn't get to talk to them, but they seemed nice."

You didn't try to talk to them. You marched yourself into the house like a good, little wife.

"Are you two dating?"

I shoved my blanket back and got up from the bed. "I don't want to talk about any of this. I think we talked enough in the kitchen."

Allie looked hurt. "You used to tell me things, Em."

And you never told me anything.

I didn't say it. I swallowed it.

"I'm your mom." Allie was almost pleading with me. "I'd like to know when my little girl has her first boyfriend."

I closed my eyes, pinched the bridge of my nose between my fingers.

"Be honest with me, okay?" I looked back at her. "I'm tired of the lies. What do you want?"

"I've never lied to you, Em."

That almost did it. I almost exploded on her.

But then I remembered Rachel. That her foster placement was in the same box as mine. That she was adopted through the church I'd attended—that my parents took me to.

"You need to tell me things, Em," Allie insisted. "I've spent every night on my knees begging God to bring you back to me. To heal our family. You need to tell me if you're dating that man."

I watched her.

Kade hadn't asked me. But I knew he liked me. Wanda told me he did. And I could feel it when he looked at me. Held my hand. Insisted that I call him if anything went wrong.

But it felt too real. Too sacred.

I couldn't cheapen something I'd just started to feel by sharing it with her... who would share it with *him*.

"I'm going to talk to your dad." Allie stood up from my bed, finally. "I'm going to see if we can try different churches. I think there's one just over the North Carolina line. I know it would be a long way to travel for church, but it would be worth it, for you girls."

She smoothed her dress out and slipped her hand into one of the seam pockets. That wasn't like her. There was something in her pocket.

"God doesn't want us..." She floundered when I met her eyes.

Paused. Shifted her hand in her pocket.

"It wouldn't be right, Em."

I clamped my teeth on my lower lip, copper biting back.

Then she pulled her hand from her pocket. She was holding a small purple and white box. "I need you to take this."

"What?"

I didn't need to step up to her. She was walking toward me, hand outstretched.

"I know there's no need." Allie shook her head. "Because I trust you—but Don wants you to take this."

I stared at the box in her hand. Big, purple letters read *One Step Pregnancy Test*.

"What the hell?" I recoiled.

Allie's brow rose on her forehead. "Emily! Why are you cussing lately? Is that how *they* talk?"

"You're trying to get me to take a *pregnancy test!*" I couldn't help my voice rising. "I told you I wasn't pregnant!"

"I know! But you know how your dad is."

"No." I shook my head. "I know how *you* are."

"What's that supposed to mean?"

I walked across my room and opened the door. "I need to be alone."

Allie put a hand on her hip, pushing a pissed off *uh* out through her nose. She stepped to the door, to me, but stopped short of leaving.

She pushed the box toward me.

"I'm not taking that." I heard the words leave my mouth.

Confident. Final.

I'd never said *no* to Allie before, not really. Not with so much certainty. Not where she couldn't talk me into saying *yes* afterwards.

She stared at me. For a couple seconds? A minute or two? Three hours?

It felt like forever we stood there, eyes locked on each other, my hand on the door, waiting for Allie to walk out.

She finally looked away. She tossed the box at my bed, it missed, hit my Goldilocks lamp on the side table, knocking it to the floor.

She didn't say she was sorry. Didn't say she didn't mean to throw the box that hard. She left.

And I locked the door behind her.

32

CRAWDAD MAN

I didn't go to dinner that night. I didn't answer when Allie came back to my door, tried the knob only to find it still locked.

"I made dinner." Her voice rose through the crack beneath the door. "If you plan on eating with the rest of us, you need to come downstairs."

I didn't answer. I listened. Waited for her footsteps to retreat down the steps.

> You still need to eat something.

Wanda texted me when I'd told her that I wasn't going to dinner with the rest of the *family* tonight.

I ate stale peanut butter crackers from the bottom of my backpack, sitting cross-legged on the floor while I looked over Rachel's file one more time.

I'd tucked the placement forms in with the file earlier. When I opened it now, they were staring me in the face.

Child's Legal Name: Emily Rose (Last Name Redacted)
DOB: 02/14/1991
Placement Date: 08/23/1994
Foster Resource: Donald Lyles and Allie Lyles

I stared at the name, *Emily Rose,* and the birth date.

I'd been so assaulted by Don and Allie's lies, I hadn't let this part sink in. I wasn't Emily Carol Lyles. I wasn't even twenty-two. I was someone else. And I had been for a long, long time.

It was jarring, staring at these pages again, with fresh eyes. Less distracted. Less shocked.

I didn't know who I was. Where I came from. What my parents were like. Is that why I always felt out of place?

I had brown eyes, like Don. But my hair—flat, brown, forgettable—it wasn't blonde and curled like Allie's or wavy black like his.

Allie was covered with freckles. From head to toe. Don's skin was fair, he burned easily, never tanned. They were both cool and pink, like shades of old porcelain.

I'd always wondered why my skin was darker, warmer. Why my face and arms held color, even in the winter.

It wasn't dramatic. Most people wouldn't notice, not at church, or at the grocery store. But in photos, side by side, under the flash, it showed.

I thought of Gracie. She fit in better. Kind of.

She was pale, at least. Always had been. In the right light, her skin looked almost translucent.

Even on the most hellish summer day, she wore long sleeves. Her skin would scorch. One summer she wore short sleeves, up to her elbows, like me, and her arms glowed almost as red as her hair.

I spent several days thinking through all this.

Things had cooled down around the house.

I didn't say much. To Allie or Don, or even Gracie. But I did go back to work.

We were at a different job site now. I wasn't painting, I was scrubbing the kitchen down. Top to bottom, degreaser on a metal scouring pad, gloves up to my elbows.

But I wasn't thinking about work.

Gracie's hair was red. So bright. So obvious. Why did that strike me like it did?

I bore down on the cabinet top, my feet planted firmly on the faux marble counter below me.

It was driving me crazy.

Why did it bother me that my sister's hair was red? Gracie's hair had always been red. But now, I couldn't stop seeing it.

"Are you okay?"

Gracie herself came into the kitchen, a brand-new gallon of yellow degreaser clutched to her chest, a couple orange plastic bags hanging from her arms.

I didn't answer her right away.

She set the cleaner down, unloaded the different scrubbers, gloves, and sponges from the bags.

"How was Hardy's this afternoon?" I didn't look up, just kept scrubbing like the top of this cabinet owed me something.

I'd have to paint the fucker anyway, I didn't know why Allie didn't let me use paint stripper. It would melt all the grease away in two seconds flat.

"Busy," Gracie answered. "But you know the leak over the hardware department?"

"Yeah?"

"They finally fixed it."

I glanced at her. "Good, I guess."

Gracie was sorting through the cleaning items. She mentioned something about the cashier at number five. She always talked to Gracie when we went to Hardy's. A sweet lady, recently a widow, she was into cozy hobbies, knitting and crochet, like Gracie.

Everything sounded normal, looked normal. Gracie's story. My hands. The steel wool. The puddle of putrid, yellow chemical on the top of this cabinet. But nothing was normal. Nothing was right.

And trying to pretend was killing me.

I glanced down at Gracie. She'd finally finished arranging all the cleaning products by size across the opposite countertop.

Sometimes it was size. Sometimes color. Sometimes alphabetically. But there was never any dumping things out and going for Gracie. Things had to be right. In order.

I watched her a minute. She surprised me when she pulled a little bag of Cajun flavored pretzels from the last orange Hardy's bag.

She popped it open and held it up to me.

"Pretzel?"

I peeled off my gloves and squatted carefully, taking a couple pretzels from the bag. Powdery, red flavoring dusted my fingers.

I didn't take my eyes off Gracie as I stood back up, bringing the salty snack to my lips. I expected it to dissolve as it touched my tongue. The bag in my sister's hand to morph into a sponge or scouring pad.

But it didn't.

I ate the pretzels, and Gracie was still standing there, nibbling hers.

"They're pretty good," she said. "I usually don't like hot things, but these aren't just hot. They taste good."

I couldn't taste them. They were salty mush oozing between my teeth.

I couldn't believe my sister was eating pretzels. The flavored kind with all those dangerous additives.

"Dad let you get those?"

Gracie shook her head, a defiant, red curl slipping from its tight bun and dancing around her neck.

"I checked out at number five while he was still arguing with the man running the carpet cutting machine in the back."

My mouth dropped open.

"He doesn't know you got those?"

It shouldn't have mattered. But it did.

Gracie raised a thin shoulder in a shrug. "They're just pretzels."

No. They weren't *just pretzels*.

Gracie had never, ever bought anything without permission. She'd never gone through a cash register line without someone with her. And she'd certainly never ingested anything Don and Allie considered *unhealthy*—food tainted by the world's addictions.

I lowered myself to the countertop, sitting down where my feet had been.

"I didn't mean to interrupt your work." Gracie popped another pretzel in her mouth.

I shook my head, but I couldn't get my tongue to say anything.

"I'm proud of you, you know." Gracie's voice dropped a little. "Things need to change."

I stared at her, remembered her hand on my knee when I lied to Don.

"You're still talking to them, aren't you?" Gracie whispered now.

I nodded.

"Did the man, Kade, get you a phone?"

I swallowed. "Gracie, how do you know that?"

"I don't. But I know you wouldn't quit talking to him."

Silence fell between us. Thick. Heavy.

I could hear Allie talking to Don outside. Arguing about money, as usual.

I thought you said you wouldn't spend that much! The credit line's almost maxed out! We have three jobs going, how are we going to buy all the materials?

"I guess I would've lied too." Gracie licked her teeth. "The first man to ever pay attention to you and *he* wants you to quit talking to him."

"I don't think Kade goes to church." My voice came out raw.

Gracie looked at me a moment, then looked back down at her bag of red pretzels.

"I applied to an online college."

I jumped off the counter. Forget the pretzels.

"What did you say?"

"I want to be a teacher." Gracie held the bag of snacks out to me. "They do get kind of hot, don't they?"

She firmly pushed the bag into my hands and dusted hers off on her dress.

I watched her grab a couple of sponges off the counter, realign all the cleaning products, and then turn to leave the kitchen.

She stopped in the doorway.

"Oh, Em?"

I thought she'd keep talking, but she waited on me.

"Yeah?"

"Every family does have its problems, but you don't need to stop digging into this one's, okay?"

I couldn't answer.

Every family has its problems.

I watched Gracie turn and leave.

I stared down at the pretzels in my hands. The happy, little man on the front of the package smiled up at me, pitchfork in hand, bright red crawdads trying to crawl out of a bucket in the other.

Did Gracie quote that... *thing*? The thing that wore her skin? That chased me from my room, clawing at me with those curling, long nails?

I blinked. The room twisted. The counter lurched sideways beside me, like the whole house had changed its mind, tilted on its foundation.

I reached for the countertop. It was going to crush me. Heavy wood and glued on plastic marble. But my hand went through it. Like paper or sun-dried cardboard.

And I fell. Hit the floor.

And then I wasn't even at the job anymore. I was back home. In my room. In the room inside the wall. Clutching my backpack to my chest.

Crawdad man was beside me, pushing a paper into my hands.

"Read it again, Emily," he grunted.

It was Rachel's. Her placement record.

The paper, once old, stained, and brittle pulsed in my hands like it was alive. Thick, fleshy, vibrant.

Highlighted in sickly, glowing yellow, three words rose off the page like oozing blisters.

Caseworker: Lawrence Biddle

33

BLEEDING YELLOW

It wasn't right.

That name wasn't on Rachel's placement record. It couldn't be. It didn't belong there.

I had the file with me, of course I did, tucked into my backpack. But I wasn't about to pull it out around *them*. Not even to sneak a glance.

I had to wait. Until I was really back at that house, not just imagining I was there. I had to wait until I was safely locked inside my room. Then I dug out the file.

Trembling, I shuffled through the pages until I found it.

Child's Legal Name: Rachel Marie Bagwell
DOB: 07/26/1970
Placement Date: 03/10/1987
Foster Resource: D.L. Emerson Ministries

My eyes darted down the page. I flipped it over. Tried to blink away the blur.

Reasons for Placement
Removal from prior placement due to overcrowding and caseworker reassignment.

Child exhibits emotional detachment and mild disordered eating. Counseling recommended.

Foster parent reports experience with "troubled girls" and has committed to long-term care.

And there, at the bottom. Highlighted in sickly, glowing yellow...

Caseworker: Lawrence Biddle

I dropped the page. Doubled over. Head to my knees. Hot tears spilling down my face. My pulse thundered in my ears. Thick, sloshing blood, too loud to think.

Shhh... Shhh... My body was trying to hush me. Telling me to shut up. To keep it inside. Lock it up.

Don't tell.

"No."

I sat up. Yanked my phone from my pocket. Swiped through the tears streaking the screen.

> The bishop was the caseworker.

He'd known her. Known Rachel.

I sent the text. To Wanda and to Kade. Then I sat and stared at the page. At the name, glowing yellow.

This wasn't highlighted before... was it?

I picked up the paper, flipped it over, eyes registering the yellow ink bleeding through the back of the page.

This was new. This wasn't washed out highlighter from 1987. It glared off the page like caution tape soaked in bile.

I touched the mark. Brushed my thumb over the bleeding yellow. It didn't feel damp. It didn't feel like ink at all. A smear that shouldn't be there.

My phone vibrated against my thigh, sharp and sudden. I snatched it up.

> Fuck, are you for real right now?

Wanda's text.

I snapped a quick photo of Rachel's placement record and sent it through the group text.

> Lawrence Biddle. He's bishop of Caster Independent Assembly.

I closed my eyes a moment.

Bishop Biddle. Brother Lawrence.

I'd sat through so many of his slow, droning sermons. Watched him for hours as he preached from the plain pine pulpit at the front of that cinderblock church.

My phone buzzed against my skirt again and I opened my eyes to read Wanda's text.

> Holy shit, you're right. I got it pulled up on my computer. He used to be a social worker back in the '70s and '80s.

> Maybe he could tell us who fostered Rachel.

Of course he could. He worked the case. He would've met Rachel Bagwell herself.

A cold chill rushed up my back.

> I cross referenced D. L. Emerson.

Wanda was texting.

> He built that house, but I can't find his name on anything to do with Rachel Bagwell.

I took a stiff breath. My lungs felt cold. Sore.

> What about D. L. Ministries?

Wanda started typing again, as soon as my text went through.

> Yeah. A lot came up on that name. Church stuff. Nothing about Rachel though.

I realized I was gripping my phone so tight my knuckles were blanched. I loosened my hold.

The last thing I needed was to break this phone too.

> When can we go meet this Bishop Biddle?

Kade finally responded to everything. Up to now, he'd silently been observing mine and Wanda's texts.

My shoulders fell as I read his message.

I don't have any way to get out of here. Allie took my keys.

There was stillness in the chat for a moment. I knew we were all thinking. Then the little blue bubbles popped up again. Wanda was typing.

> Could Kade and I stop by there?

I bit my lip.

No.

That would *not* work. I knew that without even thinking about it.

> He wouldn't talk to non-members about church affairs. Especially if rumors of murder made a former member leave the state.

My mind was racing. How could I get away long enough to go all the way to Beckham's Road and talk to Lawrence Biddle?

Would he even talk to me?

A woman. Unmarried. Without her father. Without a husband. He might not even acknowledge me beyond a civil nod or a handshake.

> I wouldn't want to go without you, anyway.

I had to do a double take at that text.

It was Kade. But not in the group chat. Just to me.

I blinked, but the message didn't disappear. It didn't go away. It was still there. Waiting for me.

I wouldn't want to go without you, anyway.

He couldn't mean that the way it sounded, could he? He certainly didn't mean it the way it felt.

What should I text back? Should I text him back at all?

My thumbs hovered over the keys, and then they were moving before I could stop them.

> Me either.

I didn't know what I meant by that. I hit send anyway. Before I could delete it.

Then I set the phone down like it had burned through my hand.

What was happening?

I stared at the wall across from my bed. The wide cedar paneling soaking in what was left of the evening light.

Two seconds later, my phone vibrated against the comforter, buzzing into the mattress.

> Let's think about it tonight, talk about it some more in the morning.

Kade.

But in the group chat this time.

> Okay. Not like we could go over there tonight anyway.

Wanda.

She was still typing.

I waited, my hands unsteady holding my phone.

> I got a test to study for, so I'm going offline for the night. Text me if you need anything, Em.

A smile crept onto my face.

> Good luck studying, Wanda.

I texted her back and then waited.

Everything was silent again. Still.

I set my phone down and rolled my neck against my shoulders. I needed something for this stiffness, the low, constant throb in my head.

I pulled open the narrow drawer of my side table and found ibuprofen. I popped a couple of the red pills into my mouth and swallowed them dry.

I didn't feel like going downstairs for water. Wasn't worth it. I'd get a sip from the bathroom sink once the house was quiet, and everyone was in bed.

My phone buzzed again, humming into the fibers of my bed.

> How are you, Em?

Something warm fizzed beneath my ribs.

It was Kade again.

In the text that was just him and me.

I didn't answer. Not right away. I couldn't. I stood by the bed and stared at the screen until it dimmed itself.

Then it was like a switch flipped inside my brain. I scooped up my phone, desperately tapping, swiping, trying to find his text again.

It sprung to life on the screen.

How are you, Em?

I stared at it, lowering myself back onto my bed without realizing. My fingers moved slowly over the screen.

I don't know.

I hovered over send. Then I deleted it.

> A little tired.

I sent that instead.

> What did you do at work today?

I swallowed. Hard.

He was asking about my day. Not about the Rachel mystery. Not about ghosts. Not about my parents' lies, or my panic attacks. Kade was simply asking about my day.

And it paralyzed me.

What did I do today?

Scrubbed years of grease off cabinets. Burned my sinuses with degreaser. Hallucinated. Talked to the crawdad guy from Gracie's forbidden pretzel bag.

> Cleaned cabinets.

I hit send before I could overthink it anymore.

> To get ready to paint?

Kade answered fast.

I couldn't help but think that he'd been waiting.

Message app open.

Watching for my response.

> Yeah. Listened to some music while I worked.

I sent the text and watched as the little blue bubbles popped up while he typed. I imagined the phone in Kade's hands. Big warm hands dwarfing the smartphone screen.

I wondered if he was in bed like I was. Or sitting on a couch, the TV on in the background. What did he like to watch on TV?

> What music do you like?

He asked another question, and my neck warmed.

> Ozzy. KISS. Rock and Roll, mainly. I like some pop, country, and blues too.

The room went silent as I hit *send*. I'd never told *anyone* what I liked. Only what I was supposed to like. Quiet gospel and hymns, none of the new stuff. No drums or electric guitar.

> You ever heard of The SteelDrivers?

> They're my comfort band.

> No, but I'll look them up.

I tucked my feet under my blankets and rested back against my pillow as my phone buzzed against my hand again.

> I guess I'll get a shower and go to bed. Four a.m. shift at the lube joint tomorrow.

I grimaced.

> That's early!

He was quiet for a moment, then texted back.

> You'd be surprised how many people stop to get their oil changed on their way to work.

He didn't text anymore after that, and I wasn't sure if I should either.

Should I say goodnight? Do people do that? I usually didn't with Wanda, we stopped texting and picked it back up when we could.

I decided that's what I'd do tonight, with Kade. I set my phone by my pillow and stared up at the ceiling. Too wired to sleep, but too tired to move.

I wondered if, somewhere across town, Kade was doing the same. Except, he had a home of his own, a job to get to in the morning.

I was stuck here, at my parents' house. I'd go back to work in the morning, probably painting the cabinets I'd spent all day scrubbing. I'd eat the bologna sandwich Allie always packed and I'd come back home to my room, avoiding everyone as much as possible.

I wondered what Kade had for lunch on weekdays. Did he pack a sandwich? Pick something up? I wondered what he liked to eat.

My phone buzzed beside me, and I almost fell out of the bed trying to grab it.

Did Kade text me again?

But there weren't any notifications on the lock screen.

I swiped and tapped, opened the message app.

Nothing.

I didn't have a message from Kade or Wanda. Everything was still and silent, like when I'd set my phone by my pillow.

I sat up, dangling my feet off my bed, pondering the phantom vibration.

Maybe I imagined it?

I didn't have socials downloaded yet, so it couldn't have been a notification from that.

Maybe the phone was reminding me to do an update.

I searched through settings and finally found the software tab. No updates available.

My back sagged. I probably imagined it.

Was I *that* hopeful about whatever this was with Kade? Was I that excited that I would imagine a text that was never there?

Probably.

I shifted on the bed. A paper slid out from the comforter and I jumped.

Rachel's placement agreement.

Holy shit, that was reckless.

I grabbed my saggy, orange backpack and found the file, slipping Rachel's placement back on top.

But then I stopped. The yellow highlighter...

I grabbed my phone, swiped through the group chat, found the picture I'd sent earlier.

There it was, bright as day. That smear of sickly yellow. Glowing. Loud.

It *had* been there.

I looked back at the physical page, lying there at the top of the file. There was no highlighter. Nothing.

Just ordinary faded type and some scribbled handwritten notes on brittle, stained paper.

No highlighter.

34

SALT ON ICE

Dip. Tap. Brush.

I let the monotony soak in.

Dip. Tap. Brush.

SKREEEEE-CHUNK

The table saw shrieked through wood, metal teeth catching, spitting sawdust like bone powder.

Even that didn't startle me. It's hard to flinch at noise when a ghost girl's been sitting next to you all day.

If it was the same Rachel from my room the other night, I wouldn't be this focused on painting.

Dip. Tap. Brush.

It *was* Rachel, I could tell by the hollow eyes and flame of tangled, red hair. But this wasn't the little girl holding Beagle in the dark.

This girl was older. The teen from the yearbook. From the pregnancy photo. Leaning on the cracked post of my bed.

But her mouth was sewn shut.

Huge, black stitches pulled her lips together. Blood oozed from the punctures, dripping down her chin and pooling beneath the cabinet where she sat.

Except... there was no blood.

I ran my black tennis shoe through the puddle. It came out clean. There was just paint-stained subfloor beneath me.

I tried talking to her when I first got here this morning.

"Rachel," I'd whispered. "Who did that to you?"

She didn't move. Didn't answer. Of course not. Her mouth was sewn shut.

"I'm trying to find out what happened to you," I told her, then we were silent most of the day.

She moved places one time, when I did.

I'd refilled my paint bucket and swapped cabinets. Put my back to her. Not to be rude... It was just hard looking at her. With all the stitches. And all that blood.

But she followed me. Now she sat on the counter in front of where I was working.

I almost touched her once, when I caught a paint run down the side of the cabinet. It stung, like ice slicing under my skin.

She flinched too. Her hollow eyes widened. The stitches pulled taut, trembling as if she were trying to speak.

"Sorry," I'd whispered.

She shifted on the countertop. I thought she'd leave. But she slipped her boney fingers under her thighs and sat on her hands.

I didn't look at her again after that, even if I knew she was still there.

She didn't leave. And I kept painting.

Allie called me from the living room a little after one.

"We're sitting down for sandwiches if you're hungry, Em!"

"I'm fine!" I called back, and she didn't say anything else.

Don didn't insist I join them. Gracie didn't come and ask if I was okay. They'd all seemed to have gotten used to me not eating with them.

I was living on crackers and apples I kept stashed in my backpack. Or the occasional bowl of leftovers I'd steal from the fridge after everyone else was asleep.

But I couldn't avoid them altogether. I had to ride with Gracie to work.

That was better than riding with Allie and Don, which I was stuck doing if Gracie was in one of her moods and too nervous to drive.

I managed to keep conversation to a minimum though, which wasn't *too* out of the ordinary anyways. I hadn't talked regularly with Allie since the whole puberty thing, when she seemed to decide she had to choose between me and her very-important-couldn't-tell-him-no husband.

My conversations with Don had never existed to start with, so this wasn't any different for us.

Gracie...

Since that weird pretzel situation on the job the other day, she hadn't really said much to me.

I wondered if she was still researching schools. Had she heard from the one she applied to? I didn't know how any of that worked. Had she applied to anymore? Had she really even applied at all?

That wasn't like Gracie, to sneak around Don and Allie. Especially for something as *worldly* as college.

"What do you think about Gracie?" I whispered, without looking up at Rachel.

I knew she couldn't answer me. Not right now. But maybe she could think about it and answer me later.

"I think she's gotten worse since we moved to Caster."

I was barely muttering my words. I put just enough breath behind them that I hoped Rachel could hear me, but anyone listening from outside this kitchen couldn't.

"She's always had her *habits* but lately..."

I let my words run off and stood back to assess my work.

Fuck.

I only had one end of a cabinet left to paint and I'd be done for the day. Of course, I couldn't have enough paint left in my bucket to finish up.

"That's my luck." I muttered and went to the five-gallon bucket of eggshell white to pour a *little* paint into my bucket.

It was heavy. I've always been awkward. I poured too much, like every other time.

"I'll have to pour it back once I'm done with this stupid cabinet."

I didn't mean to, but as I picked up my bucket to get back to painting, I glanced at Rachel. I almost dropped my paint.

Bloody tears were streaming down her face, mixing with the thick, black blood dripping from her sewn lips. The stitches strained across her mouth again. Her whole milk-glass body was heaving, thin shoulders shuddering.

I almost ran to her. Like I could help.

She's dead.

Everything in my body froze.

Rachel's dead.

I was looking at her… ghost? She couldn't die again, no matter what might be happening to her right now.

"Rachel, what's the matter?" I whispered, almost too loudly, as I stepped cautiously back to the cabinet.

I'd forgotten about painting. My brain shut down, but my hands didn't. *Dip. Tap. Brush.*

I glanced at Rachel. Bloody tears ran down her neck, stained the front of her pink nightgown.

"Is someone hurting you?"

I remembered how she looked in the rearview of Don's truck that night. How a shadow moved behind her and her face had twisted in pain.

My hands went cold.

"Is something else here?"

But that time Rachel answered me. She communicated with me. One on one.

It was only a shake of her head, but my heart almost stopped.

Up until now, I'd found some comfort in the thought that maybe I was imagining all of this.

Rachel, sitting on the countertop, moving around the kitchen with me as I worked, her lips stitched shut so she couldn't talk.

It was easier thinking I'd made her up. That all the panic and anxiety was catching up. I was going crazy—even just a little bit. Realizing she was real was so much worse than thinking I'd imagined her.

"What's the matter?" I whispered, my voice shaking.

But there was no time for her to try to answer.

I was finishing the last couple swipes of my paint brush over the side of the cabinet when Don and Allie came into the room, gentle smiles plastered on their faces.

Horror stung every cell in my body.

What if they saw her? What if they thought I'd summoned her? Sold my soul to witchcraft? Or worse—what if they could hurt her? Stop her from communicating with me?

As soon as that thought entered my head, a slow thump started at the base of my skull. Two minutes ago, I was freaking out she'd answered me. Because it meant it wasn't all in my head. And now I was scared it might stop.

"It looks so good in here, Em," Allie said, voice all sunshine. "The cabinets look brand new."

Don nodded. "You've been busy."

I looked at him. At her.

Couldn't they see her? The blood? The stitches? Couldn't they hear the sobs?

"We mean it!" Allie insisted. "You're working hard."

Don nodded again.

I finally took the chance, glanced at Rachel.

Her eyes rolled white. The blood tracked down her neck, eating away her skin, exposing chipped bone and blackened muscle.

But it wasn't any of that that made my breath snag. It was her face. The distorted, twisted turn of her features. It was pure terror personified.

I wanted to rush to her, ask her what was wrong. Who was hurting her? What was happening?

But I couldn't.

All I could do was stand there and watch as she dissolved. Like ice when you dash salt across it. She melted away until I was staring at an empty countertop. She was gone.

It hit me, way harder than I expected. Rachel wasn't beside me anymore.

It felt like all of this took half an hour to complete, but it must have been less than a couple seconds. Allie and Don were still talking to me. They hadn't seen a thing, or noticed anything about me that would cause them alarm—not my blank stare at the countertop, or my horrified gasp when I saw Rachel's face melting into nothingness.

"We want you to have these back," Allie said, softly, pressing something into my hands.

Hard.

Metallic.

"You've earned them," she whispered.

I looked down at my hand. My keys. To the house. To the work van and Don's truck.

I wanted to say *thank you,* but the words got stuck in my throat. Like they knew better than I did.

What had I earned? The right to a home I was working to keep? Transportation that I helped pay for?

"It's only because we love you." Don's voice chimed in. "We want the truth so deep inside of you that no one can take it away."

"We want to trust you again." Allie was quieter now. "But you have to meet us halfway. You can go to the library, even get coffee if you want."

"Drive-thru only," Don added.

"But we're trusting you not to talk to those people again."

I couldn't look away from my hand, cocooned around the keys, Allie's fingers wrapped around mine.

Suddenly, my mind was nowhere near here. It was already racing. I could go to the church. See if Bishop Biddle would talk to me. I'd say I was going to the library. But I'd go to the church. Find that man. Ask him about Rachel.

"Can we trust you, Emily?" Allie's question floated into my conscious just in time.

What do you think, *Mom*?

"Of course," I whispered, with as much sincerity as I could muster.

"You're growing up," Don said. "The world's waiting to swallow girls like you whole."

I didn't even hear him.

I glanced back at the spot on the countertop where I'd watched a ghostly, tormented form of Rachel Bagwell dissolve into nothingness.

"Here," Don said, pushing money toward me. "For gas."

I hesitated. This was too much. Too nice. Too fucking sudden.

"Don't make us regret this," Allie said, her voice laced with warning.

I took the bills. A crumpled twenty and a ten.

"Gracie's going to start helping more, running errands. We'd like the same for you."

Gracie? Going places by herself? That... no. That wasn't Gracie.

"Be honest with us," Allie pressed.

"We don't want to see you pulled away." Don reminded me. "The devil works through simple things. Innocent things. People that seem *nice*."

He lingered on that last word.

Wanda and Kade. I knew he was talking about Wanda and Kade.

"I'll be careful." I forced the words out, prayed for forgiveness as I articulated yet another lie to the people who claimed to be my parents.

I wasn't going to be careful. I wasn't staying away from Wanda or Kade. And I *wasn't* going to the library.

I was going to the church. To talk to Bishop Lawrence Biddle. About Rachel Bagwell's foster placement in 1987. About her disappearance. About her murder.

And I was taking Wanda and Kade with me.

35

Milk. Eggs. Bread.

I couldn't drive myself to the library that night. I'd ridden to work in the van, shoulder to shoulder with Don.

There hadn't even been a minute to text Wanda and Kade until we got home. When I finally did, I told them I had my keys back. That I'd get to the library tomorrow afternoon.

Wanda responded first.

> That's kind of weird.

She wasn't wrong. Everything about this felt off.

> They're letting Gracie go places alone now.

That was the part that made my stomach twist. But while I still had my keys, I needed to move.

Before they changed their minds. Before Rachel disappeared for good.

> I'd like to meet Gracie one day. I only know her through whatever it was that cornered us in the bathroom that day.

A chill worked up my spine. That hadn't been Gracie.

I glanced up—in time to catch the antler chandelier above my bed sway on its chain. Like it did every at night.

My phone buzzed again.

> Shit.

Wanda.

Then more bubbles. She was still typing.

> My HESI Exit Exam is tomorrow! I thought it was Thursday.

My shoulders sagged.

> Em and I could go, if you don't care.

Kade. It was the first time he'd said anything tonight.

I bit my lip. I'd never spent time alone with him. We'd texted—mostly about music, or dumb things we'd seen that day.

> I hate to miss seeing Biddle's face when you bring up Rachel, but that's fine. I'd probably blow the whole thing, anyway. I'd want to give him a piece of my mind.

I stared at the thread. I was going with Kade. To the church. The two of us.

> You alright with that, Em?

His text lit up the group chat.

> Yeah, that's fine.

I answered fast.

My pulse danced in my throat. Why was I this nervous? It wasn't a date.

We hadn't even told each other how we felt—just Wanda. I wondered if she'd told Kade that I liked him too.

> You two have fun while I wring my brain out on this test.

We were going to see Biddle. Kade and I. We were going to see the bishop of a church I hadn't set foot in for five years. To ask him about a dead girl. A girl he helped place in a foster home, using his position as caseworker, under the youth ministry branded with his church's name.

Thinking through it helped. A little.

But the next day didn't go as planned.

I'd worked hard to finish early—by three, maybe a little before. I planned to get to the library by four. Allie knew that. I told her first thing this morning. Same as I always did on days I wanted to go to the library.

Things were normal. Status quo. Until 2:45.

"Do you mind riding with Gracie to the library, Em?"

Allie asked it casually, walking through the bedroom where I was breaking my neck painting the last corner of the ceiling.

"What?" I twisted to look at her. Eggshell paint dripped onto my neck.

"I need you to ride with Gracie to the library this afternoon," Allie repeated, watching me wipe the sticky, smearing paint off my skin.

That wasn't a question. It wasn't up to me. If I didn't ride with Gracie, I wouldn't go to the library. Or to the church.

"Sure." I half-shrugged. "Gracie has someplace she's going this afternoon?"

"M-hm." Allie was already leaving the room.

I stood there, on the ladder, watching after her a moment.

Where would Gracie be going? I could go to the library alone. They'd recently added getting coffee. That's all I could do alone. Where could Gracie go?

She'd never been anywhere alone. She always stayed home. She usually went to pieces around a lot of people, loud noises, even congested traffic. She couldn't function.

I grabbed my rag and wiped my neck, still feeling the paint drying against my skin.

Oh well. Whatever it was, it would have to be fine. I'd ride with Gracie. Tell her to pick me up in three hours. She wouldn't care if Kade was waiting for me when we pulled in the parking lot.

I would've lied too. The first man to ever pay attention to you and he wants you to stop talking to him. Gracie's words from the other day echoed in my skull as I cleaned my paintbrush a few minutes later. *I'm proud of you, you know. Things need to change.*

Everything would be okay.

Even if I couldn't tell Gracie I wasn't staying at the library this afternoon. I couldn't tell her I was going to the church, to talk to the bishop, about a dead girl.

But she would understand Kade meeting me.

"Where are you going this afternoon?" I kept my voice cheerful as I buckled my seatbelt in Don's truck a quarter hour later.

Gracie prepared to drive, studying the dash like a textbook.

"Hm?"

"This afternoon," I repeated. "You had somewhere to go?"

She looked up at me, but her dull green eyes seemed far away. "Oh... yeah. Milk. Eggs. Bread. That's it."

That made me stop.

Her voice was right. But her tone was hollow. Like an echo through a dream. The words were certainly all wrong. Shopping? For things I'd seen stocked in the fridge just this morning?

I watched Gracie turn the key. The truck purred to life.

"I saw two dozen eggs and a couple loaves of bread the last time I was in the kitchen."

Gracie was stiff, white knuckling the wheel, eyes darting between mirrors as she backed out of the job site.

"Milk. Eggs. Bread," she repeated, eyes fixed ahead as we turned onto the street.

I slumped against my seat.

There was no way Gracie was going anywhere by herself. She was too nervous simply getting out onto the road.

"I didn't check the milk." I mumbled and watched my sister slowly accelerate to *just* the speed limit.

"You want me to drive?" I asked her, after a long stretch of silence.

She was slowing down forty yards from a yellow light.

"I'm driving."

Barely. I thought it, but I didn't say it.

At this rate, we *might* get to the library by five-thirty or so.

I tried to relax into the vinyl seat. Tried to ignore everything that was wrong about this afternoon.

Did the man, Kade, get you a phone? Gracie's words came back to me. *I knew you wouldn't quit talking to him.*

I closed my eyes for a brief second and took a short breath. At least Gracie trusted me.

She might not understand how *really* wrong our upbringing had been—I couldn't even grasp all of that. But I was scratching the surface. I was digging. And Gracie seemed to know that it needed done.

You don't need to stop digging, she'd said, and given me what was left of her pretzels.

"How's the college application going?" I finally summoned the nerve to ask, but I regretted it immediately.

Gracie's back went stiff against the seat, her hands bared down on the wheel, and she swerved into the next lane enough I clutched my backpack to my chest.

The passing car laid on the horn, and I grabbed the armrest on the door.

The horn died behind us, swallowed by thick silence. Like someone flipped a switch.

I couldn't hear the hum of the tires against asphalt, or the *click, click, click* of the signal as Gracie prepared to turn.

I sat up and jiggled the fan control. It was warm enough today we needed air conditioner, but I couldn't hear the *rurr* of the compressor.

I touched the vent. Cool air rushed out against my skin.

Everything was... silent.

And Gracie hadn't answered me. She'd almost had a head-on collision, but she hadn't answered me.

I waited until she'd turned off the main highway, down the little backroad that took us toward Caster, before I tried again.

"I didn't mean to upset you," I said, quietly.

Gracie glanced at me. "How did you upset me?"

I watched her profile. The hard, constant stare down the two-lane road.

"Asking about school."

She glanced at me again, her brow furrowed. "School?"

I bit my lip. Was she pretending she hadn't heard me?

"The other day. You told me you applied to an online college."

Her brow rose on her forehead, but she didn't look away from the road that time. "Em, I wouldn't do that."

It felt like she slapped me.

Shifted in my seat, I turned and leaned my back against the truck door so I could watch her.

"You came into the kitchen at the job." I tried to help her remember. "You told me you'd applied to an online school."

Gracie sat back against the seat a little, her iron hold on the steering wheel loosened.

"You had pretzels." I reminded her. "Cajun seasoned. From Hardy's."

She gave a soft, almost pitying shake of her head. "Em… I don't even like spicy foods."

It was happening again. A moment that *meant* something, like the purple blanket with her name on it, folded up in the hidden room inside the wall. But she couldn't remember it. Or claimed she couldn't remember it.

I took a breath, turning back to face the road. "Gracie, do you remember telling me that they fixed the leak in the ceiling at Hardy's?"

She nodded. "I rode with Dad the other day, to pick up carpet for the job on Nance Street."

"You got a bunch of cleaning stuff too." Hope surged in my veins, but I tried to keep my tone even, my voice down.

"For the bathroom." Gracie agreed with me.

"And you checked out at register five—without *Dad*—because you bought pretzels."

She was quiet, but she relaxed. She took one hand off the wheel, rested her elbow on the door.

I clutched my backpack tighter. Gracie *never* relaxed this much while she was driving.

She glanced at me again. "You haven't been sleeping much, have you?"

My face stung.

"Gracie!" I couldn't hold my even tone. "You seriously don't remember sharing your pretzels with me? There was a funny crawdad man on the front of the bag, with a bucket of crayfish in his hand!"

Who came to life. As I fell through the kitchen floor. And he gave me Rachel's placement paper. Which also felt alive...

I'd stopped suddenly and Gracie turned and looked at me again.

Her eyes were on me way longer than should've been possible, especially while she was driving.

Or did I imagine that too?

Then she smiled. A simple, sweet smile, before turning back to the road.

I blinked.

Did she know where my mind had gone? To the crawdad man in the hidden room? The pulsing, fleshy paper with the putrid, yellow blisters highlighting the bishop's name? Had I said it all out loud?

I had no idea anymore.

"Are you getting out?" I felt like she'd shaken me from a dream.

"What?" I looked around, out the windshield, the passenger window. We were at the library.

I spun back, checking the dash clock. Ten minutes after four.

I closed my eyes.

We hadn't left the job site until four fifteen.

"Do you want to go with me to the store?" Gracie asked, completely calm.

"No!" I grabbed at the door handle, yanking it open.

I wasn't afraid of scaring her anymore, wasn't afraid of making her suspicious.

"Hey, wait!" She leaned over and caught the door before I could shut it. "What time am I supposed to pick you up?"

My heart was pounding. I watched my sister. Waited for her nails to grow long, or her teeth to turn sharp and black. Something to tell me this wasn't even Gracie I was talking to.

But nothing happened.

She stared at me like I was being crazy.

"Three hours." My voice came out raw, it burned my throat.

"Okay." Gracie smiled at me again, her normal, natural smile. "I'll pick you up at a quarter after seven."

She pulled the truck door shut and put the thing in reverse, backing seamlessly out of the parking space.

She waved at me as she pulled out onto the road and drove away.

36

THE BIKE

I was thankful Kade wasn't already waiting at the library.

I'd thought Gracie would understand him meeting me. But after that ride, I wasn't sure she'd understand *anything*.

I slipped inside the library, long enough to make sure she was gone. Then I stepped back out and sank onto the cold concrete bench to wait.

Without distraction, I watched the digital numbers on my phone tick by for three long minutes.

I could handle seeing Rachel, her lips sewn shut, sitting on a countertop all day. I didn't *like* it, but I could handle it.

I could handle the stench of corpse bleeding into my sinuses, even if it made me vomit. I could handle watching her skin slough off as she tried to sit up.

What I couldn't handle was time slipping.

Forward or backward, it didn't matter. I hated the feeling that I didn't have a grip on reality. Like I was sleepwalking through someone else's nightmare. Like one day, I'd finally wake up and none of it would be real.

Time slips didn't happen, did they?

Ghosts? Sure. Spirits? Maybe. If God were real, if angels and the devil were real, then ghosts could be too.

But time didn't bend. It didn't vanish. Time was cruel and constant. This was my brain screwing with me.

"Hey, Em." Kade's voice made me jump.

"Didn't mean to scare you." He smiled, and the tension in my chest loosened an inch.

I shook my head. "It's fine." I stood from the bench, grabbing my backpack. "I guess I was daydreaming."

"I was inside." He nodded toward the library. "Hope you haven't been sitting out here too long."

"Only a couple of minutes." I grimaced. "Allie insisted I ride with Gracie. She dropped me off."

Kade shoved his hands in his pockets. "Well... that complicates things."

My stomach lurched. "Does it?"

"My El Camino blew a head gasket. I brought my bike."

My stomach dropped.

A bicycle. There was no way we could both ride a bicycle and no way we'd get all the way to Beckham's Road on foot.

"Would you be comfortable on a motorcycle?"

Motorcycle.

Holy *shit*.

A laugh burst out of me before I could stop it. "Oh my gosh—I thought you meant a bicycle."

Kade grinned as I laughed. "Nope. I upgraded after I got my license."

It felt good to laugh.

Too good.

Like every knot of tension inside of me had snapped all at once. The kind of laugh that verges on crying. Too much. Too fast. A release I hadn't planned for.

Kade didn't say anything. He waited, laughing a little himself, and let me burn it out.

"I feel so stupid," I muttered, wiping at my eyes.

"Nah, you're fine." He shook his head. "Lots of guys ride bikes, especially in town. I wasn't very clear."

I finally got myself under control. My stomach cramped from the effort.

"I'm sorry." I shook my head again. "I don't know what got into me. It's been a long day. And I didn't have any coffee this morning."

"You don't have to apologize." His voice was calm. Warm. "It's been a hell of a couple weeks. Nice to hear you can still laugh."

My neck flushed. I didn't know what to say to something like that. From someone like Kade.

I shrugged and mumbled that I'd never been on a motorcycle before.

"I can show you," he said. "If you're comfortable riding with me."

And that's how I ended up taking my first ride on a motorcycle—holding onto Kade Weston.

Time blurred after that.

Not like it had with Gracie. Not like ghosts. Not like memories slipping out from under me. Not like hours vanishing mid-tick of the second hand.

This time, it blurred in a good way.

Kade led me around the side of the library to where his motorcycle was parked. Gracie had driven right past it pulling in. I wasn't sure how I missed it, how I didn't put it together. Kade had mentioned his bike before.

It wasn't flashy, simple black and a little dusty, but the seat was wide, and the paint caught the afternoon sun just enough to gleam. He pulled a helmet off the handlebar and passed it to me.

"You ever worn one of these?"

I shook my head. The padding was heavier than I expected. It muffled the world as I buckled the strap beneath my chin.

"You okay in that dress?" he asked.

I glanced down at myself. A navy-blue skirt caught around my legs, splattered in faint streaks of paint. Didn't exactly scream motorcycle chic. Or even *safe*.

"I'll manage," I said.

It'd be so much easier in jeans. That quiet thought slipped in before I could shove it away.

It was the first time I ever let myself *want* to wear pants.

I hated the dresses. The capes. The denim jumpers. But I'd never let myself admit I'd wear something else. Something *worldly*. Something that would make it easier to ride a motorcycle.

I took a step toward the bike, then stopped, my heart pounding louder than the engine.

It hit me. All at once. I was getting on a motorcycle. With Kade.

I hadn't given myself time to really process what I'd agreed to. Now, he sat there waiting.

This was *not* going to go well.

I would fall. My dress would catch on some part of the bike I didn't even know existed. I'd make a fucking fool of myself.

Kade didn't rush me.

I adjusted the helmet strap again, for something to do. Then I climbed on behind him. I'd never done anything like this. Never even *thought* about it.

Don detested motorcycles, or rather, the men who drove them.

It's not transportation, it's a temper tantrum on wheels. Don would spit every time he passed a rider on the highway. *Leather jackets and loud pipes. Little boys playing dress-up, hoping someone thinks they're dangerous.*

I was finding out Don was wrong, more often than not. Kade wasn't any of those things.

I tightened my hands around his waist, surprised by how solid he felt. Warm through the soft fabric of his T-shirt.

"Lean with me," he said over his shoulder. "Especially in the curves. You don't have to grip tight, just move with the bike."

I nodded, though I wasn't sure if he could see it. The engine rumbled beneath us, low and steady, and a surge of excitement thundered through my veins.

I squeezed Kade a little tighter than I meant to.

"You ready?" He turned his head toward me.

"Yeah." My voice came out kind of shrill.

And then we moved.

The first few seconds were awkward. My arms were too stiff. My skirt caught weird under my knees. But then we rounded a turn, and Kade leaned, slightly, and I did too.

The wind hit my face as he accelerated down Caster's main street. My lungs opened up. My ribs stretched wide, like I could finally breathe.

I felt alive. For the first time since... I could remember. I didn't feel like a passenger. We felt like a team, Kade and I. And I'd never felt that with another human being in my life. Not even Gracie.

We didn't get too far down the road before Kade pulled off near a little gas station.

I recognized the place. Gracie and I had stopped here to fill up Don's truck before work sometimes. We'd stop here because there was a little coffee bar inside.

The coffee was too expensive. Allie put a stop to that right away. And Don didn't like the place either. That's when the drive-thru rule started.

"Is something wrong?" My hands shook slightly when I unbuckled the helmet.

"Nah," Kade said. "Can we spare a couple minutes for caffeine?"

"I told Gracie three hours."

"Then we get some joe." He flashed a grin. "You said you didn't have any this morning, right?"

I smiled back, surprised by how easy it felt this time.

We sat at one of the metal picnic tables off to the side, coffees between us. His was a strong Americano. Mine, a sweet and creamy vanilla latte. I folded both hands around the paper cup, letting the heat soak into my skin.

I'd paid for this coffee myself, with some of the gas money Don gave me. I would've bought Kade's too, but he insisted on getting his own.

"This church is down Beckham's Road, right?" he asked, lifting his cup for a sip.

I nodded. "It's at the very end."

"I thought so. I've been out that way. Went looking for a hunting spot one fall with a buddy from school."

He shook his head, a half-smile forming. "I think I met this Biddle guy. Somebody came storming out of the church and ran us off."

I bit my lip, tried to hide it behind the edge of my cup.

"We wouldn't have gone down there if we knew it was private," he added. "Someone told us it was public game management land. The man who came out of that shop-looking building was real clear that it wasn't."

I'd never spent much time with Lawrence Biddle. Never seen him outside the sanctuary, outside his office, outside his white collar and steel-tight smile.

But the man Kade was describing sounded less like a bishop and more like Don.

And maybe that shouldn't have surprised me.

If living with Don Lyles had taught me anything, it was that some people wore their kindness like a costume. A borrowed thing. A mask they learned to slip on and off depending on the audience.

Don could be the warmest, most welcoming man you'd ever meet—in public. At home, he'd dump his dinner in the trash because Allie said the wrong thing during prayer.

"Do you like your coffee?" Kade's question pulled me out of my haze.

"Yeah, I do." I smiled at him. "You?"

He nodded. "I always get the same thing when I come here. They have the best espresso."

"I've been here once or twice." I lifted my cup for a sip. "The coffee's really good."

My latte had finally cooled some. I took a real sip this time, the warmth of coffee and milk laced with vanilla softening something in my chest.

"That espresso'll keep you up tonight." Kade shook his head. "I guess I should've had tea or something. I go in at four again tomorrow."

I cringed. "I'm not an early riser, if I can help it. I couldn't imagine getting *to* work at four. You have to be up at three thirty or better!"

"Three fifteen," he said, and I shook my head.

I noticed he was almost done with his coffee, so I took a bigger sip of mine.

"I guess you get used to it," he added after a while. "Feels like I've been working this job forever, but it's only been a couple of years."

"You said you work at a lube place?"

"Yeah..." He shrugged. "It's monotonous. Same thing every day, just different customers. Most of them are rude. All of them are impatient. Not exactly my dream job."

"What *is* your dream?" I asked, quietly.

He looked at me for a long moment and I wondered if anyone had ever asked him that.

"Get out of Caster," he said, finally. "Go out west maybe, or up north. Travel. See places."

He downed the rest of his Americano. "I'd really like to work on bikes one day. Maybe open a shop. I guess I want something that's mine. Something nobody can take."

"That makes sense." I felt how quiet my voice was. "It sounds like you've thought about it a lot."

"I've been in Caster a long time. I went to school here. Learned to drive. Graduated. I guess I'm burnt out on it."

I'd lived in Caster for six years and hadn't seen any of it. Not really. I'd been tucked away tight in the old Dickerson house, under Don and Allie's thumbs, apron strings tied up tight.

But I didn't have any real interest in Caster. I'd dreamed of traveling too. Getting away from here.

But, for me, dreams had always been just that, dreams. A figment I could visit, but never live in.

You didn't act on dreams. Not in the Lyles' household. You stayed put. In your place. Waiting your turn. Even if your turn never came.

"What about you?" Kade surprised me. I looked up from my latte to see he'd been watching me. "What do *you* want to do, Em?"

The words sat heavy on the table between us.

How could I possibly explain everything my brain had run through? Kade wouldn't understand it. Not being allowed to dream. And me not doing anything about it. Not trying to grow out my wings. Not trying to fly. Just... waiting.

"I... I don't know."

Kade was quiet. Like he knew I needed a moment to think, to find my words. He fidgeted with the black plastic lid of his cup and waited on me.

"I've never been allowed to think about it," I finally admitted. "I'd want to travel, I know. Go somewhere and not have to ask permission. Somewhere that's not *here*."

He nodded like he understood.

When we got back on the bike, I settled behind Kade without hesitation. The wind rushed past us as we took the main road again, this time toward Beckham's.

Toward the church. Toward answers. Toward something that felt a little bit like freedom. Or maybe, that was already inside of me.

A tiny seed taking root, pushing upwards. Out of the dark. Out of everything I was told I had to be. Maybe I didn't know where I was going. But for the first time, I really wanted to go.

I wanted more than survival. I wanted something real. A life that was mine.

37

STEPPING BACK INSIDE

The ride down Beckham's Road wasn't as rough as I'd imagined, even with the red clay ruts and loose gravel.

I clung to Kade's jacket as he weaved around every pothole and washboard strip like he'd done it a thousand times.

"I thought this would be hard to drive on a motorcycle."

It was the first time I'd tried talking while he was driving, raising my voice over the growl of the engine.

"Nah, she's a DR-Z," he called back over his shoulder. "Not a street princess. She eats gravel for breakfast."

I had to smile at that. Kade must've felt it, because I swear he smiled too.

When we took the last turn on Beckham's, and the cinderblock church came into view, I was surprised to see the gravel lot full.

Rows of pickup trucks and dented sedans sat in slanted lines, halos of dust clinging to their windshields. The sun hung low behind the pines, casting long, ghostly shadows across the parked cars.

Kade cut the engine. For a minute, we sat there—on the bike, me still holding onto him—staring at the full lot.

"I haven't been to a church in a while." He rested a hand absently over mine. "But I thought it was Sundays and sometimes Wednesdays."

I groaned, the memory clicking into place. "It's the first Tuesday of the month."

I swung off the bike, but the ground didn't feel steady under my feet.

Kade climbed off too, taking the helmet from me. "Okay...?"

I took a breath and focused on the gravel beneath my shoes. "It's foot washing," I told him. "They do it every first Tuesday."

His brow rose. "Foot washing?"

"Yeah. Jesus washed his disciples' feet before he was crucified." My voice caught. "They take that part literally. 'I have given you an example, that ye should do as I have done to you.'"

Kade watched me.

"It's about humility." The more I tried to explain, the stupider I felt. "To show they're willing to serve each other."

Silence stretched between us.

"That's what they say, anyway." I shrugged one shoulder, my voice too quiet.

"I thought stuff like that in the Bible was symbolic," Kade said finally. "Not... like, the whole church actually doing it."

I tugged at my sleeves, suddenly too aware of the skin showing above my elbows.

"It's crazy," I said, forcing a smile. "You wanna just go? We can come back another time."

Kade glanced at the quiet cinderblock building. He ran a hand through the wild mess of dark curls on his head, barely taming them.

"We came to find out about Rachel, didn't we?"

I remembered her face. Bloody tears. Skin peeling like tissue paper.

I hadn't told Kade about that yet. That she'd spent the whole day beside me, quiet, watching me paint. Until Don and Allie walked in.

Then she warped and twisted in pain, silent sobs shaking her body.

When Don and Allie came into the room.

I paused. I thought something else had been hurting her. Something I couldn't see. Something that had sewn her mouth shut. But I asked her. And she'd shaken her head.

Could it have been... them? The church blurred around the gables. Was Rachel afraid of Don and Allie?

"If you're not comfortable..." Kade started but cut himself off. "We can come back another time."

I looked at him. His words felt far away, like I had to reach through fog to grab hold of them.

"No," I said quickly. "If you're okay going in, I'll be fine. We need to find out what Biddle knows."

Kade nodded, but he didn't move until I did. He waited for me to take the first step.

I wasn't even thinking when, halfway across the gravel lot, I reached for his hand. He linked his fingers through mine, warm and steady, and I squeezed his.

"They split the men and women up," I muttered, and he looked at me. "For every service."

"It'll be okay." He brushed a thumb over the back of my hand. "It can't last that long, can it?"

He was right. Foot washing was usually a shorter service, forty minutes or so at most.

"We go through the motions and then find Biddle," Kade said, beneath his breath, as he let my hand go and pulled open the door.

We stepped inside, and just the smell of the place—it hit me hard.

Old hymnals and musty carpet. Faint undertones of pine-scented cleaner and stubborn mildew. The sterile tang of aluminum chairs scrubbed down with no-splash bleach.

It smelled like my childhood. Every Wednesday night, twice on Sundays, and every revival and purity meeting in between.

Proverbs 31 apprenticeships.

Saturday night girls' club. Modesty studies in Biblical Womanhood. Memorizing verses and the basic principles of life.

What parts of the body must be covered to honor God?

What message are you sending if your shirt is too tight?

Booklets with pages full of sketches of worldly girls. In V-neck sweaters and tight jeans. Swimsuits and form-fitting jackets.

Could a brother in Christ stumble if he saw you in this outfit?
Explain why a knee-length skirt reflects a heart submitting to God.

I blinked hard.

The air was too still. Too quiet. Even with the soft hum of conversation coming from the sanctuary down the narrow hall, something about the place felt suspended, like time stopped here.

A chill ran up my spine.

"You okay?" Kade whispered beside me.

I hadn't realized I'd stopped, just inside the door.

The overhead fluorescents buzzed faintly, casting the dim hall in an eerie glow. At the end of the hall, the light ended. The sanctuary was lit only by the windows—long, narrow rectangles that cast watery, dust-filled beams onto the worn carpet floor. Or, late at night, by small flickering candles placed on the windowsills.

I could see it, without even stepping inside.

"Em, are you sure you want to do this?" Kade put a warm hand on my arm, and I finally realized I'd never answered him.

"Yeah." My voice got stuck in my throat, choked the last bit of the word.

He tilted his head, looking at me doubtfully. "You sure?"

I closed my eyes for a second. Took a deep breath.

"I haven't been here in like five years," I whispered. "I'm okay though."

I nodded toward the sanctuary. "Let's go."

38

A Shame To Speak

Kade followed me through the narrow doorway, his boots silent on the faded green carpet. I could feel the weight of his presence as he stepped to my side.

The sanctuary was full, but quiet.

A woman in a long navy skirt passed us, her arms full of neatly folded white towels. She looked at me, and her tired eyes lit with recognition before flicking to Kade.

"Oh, hey, you're Brother Lyles's daughter, aren't you?" she asked, her voice barely above a whisper.

"Yes. Emily." I nodded, mind racing, trying to place who this woman was.

"Emily, that's it!" Her smile was genuine. "It's been too long! You're grown!"

I was practically grown the last time I came here—seventeen—but I didn't bother pointing that out.

"You brought a visitor?" She glanced at Kade again.

"A friend." I looked at him. "Kade Weston. Kade, this is... Shirley." The name popped out, and I prayed every prayer I knew that I had it right.

"Nice to meet you, Mr. Weston." Either I got her name right, or she was too polite to say otherwise. "We're having our foot washing tonight. You're welcome to join in. Brothers to the left, sisters to the right."

"Thank you." Kade nodded. "Nice to meet you too."

"I have to get these towels to Sister Ann." Shirley smiled. "Hang around after church, Emily. We can catch up."

I lied and told her I'd love that, my throat going dry as she walked away.

"I don't even know if that was her name..." I whispered to Kade, finding his hand between us.

Even married couples didn't hold hands. Not here.

I was suddenly very aware of how close we were standing, how sweaty my hand was, and how everyone seemed to be looking right at us.

Even with so much going on, everyone in the place seemed to take a moment to turn and look.

Shirley must have spread the news like wildfire.

Don Lyles's daughter is here, and she brought a worldly man with her.

"Do we take our seats?" Kade asked under his breath.

I tried to look around the sanctuary, at what was happening, and ignore who was looking my way.

White plastic dishpans were being laid out between the rows of metal chairs. Younger girls helped the older women.

A gray-haired woman in a solid black dress knelt, filling each pan with an inch of water. She was being helped by a younger woman, a tired-looking girl who couldn't have been over seventeen.

She had a baby on her hip, a little boy with a tuft of brown hair. I wasn't surprised when she turned and I saw she was close to giving him a sibling. Six or eight months along with her second child.

I felt a pain I hadn't felt in a while. A sting in my chest. I was twenty-two. Twenty-three, really. But in this room, I felt fourteen again. I was so far behind where I should be right now.

I sucked in a breath.

"I think we can," I answered Kade and let his hand go.

Somewhere near the front, a microphone crackled, then whined.

A hush swept the sanctuary. A woman gently shushed a squirming toddler, and a baby began to whimper.

That whimper, it crawled straight up my back like a spider.

"Are you going to be okay, Em?"

I couldn't look at him, but I nodded.

Then we parted. Kade to the left, with the brothers. Me to the right, with the sisters.

I sat on the last row of chairs, at the very end, closest to the men. Kade took the seat directly across from mine.

The aisle, three metal chairs wide, separated us. Kept the men and women apart.

I tried to breathe. In through my nose. Slow, steady. Out through my mouth. Measured. It didn't help. I felt like I was choking on the smell of mildewed hymnals and moldy carpet.

I couldn't believe where my mind had gone, watching the girl toting her toddler as she filled dishpans for foot washing.

My hands went cold.

Was it that easy for me to get caught back up into feeling like a failure? Into feeling like I wasn't good enough?

Because I wasn't married yet. No man had even asked Don for permission to court me. At least, he hadn't told me of any. I certainly wasn't anywhere near having my first child, much less my second or third.

I looked around the room as members began taking their seats. Women settling into their chairs, herding their kids into a row.

Older women with six or eight little ones. Mrs. Harold Marsh was still here. She was always given a white carnation for Mother's Day, a celebration of her status as *mother with the most children.*

She and her thirteen offspring sat across the very front row, as always.

The youngest moms all had at least one child. Most of the girls my age had four or five little ones crowded around their knees, pulling their skirts, each demanding their turn to be held.

Across the main aisle, the men were child-free. Except for older boys, at least twelve, all the children sat with their mothers through every service.

And there was no such thing as children's church or Sunday school. Children needed to be in the congregation, hearing the Word.

I slumped against the cold metal of my chair.

You fit in.

I glanced across the aisle.

Kade sat up straight, quietly taking in the room around him, hands resting on his thighs. His boots, scuffed and caked with red clay dust, looked too loud for this drab room.

He'd shed his leather jacket, hung it over the back of his chair. The soft white T-shirt he'd worn underneath hugged the muscles in his arms, the bold lettering faded from too many washes.

His curly black hair hadn't been tamed. It fell down his neck and a little past his shoulders. It wasn't cut off short, parted down the middle, and neatly combed to one side.

He did *not* look the part.

Button-down shirts and black slacks. Plain black shoes. No jewelry, not even a watch.

Kade looked like he'd been dropped into this sea of unspoken uniformity from another world.

I looked like I belonged here. With these people. With their rules.

The ankle-length hems. Necklines that followed the four-finger rule—no lower than four finger-widths below the collarbone. No slit up your skirt. Ever.

Muted colors. Tame. Nothing that might draw attention.

No sleeveless tops. Nothing that clung. Definitely no pants, not even under a skirt.

Uncut hair twisted into a bun pinned so tight to the back of my head it gave me headaches.

I closed my eyes as pain bloomed behind them. I wanted to run. To grab Kade's hand and bolt from this place and never look back.

This used to be sacred. The rules. The quiet. The order. Now it felt like a trap. And I felt like an animal who'd stepped inside to nibble the apple, and the cage door had slammed on my ass.

My lungs tightened against my ribs. I took a long breath in, trying to slow the pounding in my temples.

"It's good to be here tonight."

Lawrence Biddle's voice cut through my shaky resolve.

"We have a full house. That's a thing of beauty for these old eyes, let me tell you."

I looked.

The man stood behind the narrow, wooden podium. White hair sat neatly combed on his head, hiding the thinning spot near the top. He wore a white collared shirt, the sleeves long and buttoned at the cuffs. Black slacks. Black shoes.

But I wasn't paying attention to what he was wearing. I wasn't seeing his clothes. I could hardly hear his voice. There was a low hum outside my ears. Like when you listen to a seashell and hear the ocean.

He was looking right at me. Narrow-set eyes staring into my soul over the heads of all the other women I blended in with.

This man knew Rachel Bagwell. He had been her caseworker. He had gotten her a foster placement, through this very church.

Was he bishop then? Did he hurt her? Did he turn a blind eye to someone else hurting her? The great and mighty D. L. Emerson, maybe?

"And as always," Biddle said, voice calm and sure, "I ask that sisters refrain from speaking, in accordance with First Corinthians, chapter fourteen."

Suddenly I could hear him.

His voice was loud, thundering, booming into my ears like he was standing right beside me, thin lips to the side of my head.

"Sisters, be in prayer, and if you have any questions or learn anything, go to your husbands, your fathers at home. Seek the men God put over you to protect you. For it is a shame for women to speak in the church."

Then he bowed his head in prayer.

I couldn't close my eyes. Couldn't play along.

How had I never *heard* those words before?

I'd heard them, they were spoken every single service. A reminder for anyone without a dick in their pants to keep their mouth shut.

To stay in their place. Under. Beneath. In silence, with all subjection.

For I suffer not a woman to teach, nor to usurp authority over the man, but to be in silence.

Those words, those verses, they had never sunk into my head before. I'd heard them so many times, but I'd never really listened.

Never really heard what they were saying. What they were asking of half the congregation.

The ones herding the children. The ones on their knees filling the dishpans for foot washing. The ones scrubbing the church toilets every Saturday night, not worthy to be heard by Sunday morning.

I glanced across the aisle. I didn't care that Biddle was still praying. Didn't care that someone might see me, my head not bowed, my eyes wide open.

Kade didn't seem to care either. His dark eyes met mine, and I felt the question in them.

Do you need to leave?

I swallowed hard, my throat burning like I'd forced down shards of glass.

The prayer dragged on. The words thundering over my head like rain pounding on a metal roof. My ears still ringing with the word *silence*.

I was on the edge of my seat. Fists gripping my skirt. So close to nodding at Kade. Getting up. Walking out.

Then I saw her, standing behind him.

Hollow milky eyes watching the man at the podium. She was screaming at him, pointing a bony finger.

But no one could hear her. No one listened.

I think Kade could tell something had shifted. Something in those seconds had changed.

I shook my head, barely, and looked away. I would stay. I would survive this service.

And I'd find out what happened to Rachel.

39

THE COVER GIRL

The rest of the service blurred.

The woman beside me knelt on the carpet, hushing her three kids while I slipped off my shoes and socks.

She whispered apology after apology, breathless, as her youngest kept sliding off his chair toward the dishpan. A couple of times, he even tried to tickle my feet.

Her face flushed red. Mortified.

I told her it was okay, that she was doing a good job with her kids. She was a good mom. I don't think she could hear me.

Her bare hands trembled as she washed my feet, then dried them with a towel.

I knelt and mirrored her, surprised at how steady my own hands were.

She held her squirming boy on her lap, whisper-scolding as he made faces at me and giggled too loud.

Then the dishpans disappeared. Towels vanished into the arms of teenage girls in denim jumpers.

And Biddle preached.

I heard none of it. Didn't sing. I was trying not to stare across the aisle.

Rachel hadn't moved. She was still behind Kade's chair. Bloody tears streaked her papery cheeks. Pointing. Mouth open in a silent scream.

I glanced at Kade. Could he feel her behind him? If so, he didn't let it show.

I wondered what he'd say—once we left, once the door closed behind us. What he thought about all this. How it felt to him.

It didn't take long for Lawrence Biddle to find me once the final prayer was said. I'd barely rejoined Kade, and we'd made it only a few steps down the hallway when...

"Miss Emily Lyles!" Biddle's voice rang out behind me. It didn't startle me, didn't make me jump.

It made me burn.

So much joy. So much fake cheer wrapped around those syllables.

The same voice that silenced every woman here tonight. The same voice that may have silenced Rachel.

I swallowed it all, then turned and faced him.

"Hey, Bishop." I used the title. He smiled.

"It's been way too long!" he said, extending a hand.

I shook it. Firm. Steady. Stronger than I thought I could be.

"We've missed your sweet family's presence in the Lord's house." Biddle smiled at me, releasing my hand.

He asked about my *parents*, about Gracie. If we were in good health. If we were staying *in the Word*.

He hadn't said anything to Kade. Hadn't even acknowledged him.

Until his script dried up.

"Aways a blessing to see our young ladies bringing a soul into fellowship." Only then did he offer Kade a handshake.

"Kade Weston." I introduced him for the second time tonight. "Kade, this is Bishop Lawrence Biddle."

"You look familiar." He didn't let go of Kade's hand. "Where do I know you from?"

"I came down in here with a friend," Kade said, "As a teen. We thought this was game management and were looking for a place to hunt."

Biddle's face lit up. "Oh... that's right. That's right. I knew I'd seen you before! It was good to have you come worship with us tonight."

Kade pulled his hand free without answering.

"Bishop, we actually came to talk to you." I took advantage of the couple of seconds when Biddle didn't seem to know what to say. "I didn't know who else to go to..."

I let it hang, let the unease seep in. The old man's face shifted—concern, or something close enough to pass for it.

"Of course." He nodded toward a room off the hall.

The girls' classroom.

"Let's talk in here. It's more private."

He pushed the door open, but stepped back to let us go in first.

"Let me tell Elder Marsh I'll be a few minutes," he said, as he flipped on the light. "I'll be right back."

We watched him go. The door clicked shut behind him, a thin echo in the empty room.

Kade was already scanning the room. He shook his head at me.

"What the hell is this?" He gestured at the blackboard, which took up an entire wall.

On it was a series of questions.

I recognized them. They were test questions. A pop quiz on the basic principles of life.

Explain why an ankle-length skirt reflects a heart submitted to God.

What message are you sending when your shirt is too tight across the chest?

Makeup is a tool of seduction. Who are women trying to please when they apply it?

If your outfit causes your brother in Christ to stumble, who will God hold accountable for that sin?

"They're test questions," I mumbled, stepping behind the desk. I found a workbook lying open. I flipped it closed and showed Kade the cover.

Basic Principles of a Biblical Life

"Em, I don't mean to be..." He didn't finish the sentence.

I met his eyes.

"This is a fucking cult," he said. "Not a church."

My heart doubled up in my chest. I couldn't answer him. I dropped my eyes to the thin paper booklet in my hands, staring at the young woman on the cover.

High neckline. Muted green dress. Sleeves down to her wrists. Her skin was waxen. Drained of sun, of life. Her lips matched. Bloodless and bare. No touch of pink, no breath of warmth.

Her eyes were lifted heavenward, wide and expectant, like she was waiting for something.

Acknowledgement. Praise. A pat on the head for knowing her place and walking it in silence. For honoring her father's authority without question. For preparing for her calling, to be a respectful, silent helpmeet to her future husband.

I took a breath, but it caught sharply in my chest.

I was her. I had been her. Twenty-some years of smiling silence. In a cult?

Kade stood silent, but his words echoed in my skull. Over and over.

This is a fucking cult. Not a church.

On the booklet in my hands, beneath the woman's picture, words stared at me in heavy, black type.

A Foundational Curriculum for Young Women

The cheap paper curled at the edges. I ran my thumb over the bottom corner, smoothing it.

And there, in tiny print—*A publication of D. L. Ministries.*

"Oh my gosh, Kade."

He'd wandered down the classroom a little. I stepped up and grabbed his arm, pressing the booklet into his hand.

"I knew it." I pointed at the tiny print. "They print all the curricula."

Kade didn't say anything. He was flipping through the pages.

"I knew I recognized that name," I said quietly.

"Do these people do anything *but* run women into the ground?" Kade snapped. "Everything's about sex. That's all women are for. And how they need to avoid being…"

His words trailed off. He slapped the booklet shut.

"*Being*. It's like they don't want women to even exist—until they want them to."

I stood there, staring at him. I couldn't peel my tongue off my teeth. Couldn't drag any words from my throat.

Kade had just said what I'd spent so many years feeling. So many years fighting. Trying to un-think it. Trying to be *thankful* for it.

Because that's what I was told I should be. By the bishops, the pastors, the elders. The thin haggard woman sitting with her thirteen kids on the front row.

I should be grateful for protection, for boundaries.

Thankful to be a daughter living under authority, waiting for my father to hand me off like a wrapped gift. Something to be unwrapped on my wedding night and finally allowed to exist—as long as I did so in all *subjection*.

My chest tightened.

I looked at the girl on the cover again. The pages were wrinkled now, from Kade's grip. But I could still see her.

Bloodless lips. Glowing face. Eyes aimed toward Heaven. I had been her.

"I'm sorry." Kade's voice softened. He smoothed the booklet and tossed it back onto the desk. "I know all of this is way harder for you than it is for me. I shouldn't be so blunt."

I shook my head. "No."

He stopped and looked at me.

"I needed to hear it," I said, my throat raw. "I've never let myself say it. Not out loud."

Kade's shoulders sagged. "Em, I'm so sorry you've been treated like this your whole life."

I tried not to let the chill in. Not to shake. But my back ached. My eyes burned.

His hand brushed my arm, and I stepped closer. He pulled me into him, strong arms holding me close. I pressed my face against his chest and held on, arms around his waist, breath ragged in my throat.

But I didn't cry.

I let myself soak in his warmth, his strength, his quiet steadiness.

And I didn't cry.

"We're here for Rachel." I whispered, pulling back as resolve slipped back into my limbs. I pinched the bridge of my nose.

"Yeah, we are." Kade waited for me to meet his eyes. "But this is your life too, Em. You're allowed to feel it."

I dropped my hand from my face and looked at him. Really looked.

He meant it. And it cracked something in me. Just a hairline fracture. But enough to breathe through.

"I'm scared of what else we're going to find," I admitted. My voice was thin, small.

"Then we'll find it scared. Together." Kade was quiet too.

Together.

40

SPINE OF THE MINISTRY

The door creaked open behind me. Biddle stepped into the room, his smile back in place. He eased the door shut behind him.

"Sorry about the wait. What can I help you with, Miss Emily?"

He wouldn't talk to me if I asked about Rachel. Not directly.

"I really miss coming to church, Bishop." I softened my voice. "I wanted to come by tonight to experience foot washing again, and to ask you why my family and I aren't allowed to be members here anymore."

His smile faltered. For a second. He moved to the teacher's desk at the front of the classroom and leaned against it, arms crossed over his chest.

"Emily, I never said your family wasn't welcome here." His voice was quiet, assuring, *grandfatherly*. "You, your father, mother, and your sweet sister, Gracie, are always welcome in this church."

"But... we haven't been allowed to attend for five years."

Biddle grimaced.

"I don't know how much I should say, Miss Emily." He said, sadly. "If your father hasn't felt the need to disclose his reasons for not attending this church, I'm not sure I should violate that by sharing with you the part I played in that decision. Brother Don is the head of his house, and he'll share what he feels you need to know."

Kade shifted beside me. I could feel it, the anger coming off him.

I searched my soul for an argument, a plea.

"Bishop, we haven't been attending anywhere," I said quietly. "I'm twenty-two now. Gracie turned twenty-five this past October. I miss the fellowship, and we both need... opportunities."

Biddle's narrow-set eyes shifted to Kade for a quick second, and I knew I'd found my angle.

He shook his head, looked down at the tightly worn carpet at his feet and sighed.

"I know God has given me a responsibility to all the sheep in this fold. I don't believe I would be a good steward if I didn't at least try to clear some of this up for you."

He paused for a moment and then looked up at me.

"Your father has a very strong calling on his life, Emily. He has served God and His people for decades through his devotion to our youth all over the country."

Biddle shook his head again.

"But I can't allow him to serve *here*. I gave him letters to a couple of churches in North Carolina and one in Georgia. We need his work. We need him in our churches, teaching our youth, guiding our young people to the fullness of the experience of Christ."

Something shifted. Not in Biddle's words, but in the air itself. A pressure change. Cold rising from the floorboards. It happened so quickly, so softly, I almost didn't notice. The slight coolness along the back of my neck. The flick of static near my elbow.

The hair on my arms prickled.

"Having your father here, a member of our church, is one of the greatest honors I've ever had during all my years in ministry. His first years here put our little church on the map. Up until your father took the step out, acted on the calling that was on his life, no church south of Richmond had much pull in the big conferences."

He smiled a little, spread his hand out toward the room.

"We're a tiny, cinderblock church at the end a red clay road in a run-down, little town in South Carolina. I couldn't even vote at conference assemblies until God used your father in the mighty way He did."

The corners of the room were darkening. The light didn't reach the far wall anymore.

Biddle's face was blurring.

His first years.

Don only served in this church for *half* a year, right after we first moved to Caster. Then we left. Stopped going to church. Started having quiet services in our home. Us four.

"It broke my heart to have to go to Brother Don with what God laid on me." Biddle continued, quietly. "But I do not serve man. I wished—prayed—he would have taken it better than he did. I've prayed for him every day since, and every service I faithfully expect to see him, and his beautiful family, come through those doors."

This wasn't a draft. This was cold, icy cold. It curled around my ankles, seeping under the classroom door.

My lungs pulled tighter. I tried to measure my breaths. I didn't want to show it. My unease. The gnawing sense that something was *not* right. That Biddle was telling me something he thought I already knew—something I should *not* know. And that something in this tight, dim, little room didn't like it.

"God told me that, for this church, it was better if Brother Don was *not* in a titled leadership position."

The old man pushed himself up from the desk and Kade moved half a step closer to my side.

"Any other church, any other town, any other state, God knows Don Lyles could serve in any titled position he felt led." Biddle sighed. "I wish I could offer that to him here, especially with this church being his home, the root of his ministry. But after everything that happened before..."

He stopped, and his eyes looked far away, clouded. It only lasted a moment, then he shook his head and looked back at me.

"I couldn't offer him a titled position. It wouldn't look good for our church. The community would *not* understand."

I swallowed, but saliva stuck in my throat, meeting the bile trying to come up.

I had to look away. From Biddle. From the curl of black shadow rising up behind the desk.

I wanted to ask. Point blank ask. Get this man to clarify what he was beating around the bush to say.

"I'm sorry things went the way they did, Emily." Biddle was quieter now, a shade of regret lacing his words. "Your father didn't want to serve without full creative authority over his classes."

I bit my lip, stared at the tight weave of the carpet beneath my black tennis shoes.

"I don't blame Brother Don." Biddle was still talking. Still explaining. Still assuming I already knew.

"He *should* have full authority over his own classes. He shouldn't have to defer to anyone else, not even nominally."

His classes. The attic. The booklets. That tiny line of text: *A publication of D. L. Ministries.*

D. L. Emerson.

Don Lyles.

I was shaking now, no use pretending otherwise. Kade slipped his hand into mine and squeezed.

How hadn't I seen it? The signs weren't subtle. They were flashing red.

D. L.

Don Lyles.

D. L. Ministries.

The ministry that saved souls. That molded youth. All over the country. This little town—*the birthplace of a great ministry.* Founded by the man who raised me.

Biddle's voice sounded far away now, like it had to cross some icy gulf to reach me.

"None of the other ministries would've even gotten off the ground without your father's vision, Emily. The whole Basic Principles curriculum—modesty guidelines, pillars of purity, study tracks, the church youth placement system, helping struggling young people have a chance at a better life—everything came out of the work he did here. Out of this church."

It all started here.

Don sang D. L. Ministries' praises when we moved to Caster six years ago. Recounted the history of that *divine working*.

"When D.L. Ministries started publishing on a national level, reaching churches all the way from New Mexico to North Dakota, your father didn't even want his full name listed. He said it wasn't about *Don Lyles*. It was about the message."

Biddle was still talking. But I heard it all in Don's voice.

The books in the attic. D. L. Emerson. *The Doctrine of Spiritual Purity*.

Wanda's face flashed in my mind. The pain. The anger.

Why races must not intermarry.

Don's words. Not a quote. Not a reference. His own words. Not borrowed. Not inherited. They were written, preached, printed—by *him*.

Don Lyles was D. L. Emerson. He *was* D. L. Ministries.

It hit me like a boot to the stomach.

A slow wet breath curled into my ear. Raspy. Murmuring a sentence I couldn't make out.

I gripped Kade's hand tighter. Tried to stop the spinning.

From somewhere behind the desk—behind the bishop—a shadow peeled itself from the floor.

Kade tensed beside me. Just a little. Could he see it too?

She had no form. But I knew who it was. I knew who brought the cold. Rachel. Angry. Icy. Bitter. The static spiked, dancing across my skin.

Something ticked near the light switch, soft, like a filament about to blow. The overhead light flickered. Once. Twice. Then steadied.

Biddle glanced up, brushing the back of his neck like he felt a draft. He looked over his shoulder.

But he didn't see her. He didn't see Rachel rising above the desk behind him.

"I'm sorry you're struggling with all of this, Emily." His voice was warped now, muffled like I had glass pressed over my ears. "I hope I've been able to bring you some peace."

He flicked at his neck again, like he felt a fly.

"Or at least, some understanding."

"I know my father's struggling. Maybe more than I am."

I made myself say it. Lying was getting harder. I needed the truth.

I was so close to breaking. To tossing the game board. To grabbing Lawrence Biddle by the collar and demanding the truth.

Did Don Lyles know Rachel Bagwell? Did he foster her? Was he accused? Shamed? Did the man I called father bury her memory and walk away?

But I didn't have to ask. Didn't have to scream. Because my careful play worked.

"My heart breaks for Brother Don," Biddle said softly. "I know he did his very best by Rachel."

Even if I'd *wanted* to know, the words still hit me like the man had backhanded my face. I tore away from Kade's hand. Staggered a few steps back.

I needed air.

"He's lived haunted by it," Biddle added, like that explained anything.

Haunted? Don wasn't haunted. He was clean. He was polished. He was *praised*.

He had a box full of awards and a drawer full of porn and *not one single memory* of the girl who died in his care.

I bit down so hard on my tongue iron tingled between my teeth. But the air around me changed.

The cold was waking. The stillness moving. The shadow behind Biddle stretched and rose.

"That's the main reason he can't be in any titled position here at church," Biddle said. "After all those rumors when Rachel disappeared… it wouldn't look good. Not in a town this small."

Disappeared.

I looked up.

Rachel was no longer a shadow. She crouched on the desk behind Biddle. She was too tall, too thin, limbs bent at sharp angles like a broken marionette.

Her bare feet pressed flat against the wood, her hair soaked and clinging in rusty ropes to her skull.

And her face, it was too familiar. Not because I'd seen her so many times. This was something worse. The angle of her jaw. The freckles dusted across her papery nose. Things I hadn't noticed before. But they were things I *already knew*.

And then her eyes. White. Blistered. They locked onto mine like she never planned to look away. Like she'd been *waiting*.

I held her gaze.

"I'd love to know more about Rachel," I said aloud, my voice somehow steady. "I'd love to find out what happened. Where she went."

I kept my eyes on hers.

"To clear Dad's name," I added. "I hate that he's been burdened for so long."

Rachel didn't blink. Didn't move.

My teeth were clenched so tight, I thought I might break them.

Biddle didn't seem to notice. He sighed, sorrow softening his breath.

"That's an admirable thing for a daughter to do." He nodded slowly. "I wish I could help more."

He paused and I thought for a minute he wouldn't say anything else, but then he looked up at me. "Rachel was a sweet girl, Emily. I feel... partially responsible for what happened to her. I was her caseworker, back when I worked for the Department of Human Services."

His voice stayed calm, measured.

But my breath hitched.

"I let my coworkers sway me," he said, shaking his head. "They insisted on public school that first fall, said it would help her adjust."

He looked regretful, like he'd spilled a drink.

"I knew better. Rachel came from a worldly home. She'd passed through several worldly placements. She hadn't been taught to protect her purity, or to guard her heart."

Another shake of his head.

"She needed time to prepare. Especially coming to our congregation as a teen. A troubled one."

Rachel's eyes broke from mine. It was like she'd been holding me up and suddenly let go. I stumbled.

Kade noticed. He looked at me, eyes sharp with concern.

Are you okay?

I couldn't nod. Couldn't answer.

The world tilted.

Biddle started to cough. Violent choking. His face flushed crimson, one hand clutched to his chest, the other raised in a wordless apology.

But I wasn't watching him anymore.

I was looking at Rachel.

Her long bone-thin fingers wrapped Biddle's neck, squeezing, sinking in like roots searching for water.

I could see blood, coming from the fingerprints, oozing out around Rachel's fingers, down her hands.

Biddle hacked up huge black clots. They hit the carpet. Then vanished. I blinked and the blood was gone.

Completely.

But Rachel was still there, and Biddle was still choking.

"Oh heavens." He stepped away from the desk, but Rachel didn't let go, he was dragging her with him. "I must've inhaled sideways. I'm so sorry."

I shook my head, but couldn't get any words to come, couldn't look away from the shadowy form of Rachel Bagwell strangling Lawrence Biddle.

That's when Kade saw her too.

"Holy shit..." he whispered, breathless.

Biddle opened a mini fridge in the corner. "What was that?"

"I said don't worry about it," Kade lied smoothly. "Happens to the best of us."

Biddle sipped his water, stepping back toward the desk, still dragging Rachel.

Kade looked at me, eyes wide.

You see her too?

I bit my lip.

"We were talking about poor Miss Rachel." Biddle's voice had roughened, hoarse from coughing, but he pushed on.

"Before your father could remove her from public school, some worldly boy got her pregnant."

His tone turned almost mournful. "That's why we teach our girls to guard their purity. One wrong influence... one step outside the covering of authority, and the devil already has a foothold."

I swear the bastard glanced at Kade.

Then choked again. Graceless, guttural.

Rachel tightened her grip.

Her fingers had vanished inside his throat. Elbows latched over his shoulders. Legs wrapped around his waist, like she'd grown from his spine.

"It was a difficult time for Brother Lyles." Biddle rasped. "His first wife, Barbara, had backslidden. Left him. Taken his daughter. Moved out. It wasn't a calm home for a displaced teenage girl."

He drank again. Tried to sigh, but it caught. He coughed into his hand.

I watched Rachel's thin arms ripple under his skin.

"But I believed it would help him. Having a new face in his home. A new calling. A youth to guide."

He emptied the bottle.

"I had no idea she'd disappear. Or that Brother Don would face such wild rumors—murder, of all things!" Biddle laughed weakly, a hand pressed to his chest. "The devil was after him hard in those days. The more a man serves, the more the enemy attacks."

I couldn't take any more. I looked at Kade.

"We need to go."

Before he could answer, Biddle stepped forward, sliding between us.

"It was so good to see you again, Miss Emily. Thank you for coming tonight."

Kade moved to the door. Opened it. I followed.

"Tell your father and mother I said hello," Biddle croaked. "I'm very sorry about this coughing fit interrupting our conversation."

I looked at him. At Rachel, still wrapped around his body, her hands buried deep in his neck.

"No worries, Bishop." My voice came out quiet, flat.

We turned. Kade stepped through the door. But Biddle's hand shot out. Closed around my arm.

"Emily," he said my name heavily, "do your parents know you're here tonight?"

"They know I went out." I pulled away.

His grip tightened, then let go.

"Do they know you're with *him*?"

I sucked in a breath. Kade had stepped back into the doorway. I don't know if he heard.

"No. They don't."

Biddle's face faltered. He cleared his throat, eyes darting to the wall behind me.

"You're a lovely girl, Emily. A godly young woman." He hesitated. "Don't become a Rachel."

He choked on her name.

Rachel had tightened her hold again.

I didn't answer. Just walked to Kade, linked my arm through his, and faced the bishop.

I smiled.

"Goodnight, Bishop," I said. "I'll be praying for you."

41

A Hand In The Dark

The church door clicked shut behind us. The hum of voices and the echo of Biddle's choking died as we stepped off the porch into the cool night.

Kade exhaled like he'd been holding his breath since the first prayer and scrubbed both hands through his wild curly hair.

"You were solid in there, Em." He looked back at me, a smile slowly forming on his face.

I didn't answer. My fingers were busy yanking the sharp pins from the bun twisted at the back of my head. Each one pulled free with a tiny sting. I let them fall—left a breadcrumb trail of iron teeth in the gravel as we walked toward Kade's bike.

"I mean it." He turned and walked backward, hands shoved in his pockets. "That took guts. You *grew up* in this shit."

I watched him as I tore through the braid, uncoiling it like a snake wound through my hair. My scalp ached from the tension. So did the rest of me; my arms, my chest, my lungs.

The pins were gone. The braid was gone. The pressure on the back of my head had disappeared, but I still couldn't breathe.

"He's... it was *him*." I stumbled the last few steps to Kade's bike at the edge of the lot.

My knees buckled. I sank into the weedy grass where the gravel ended.

"Don." I looked up at Kade, as he settled beside me. "He fostered Rachel. *He* was the man accused of murdering her. He built that fucking house."

Kade nodded, but he didn't say anything. My mind was flooded. I wouldn't have heard him anyway.

"How did I *not* know that?" I laid back with a *thump* on the ground, staring up at the stars glinting in the early night sky. "I should've known when we found out I was adopted—when we found Rachel's placement papers in the same box as mine."

I didn't even realize I was crying, until I felt the damp on my cheeks.

"Hey," Kade said softly. "Your brain wouldn't jump from *he hid my adoption* to *he was accused of killing a girl*."

"It should've," I groaned. "They didn't just hide things, Kade. They lied. Made up stories about my first birthday, learning to walk—my whole birth story."

I spilled it all out in one breathless rush.

"What kind of person lies in that much detail?" I wiped my eyes, the stars above us blurring. "And how do two people keep that many lies straight for so long?"

Kade didn't answer right away. He stared up at the stars.

"That's messed up."

His words sat there. Too heavy to ignore, too true to disrupt.

"Do you think Allie knew Rachel, too?" After a while, Kade broke the silence.

I sighed, like I'd been holding my breath.

"I don't know. Gracie was born October 1988. They said they met in December 1987, but… I don't know what to believe anymore."

"None of it, probably." Kade murmured.

I lay there, eyes dry now, staring at the sky. I didn't even remember reaching out, but my hand was in his, our fingers threaded together in the dark.

We laid there a long time. His bike a buffer between us and the slowly emptying gravel lot.

Evening was deepening into night. Members were leaving. Taking their drab-colored old cars packed with kids home to fight bedtime.

Soon, the lot would be empty. The church abandoned. And darkness would swallow this red clay road.

Kade rubbed his thumb over mine. I looked over, but his eyes were still on the stars.

"Did you see her?" I asked.

He looked at me and nodded. "She wasn't the little girl in a pink nightgown I saw before."

"No." My voice had choked down to a whisper.

We both went quiet again.

"Did you ever figure out where that fabric came from?" Kade asked me, after a couple minutes.

"It fell out of one of those *D. L. Emerson* books."

I felt the weight of what I said as soon as the words left my mouth.

He kept a piece of her nightgown.

Kade was quiet again and I closed my eyes.

Was it regret? Grief? That made Don Lyles keep a piece of Rachel's nightgown? While he erased every other memory of her? Or was it something else? Something my mind didn't want to fully articulate. Something dark, twisted. Silenced.

I wondered if Rachel ever went to Biddle for help.

Maybe, if she did get pregnant in high school, Don didn't take it well.

A brief chill skitted up my spine as I thought of the hell I'd go through if I turned up pregnant, like Allie thought.

Maybe that's why she was so convinced I was hiding a pregnancy. Because she knew about Rachel. And Don hadn't taken it well.

Maybe Rachel had gone to Biddle, her pastor and caseworker. Maybe she wanted to move.

Had he made excuses? Explained how, if she would only submit more, pray more, and trust God more, her life would be easier. Her sins would be forgiven.

Had he silenced her?

Let your women keep silence in the churches: for it is not permitted unto them to speak; but they are commanded to be under obedience.

I'd heard it so many times. It was second nature to quote it. Like radio static at the beginning of every service.

I suffer not a woman to teach, nor to usurp authority over the man. But to be in silence.

Seen, but not heard.

Good enough to cook all the church meals and wash dishes for eighty people, but not worth enough to whisper a prayer when a man was present.

I rolled to my side, toward Kade.

"You were right."

He raised an eyebrow.

"This is a cult."

He grunted, like he regretted saying that word. Then he rolled to face me, squeezing my hand.

"I don't like fitting in here," I said. "I hated it. Sitting in there, looking like one of them."

He was quiet, watching me.

"You stuck out like a sore thumb." I couldn't help but smile.

Kade gave a short laugh. "Yeah... I noticed."

I shuffled a little closer to him, brought my second hand over his.

"That's a good thing."

He was quiet again. We were both listening to the sound of tires against gravel, as the last couple minivans pulled out onto Beckham's Road.

I thought of how many times that had been me.

Tucked in the back of Allie's twenty-year-old Astro, clutching my worn-out Bible on my lap. I'd listen to Don mumble about words Brother Biddle pronounced wrong, or how he should've gone *deeper* into a particular verse, or used a different analogy to get his point across.

I blinked. The stars came back into view. Brighter. Closer.

"I'd go buy clothes tonight if I could," I mumbled.

"I'll take you," Kade offered.

I wanted to go.

To shop for normal clothes for the first time in my life. To leave this cape dress in the dressing room and walk out someone else.

Emily Rose, not Emily Carol.

But if I walked through their door in jeans and a T-shirt, Allie and Don would explode.

Everything would change. And not in my favor. They'd ground me for life. Take my keys again. I wouldn't be allowed to leave the house unless someone was with me.

I shook my head. "We need to find out what happened to Rachel first."

"First?"

I nodded. "Then, once we find out, can you take me shopping?"

"I sure can." Kade smiled a little, but it faded fast. "Em, I'm worried about you going back to that house."

I bit my lip. That was the one thought I'd been avoiding all evening.

"A girl disappeared under Don Lyles's care." Kade was quiet. "You're digging into something he's had covered for almost three decades."

But they don't know.

The second I thought it, I saw Don's face in the attic doorway. Blocking me.

Kids always end up where they're not supposed to be.

And my diary... the one I found burned in the fireplace. The one I thought I'd dreamed.

"I'll be careful," I whispered.

Kade grimaced. Like he'd hoped I would have said something different.

"I have to know what happened to her." I squeezed his hand. "But I'll be careful."

He nodded.

"We should probably get back to the library." My voice came out begrudgingly.

I would've stayed here, like this, with Kade, all night. Never gone back to that house. Never saw Don or Allie again.

Kade pulled himself up, and then me, but I didn't let his hand go.

We both watched the church across the gravel lot. A silent cinderblock box, windows dark like rows of empty black holes.

I didn't know where Kade's mind had gone. Maybe back to Rachel. To her thin, shadowy form wrapped around her ex-caseworker, hands sunk into his throat.

But, for a minute, I didn't want to think about Rachel. Or Allie and Don. Or D. L. Ministries.

I looked at Kade.

His jaw was set, in that quiet way it got when he was thinking too hard, his eyes shadowed with the darkness settling in around us.

Wherever his mind had gone, he was still holding my hand. Like it was the most natural thing in the world. It felt like it was. Like we'd held hands for years. Like we'd known each other for years.

Maybe it was the night. Or the weight of what we'd just lived through inside that church.

But for a moment, watching Kade, something in me went still.

42

AT THE ALTAR

"Oh damn."

I was strapping on the helmet when Kade cursed. "You okay?"

He gave a wary glance back at the church, now draped in shadow. The last of the taillights had blinked out of sight on Beckham's Road several minutes ago.

"I think I left my jacket."

I felt my shoulders drop.

He was right. His black leather jacket. He'd worn it in, but we'd left so fast, he hadn't grabbed it on the way out.

"I'll buy another one," Kade muttered, tugging on his riding gloves.

"Aren't they expensive?"

He shrugged. "Yeah. But I don't like the way it felt in there." He looked at me. "It's more than Rachel."

I paused, fingers frozen on the strap under my chin. "You saw something else?"

Kade shook his head. "No, but the whole place has a... vibe." He rubbed the back of his neck, gaze distant. "Like it doesn't want us there."

I didn't answer right away, and he shook his head again. "I know it sounds dumb..."

"No." I cut him off, too fast. "Kade, I've seen so much dumb shit this past month, I don't doubt anything anymore."

Knocking. Scratching. Faces in mirrors that didn't belong. Hidden rooms inside walls. My sister's memory blinking in and out like a skipping cassette tape.

And the ghost girl. Sitting next to me all day at work. Her mouth sewn shut with jagged black thread.

I blinked hard, trying to blur that image, but it clung.

"Remember the thing that pretended to be your sister?" Kade asked.

My breath hitched. "Yeah..."

"What was that?"

The mimic. The voice. The perfect copy of Gracie's face... until it wasn't.

"The spirit of the house?" I offered, but it sounded weak even to me.

He shook his head slowly. "Inanimate objects don't have spirits, Em."

A shadow crossed his face. Maybe only moonlight, warped by a drifting cloud. But I swore it was something deeper, a resurfaced fear. Or a stinging memory he hadn't shared.

"Do you think it was another ghost?" I asked.

Kade turned toward the church. The silence stretched.

"I don't know. But whatever it was, it wasn't good. And I felt it again, while we were in there." He glanced at me. "I kept waiting for whatever it was to show up while Biddle was preaching."

I'd been so focused on how disgusting it felt to fit in, to blend seamlessly back in with that world, I hadn't noticed what Kade had.

Or maybe, I was so used to surviving inside of rot, I didn't smell it anymore.

Like when it wore Gracie's skin. I didn't feel a thing—until I was right on top of it.

A night breeze stirred a thin wisp of gravel dust across the lot. I still had to live in that house. Sleep there. Even with that thing there. Watching me.

"But we can run in just for your jacket, right?" I asked.

He grimaced.

"You need it for the ride? Bugs or whatever?"

He cracked a small smile. A little tension left his neck. "Yeah, I guess." He shrugged. "I just like it 'cause it's cool."

I slipped the helmet back off and set it on his bike seat.

"I didn't plan on ever going back in there," I said, circling around to meet him. "But it's your jacket. No one's here."

I looked across the empty lot and took his hand.

"It's not the people I'm worried about." He shook his head.

"We're not snooping," I whispered. "We were digging into things when whatever that was wore Gracie's face."

I stopped and watched Kade's dark eyes.

"They always keep the back door unlocked," I added. "In case someone needs a place to stay or get out of the weather. We're walking in, grabbing your jacket, and walking out."

A pause. Crickets chirped in the woods beyond the church clearing. Oblivious.

Kade finally nodded. "Let's make it quick."

I started across the gravel, still holding his hand. The rocks crunched beneath Kade's heavy boots, but I felt every pebble through the thin soles of my sneakers.

Night had brought a chill, but for March, it wasn't as cold as it could've been. Almost like an early summer night. But the cloudless, starry sky promised a frigid morning.

"You think Biddle's gone?" Kade asked as we rounded the back of the building.

I looked to where the bishop always parked—under the old oak hunched at the far edge of the gravel.

"His car isn't here."

We reached the back door. Kade nodded, like he'd finally resigned himself to going back in.

"Okay. Hurry."

I knocked lightly and waited.

"No one's here," I said over my shoulder, turning the knob.

The door swung open, yanking the cold metal from my hand. Or maybe I pushed too hard.

I stood still, trying to swallow my heart.

"I think I shoved it," I whispered.

Kade stepped around me. "Let me go first, Em."

Cold sweat bloomed across my neck. I cursed myself for being a coward but still let him go ahead.

He switched on his flashlight app. I did the same.

The sanctuary was mostly dark now. Pale beams of moonlight filtered through narrow windows across rows of empty metal chairs and worn carpet.

I stood there, something scratching at my brain. Something wasn't right.

"It's still there," Kade muttered, stepping past the wooden podium and up the aisle.

My feet wouldn't follow. The carpet clung. Like if I took one more step, I'd become part of the building. I wouldn't be able to leave.

That's when I saw them. All the little, battery-powered candles in the windowsills. They were still on. Why would the bishop leave them on?

I watched Kade grab the jacket. His light swung back and caught my skirt.

"Got it," he said.

I nodded, then stilled. A sharp, off-tune note sounded by my ear. A piano?

"Shit," Kade muttered, moving faster.

He'd heard it too.

My vision flickered, like an old VHS tape warping. Like I was blinking into another timeline. One I wasn't meant to see.

The windows were bright with sunshine. The metal chairs were full. Women and children on the right. Men on the left.

And there, seated in the front row and clutching a ragged teddy bear, was teenage Rachel Bagwell. A plain beige dress fell to her ankles. A high, tight neckline choked her.

She looked like she was trying not to draw attention, but she was struggling to breathe. Gasping for air through cracked lips.

Her bright eyes, the same ones from that old photo at Niagara Falls, were glazed. Her thin fingers trembled where they gripped the bear.

Beagle.

My bear.

I tried to blink. Tried to breathe. Tried to scream. But I couldn't move.

Rachel started crying. I knew that fear. That choking need for oxygen. The cold that bites deep. The cramps from shivering too long. The same drowning feeling that crippled me in the library with Wanda—when I saw Rachel's face in the microwave door.

The day I met Kade.

"Hey."

It was his voice, but I couldn't see him.

"Em!"

He wasn't in the sanctuary anymore.

It was only me, standing at the foot of the podium, watching Rachel Bagwell break apart.

Men moved toward her. Elders. Lawrence Biddle. Don Lyles.

They *encouraged* her to go to the altar. *Helped* her to her knees. Prayed the devil out of her.

"It's a panic attack!" I tried to scream at them, but no sound came. I was choking.

"Hey!"

Kade's voice, louder now, shattered the vision. It fell apart like broken glass, darkness rushing in behind the pieces.

I was on the floor. Back against the threadbare carpet, eyes to the plain white ceiling.

"Holy shit." Kade was beside me, his arm braced under my neck. "Em, are you okay? What happened? You stopped breathing."

I was crying now, broken sobs between gulps of air.

"She was here," I gasped. "They dragged her up to the front and prayed over her."

"Rachel?"

I grabbed his arm. "Kade—she was having a panic attack. She had Beagle. A teenage girl, holding a teddy bear in church. She was terrified."

"Okay." Kade's voice was gentler now. "She's showing you what happened. She can talk to you. But you need to breathe, Em. Just for a second."

He helped me up. I was still gasping, legs wobbling, my mind scrambled.

I wanted out.

My eyes snapped to the door. Only a few feet away. Still open. The night air whispered through, cool against my face.

We could make it. A few steps. One quick dash. And we'd be out. I braced to run, muscles tightening—but my feet didn't move.

"What's the matter?" Kade asked. His hand was steady on my arm, but his voice cracked.

I shook my head. "My feet..." I looked down.

Thick black tendrils erupted from the floorboards, coiling tight around my ankles. I couldn't feel my feet. Couldn't move. The vines spasmed, tearing through carpet, inching higher. Climbing my legs.

"Kade!" It was like I was trying to scream underwater. I choked, coughed, tasted blood.

The vine had wrapped my throat and yanked my head to one side. I cried out, the crunch of my neck loud in my ears.

But I wasn't dead. My neck wasn't broken.

I sucked in air, desperate, ragged. But I couldn't turn my head. It held me, forced me to look.

My tear-blurred eyes tracked the thick, crawling mass across the splintered church floor... to the altar.

And I saw a foot. Bare. No shoe. No sock. Thick black veins pulsed around the ankle—like they were dragging him down. Through the floor. Into the ground. Into hell.

I squinted, straining to see.

A man. Black slacks. A white shirt, wrinkled and untucked. My heart jolted.

It was Lawrence Biddle.

One lifeless hand stretched forward. Blood foamed at his mouth. Lips frozen mid-scream.

I screamed Kade's name again, but the vines yanked me back.

I was rising. Above the floor. Above the vines. Above Biddle's body.

Then... cold. Freezing cold.

Icy air slapped my face like a thousand tiny needles. My lungs unlocked. I gasped, and the sobs broke loose.

"We're outside, Em."

Kade's voice. His arms were around me. Carrying me.

This was real. Not a vision or a dream. Not some imagined shadow. We were outside. The church behind us.

Kade set me down gently at the edge of the lot, steadying me.

"Can you stand?" His voice was deep. Calm. Grounding.

I shook my head, as my knees buckled. I collapsed into a patch of clover near a tree.

Kade helped ease me down.

"Are you okay, Em?"

I shook my head again, breath stuttering. "I saw Biddle. He was there. Lying across the altar. In the dark. Dead."

He held my hand. "It's okay."

I closed my eyes, inhaled slow. Let his voice settle into me. I squeezed his hand, felt his thumb brush mine.

When I opened my eyes, Kade was pulling out his phone.

My stomach dropped.

"What is it?"

I'm calling an ambulance. You need help. You're not well, Em.

But he didn't say any of that. He looked at me, fingers already dialing.

"I'm calling the cops."

"What?" My hand locked around his arm—too tight, too fast.

"There's a dead man in there, Em." Kade didn't blink.

"We need to call the police."

Thank You

Thank you for giving my words a chance.

If *The House's Daughter* moved you, haunted you, or stayed with you longer than you expected (either positively or negatively) I'd be so grateful if you'd leave a review on Amazon or Goodreads.

Reviews help indie authors more than you know. They tell the algorithm this story matters, and they help other readers decide to take the same risk you did.

Even a sentence or two (or just a star rating) makes a difference.

Thank you.
—April

Leave a review on Amazon
Or Goodreads
Tag me on Instagram or TikTok. I'd love to hear what stuck with you.

WHAT COMES NEXT

Continue the story in...

Let Her Be Silent
The House of Prey ***Origins Duology*** *Book Two*
Pick up your copy here.

Turn the page for a peek at the first chapter...

LET HER BE SILENT

The House of Prey

Origins Duology – Book Two

April Boulware

Sirens Screaming

The sirens didn't sound real. Not at first. They screamed up the long narrow stretch of Beckham's Road, like a warning from someone else's nightmare.

I didn't know where I was, only that Kade was there. That part was real.

His shoulder was warm, brushing mine, the only proof the world around me wasn't just a dream.

The ground beneath me was freezing. Concrete, or gravel, or maybe just the worn carpet of the church floor. It scared me that I couldn't tell. The cold leeched through the layers of my skirt. My legs were numb beneath the yards of drab blue fabric gathered at my waist.

I looked down. The double-layered bodice was crawling up my throat, choking me. The stiff seams pinched my skin.

I blinked and saw Bishop Lawrence Biddle's face, blotched red as he tried to catch his breath. Just enough to sing his praises.

The praises of the man who fostered Rachel Bagwell. The man I had called *father* for so many years. The man who lied to me. The man accused of murdering her.

Don Lyles.

The devil was after him hard in those days. Biddle's voice was harsh and brittle. *The more a man serves, the more the enemy attacks.*

I hadn't wanted to hear it. But I needed to. I needed to know.

Rachel hadn't wanted to hear it either. And she'd done her best to silence him.

She'd crouched on the desk behind Biddle. Too tall. Too thin. Limbs bent at sharp angles like a broken marionette. Her bare feet pressed flat against the wood. Her hair soaked and clinging in rusty ropes to her skull. White, blistered eyes locked onto mine.

The more the bishop talked, the more he coughed. Violent, graceless choking. His face flushed crimson, one hand clutched to his chest, the other raised in a wordless apology.

But I hadn't been watching him anymore. I was watching Rachel.

Her long, bone-thin fingers wrapped around Biddle's neck, squeezing. Sinking in like roots searching for water.

Blood oozed out around Rachel's fingers, down her papery hands. And I couldn't look away. I watched his words fall apart. Wheezing. Gurgling. Gasping for enough air to speak.

"I had no idea she'd disappear," Biddle sputtered. "Or that Brother Don would face such accusations. Murder, of all things!"

He hacked up huge black clots. They hit the carpet. I saw them—blood leeching into the faded green nap. But when I blinked, nothing was there.

Nothing at all.

But I'd seen it. All of it.

Rachel tightening her grip. Her fingers vanishing inside Biddle's throat. Elbows latched over his shoulders. Legs wrapped around his waist, like she'd grown from his spine.

How could I see a ghost? A dead girl? Rachel? Someone hacking up blood that didn't exist? Suffocating at the hands of the raging spirit of a forgotten young woman.

My heart was thumping, beating against my ribs. My head pounding like my brain would explode, burst out my ears like overripe fruit stomped flat.

Is this how Biddle felt? When Rachel tightened her grip and choked the life out of him?

The edges of my vision darkened. Blackness crawled in. Everything blurred.

I looked down. The high neckline kept climbing, tightening, cutting off my air like Rachel had strangled Lawrence Biddle.

Higher. Tighter. I couldn't swallow.

"Kade!" I twisted too fast, clawing at my dress. My head slammed into something behind me—hard. A tree? Pain flared behind my eyes.

"Whoa, Em!"

Strong hands closed around my arms.

I couldn't see what I was doing, but I heard the fabric tear. Felt my throat loosen. My lungs filled with air, like I'd pulled a noose from around my neck.

The cold night air stung my skin. I blinked away the last of what I'd seen. Rachel. The bishop. Don Lyles and the elders.

Kade knelt in front of me, slipping out of his leather jacket.

"Here." He dropped it around my shoulders and pulled it closed.

I felt the weight. It smelled like him. Leather and pine. Something citrus and sweet. I could finally focus on his face.

"Hey," he said. "I'm here, okay? I'm not going to let anything happen."

I believed him.

But the sirens were louder now. Sharper. Real.

"He's dead, isn't he?" My eyes were burning with tears I wouldn't let fall.

Kade nodded. "Biddle is."

"Rachel killed him." I was shaking. I folded in on myself, arms crossed over my stomach, knees pulled to my chest.

Kade shook his head. "We don't know that."

Lights pulsed behind him, blue and red.

"You saw her." I watched his face.

I'm not crazy. Rachel was there. She strangled Lawrence Biddle. With ghostly, shadow hands.

"I saw her," Kade said softly. "But let's hope it looks like natural causes. We went in to get my coat, right?"

He waited for me to nod.

"Then we found him there, already gone. We had talked to him after the service, caught up and asked about your dad's fallout. It went well. He was fine when we left the church." He paused, searching my eyes. "The cops are coming, Em."

It struck me what he meant, why he was going over what happened. Like a bullet. Hard and fast, it stole my breath.

We were outside the church. The quiet little cinderblock church at the end of Beckham's Road. Just me and Kade—and the dead bishop.

The bishop of a generally respected, even admired, congregation.

No matter how much outsiders misunderstood them, the members of this church were looked on with a lot of respect.

They were hard working, *honest*, down to earth people.

With their simple clothes. Families with so many children. Quiet lives. No televisions. No modern distractions. Just the important things. Family. Church. Service to their fellow humans.

The world warped. There were so many lies. Tucked away in careful little boxes. Wrapped up with neat, tight bows.

Kade was an outsider.

I was the youth minister's daughter. The same man who'd butted heads five years ago with the bishop now lying dead at the altar.

Engines roared. Diesel and gasoline stung my sinuses. Tires crushed gravel. It was all too loud in the silence that followed the sirens.

Cops and EMTs crowded the back lot. Headlights swept across us—me and Kade, huddled under the oak at the edge of the gravel.

Maybe ghosts didn't leave fingerprints on throats when they strangled people. Maybe ghosts didn't bruise skin.

Maybe Kade and I wouldn't be facing murder accusations.

Like Don Lyles had.

A broad-shouldered policewoman slammed her cruiser door. "You made the call?" she shouted to Kade.

"Yes, ma'am."

"Where's the body?"

"Inside the church," Kade said, pointing toward the back. "At the altar."

"Is there anyone else inside?"

"No ma'am."

Things started to blur again.

"Anyone armed? Any threats you're aware of?"

"No ma'am." Kade's voice again. Deep, resonant. I think I was leaning against him. I could feel his words in my chest.

I heard the sharp beep of a radio. "Unit 13—two entering to clear."

Police filed into the church, I could see that much, but two figures peeled off toward us under the tree.

"Thank you for making the call." The officer's voice was strong. "Is anyone hurt here?"

"No, ma'am." Kade shook his head, wild curls brushing his shoulders. "She's just... really shaken up."

"Alright. I'm going to have EMS come over and take a look at you, okay?"

I think she looked at me, but her face was blurred.

The crackle of her radio was loud as she stepped a couple feet away.

"Scene secure. One deceased. No other persons."

It sounded far away, but I could still see her—or someone—just on the other side of Kade. A blur of navy.

"Is it alright if I check you out, ma'am?"

I thought the voice came from the radio again, tinny and too loud. But when I looked someone had crouched on the ground beside me.

It took a minute for it to register that he was talking to me. No one called me ma'am.

I was just Em. Or Emily Carol.

I tried to nod, but my neck wouldn't move.

"Can you tell me your name?" His voice was calm. Gentler than Kade's, but it didn't have his steadiness.

"Emily." My voice burned my throat. Emily...Carol? Rose? Lyles?

I didn't know my name. Not really. Just the name they gave me. And I couldn't get the syllables off my tongue.

The man waited a beat, then nodded. "Okay, Emily. My name's Mark. I'm a paramedic. Is it alright if I give you a blanket?"

I nodded. Watched his hands move. He wore a square smartwatch, wrapped in a red Velcro band. He unfolded a thick gray blanket and held it out to me.

It was heavy on my lap. Soft. I curled my fingers into it.

"May I check your pulse, Emily?" The EMT held up his hand, pointed to his wrist. "Just two fingers on your wrist, okay?"

He waited for me to nod. "If you're uncomfortable, just say no and I'll stop, alright?"

I nodded again and rested my arm across the thick blanket.

His fingers found my wrist. I could feel it—my pulse, thudding against his touch. I filled my lungs. Full. In through my nose. Out in a slow, steady wisp through my lips.

"That's good." The EMT nodded. "Just like that. Breathe."

Slowly, my pulse leveled. The stuttering stopped. The pace felt more natural.

"I'm just here to make sure you're not hurt, Emily. You're not in any trouble, alright?" The EMT reassured me.

"If it's alright with you, I'd like to check your blood pressure. It just takes a minute, this cuff will go around your arm and squeeze gently, okay?"

He waited for me to nod. "You can say no at any point."

Then he wrapped the cuff around my arm.

The Velcro hissed, too close to my ear. My heart skidded.

I blinked and saw a man's hand where the cuff should be. Tight. Hard.

The rubber bulb wheezed.

Hssst... Hssst...

Like a heavy breath.

The hand tightened on my arm.

Hush... Hush...

A voice I couldn't remember. My racing mind couldn't place it. But my body already had.

I don't know what happened after that. My hands were clawing the cuff off before my brain caught up.

The policewoman's voice cut through the buzzing in my ears, but it was steady and quiet. "Can you tell me what happened to her dress?"

"She tore it." Kade's voice. Close to my ear. He was holding me. Or maybe I was holding him. Clutching him. His faded T-shirt twisted in my fists.

"How?" The policewoman, calm and collected.

"She grabbed it with both hands and ripped it off her throat."

Kade again.

"Just like she did the blood pressure cuff. Just now."

What was happening to me? What was wrong with me? Had I completely lost my mind?

"Okay." I could hear the nod in the policewoman's voice. "And your name?"

"Kade Weston."

"Thank you, Kade."

She must have stepped aside. I don't know where the EMT with the blood pressure cuff went.

I think we were mostly alone because Kade's arm tightened around my shoulders, then he pulled back to look at me.

"They're gonna want to talk to us separately." Someone must've still been close, because he whispered.

But I couldn't see anyone else. All I could see was Kade. His face illuminated by blue and red lights, harsh against his skin.

"It'll be okay." He saw the panic in my eyes. "They're just gonna want to know what happened. They won't hurt you, Em. They're here to help."

I watched his face. The steady light in his dark eyes. His wild curly hair falling over his shoulders. The smooth curve of his jaw. The way his lips were parted, just a little, taking in air.

"It'll be okay," he repeated. He must've seen the fear in my eyes.

I didn't even know what I was afraid of. But it was there. In the pit of my stomach. Eating at me. Gnawing its way up.

If you liked this first chapter, you can pick up your copy of
Let Her Be Silent
Here

A Little About April

April Boulware writes haunting psychological horror with a heartbeat.

She blends gothic atmosphere, slow-burn suspense, and raw emotional depth to explore what it means to survive the unimaginable, and still hope. Her work often centers on women reclaiming their stories after spiritual abuse, trauma, and isolation, with threads of found family and quiet romance woven through the dark.

April draws inspiration from her own past in a cult-like, abusive environment, and the long road of healing that followed. When she's not writing or reading something ghostly, she's probably reorganizing her planner, sipping strong coffee, or chasing a story idea down a rabbit hole.

She lives in rural South Carolina with her husband, three children, and a bunch of chickens, where she homeschools by day and writes by night.

The House's Daughter is her debut in the House of Prey series, a gothic psychological horror saga about faith, memory, and the girls who were never meant to survive.

You can read more in her newsletter Letters from Behind the Wall, or by following along on Instagram or Tiktok

A Letter from Me

Hey lovely reader!

I hope this note finds you well, and that you enjoyed the first half of Emily's origin story.

If you did (or didn't!) please take a minute to leave a review—or even just a star rating!—on Amazon and/or Goodreads. Reviews *are* for readers, but they help authors tremendously, especially indie authors running small businesses, trying to get our words out into the world.

I'm sure you've guessed by now (if you didn't already know from following me on Instagram or reading my newsletter) that this book is not an autobiography.

I think I would need a lot more than a daily dose of Lexapro and Wellbutrin if I ran into an entity wearing my sister's skin like Emily did!

That's not to say I haven't seen my share of apparitions or heard my name called by disembodied voices, but that's a subject for an entirely different book. (Given my mental health history, some people say all these things are hallucinations... I beg to differ. I've experienced both visual and auditory hallucinations, and this is something different. I lean more towards Kade's point of view. There's a spirit world out there. But like I said, the arguments for and against these topics could create a book on its own.)

But even if the supernatural parts of this book *are* fiction, other aspects of it are not.

Some of the things Emily goes through, parts of her trauma—and certainly most of the struggles with her family because of their cult-like belief system—I lived through myself, and I know a lot of other women have too.

Not everything Emily faces is my personal experience. And though much of her memories and trials are, I'm not comfortable naming off point for point what is drawn from my life and what isn't, because a lot of it is so deeply personal.

Just know that so many women have lived through similar, or worse, situations because of the belief system they were brought up in or unknowingly married into.

Purity culture, misogynist cults, and even non-religious narcissistic and abusive men create a world of hell for women to try to survive in. We're expected to bear so much, just in our day to day lives as females. Our psyches weren't meant to handle the abuse so many of us face from the people who claim to love us the most.

My hope is that my stories will be a voice for these women who have had their voices taken away. Maybe you're living this today, or you only recently broke free. Maybe you've been free for decades, but you still carry the scars in your physical body and your mind. Maybe you'll see yourself in Emily, even just a little, and my words will help you feel like your story has been shared too.

On another note, I've had a lot of comments and messages on Instagram and Facebook assuming I hate God because I'm sharing bits of my story on social media, and a lot of it through the lens of Emily's life.

I know many people who have gone through similar situations have found their peace outside of religion completely.

Personally, I have not. I'm still a Christian. I love Jesus very much, attend church regularly, read my Bible, and pray. That's just where I've found my peace and hope.

In the name of full transparency, I'm actually an active member of a more charismatic denomination. I believe in things that were denounced when I was growing up. Speaking in tongues, dancing, clapping your hands during worship, etc. There's also laying on of hands, anointing of prayer cloths etc., for the sick or those who need special prayer. This does not mean we drag people to the altar, push them down, and claim they're slain in the spirit while everyone flaps their tongues and screams. (No, I don't believe in snake handling either, I think that's stupid.) There's a lot of faking in my denomination, and I'm aware of that.

I'm also aware that many of you reading my books were probably hurt through churches claiming the denomination I'm now a part of. I've also been in some offshoot churches, nondenominational, ultra conservative, frankly disgusting. In every denomination there will be people who take parts of the belief system and run off the deep end with it. We see this all the way from Fundamental Baptist to Pentecostal Holiness and everything in between.

I'm sorry if you were hurt through a church, especially one claiming the denomination I'm now a member of. I hope you've found your peace, no matter that looks like for you, and I hope you're healing.

For me, personally, the church I'm now a member of is the complete opposite of what I was raised in. Which is probably why I've found my peace there. If I'd been raised in a charismatic church, where people pulled snakes out of the altar, rolled around on the floor, screaming and dropping tongues like they were losing their minds, I probably would have found my peace in a denomination that's more structured and quieter. But I was forced to be quiet all my life. So, being in a church where I can express myself (if I want to) has been freeing for me, personally.

Being in a church *period* has been freeing for me. I was raised that *church* was evil. I couldn't even say the word "church" in reference to a building. It was treated like a cuss word. My dad didn't believe in the *pastor system* (because he couldn't handle anyone being over him). My parents didn't believe in being a *member* of a physical church, and *denominations* were of the devil.

Everything I believe now is against what I was raised in. I mean, you had to grow up really sideways when *joining a church* feels like rebellion.

That's not to say I haven't struggled—and still do—with my faith because of how it was weaponized while I was growing up. I can't read a KJV Bible. I read NLT. I don't agree with everything my church teaches, but I really want to be in a denominational, holds-services-in-a-building church, so I've realized you'll never agree 100% with everyone, no matter where you go. (I've learned that in my life in general. I was raised that my parents were *right*, and everyone else was wrong. Learning that people having differences in opinions isn't evil has been a lesson I've had to learn as I broke free from the brainwashing.)

And... last but *not* least, I still read over those verses in 1 Corinthians and wonder why God hated women so much that He would let verses in the Bible be included that silence and degrade us. Yet later, include verses that say that in God's view there is no male or female. If there's no male or female, why does it is say, "I suffer a woman not to speak or usurp authority over a man"?

My take on this is that Paul was just a man. Yes, he was a founding father of the church, but he was still just a man. I think these verses silencing women were written from his own mind, not God's.

I mean, I'd like Paul to have gone back into Old Testament times and stood in front of Deborah while she led the entire military force of Israel, and told her, "You know what, step down. Because you don't have a penis, you can't tell these men to go fight in this war."

I'd like to see how that would've gone. She probably would have shot him. Or speared him. Or whatever kind of weapon they had back then.

But I'd also like to hear how some of these men today who cite Paul's words from the New Testament as a weapon to silence their wives and daughters, would explain Deborah's complete power over the Israelite army.

Or the fact that God spoke to Manoah's wife instead of to him, in Judges 10. Not only spoke to her but came back *to her* when Manoah was like "God, let this angel come back to *us* (not just my wife) and tell us what we're supposed to do!"

The angel came back, but to *her*, while her husband wasn't anywhere around. That dumb man still didn't believe her until he saw the angel for himself, and insisted the angel repeat exactly what was told to his wife, to him.

I mean, how dumb can you be? How prejudiced by what's between somebody's legs? And where is the proof that God even gave a shit?

Bill Gothard? Got any thoughts? Oh that's right, you had to step down from leading your cult because you were accused of molesting underage girls...

Never mind.

Anyway. I just thought I'd share some of my thoughts. Clear up some things I've been asked about several times on Instagram and Facebook.

No, this isn't my life word for word.

Yes, I'm still a Christian, but I consider myself an enlightened Christian.

Hell no, I don't write Christian fiction. (Not that I'm yucking someone's yum, if you like Christian fiction, more power to you. It's just not for me.)

Oh, and I don't hate my parents because of how I was raised, or what I went through when I tried to break free, or what my husband and I went through together simply because we met and tried to date.

I did hate them at one time. They stole a lot of things from me—experiences, time, things I can't get back. But part of healing is forgiving. Moving on. Holding onto anger only hurts the person holding onto it.

I still talk to my mom some. She's said she's sorry. That she wishes she'd done differently while I was growing up. She's doing things somewhat different now, for herself.

And I love that for her.

But I needed a mom back then. I still do now. You never get old enough that you don't need your mom.

Today, I need space to heal. Because, even with the changes she's made, my mom has not fully removed from the cult mindset. And my dad hasn't changed at all. They still believe men are better than women, men are over women, and good wives *submit*. Among other things that I'm not going to get into here.

There's also the abuse aspect, the narcissistic side of things I don't believe either of them have taken any steps to heal. They still don't really "believe" in Christians struggling with their mental health.

So I've learned to mother myself. Which is hard.

I've made changes in my life and gone through a hell of a lot of shit directly *because* of the cultish, abusive upbringing I survived. And I've had to do that on my own.

(On my own, but with my husband's support. I'm thankful every day that I met Chris when I did. He truly is the other half of my soul, my rock, and my best friend. He sees my trauma, gives me space to be heard and seen, listens when I need him to, and encourages me to be the person I truly am instead of who I was raised to think I was. If you're reading this, Chris, I love you very much and I don't know where I'd be without your support and love.)

Has it been hard? Hell yeah. Every day is hard.

I still can't go through a drive-thru by myself.

I break into a cold sweat if I have to pump gas alone.

My heart races uncontrollably whenever I have to make a phone call.

And I still struggle to look men in the eyes.

But it's made me who I am today, I guess. I'm still trying to heal, for myself and for my kids. I want them to look back one day and be able to say, "You know, Mom didn't get it right all the time, she struggled, but she worked hard to heal herself."

And it's given birth to this book, and whatever books come after it.

Do I wish I hadn't gone through the hell I did?

Of course.

I'd probably be writing paranormal thrillers right now. This book would've been the story of a woman inheriting an unknown great-aunt's mansion somewhere near the Arctic Circle, and then realizing it's haunted not only by ghosts but also by a serial killer who's lived in the place, framing himself as the caretaker for thirty years.

Ooo.

I think I just had a book idea.

But even if I wish I'd had a normal life growing up, and didn't have anxiety today, or fragmented repressed memories, or major depression... Since I did, and I do, I can at least use it for something good.

By helping others who lived through similar—or worse—feel seen through the pages of my stories.

I hope you enjoyed this book, and that you're ready to read the rest of Emily's escape.

It's going to be a hell of a ride.

April

Printed in Dunstable, United Kingdom